Two fabulous
from two treme

JOAN HOHL
DIANA PALMER

It's the season for love and for Matilda Wolfe
that means meeting her match in the dangerous
new reverend, Mac Macdonough—sparks are
sure to fly off this pair.

For Lisa Monroe this special time finds
her arousing a fiery passion in formidable
mercenary Cy Parks, proving that *this*
winter soldier's heart *can* be melted.

That's

Winter
LOVING

Winter
LOVING

JOAN HOHL
DIANA PALMER

SILHOUETTE®

*Silhouette and Colophon are registered trademarks of
Harlequin Books S.A., used under licence.*

*First published in Great Britain 2001
Silhouette Books, Eton House, 18-24 Paradise Road,
Richmond, Surrey TW9 1SR*

WINTER LOVING © Harlequin Books S.A. 2001

The publisher acknowledges the copyright holders of the
individual works as follows:

Wolfe Winter © Joan Hohl 1998
The Winter Soldier © Diana Palmer 2001

ISBN 0 373 04729 0

128-1101

*Printed and bound in Spain
by Litografia Rosés S.A., Barcelona*

Wolfe Winter
by
Joan Hohl

JOAN HOHL

lives in south-western Pennsylvania, where she was born and raised. The best-selling author of over forty novels, including over twenty-five for Silhouette®, Joan has won numerous awards, including the Romance Writers of America Golden Medallion Award and two *Romantic Times Magazine* Reviewer's Choice Awards. One of the industry's most popular authors, Joan writes both historical and contemporary romance.

To law-enforcement officers everywhere, with thanks
for their dedication and bravery in the line of duty.

Chapter 1

The call came through ten minutes before the end of her shift, directing her to investigate a reported desecration of property at the new church just outside town.

Officer Matilda Wolfe—Matt to her family and friends—grimaced. Acknowledging the directive, she whipped the patrol car into a tight U-turn and headed north to the sight of the crime. She did not activate the siren or the bar of flashers on the car roof; there seemed little point in doing so, since the late-night traffic was sparse and the perpetrator of the crime was probably long gone.

"Ten minutes," she muttered, her sharp gaze skimming the road before her and the bordering sidewalks; everything appeared peaceful and quiet, as it should at that time of the workweek night.

"Just ten lousy minutes," she continued her muttered grousing. The clustered buildings thinned, the area becoming more rural. "I'd have been back at the station, smirking at Uncle Jake, my venerated chief, while my replacement was making this run."

Feeling somewhat better for having vented her annoyance, Matt steered the car onto a black-topped secondary road, and allowed a soft smile to ease her tight lips.

The smile was in response to her thought about the man who was her chief, and her uncle. Jake Wolfe was at the station unusually late, having gone in after being notified of the apprehension of a rape suspect.

Her uncle had started as a rookie patrolman with the Sprucewood Police Department over twenty-five years ago, when the town was a lot smaller and the police force consisted of only a handful of men. He had worked himself up through the ranks as the town and the force had grown and expanded. Jake had made chief two years before Matt had graduated from the police academy and joined the force.

At that time, Cameron, Matt's father, and the eldest of the four Wolfe brothers, and a special agent for the FBI, had been, and still was, bureau chief of the Denver office. He'd held that position since before his marriage to Matt's mother, Sandra.

Along with her paternal grandmother, Matilda, for whom Matt had been named, her uncle Jake and his wife Sarah, had happily assumed the role of surrogate parents of Matt while she attended the police academy.

Recalling her early days on the force, Matt laughed aloud. Her uncle Jake had been tough on her, tougher than he'd been on the other rookies. But he'd done so only because he demanded the best from her, expecting her to uphold the family tradition of excellence and dedication to law enforcement principles.

While Matt had suffered moments of resentment for being judged by such high standards, passing the rigid Wolfe mettle test had endowed her with the satisfying rewards of self-esteem, value and worthiness.

Matt was a good cop—a darn good cop, and she knew it. So did everyone else.

She had earned the unqualified respect of every member of her family; aunts, uncles, cousins, but most importantly, her parents and her sister, Lisa, who had followed their mother into the practice of law.

The thought of her parents, her sister, sent a thrill of anticipation through Matt. She would be seeing them soon, as her parents and Lisa were coming east in a few weeks for the holidays.

Another thought made Matt grin. Along with having earned the respect of her entire family, she had earned the right to smirk at her chief on occasion.

The thought was more warming than her police-issue leather jacket.

A few minutes later she reduced her speed to a crawl, then made the sharp turn onto the curving driveway leading to the church that had been built just a few years before. Its profile gleamed stark white in the glow of the spotlights strategically positioned in the grounds.

Bringing the car to a stop, Matt took note of a dark shape emerging from the shadowed church entranceway. The figure was male, and large. As she stepped from the car, she slid her hand to the holstered police-issue pistol strapped to her waist.

* * *

That is one extremely tall woman.

The Reverend David Macdonough—Mac to his friends, and most of his parishioners—made the observation while watching the uniformed woman stride toward him. Gliding a swift but comprehensive glance over her imposing length, Mac judged her to be some four or five inches shorter than his own six feet four-and-a-half inches. Which placed her at close to six foot.

Oh, yeah, she was tall, all right, he reflected, feeling a little jolt as she moved from the darkness into the glare of the spotlights. Tall and shapely and drop-dead gorgeous.

Admiring the spun gold color of her hair beneath her regulation hat, Mac extended his hand as she came to a halt a prudent distance from him.

"Good evening," Mac said, offering her a smile as he took a careful step closer. "I'm David Macdonough, pastor of the church. I placed the call to the station. Sorry to have had to bring you out here so late, and on such a cold night, Officer…"

"Wolfe," she readily supplied, removing her hand from the weapon at her waist to grasp his in an unsurprisingly firm grip. "And responding is

my job, sir, time and cold weather notwithstand-
ing.''

Mac liked the sound of her voice. It was low,
kind of throaty, with a sexy hint of smokiness. He
liked the feel of her hand, too, the strength beneath the softness of her skin. He felt regret, along
with a tingling sensation, when she slid her palm
from his.

''The report said there's been an act of desecration,'' she said in brisk tones. She raised
golden, delicately arched eyebrows over eyes that
appeared to be the exact shade of dark, rich chocolate.

''Yes, that's correct.'' Brought back to the reality of why she was there, Mac suppressed a
sigh. Turning, he indicated the crèche set up off
to the side of the walkway in front of the church.

''If you'll follow me?''

To the ends of the earth.

Startled by the errant thought, coming as it had
on top of the jolt she'd experienced by the touch
of his hand, Matt compressed her lips and trailed
after the right reverend across the frost-stiffened
lawn.

Why in the world would she have felt that elec-
triclike zing from his hand against hers, or had

such a thought about a stranger? Or any man, come to that. It was a new experience for Matt— and one she felt she happily could live without.

She wasn't interested in feeling intrigued by a man. Matt had grown up in a family of law enforcement officers. She knew, better than most, the constant fear *their* life partners lived with every day.

When she had taken the oath to the force, Matt had added another oath to herself—that of walking her chosen path alone, without the emotional baggage of a constantly concerned husband or significant other.

And she certainly didn't need the distraction of a zing of awareness now. This particular man was an ordained pastor in the bargain, Matt upbraided herself, her now-wary eyes measuring his impressive figure.

Of course, he didn't look anything like her idea of what a minister looked like; he certainly didn't look anything like her pastor. That gentleman was elderly, almost fragile in appearance, thin and rather smallish.

The Reverend Macdonough was the exact opposite of elderly, fragile, thin and small.

Matt's trained eye swept from the top of his head to the running shoes on his big feet. Six-five, she decided, and approximately one hundred and eighty pounds, give or take a couple of ounces. And, unless she missed her guess, precious few of those pounds were made up of fat, but pure toned muscle.

He wasn't bad to look at, either, if one found attraction in a dark-haired man with a harshly hewn bone structure, a long, thin, aristocratic nose, sculpted lips, and piercingly direct dark blue eyes.

"—as you can see."

The deep syrup-over-shrapnel sound of his voice snagged Matt from the mists of reverie. Fortunately, his pointing finger showed her the damage inflicted, sparing her the embarrassment of having to ask him to repeat the first part of his remark.

Oh, yes, Matt could definitely see, and the sight instilled in her both a feeling of sickness and a flash of outrage.

The crèche was constructed entirely of wood, from the cradle to the attending figures to the stablelike shelter in which the figures of the Holy Family were set. The figures themselves appeared to Matt to have been cut from one-half- to three-quarter-inch plywood, and were scaled slightly larger than life-size. They stood well over six feet tall, most likely, she figured, to be clearly seen from the road. The paint on the flat surfaces used to depict clothing and facial features had been applied by a steady hand, and a talented eye for detail.

The single figure in the scene not constructed of wood was that of the child. The infant Jesus was represented by a toddler's soft-skinned baby doll. It had been lovingly wrapped in a large woolen shawl—probably belonging to a parishioner or the pastor's wife, Matt mused. She ignored a disquietening sensation instilled by the likelihood that the reverend was married.

Collectively, the crèche was a beautiful and reverent piece of work, worthy of admiration and praise, not wanton vandalism.

After years on the Sprucewood Police Force, Matt had witnessed many scenes of destruction, the results of violence, the aftermath of accidents of all kinds. She had reacted to those scenes with revulsion for the sheer stupidity of it all.

But this…this scene before her had a different, deeper effect on Matt. Her sense of outrage stemmed from an inner spirituality unrelated to any particular religious belief or denomination.

Appalled, a sadness constricting her chest, Matt stared for long silent moments at the figure depicting the Virgin Mother. A protest rose in her throat against the hate that had directed some obviously disturbed person to obliterate the Virgin Mary's face with flat black paint.

"Sickening, isn't it?"

"Why?" Matt wasn't even aware of giving voice and substance to her despair and confusion.

"I've asked myself the same," the Reverend Macdonough murmured. "You can't help but wonder what's going on inside the head of a person who could do that."

Matt slanted a glance at him and discovered his expression reflected her feelings. The Reverend Macdonough was experiencing a similar confusion and despair.

No life had been wasted. No innocent had been defiled. No person had suffered physical damage. And yet, on some level, the desecration was almost frightening.

A gust of cold December night wind shivered through the surrounding evergreens. The chilled air drew Matt from her spiritual anguish and back to the reality of her purpose here.

"You've not touched anything?" She shot another, sharper look at the pastor.

He shook his head. "No, of course not. And I didn't walk up to it for a closer look." His smile was wry. "With the frost, there should be foot-prints."

Matt agreed with a brief nod, relieved that the man of the cloth appeared to possess some practical intelligence.

"There probably won't be much evidence to go on," she felt duty-bound to admit. "A dash to the figure, a few quick blasts from a can of spray paint, and then a hasty retreat." Sighing, she turned from the unsettling scene and headed for the car. "I'll toss the ball into the lab crew's court, then tape off the area."

To Matt's surprise, the pastor matched his long stride to hers.

"Can I be of assistance?" he asked in response to her questioning glance. "It's getting colder, and we could cut the exposure time in half."

"Thanks but..." She paused to catch her breath as another gust of wind smacked her square in the face. Pulling the car door open, she dove inside, grateful for the warmth blasting from the heater of the idling car. She was reaching for the two-way when the pastor slid into the passenger seat.

Eyeing him, she flicked the button on the control. "Four-one," she said, identifying herself to base.

The two-way crackled. "Go ahead, four-one."

While making her report, Matt avoided looking
at the silent man next to her by staring at the
dashboard. Her gaze settled on the digital clock;
a groan vibrated her throat; she swallowed it.
Groaning would not change the fact that she
should have gone off shift thirty-five minutes ago.

"So now what?" he asked after she had finished and replaced the handset. "The tape?"

Matt angled her head to gaze at him. "Yes, the
tape first."

"And then you'll have to interrogate me?"
Amusement gleamed in his eyes.

"I'm afraid so, sir." Her tone gave clear indication that, though she respected his profession,
she would follow procedure. "Sorry."

"No need to be," he assured her. "I do realize
that, for the moment at least, I am a suspect."

His approval rating went up a few notches on
Matt's personal judgment scale. The Reverend
Macdonough was neither arrogant nor a fool, believing himself above the law because of his profession.

Thanks to the surrounding trees, and the pastor's assistance, the taping-off went swiftly. Still,
feeling the bite of the frigid wind, Matt was
chilled to the bone by the time they finished. She
was both relieved and happy to turn the scene

over to the lab crew when they arrived a few minutes later.

She turned to the pastor, but before she could voice her first question, he offered an invitation.

"Would you like to step inside, out of this wind? That's my place, over there." He indicated a house set a short distance to the side of the church. "I don't know about you, but I'm freezing."

"Well…" Matt slanted a glance at the lab crew, fully aware they didn't require her presence. "There's no rule that says you can't have a hot drink while interrogating someone, is there?"

"No, there are no rules against that…so long as the drink is nonalcoholic," she said, smiling.

He smiled back. "Wouldn't dream of offering alcohol to an officer on duty," he said, striding off toward the house. "Come along," he called over his shoulder, "before we both freeze fast to the ground."

The house was neither large nor small, but average. Though of good quality, the furniture was decidedly masculine, a lot of leather and wood. There were few adornments, knickknacks and the like. Yet it had a welcoming ambience, and was deliciously warm.

"Oh...feels good," Matt murmured, rubbing her cold-numbed fingers.

A quirky smile tilted the pastor's lips. "I noticed a pair of gloves on the seat of the car," he said, a teasing light springing to life in his eyes.

Matt gave a careless shrug—at least she hoped it looked careless. Considering the flutter his gleaming eyes had activated in the vicinity of her heart, she wasn't sure she had pulled off the careless appearance.

"I seldom wear them," she admitted, breathing easier when he turned away, motioning her to follow. "They're too bulky," she went on, trailing him into the kitchen.

"Hard to hold a police issue .38 with fingers stuck inside lined leather, huh?" His voice was serious in contrast to the dancing light in his eyes.

"Something like that," Matt agreed, averting her eyes as she dug a notepad from her pocket.

"Coffee, tea or hot chocolate?"

Matt glanced up, and felt her breath catch in her throat. Heavens, she thought. For a man of the cloth, he has wicked eyes.

"What's your pleasure?"

Matt was tempted—sorely tempted—to find out if she could shock and rattle him with an outrageous response, but she quashed the impulse.

"Hot chocolate, please," she said, sticking with propriety, and wondering why she'd been tempted in the first place. "If it's not too much trouble."

"No trouble," he said, opening a cabinet above the stove and removing two packets of the mix from a box. "Take off your jacket and hat and have a seat. This will only take a few minutes in the microwave."

"Thanks." Placing the notepad and pencil on the table, Matt removed her hat and set it next to the notepad. She shrugged out of her jacket and hung it over the back of a chair, then settled on the seat.

Hands folded on the tabletop, she watched as he prepared the two cups of hot chocolate, appreciating his efficiency. His spare, competent movements reminded her of her father and uncles—four men fully domesticated by a shrewd mother.

A gentle smile curved her lips.

"Pleasant thoughts?"

His question scattered the memory clouding her mind. "Hmm," Matt hummed, nodding. "I was thinking about my family...my father."

"I like that." His voice was warm with approval. Smiling, he set a steaming cup of hot chocolate in front of her, then circled the table to sit opposite her.

"You like...what?" Matt frowned.

"The sound of your voice when you said 'father,'" he said, raising his cup to his mouth for a tentative test taste.

She laughed. "How did it sound?"

"Oh..." He shrugged. "Warm, loving...with perhaps a hint of longing."

"They're in Colorado."

"'They'?"

"My folks," she explained. "My mother and father, and my sister."

He took a swallow of the chocolate drink, studying her with contemplative eyes. "They're on a winter vacation?" he asked.

Matt gave a quick shake of her head. "No, they live there, have since before I was born."

"And yet, you're on the police force here, in Sprucewood, Pennsylvania," he said, a frown drawing his dark brows together.

"Hmm," she murmured around the chocolate sip she'd taken into her mouth.

"Might I ask why? I mean..."

Her soft laughter silenced him. "I know what you mean," she said when her laughter subsided. "But it's not as puzzling as it may sound." She took another sip before continuing. "My father is originally from Sprucewood. His mother still lives here, as does his youngest brother. I spent most of my summers here while I was growing up." She grinned. "And I like it here."

He grinned back at her. "So do I."

"You're from around here originally, too?" Matt asked, figuring if he could probe, she jolly well could, too; she was a cop, wasn't she?

"No." He shook his head. "I was born in Virginia, but I've lived all over the world." His smile was wry. "My father was a career serviceman— marines."

"Was?" She raised an eyebrow. "Retired?"

"No." His expression and voice were somber. "Deceased. He died from injuries from a car accident."

"I'm sorry." The sentiment seemed inadequate, but what else was there to say?

"Yeah, me, too." He sighed. "We lost my mother to cancer the year before."

Matt felt terrible, knowing how devastated she'd feel in the same situation. "That's...awful."

"For me...yes," he said, his eyes bleak. "But, in truth, I had already lost my father. The life had gone out of him before the accident—he just seemed to fade after my mother passed away.''

''Too bad,'' Matt murmured, somehow knowing it would be the same for her father in the unthinkable event that he should lose her mother. The mere thought sent a chill down her spine. She hastened to change the subject.

''My father is a career law enforcement officer.'' Her smile was tentative yet wry. ''FBI.''

''Whoa. Impressive,'' he said, lifting his cup to drain the last of his drink.

Matt couldn't tell from his tone of voice whether or not the reverend was being facetious, but she kind of suspected he might be. So, just in case he was, she decided to impress him a little bit more...then get on with her interrogation.

''Not really,'' she said, coolly insouciant. ''You see, law enforcement is something of a Wolfe family tradition. Other than my grandmother and my aunts, we're all in some form of it.''

''All?'' His drink finished, the reverend leaned back in his chair and stretched his legs out under the table, looking for all the world as if he were settling in for a lengthy discussion. ''How many law enforcement Wolfes are there?''

Matt was tired. She still had her reports to fill

out before she could go home, and she felt certain her captain would rip a verbal strip off her for taking so long on this assignment. Nonetheless, since she had offered the tidbit of information about her family in the first place, she thought it would be unfair not to respond.

"There are eleven of us working on the front lines, so to speak, and two behind the lines," she said, stifling the need to yawn.

"Eleven..." He looked astonished, then frowned. "Would you care to sort them out for me?"

"Another time, perhaps," she answered. Pulling the notepad toward her and picking up the pencil, she gave him her most professional, no-nonsense look. "Now, I think we'd better get on with the interrogation."

He muttered something she didn't quite catch, something moreover that she felt certain she had misunderstood.

"I beg your pardon?" she said, convinced she had to have misunderstood, because it had sounded to her like he had said, "Dammit to hell." Nah, she decided, she was tired, that was it.

"Don't have much to tell," he said, the corners of his lips again twitching with that quirky smile.

Something about that smile bugged Matt. Her
spine growing rigid, she gave him a drilling stare.
His expression was benign, innocent. Hmm, too
innocent, maybe? she mused.

"Are you planning to begin anytime soon?"

"What?" Matt frowned.

"The interrogation," he reminded her, his expression now somber and serious. Although a
spark of that wicked light still gleamed in his dark
blue eyes.

"Oh, yes, of course," she said, advising herself
to get a grip. "How did you happen to discover
the act of desecration?" she asked briskly.

"I was returning home from visiting a parishioner," he began when she interrupted him.

"The parishioner's name?"

He gave a name, a female name. Hmm, Matt
thought again as she jotted down the name. Then,
shoving speculation aside, she said, "Go on."

"Right." He nodded. "If you noticed, the
driveway leads from the road, then up to and
around the side of the church, where it branches
into two lanes. One leads to the parking lot in
back, the other to my garage."

Matt's brief nod indicated that she had noticed.
How could she not have?

"Well, when I drove by the crèche, I caught a

glimpse of something that didn't look quite right,'' he said.

''So, after I parked the car, I walked back along the drive for a closer look.'' He moved his broad shoulders—Matt couldn't help but note their width—in a light shrug. ''And that's about it.'' He smiled. ''I will confess I was tempted to walk up to the figure, touch it to see if the paint was still fresh and tacky...'' His smile widened. ''But I resisted the temptation.''

''Commendable of you.'' Matt favored him with a dry-as-dust look. ''And that's when you called the report into the station?''

''Yes.''

''Could one of your parishioners be nursing a grudge against you, or be disgruntled with church policy in general?'' He frowned.

''It's possible I suppose,'' he admitted. ''But I believe I'd be aware of it if someone did. I know them all fairly well, at least the ones who regularly attend services. The congregation's not very large.''

''Do you have any known enemies—some person or persons seeking to strike at you?''

''No.'' His shook his head. ''As stated, I'm relatively new to the area.'' A wry smile tugged at his very masculine and attractive lips. ''I haven't been around here long enough to make that sort of enemy.''

"No one knows you well enough yet to hate you, huh?'' she drawled.

"That's about it.'' He laughed. The deep, rich sound having a strangely exciting effect on her.

"Okay.'' Matt flipped the notepad closed and pushed her chair away from the table. Rising, she settled her hat on her head and shrugged into her jacket. "If you should think of anything else, or if you notice any suddenly odd behavior or attitude in one of your parishioners or personal friends, let us know.''

"Certainly, although I can't imagine either a friend or parishioner committing such a wanton act,'' he said, plucking his jacket from the back of a chair.

Matt gave him a quizzical glance, but started for the front door.

He was right behind her.

"Will you keep me apprised of any progress you make?'' he asked, following her outside.

"Yes.'' Matt started walking, and frowned when he stepped to her side. Sure of his intentions, she angled a sidelong look at him.

"Your lab crew has left,'' he said by way of an explanation.

"So I see," she murmured. "Still, it's not necessary for you to escort me to the car, Reverend Macdonough." She lifted her right hand to brush her fingers over the butt of her holstered pistol. "I can take care of myself."

"I'm sure you can." He ran a telling glance over her tall, imposing—some might say, intimidating—form. "And the name's David," he said, smiling. "Or, if you like, Mac. Most people call me Mac."

"Hmm," she hummed, by way of avoiding committal or reciprocation.

Reaching the car, she grasped the door handle, hesitated, and then turned to bid him good-night.

He didn't return the salutation. That quirky smile was back in place at the edges of his mouth. "What do most people call you?"

"Officer Wolfe," she said, deadpan, pulling the door open and sliding behind the wheel.

He laughed aloud.

"Good night, Reverend Macdonough." Matt shut the door, fired the engine, released the hand brake and set the car in motion, backing around to head down the driveway to the road.

The deep, rich, disturbingly exciting sound of his laughter reverberated inside her head all the way back to the station.

Matt didn't like it…because she found it much, much too attractive, and him much too stimulating. And the very last thing she wanted was to find herself stimulated by or attracted to him, or any man, for that matter.

In Matt's belief, and oft-stated opinion, she was better off walking the law enforcement road alone.

Chapter 2

He'd slipped again.

His laughter dwindling to a lopsided smile, Mac ambled back to the house. His smile changed to a fleeting grimace as he passed the crèche.

Why? he asked himself, heaving a sigh. Why would anyone...

His thoughts fractured. Why wonder why? There were people in the world, disgruntled, disturbed, and flat out fanatical, that was why.

Mac knew, better than many, about people like that. He knew more than he wanted to know. Serving in the Armed Forces' Special Services had given him an in-depth education on the aberrant mental workings of a whole spectrum of different peoples.

Hadn't someone once said that it took all kinds?

Well, Mac had seen all kinds. The observations had finally gotten to him.

Hadn't someone else said something about man's inhumanity to man?

In the line of duty, Mac had stood witness to the truth of that saying. His service time had toughened him, hardened him, and in the end, sickened him, in mind and spirit, tested his innate belief of the ultimate goodness of the species called man.

A child shall lead them.

In the end, that prophetic verse had borne bitter fruit inside Mac.

Mac had experienced his crucible on sight of the large, imploring eyes of a small child. The poor mite had been rendered to the point of starvation by the deliberate acts of the greedy and ruthless leader of the child's ill-used and confused people.

Thoroughly disgusted with the world in general, Mac had done what, for him, previously would have been the unthinkable. He had quit, simply walked away from responsibility, duty, pride.

After first wallowing in the sins of the flesh, free-falling in a downward spiral until hitting rock bottom, the quitting had eventually proved to be the path of his salvation.

While losing himself, Mac had found redemption.

Cleansed and strengthened by renewed belief, and armed with a sense of purpose, he had set about putting himself back together by cleaning up his act.

The struggle against his own inner demons was now five years past.

But Mac still had moments when he slipped...as he had earlier, with his impulsively muttered remark to Officer Wolfe.

The lopsided smile was back in place when Mac reentered his house.

Yes, he had slipped with the muttered, ''Dammit to hell,'' but... Mac shrugged—off the remark and out of his jacket at the same time.

He had felt frustrated by her reluctance to give him a rundown of her various family members involved in the business of law enforcement.

Mac even acknowledged why he'd felt frustrated. He was interested, but not from an over-

riding curiosity about her family. In truth, he had
felt an immediate interest and attraction to the
woman herself.

Bemused by the self-realization, Mac went
about the business of clearing away their hot
chocolate mugs. He secured the house and prepared for bed with his usual, if absent, efficiency.

It had been some years since he had experienced so much as a glimmer of interest in a
woman, let alone a twinge of physical attraction.

His disinterest had had nothing to do with the
tenets he had embraced upon his salvation. His
church, his denomination, did not demand abstinence.

Mac had been celibate by choice ever since his
emotional enlightenment and emergence from the
depths of degradation over five years ago.

His own personal, earthly savior, that incredible
person who had been the means of Mac's salvation, though compassionate and sympathetic, had
adhered to the principles of tough love.

Mac, compassionate and sympathetic, as well
as understanding, also practiced tough love in his
dealings with his fellow humans. But he practiced
the hardest on himself.

Not once throughout those years of abstinence

had he been visited by the allure of sensual temptation.

Until tonight, on sight of Officer Wolfe.

Weird.

Lying on his back in his bed, Mac stared at the shifting patterns of moonlight on the white-painted ceiling of his bedroom. He contemplated the stirring desire quickening his mind and body.

After so many years the sensation felt strange—not unpleasurable, just strange.

And he didn't even know her given name.

Strange indeed.

Mac's eyelids felt weighted, and they slowly drifted shut. Yet his mind remained active, dissecting this startling phenomenon of attraction.

In this case, "phenomena" perfectly defined the condition, he mused. For he felt the attraction on different and distinct levels.

There was, of course, the physical level, and Mac's attendant discomfort. Yet there were clear indications of interest on an intellectual level, too. In the brief amount of time spent in her company, Mac had detected elements of Officer Wolfe's sharp intelligence and keen wit.

And there was an emotional level, as well; the deep, abiding emotion of family love. The note of unqualified love in her voice when she'd spoken of her family—her father, her mother, her sister, and who knew how many others—had struck a deeply buried chord inside Mac. He was achingly aware of being without family or close friends, a man alone in the world.

A soft sigh escaped Mac's guard, breaking the silence of the cold night.

Though in a secret place inside him Mac would always mourn the loss of his parents, and then his younger sister, his only sibling, in a fiery auto crash, as well as the subsequent loss a few years ago of his benefactor and mentor, he seldom gave a thought to being alone in the world.

His faith, all-encompassing and comforting, had sustained him. It had strengthened him, accompanied him along the path he had freely chosen to follow.

While accepting the sorrow of personal loss, Mac had not felt bereft of the loss of the bonhomie of close, personal friendships or the intimacy inherent in relationships with members of the opposite sex.

Even with Corine Baxter, the still young and pretty widowed parishioner he had visited earlier that evening, Mac had not felt so much as a hint of an attraction, physical or emotional. Even though he couldn't help but notice that she had

sent out unmistakable signals of a personal interest in him, he simply was not interested. He
hadn't been in a long time.

Until now.

The stirring intensified in the lower regions of
Mac's body; he shifted in a fruitless attempt to
ease the discomfort.

Why? Mac frowned. There were lots of whys
scurrying around inside his head.

Why now?

Why her?

Why not?

A faint smile of amusement tickled the edges
of his mouth—self-derisory amusement. After all
this time, the reactivation was almost funny. But
not nearly funny enough to distract his mind from
the acute discomfort of his body.

Unbidden, and unwelcome, considering he was
trying to decrease the ache, not expand it, an image of Officer Wolfe grasped control of his mind
and senses.

With amazing clarity, Mac could see her as
clearly as if she were standing at the foot of his
bed…or lying beside him on top of it.

His imagination re-created a tormenting picture
of her as she had appeared seated beneath the
glare of the kitchen ceiling light. Her delicate fea-

tures had been cast in stark relief, the creamy
smoothness of her skin accentuated by the hun-
dred-watt bulb inside the frosted globe of the ceiling fixture.

And her hair...after she had removed her hat,
her hair, brushed back and twisted into a knot at
her nape, was tawny in color, shot through with
shards of gold.

Mac felt a sharp, intense desire to see her hair
freed from that knot, to curl his fingers into the
silky gold-streaked mass.

He flexed his fingers, and half groaned, half
laughed at himself. Sighing instead, he ordered
his brain to continue its mental examination of
her.

Free of lipstick, her lips were a tempting pink,
ripe-looking and luscious. And her eyes were the
exact shade of dark rich chocolate. Deep and inviting.

Her androgynous uniform could not conceal the
allure of her full, high breasts, the enticing curve
of her narrow waist, slender hips, rounded bottom,
and below.

Below. Mac unconsciously heaved a yearning
sigh. Even with the concealment of the straight-
legged pants, it was obvious that her legs were
long. Never having seen them, he just knew her

legs were those of a kind to set a man's imagination, and libido, into overdrive.

He sighed again. Overall, his imaginations revealed the tall form of one very appealing and sexy woman.

And a sexy-looking woman who appealed to him was the absolute last person he needed to encounter at this particular juncture of his life. He had dedicated himself, his life, to his mission of salvation.

A shudder ran down the length of Mac's body as a groan of protest rose to lodge in his throat and echo inside his head.

Why her?

Why now?

Why me?

Even while the questions plagued his brain, Mac attempted to distance himself from the physical torment by concentrating on the amusement factor.

It, too, would soon pass, he assured himself...and then, he would laugh.

"I'm home, Gram," Matt called, pulling the kitchen door closed behind her and shutting out the wind.

"About time, too," Maddy Wolfe called over

the sound of the TV set. "You get an assignment right before quitting time?"

Matt smiled as she removed her hat and slipped out of her jacket. This wasn't the first time she'd felt grateful to be living with someone who understood the demands placed upon the life-style of a police officer.

"Yeah," she answered, unbuckling her gun belt as she walked into the living room. Setting the weapon on an end table, she crossed the room to the white-haired woman ensconced in a flower-patterned, wing-backed chair. "Ten minutes before quitting," she went on, bending to place a kiss on the woman's lined but still soft cheek. "Can you believe it?"

"Of course, I can believe it." Her smile soft and loving, Maddy patted Matt's hand. "In the early years, before he was promoted to sergeant, your grandfather was often assigned to investigate right around quitting time." Her smile sad with memory, she flicked off the TV. "Come to that," she went on, smothering a yawn as she rose from the chair, "things didn't change all that much after he moved into the narcotics division."

Matt felt a sympathetic pang in her chest for her beloved grandmother. After all these years, Maddy Wolfe still mourned for her husband, who had been cut down during a drug bust, giving his life in the line of duty.

Maddy straightened to her full height—just a few scant inches shorter than Matt's own six feet. Her grandmother, now in her eighties but with the vigor of a woman twenty years younger, sighed with acceptance.

"I'm sure your father, your uncles, and every one of your cousins has put in their share of overtime." Her smile turned teasing. "So don't go feeling like the Lone Ranger of the force."

Matt laughed, as she always did each and every time her grandmother offered the same advice.

Maddy laughed with her, then covered another yawn. "Well, now that you're home safe, I'm for bed." She raised her eyebrows. "Unless I can get you something to eat, or a hot drink?"

Always the caregiver, Matt thought, shaking her head. "No, thanks, Gram. I had a cup of hot chocolate a little while ago." Feeling, for some incomprehensible reason, unwilling to explain how she had come by the hot drink, she quickly added, "I'm bushed. All I want is a shower and my bed."

"Then I'll say good-night." Maddy turned and started from the room. "Sleep well, dear."

"I will."

After a soothing hot shower, Matt stepped into sleeping shorts, pulled on an oversize T-shirt emblazoned with the promise Chocolate Cures Curious Cravings, and burrowed beneath the covers.

Sighing, she let her body relax and closed her eyes, certain she'd be out within seconds. And she might have been—if a vision hadn't swirled, then settled in, firing her imagination.

Against her will, an image of David Macdonough formed front and center on the stage of her tired mind.

Go away, Matt thought on a silent groan.

The image smiled at her, displaying a flash of white teeth in concert with a blaze of blue eyes.

Lord—but he was good to look at.

The admission was as good as a declaration of surrender; the image settled in for a long visit.

Captive to her own imaginings, Matt examined the vision with her inner eye. Resentful of her captivity, she searched for surface flaws.

There weren't many. Oh, perhaps his jawline was a mite too squared, too hard-looking. And yes, maybe his lips were too defined, the line too set in determination. But, other than those…

Face it, Matilda Wolfe, he appeals to you, she told herself, reluctantly surrendering to the sheer male attractiveness of David Macdonough.

That wicked light sprang to life in the blue eyes of the image, that sensuous light she felt positive didn't belong in an ordained minister.

But, ordained ministers were men. Human. With all the frailties of the species. Weren't they?

The question brought a sigh. Matt felt much too tired to theorize on the basic humanity of those who had felt the calling. She was too wary of the pull on her senses by an individual who had apparently heard the call.

Yet it was there. Whether she liked it or not her attraction for David Macdonough was strong, physical, and emotional in nature.

And Matt didn't like it.

Go away, she thought again, blinking.

She felt both surprised and chagrined when the image vanished.

Then it was the inner conflict that kept her awake.

Considering the few hours' restless slumber she received, Matt was not her usual bright-eyed and bushy-tailed self when she began her shift early the next afternoon.

Reading the report from the lab crew's assessment of the church merely abraded her already chancy mood.

The crew had verified the paint was of the spray variety of a well-known brand that was readily available everywhere. They'd also found a couple of toe imprints from hard-worn sneakers. The size of the imprints indicated the sneaker wearer was either a child or a small, thin adult.

A child? Matt thought with dismay as she studied the brief report.

Naturally, after four years of wearing the badge, Matt knew full well there were kids, some appallingly young, who angrily and willfully wreaked havoc and destruction on humans as well as inanimate objects.

For Matt, it was heartbreaking because the majority of young offenders she had dealt with had committed the random acts in a desperate cry for help.

On an intellectual level, Matt accepted the fact of a young person's capability to commit acts of physical violence and vandalism. But emotionally, she cringed at the very idea that a young person would think to desecrate a religious symbol.

In a perfect world, children would be lovingly cared for and protected, their innocence inviolate until they'd had a chance to grow and mature.

Grow up, Wolfe, Matt impatiently told herself,

sighing as she set the report aside. Sadly, the real world was far from perfect.

Come to that, she reflected, settling her hat on her head and waving an absent goodbye to the desk sergeant before exiting the station, the opposite seemed to apply.

She heaved a sigh as she slid behind the wheel of her patrol car to begin her regular rounds. On really bad days, Matt had the scary feeling the human race was hell-bent on a downward spiral into chaos.

Her normal optimistic outlook dimmed by deprivation of sleep and her depressing ruminations, Matt viewed her route with less than her usual enthusiasm.

The day was as gloomy as her thoughts; overcast with clouds the particular odd shade of gray that threatened snow before nightfall.

Thankfully, this was the last day of her shift and she would have two whole days free before starting another. Actually, her off time amounted to three days. Her first day back would be Sunday, and she'd be working the dead-man's shift so she wouldn't have to report in until midnight. The thought of her approaching downtime was the one bright spot on the otherwise dark terrain of Matt's mind.

Brooding, Matt made the turn off the blacktop country road onto the church driveway without conscious decision.

She frowned; then shrugged. What the heck, she mused. Since she was in the vicinity, she might as well stop, relay the lab report to the reverend, and ask if he had thought of anything that might help.

As excuses went, it was as good as any other.

Telling herself wryly that self-deception was a fool's pastime, she brought the car to a stop on the driveway near the crèche sight.

The figure of the Virgin Mary had been restored to its former beauty. Not a trace of the marring black paint remained. A satisfied sigh whispered through Matt's lips. The careful hand of the artist had wrought a loving serenity to the delicate features.

Her spirits lifted by the restoration, Matt drove on to the parsonage. Stepping from the car, she started for the house. The front door opened before she was halfway along the walk.

"Good afternoon, Officer Wolfe." The Reverend Macdonough was every bit as appealing in the light of day as he had been the previous night. Truth to tell, he was even more attractive…in a rugged, rough-hewn way. Matt's spirits ratcheted upward another notch.

"Afternoon, Reverend Macdonough," she returned the greeting, and his welcoming smile.

"Mac...or David...please." His smile chided.

Matt hesitated, then gave a brief nod. "All right, David, if you insist."

"I do." He waited, one eyebrow hitched.

She sighed. "Okay, David, my given name is Matilda..." Her eyes narrowed at his quickly concealed surprise. "My friends call me Matt."

His gaze swept her form, from the flat top of her cap, to the mirror-shine on her shoes. A slow smile teased his lips—and her nerve endings.

"You don't look like a Matt," he observed in a dry-voiced drawl. "But you don't look much like a Matilda, either."

"What, exactly, does a Matilda look like?" Her voice matched his for drawling dryness.

"Somebody's grandmother," he responded at once.

"Bull's-eye." She laughed. "That somebody is me. I was named for my father's mother."

"Mmm. And she's already got the nickname Matty...right?"

"Maddy," she corrected. "And, since Maddy and Matty are too similar, I got stuck with Matt."

"Ah...now I think I understand."

"Understand what?"

"Why you chose David instead of Mac," he explained. "Mac and Matt are also too similar, right?"

"Yes, of course."

"Uh-huh." He nodded, obviously suppressing a grin. "How about a cup of coffee...Matt?"

"I'd appreciate it...David."

Stepping back, he swung the door wide and invited her inside with a sweeping movement of his arm. As she moved past him, Matt caught a whiff of his scent, an intoxicating mixture of tangy citrus and healthy male.

Her reaction to his distinct smell was both confusing and unnerving. For an instant, Matt felt light-headed. A hollow sensation invaded her stomach and robbed the strength from her legs.

What the heck! she thought, locking her knees to remain upright. She had never...until now. Must be because her stomach was empty. But, telling herself her response to him was caused by the lack of nourishment, and believing it, were altogether two different matters...especially after the night she'd spent.

Her movements stiff, she entered the house, then paused, waiting for him to precede her.

"Kitchen okay?" he asked, cocking an eyebrow.

"Fine." She wet her lips; shivering in response to the intent stare he fastened on her mouth.

"Thirsty?" David's voice was low, husky-sounding. His eyes were dark, hooded.

"Y-yes." Rattled, her throat suddenly parched, bone dry, Matt swallowed.

His steady gaze monitored the convulsive motion of her throat. When he raised his eyes, the darkness was gone, replaced by a speculative gleam.

"Are you...upset about something?"

"No." Matt shook her head, too quickly, too hard. "No, I'm fine, really." It was a lie; she wasn't fine. She felt odd, jumpy, as if every nerve ending was quivering in anticipation of...something. Why? She was afraid she knew...and that rocked her inner peace.

He arched that same eyebrow again, only this time it had a quizzical slant.

If her behavior puzzled him, which it appeared to do, she couldn't blame him. She felt every bit as confused as he seemed to be.

"Did you have lunch?"

Matt blinked, thrown by the suddenness of his question, the briskness of his voice, and the cor-

rectness of the conclusion he had reached. Without delving into the possible reason for it, she
answered at once, and with complete honesty.
''No.'' She wasn't about to admit that she'd had
no breakfast, either. She opened her mouth to in-
quire as to why he'd asked, but he didn't give her
time.

''That's what I figured.'' A half smile quirking
his lips, David turned away. Striding into the living room, he called to her. ''Come along, Officer
Matt, I'll give you something solid to go with
your coffee.''

Chapter 3

Matt felt like a fool. Holding her spine rigid, she fought an urge to bolt from the house, from his presence. She trailed behind him, her reluctance evident in her slow, stiff and measured steps.

"Have a seat, Matt. Relax, it's no big deal." Although David was standing at the kitchen counter, his back to her, his advice came through loud and clear.

But it was a big deal, she silently argued, sinking onto a chair and frowning at his back—his broad, muscular back. Not understanding what the hell was happening to her—or what it was all about—*made* it a big deal. An extremely big deal.

Finished fiddling with the coffeemaker, he walked to the fridge and swung open the door. "Want to share a cheese and mushroom omelet?" He turned to face her, eyebrows raised, expression hopeful.

"Yuck." She shuddered.

"You don't like eggs?"

"I love eggs."

"You don't like cheese?"

"I love cheese."

"Ah, it's the mushrooms."

"I hate mushrooms."

He grinned. "It's heavy-going here, but we are learning things about each other."

Talk about your big deals, Matt muttered silently. Keeping the thought to herself, Matt decided to pass on his remark. "I'm really not very hungry, David, but I would love a cup of that coffee."

He shifted his gaze to the glass carafe. "It's not finished yet. How about a sandwich?"

She shook her head.

"If you missed lunch, you should have something." He arched that eyebrow. "A toasted English muffin? I've got cranberry," he added as inducement.

"I'm on duty, you know," she reminded him, making a show of glancing at her wristwatch.

"It'll only take a minute to toast a muffin." He thrust a hand into the fridge and pulled out a long container in a plastic sleeve. "I'll just pop one into the toaster for you," he said, prying apart two muffins and dropping them into a four-slot toaster. "You need nourishment to perform your duty to the best of your ability."

Matt rolled her eyes, but didn't bother protesting, certain it wouldn't do her any good anyway. She was the authority here, wasn't she? So when had she lost control of the situation?

While she was trying to figure that one out, David poured coffee into two cups. The muffins popped up in the toaster as he set a cup in front of her.

"See that?" He grinned. "Perfect timing."

Perfect teeth, too. And flashing to advantage in a perfectly demoralizing grin. The observation created a hollow feeling inside Matt.

At that moment David set a plate with two steaming, aromatic halves of muffin next to her coffee cup. The scent of cranberries blended with the healthy male aroma of him, activating her taste buds.

For the muffins...or for him? Shocked by the

thought, and the curl of sensuality it caused deep inside her, Matt felt weak with relief when he moved to take the chair opposite her.

"Thank you, it smells wonderful." She forced herself to look up at him, and felt the bottom fall out of her stomach. He looked so…so…appetizing.

"So do you."

Matt jolted, alarm streaking through her. Had she spoken aloud? Or had her expression reflected her inappropriate thoughts? He was a minister, for goodness' sake, a man of the cloth.

"Smell wonderful, I mean," he clarified—to her undying gratitude. "Your scent is light, enticing. Not heavy with musk or the badly combined and overpowering, funereal fragrance of flowers."

His observation of scents so closely paralleling her own, Matt was struck speechless. She simply stared at him—gaped, actually, since her mouth was already open in preparation of taking a bite of the muffin.

"Yes?" David prompted, obviously expecting a comment of some sort from her.

Matt's mouth snapped shut. She shook her head. "Nothing…it's just…" She shrugged.

"Well, that certainly clarifies everything." His

voice held a droll inflection; his eyes laughed at her. "It's just...what?" he persisted.

"It's just...that...well, it struck me as odd. I mean, your opinion on scents is so similar to mine...it just seemed...strange, somehow, er—" Matt broke off, floundering in her own inadequacy. Was she babbling? Yes, of course she was babbling. Dammit. What was wrong with her? She never babbled.

The laughter she had seen lurking in his eyes escaped from his throat. The wholly masculine sound of it danced on the air and down her spine.

For an instant Matt teetered on the fine line between offense and amusement.

Amusement won. A smile tickled her lips, then quickly expanded into a chuckle.

"I sound like an idiot, don't I?"

He shook his head, getting himself under control before responding. "An idiot? Not likely. You sound human, with all the frailties entailed." He valiantly fought back another bout of laughter. "You do such an excellent job of projecting the image of the stern, no-nonsense officer of the law, that it's a relief—a revelation—to discover the woman inside the cop."

His explanation left her stymied, groping for a response, and refusing to acknowledge a sudden

need to know what he *thought* of the woman inside the cop.

"I like her."

Matt caught herself just in time to keep from
revealing the shock wave his remark set off inside
her. Was she so transparent? Once again he had
appeared to read her like an open book, and she
didn't like it, the sense of vulnerability it instilled.
Besides, cops weren't supposed to wear their
thoughts on their expressions, for everyone to pe-
ruse.

"You really don't know that woman," she
said, rather pleased with the repressive tone she'd
inflected into her voice.

"But I'm beginning to," he countered. "I
know she doesn't like heavy, cloying scents. I
know she does like chocolate, and coffee, cranberry muffins, eggs and cheese..." He smiled.
"And I know she does not like mushrooms."

"Food preferences." Matt flicked a hand in a
gesture of dismissal. "Fragrances."

"And I also know," he continued, his voice
soft, intense, unaffected by her dismissive tone,
"that she can feel deeply affected by the senseless
desecration of a religious symbol."

Too close.

He was getting too close, Matt thought, tamping down an edgy sensation. She must be slipping. It wasn't good, safe, for anyone to be able to read her so accurately—not even a man of the cloth.

Most particularly *this* man of the cloth.

But David had, however unwittingly, offered her the means of redirecting the line of conversation. She could turn it away from her, personally, and to the reason she was there in the first place.

Yeah. Right.

Ignoring the unsubtle nudge from her conscience, Matt polished off the muffin she couldn't remember eating, or tasting, then got to the business at hand.

"That was good, thank you," she said. "But it really wasn't necessary. I only stopped by to tell you the gist of the report from the lab crew."

For an instant his expectant expression was altered by a flash of something. Disappointment? Then it was gone, replaced by a look of interest, and the raising of both eyebrows, leaving her strangely excited, pondering the portent of that fleeting expression.

"Did they find anything that might be helpful to the investigation?" he prompted, his intent gaze probing *her* expression.

"Not much," she said too quickly. "The paint

was a well-known, common brand,'' she continued, instilling brisk professionalism into her
voice. ''But you were right about the ground.
They were able to retrieve footprints.'' She
sighed. ''Unfortunately, all they found were toe
marks left by worn sneakers, the size and inden-
tation indicating a small, thin adult...or a child.''

''A kid?'' He revealed another flicker of emotion, clearly pained, before his eyebrows drew together in a frown.

''Kids have been known to commit random
acts of vandalism with spray paint, you know.''

''Of course, I know,'' he snapped, giving her
a mild shock with the show of impatience. ''Being
a minister does not necessarily equate with na-
iveté, Officer Wolfe. Because of the very nature
of our work, we pastors deal with all kinds of
aberrant behavior.''

Well and truly chastised, Matt inclined her head
in silent acknowledgment of his claim.

''It's not much to go on, is it?''

Grateful to him for letting her off the hook,
Matt shook her head.

''No,'' she said, pushing her chair back and
rising. She shrugged into her jacket.

''Could they get a make on the shoes?''

''Yes, they did. The shoes are a brand sold in

discount stores.'' She settled her hat on her head, and gave him a tight smile. ''The kind kids call Bobos.''

''And could have been purchased in any number of places,'' he concluded.

''Right.'' Matt nodded.

David exhaled a sigh. ''A tough one.''

She nodded again, then arched her eyebrows. ''Unless...you can recall one of your parishioners—one who might be dissatisfied about something—who fits the 'small, thin' description?''

He thought about it a moment, then slowly shook his head. ''No...as I said last night, offhand, I can't think of anyone, small and thin or otherwise.''

She sighed; there really wasn't much to go on.

''You could stop by, check out the congregation,'' he suggested. ''You never can tell, you might pick up on something. You're trained to recognize unusual behavior, aren't you?''

Matt ignored the latter to question the former. ''Stop by? You mean for church services?''

''No. You're always welcome, of course,'' David was quick to assure her. ''But I had a more informal atmosphere in mind...like the supper for instance.''

She frowned. ''The supper?''

He nodded. "The Christmas craft and cookie sale, followed by the spaghetti supper," he explained. "The church has it every year at this time."

She looked blank; he laughed.

"You had to have seen the sign while on patrol." He chuckled. "It's too big to miss."

"The sign," Matt repeated. Then the light went on. "Oh, you mean the sign along the road, right off the end of the driveway."

"The very same," he concurred, lips twitching with amusement, eyes laughing at her.

Matt was getting pretty darned tired of feeling foolish. Her spine grew stiff; her voice grew frosty. "Yes, I noticed it. I just didn't read it. When is this event to take place?"

"Saturday—one to whenever." He hesitated. "Of course, people may react to the uniform." He shrugged. "But by then the church regulars will be aware of the incident, so they shouldn't be too surprised."

"I'll be in street clothes—since I'll be off duty on Saturday."

"You'll stop by?"

"Yes." Matt smiled. "I might even bring my grandmother with me. Gram loves church socials, and eating out. And spaghetti's one of her favorites."

"I'll be looking forward to meeting her," he said, sounding as if he really meant it.

"Hmm," Matt murmured in her unconscious, habitual, judicious-sounding hum. "Now, I must go." She turned and headed for the door.

David was right behind her. "Afraid they'll put out an all-points on you?" he drawled, striding around her to open the door.

"No. They know where I..." Her voice faded as she moved to the door. "It's snowing."

Big as half dollars, the lacy white flakes looked like tiny ballerinas swirling on the breeze.

"Beautiful, isn't it?" David murmured, stepping out to stand beside her. "Not laying yet," he said, sweeping a glance over the ground. "Must have just started."

"Beautiful, yes," Matt agreed, sighing. "But if it continues, it'll make a lot more work for me." She slanted a smile of acceptance at him. "I'll probably spend my shift chasing fender-benders." With a light shrug, she walked to the patrol car.

"Drive carefully."

Matt paused in the act of swinging open the car door, surprised by the seriousness of his tone. She glanced over her shoulder at him, a mocking smile on her lips.

"I'm always careful, Reverend Macdonough," she said, her voice tinged with a note of warning. "I'm a very careful person...in and out of the car."

"Prudent," he said, nodding. A spark of understanding flared to life in his eyes, baffling Matt. She wasn't certain she understood what, exactly, she was warning him about.

Time to retreat, she advised herself, pulling open the door and sliding behind the wheel. A thought occurred as she flipped the ignition, firing the engine. She rolled down the window and stuck her head out.

"About Saturday," she called to him. "What if there's an accumulation of this stuff?"

"Unless it's up to your tush, the social's on," he said, grinning at her start of surprise.

"Uh-huh," Matt muttered, switching on the windshield wipers, then releasing the hand brake. "Then I suppose I'll see you Saturday."

"I'm looking forward to it."

Innocent enough response, Matt mused, steering the car along the driveway at a sedate speed. Yet there had been an underlying something in his tone that had sent a thrill tingling down her spine.

What was that all about?

Frowning, Matt brought the car to a stop at the road at the end of the drive, to stare, as if mesmerized, at the back and forth swish of the wipers. She spun her mental wheels, trying to figure out what had so unsettled her about those innocuous fifteen minutes or so she had spent in the parsonage.

And it had been innocuous. Nothing remotely out of the ordinary had happened to cause this churned-up sensation inside her. Nothing.

Strange.

And yet, Matt had to admit that from her first sight of him last night stepping out of the church, she had experienced an unusual reaction to him. And that reaction had remained in play, keeping her edgy and restless throughout most of the night.

In fact, she felt a curious, quivery and inexplicable excitement just being in David Macdonough's company.

And maybe she had just hit on the answer. Being in David Macdonough's company.

The man unnerved her, simple as that.

Or, perhaps, not so simple at all.

By a mile, David Macdonough was the most attractive and interesting man she'd run across. And good looks alone had nothing to do with it.

Matt knew plenty of flat-out handsome men, men with smoother, less rough-edged good looks...a few with the added attraction of wealth. Yet, not one of those men had ever made her feel shaky inside, overwarm, even in the winter cold, foolish, and too alive.

The tingly thrill tiptoed down her spine once again, causing a delicious little shudder.

David was a minister, she sternly reminded herself. A man of the cloth.

Forbidden fruit... Wasn't there some old saw about the most tempting fruit being—

"Four-one?"

Matt blinked, jerking alert at the summons from the two-way. Get it together, Wolfe, she chastised herself with chagrined impatience, reaching for the handset and depressing the call button.

"Four-one," she replied.

"What kept you?" the dry voice of the dispatcher, Dina Marsden, asked in an inquisitive drawl.

Matt was nothing if not scrupulously honest. "The reverend invited me to have a cup of coffee and an English muffin while we talked."

"What flavor?" Dina's voice had gone from dry to wry—with a hint of laughter thrown in.

"Cranberry." Matt's lips quirked.

"Yummy. You cops have all the breaks," Dina muttered. "Are you back on patrol now?"

"Yeah." The quirk worked its way into a grin.

"Oh, goody."

Matt waited, thirty seconds. Then she sighed. "You got something for me?"

"Yeah," Dina returned sardonically. "Check out a vehicular accident at the intersection of Chestnut and Willow Run. No reported injuries— just a lot of shouting and accusations flying back and forth."

"I'm on it." Flipping the call button to off, Matt replaced the handset. As she pulled onto the road, she spared a quick glance at the big sign, reading it aloud as she slowly drove past.

"'Annual Christmas Craft and Cookie Sale. Spaghetti Supper To Follow. Everybody Welcome.'"

Matt grinned again, adding, "Even cops."

Chapter 4

David.

Bemused by the distinctive, smoky sound of her voice saying his name echoing inside his head, Mac watched the squad car until it was lost to his sight around the curve in the driveway.

He liked the sound, liked the warm sensation it generated deep inside him. There were only ever two people who had called him David—his soft-spoken, gentle mother, and the tough-talking woman who had picked him out of the gutter and saved him from himself.

And now, Officer Matilda Wolfe chose to call him David rather than Mac.

A portent? Mac didn't know, nor really care. All he did know was that he liked it...and her. Matt turned him on, an amazing feat, under the circumstances.

A large, delicate snowflake came to rest on his left eye, and tangled in his lashes.

Smiling, he brushed the moisture away, then stared up at the leaden sky.

Was that a blessing or a condemnation, Sir? Mac asked, addressing his Maker in his usual method of silent communion. *After all these years of my disinclination and disinterest in the opposite sex, do You approve or disapprove of this unexpected and unsought reactivation of my libido?*

There was no answer from above, no rumble of thunder, no streak of lightning.

Mac hadn't expected such a display. Grounded within his faith was the belief that mankind had been endowed with a reasoning mind for the purpose of applying it. What was the point, otherwise?

In effect, at least for Mac, his answer was in the point, and the point was crystal clear: each man—and woman—had to think for themselves.

There were guidelines, of course, writ in stone by a finger of fire.

Having embraced those guidelines, Mac adhered to them…and there was not one *Shall Not*
pertaining to a single man's interest in a single
woman.

But was Matt Wolfe a single woman?

Mac frowned at the thought. He had noted
many things about her person and personality,
but, offhand, he could not recall if revealing rings
had adorned the third finger of Matt's left hand.

Unconcerned with the wet stuff pelting his face,
Mac continued to stare at the sky, deciding he'd
take it as a good sign if it turned out that Matt
was not only single but unattached.

Ah, the mental games we mortals play, he
chided himself, shaking his head at his own
frailty.

Nevertheless, Matt did turn him on.

And, after all these years, Mac rather enjoyed
it.

Shivering, he turned to reenter the house, hoping the snow wouldn't amount to much because
now, even more than before, he was anticipating
the church social.

For Mac, Saturday couldn't come fast enough;
but, in the meanwhile, he had a sermon to write.

If the number of cars parked on the church lot
was an indication, the social was a resounding

success.

Maneuvering her midsize car into a minisize space, Matt set the hand brake and flashed a grin at her grandmother.

"Proud of yourself, are you?" Maddy Wolfe asked in a toast-dry tone of voice.

"It's in," Matt replied. "And without a scratch, or even a bump."

"Uh-huh. It's in," Maddy drawled. "Now the trick will be us...getting out."

"It was the last space, Gram."

"I know," Maddy agreed, releasing the seat belt.

A concerned line drawing her brows together, Matt glanced to the right, studying the narrow space between the car and the one parked next to it.

"I should have let you get out before I pulled in," she said in apology. "In fact, I suppose I should have let you off at the church entrance." There was no force on earth that would have made her admit that she had been distracted by the thought of seeing David Macdonough again.

Stupid...but there it was.

Maddy merely gave her a pained look. "Think I'm too old and decrepit to squeeze out of a cramped space or totter across a parking lot, do you?''

''No...I—'' Matt began in protest, only to break off when she noticed the sparkle of laughter dancing in her grandmother's faded blue eyes. ''Oh...you.''

''Still rise to the bait,'' Maddy chided, carefully inching the door open so as not to bump the shiny new car next to Matt's. ''Come Christmas, your cousins will have a field day teasing you.''

''They'll try,'' Matt conceded, inching her own door open. ''But I'll be prepared for them,'' she said pointedly, sinuously working her way out of the car. ''I wasn't expecting it from you.''

''I know.'' Maddy tossed her a smug look before exiting the vehicle with just a smidgen less agility than her granddaughter. ''But, you see, I consider it my duty to keep you on your toes.''

Laughing, Matt circled the car to the older woman's side. ''You're a hoot, Gram,'' she said, linking her arm with Maddy's. ''You know that?''

''I do my best, honey,'' Maddy said, her steps a far cry from tottering as they made for the side entrance to the building where a large sign read Social Room.

The room was spacious—and packed.

The spicy aroma of spaghetti sauce permeated the air and activated Matt's appetite.

"Smells good," she murmured, her mouth watering as she inhaled the distinctive scent.

"Yes, and they have a good turnout for it," Maddy said, patiently waiting behind a group crowding around the cloakroom.

"Excellent," Matt concurred, unobtrusively taking a protective stance behind the older woman. "I'm glad that snow Thursday evening was a fizzle. If it had continued, this affair might have been a washout."

"Maybe not," Maddy observed, glancing around her. "This appears to be a hardy bunch."

"Yeah." Matt's gaze tracked her grandmother's over the bright, expectant faces of the milling crowd. "They look hardy and hungry. I hope they've prepared enough spaghetti for the supper."

"You wouldn't be so worried about it, if you'd eaten something for lunch," Maddy said, moving forward as the group in front of them dispersed.

After handing their coats to the teenage girl manning the cloakroom, they moved on to a young man stationed at the doorway, selling tickets for supper.

Standing in line again, Matt purchased two

tickets. Then she and Maddy trailed the crowd, wending its way around the long tables set up to serve supper in the center of the large room.

Servers, mostly teenagers, were bustling about, placing utensils wrapped in paper napkins, small bowls of salad, and covered baskets of bread on the tables.

"From the looks of it," Maddy observed, indicating the youngsters, "we won't have long to wait."

"Mmm," Matt agreed, nodding, then slanting a grin at her grandmother at the low growling demand for sustenance from her stomach.

Maddy merely shook her head.

From the big room, they shuffled into a smaller adjacent room, where other tables were laid out with the crafts and baked goods on sale.

Content to follow wherever her grandmother chose to go, and growing hungrier by the minute, Matt surreptitiously skimmed the faces around her in the room. She was looking for one person in particular, a man even taller than herself.

Her perusal proved fruitless, and quashing an unacceptable sense of disappointment, Matt centered her attention on the hand-crafted Christmas tree ornament her grandmother was examining.

Maddy bought the ornament, then moved on to

the next table, Matt playing the shadow in her wake.

"Those cookies look good," Maddy said at one of the tables, indicating a plastic-covered tray.

"Yes, they do," Matt agreed, but went on to quantify, "But I can't imagine any cookies tasting better than yours always do—and you've baked I don't know how many dozens these past couple of weeks."

"About twenty or so," Maddy said, chuckling. "But remember, in addition to your parents and sister, all your uncles, aunts and cousins will be at the house on Christmas. I know how quickly cookies can disappear when my sons and grandsons are around."

"Point taken," Matt conceded. She laughed, feeling a quickening anticipation for the visit from her family with the approaching holidays.

"Besides," Maddy went on, flicking a hand at the goodies under discussion. "I've never baked that kind, and they look delicious."

Obviously having overheard the conversation, the attractive blond woman behind the table offered one of the sweets to Maddy. "Try one," she invited, smiling. "The recipe's been in my family for generations—my great-great-grandmother brought it with her from Sweden."

Accepting the cookie, Maddy thanked the woman with a delighted smile.

While her grandmother enthusiastically consumed the sweet, Matt exchanged smiles with the other woman. She couldn't help noticing when her eyes suddenly lit up as if someone had turned on a switch behind them. She was wondering what had caused the bright animation when a velvet-cloaked, gravelly voice from behind her sent a thrill skipping up her spine.

"Well, Corine, as usual, you don't have to sell your baked goods, they sell themselves."

"Hi, Mac," the woman he'd called Corine responded, her voice breathy, her eyes even brighter than before. "How are things going in the kitchen?"

"The usual chaos." He laughed, and then his voice lowered to a rich, warm honey. "I'm glad you could make it today, Matt. Is this lovely lady your grandmother?"

The sound of her name on his lips affected Matt in a manner way out of proportion to the context of his remarks. She felt an immediate weakness, a searing warmth. So, of course, she steeled her spine and infused a chill reserve to overlay the inner heat.

"Hello, David," she said with cool composure

she was light-years from feeling. "And, yes, this is my grandmother." Catching the gleam of sharp interest in Maddy's eyes, she went on. "Gram, this is the Reverend David Macdonough, the pastor of this church. David, my grandmother, Maddy Wolfe."

A smile twitching the corners of his too attractive mouth, David extended his hand to the older woman. "A pleasure, Mrs. Wolfe."

"Maddy," she said, taking his hand in a grasp Matt knew to be surprisingly strong for a woman in her eighties. "And the pleasure is mine, Reverend Macdonough."

"Mac...please, Maddy," he returned, a startled burst of laughter erupting from his throat. "And you have one impressive grip there, lady."

"Why, thank you, Mac." Maddy beamed at him in an instantly besotted way that had Matt choking back a groan. "Comes from handling a passel of strong sons and grandsons." She eyed Matt's imposing form, and grinned. "Not to mention granddaughter."

His blue eyes shimmering with amusement, David regarded Matt, running a glance the full six-foot length of her slender body. When his gaze returned to clash with hers, his eyes appeared to smolder with blue fire.

"Strong, are you?"

His eyes, his sexy voice, sent the heat tearing through her self-imposed chill reserve to slam into her with the force of a .44 slug. Stunned, Matt felt the heat radiating from within, singeing her cheeks.

Dammit. She hadn't blushed since she was fourteen. Desperate, she imposed an icy surface control.

"And hungry," she retorted, employing the steely tone she manufactured on the rare instances she had to deal with real hard cases. "Will you be serving supper anytime soon?"

"Matilda." The shocked-sounding murmur came from Maddy, who only ever used Matt's given name when she was out of patience with her.

In truth, Matt hadn't heard her Christian name from her grandmother for some years. At any other time, Matt would have heeded the exasperation in Maddy's voice. But not this time, not with this man.

Not even sure why she felt so threatened, so intimidated by the strength of his magnetic appeal, Matt narrowed her eyes and met his smoldering stare head-on.

David had the sheer masculine audacity to laugh in the face of her open defiance.

Matt's temper simmered.

"You'll have to excuse my granddaughter's rudeness, Mac," Maddy said, recognizing the signs of Matt's pending temper explosion. "She skipped lunch…" She paused to level a hard look on Matt. "I'm afraid she must be suffering a lack of nourishment to her mental capacity as well as her body."

"No offense taken, Maddy," David smoothly assured the older woman, sparing a gentle smile for her before returning his gaze to Matt.

Rebelliously refusing to back down, Matt arrogantly quirked a brow at him.

The corners of his lips twitched once more. "You're in luck, Matt," he said, laughter woven through his honeyed tones. "I came out of the kitchen for the express purpose of announcing that supper will be served in—" He broke off to glance at his watch. "In about ten or so minutes," he went on, motioning toward the larger room. "Why don't you escort your grandmother to a good table?"

"Thank you." Matt clipped the response. "I'll do that." She broke his unsettling eye contact to turn to her grandmother. "Ready, Gram?"

"In a minute," Maddy said, her eyes bright with speculation as she glanced from Matt to David. "I want to buy some of these cookies." She shifted another sharp-eyed look between the pair before turning to give her cookie order to the woman behind the table.

"That is one shrewd woman."

Matt started at the low, intimate sound of his voice close, too close, to her ear. Her heartbeat accelerated with the moist sensation of his warm breath feathering her skin. Her voice eluded her at the realization of how very close his mouth was to the curve of her jaw.

"Y-yes," Matt finally responded, damning the weak, fluttery sound of her own voice. The compelling urge to step aside, out of harm's way, both confused and annoyed her.

"And maybe even as strong as you."

Good grief. Matt stifled a protest. He had moved his head even closer to hers; his voice a mere whisper curling around her senses. Although he was not touching her, Matt could feel the heat from his body, smell the sheer male scent of him.

Excitement flared to life inside her...deep inside the most feminine part of her. She ached with a sudden and compelling need.

This is insane, she thought, gritting her teeth in

an attempt to reassert control. Why on earth was she experiencing this wild, almost abandoned response to him? David's comments had been innocuous—but his voice, his tone...

"Forewarning, Matt Wolfe." The sound was little more than a breath. "I am stronger."

A challenge? Relief shivered through Matt—at least she assured herself the feeling was relief. She could deal with a challenge.

Drawing herself up to her full, squared-shouldered height, Matt stepped away, but only to allow herself room to turn and rake his admittedly impressive form with an unimpressed, sweeping glance.

"Indeed?" she drawled, her expression disdainful. "Don't bet the parsonage on it."

He laughed. "Oh, I think that would be a safe—"

"I'm ready now," Maddy said, unwittingly interrupting him. "Let's go find seats...before the stampede that's sure to follow Mac's announcement."

"Which I'd better get to," he said. He started to turn away, then slanted a sparkling look at Maddy. "May I join you ladies for supper?"

No. The refusal shouted inside Matt's head but her grandmother beat her by replying first.

"Why, we'd be delighted." She blessed him with a bright smile. "We'll save you a seat."

"Thank you," he responded, not sparing so much as a glance at Matt's set expression. "I'll only be a few minutes." Raising a hand, he smiled at the woman behind the table. "See you, Corine." Then he was gone.

"Yeah, see you."

The note of dejection in the other woman's voice snagged Matt's attention. Unaware of being observed, Corine's gaze was fastened on David's retreating back, a desolate, pained look in her eyes.

She's in love with him.

The realization caused conflicting emotions inside Matt. Because David had shown no signs of a reciprocal emotional involvement, she felt sympathy and compassion for the woman. She also felt something else, something unfamiliar.

While escorting her grandmother into the larger room, Matt mused in uncomfortable silence on the strange new sensation.

This feeling...surely it couldn't be jubilation? A sense of extreme exhilaration because David apparently did not return Corine's affection?

Appalled at the very idea of feeling so much as

a tinge of satisfaction in response to another's rejection, Matt dismissed the concept out of hand.

Even so…

"Why don't you sit over there?" Maddy's question broke through Matt's unpalatable introspection. "I'll sit here and save this seat for Mac."

Collecting herself, Matt took the end seat at the long table. She frowned at the empty chair opposite her, on which Maddy deposited her purse and bag of cookies.

"This table doesn't suit you?" Maddy asked, obviously noting Matt's expression.

"The table?" Matt's frown darkened. Then, realizing she was causing her grandmother concern, she dredged up a smile. "It's fine, Gram. I'm sorry, I was…um, distracted."

"Is something wrong?" Maddy raised her eyebrows.

"No, no, I…"

"May I have your attention, please?" The sound of David's voice, deep and exciting even over the PA system, saved Matt from her sense of ineptitude.

"Supper will be served in approximately five minutes. It's open seating in the social room.

Please place your meal ticket on the table. Thank you, and we hope you enjoy your meal.''

Matt dug in her pocket for the tickets she had purchased and placed them on the table.

''Mac is one very attractive man,'' Maddy said, almost too casually. ''Isn't he?''

''I suppose.'' Matt managed an equally casual tone, and a disinterested shrug. To underline her lack of concern for the subject, she speared a wedge of tomato from her salad bowl and popped it into her mouth.

''The devil dances in his eyes.''

Matt started, nearly choking on the partially chewed tomato.

''Gram, really. The man is an ordained minister of the church,'' she protested, even though she herself had noted the devilish light in his eyes.

Maddy gave her a wry look. ''I don't want to shatter any preconceptions, dear, but ordained ministers who have not taken a vow of celibacy are as subject to human frailties as the rest of us,'' she said with gentle humor. ''Or have you forgotten that our own church pastor has three children and five grandchildren?''

Matt gave an impatient shake of her head, and gulped down the mangled tomato wedge before attempting to answer. ''No, of course not, but...''

"Why don't you go get us some water?" Maddy inserted into Matt's sputter. She waved at a small table along the wall on which pitchers of iced water and stacks of brightly colored plastic cups were set. "I think you need a drink."

Grateful for the reprieve, however short-lived, Matt jumped up and went for the water.

Her smile serene, innocent, Maddy waited until Matt had returned with the drinks and had taken a sip of the cool water, before broadsiding her with another question.

"You're having trouble with the concept of our pastor as a sexual being?"

Matt was glad she had swallowed the water, for she surely would have sprayed the table with her jolt of surprise at her grandmother's phrasing. And, the thing of it was, Maddy seemed so comfortable with the topic.

"Well, no," Matt said, striving to appear as blasé as her grandmother. "But…"

"What?" Maddy grinned.

"I don't know." Matt was floundering, badly, and she knew it. Why she was floundering, she was afraid to delve into. "I just can't imagine anyone ever having given a thought to our pastor in that way…or noting the devil dancing in his eyes."

"But then, you didn't know the man when he was young," Maddy noted pointedly. "I did."

"You're kidding?" Matt exclaimed, surprised and amused by the very idea of the gentle, timid pastor she knew revealed in this new light.

"No," Maddy said complacently. "He was quite the dapper fellow...when he was young. But, mind you, he was always a fine man and pastor."

"I don't doubt it," Matt said, fascinated by the dreamy look on Maddy's face.

A smile, youthful, wholly feminine, curved her lips. "I must admit, though, that he was never as fine a figure of a man, or nearly as good-looking, as Mac."

Matt simply stared at her grandmother's rapt expression, then her attention was caught by two doors being swung open at the far end of the room. A line of servers, ranging from early teens to middle age, each bearing large serving trays, exited the kitchen. Her stomach gave a rumble of appreciation.

She shifted her gaze back to her grandmother, to inform her that supper was being served. Her words were lost to the speculative look on Maddy's face.

"Yes, Mac is one good-looking, tough-looking,

sexy-looking man," Maddy reiterated—with a flourish.

Matt had to laugh, despite herself. "Why, Gram. Darned if you don't sound smitten with the man."

"In a certain way, I guess I am," Maddy said enigmatically, her eyes fairly dancing with some inner delight. "But, more importantly, are you?"

"Me? I?" Matt blurted. Oh, hell, she thought, suddenly feeling cornered.

Smitten with the man...with David?

Ridiculous.

"Gram, really," she said, trying—and failing—for a note of repression. She was reaching, and the only defense she could grab hold of was a factor her consciousness had secretly acknowledged from the beginning.

"The man has got to be ten, possibly...probably, more than ten years older than I am."

"Indeed?" Maddy's smile was unruffled. "What a coincidence. Your grandfather was twelve years older than I am. And I took one look at him and knew."

Knew? Knew? At that moment, the only thing Matt knew was that she felt disoriented, confused, leagues out of her depth. No, she corrected herself. That wasn't quite all she knew. She knew, as well, that there was a magnetic quality about David Macdonough that drew her in some inexplicable, irrevocable way.

The very thought of an inevitable attraction was unnerving, almost frightening. Seemingly without effort, he generated an excitement inside her unlike anything she had ever before experienced.

But what was even more unnerving to Matt, was her apparent transparency. If her grandmother saw her unwilling response to him, did David see it, too?

Stunned by the idea and the ramifications it implied, Matt maintained her grandmother's bright gaze for some seconds. When she glanced away it was only to have her breath stolen. For her vision was filled with the sight of the very man they were speaking of striding along…and heading directly toward her.

Matt had a compelling impulse to bolt.

Chapter 5

Maintaining her seat, and her fragile grasp on her composure, Matt managed a strained smile. She murmured "Thank you" to the thirty-something-year-old man who deposited three heaping plates of steaming, aromatic pasta onto the table.

David waited until the man had finished serving the others seated at the long table. Then the handsome pastor slid into his seat opposite Matt.

"So, how was the salad, ladies?" He raised his dark brows and shared a smile between Matt and Maddy.

"I enjoyed mine," Maddy replied in a rather wry voice that matched her smile. "I don't know about Matt…since she barely touched hers."

He glanced at the bowl in question, then fixed a probing look on Matt. "It's not to your taste?"

"It's fine," she said, shooting a reproachful look at her grandmother.

"But then—" he began.

"I didn't want to take the edge off of my appetite," she cut in, her tone sharp. "Okay?" she demanded, wincing as her companions responded in unison.

"Matt!" Maddy reprimanded.

"Sure." David shrugged.

Matt felt both chastised and childish. She didn't particularly like the feelings. So, of course, she lay the blame on him…to herself, at any rate. She wasn't about to incur more disfavor with her grandmother by voicing her thoughts out loud.

"Sorry, but I am hungry." She made the half-hearted apology, and followed it with a muttered request. "Does anyone mind if I eat…before it gets cold?"

Maddy shook her head in despair of her granddaughter's display of bad manners.

"Dig in," David invited, his lips curving in a blatant and thoroughly sexy male grin.

The strange sensation that coiled through Matt's stomach had nothing whatsoever to do with the tantalizing smell of the spaghetti.

Darn his attractive hide. What did he think he was doing? Matt railed in silent frustration while making a performance of coolly twirling the saucy pasta onto her fork. *He was a minister, for goodness' sake.*

Matt raised her eyes to his as she slipped the fork into her mouth. An electrifying jolt sizzled through her from the heat in his eyes, which were fastened on her lips.

Oh, mercy, she thought, shivering in response to the fiery gaze searing her mouth.

"Good?" David's voice held pure innocence while his eyes conveyed the exact opposite.

Matt felt another jolt zip through her, leaving her weak, quivering, aching for...

Chill out, Wolfe, Matt told herself in exasperation. Tearing her gaze from his, she quickly tried to repair the breach in her defenses. With intense concentration, she chewed the pasta and swallowed.

"So?"

Matt glanced up, frowning at the prompting tone in his voice. "So what?"

David blessed her with a gentle, infuriatingly tolerant smile. "Do you like it?"

Distracted by his annoying smile, Matt missed the point of his question. "Like what?"

Maddy made a snorting sound and rolled her eyes.

"The spaghetti, Officer Matt," David said in obvious amusement. "What else?"

Lord help her, for it was apparent she was too addle-brained to help herself, Matt reflected miserably. What had she done? What grievous sin had she committed to be condemned to the punishment of this overwhelming attraction to David Macdonough?

Maddy sighed into the lengthening silence. "The spaghetti is delicious, Mac," she said, a tinge of youthful impishness in her smile. "The sauce is almost as good as my own."

"High praise, indeed, I'm sure." David flashed his pearly whites at Maddy, but quickly returned his drilling gaze back to her granddaughter. "Do you agree, Matt?"

She blinked, feeling dumber by the second. "About it being high praise? Yes, of course."

"No, Matt, not about the praise," he said kindly, as if he were addressing a sweet but rather dull child. "I meant, do you agree that the meal is delicious?"

Good night nurse, Matt groused to herself. Why was he so blasted intent on getting her opinion, anyway? Feeling badgered, she heaved a sigh.

"Yes, David, I do agree," she replied, her tone one of long-suffering exasperation. "The meal is delicious. I'd love to be allowed to savor it in peace."

Maddy arched a brow in warning.

To Matt's chagrin, the aggravating man had the gall to grin at her.

"Glad you like it," he drawled, as if, after all his probing efforts, it was of little matter or concern to him.

On the very edge of exploding, Matt gritted her teeth and turned her attention to her supper.

Fortunately, for her peace of already rattled mind, David followed her example. The remainder of the meal was consumed in nerve-settling quiet.

In truth, Matt did agree that the spaghetti was delicious. She cleaned her plate of every piece of long, thin pasta and every morsel of meatball. Stuffed and contented, she placed her fork on her plate, convinced she could not eat another bite.

However, no sooner had she sat back in her

chair when the troop of servers returned. Working
like a well-rehearsed unit, one group whipped the
plates from the table, only to be followed by another group, some serving smaller plates contain-
ing individually wrapped slices of Neapolitan ice
cream, others steaming cups of coffee and tiny
cups of half-and-half.

Although her table companions appeared to
welcome both, Matt accepted the coffee but
passed on the ice cream with a murmured, ''No
thanks.''

Carefully sipping the hot, full-bodied brew,
Matt studied her grandmother, noting the telltale
signs of weariness about her eyes and mouth.

Time to go home, she thought, reminding herself—as she often had to do—of her grandmother's age. In light of Maddy's robust health
and sharp mental activity, her advanced years
were easy to forget.

The woman was obviously beginning to tire
and, ever protective of her beloved grandmother,
Matt suggested leaving as soon as Maddy finished
her dessert and coffee.

''I've got a few things to do yet tonight,'' she
tacked on, so that her grandmother wouldn't think
she was being too overprotective.

''Yes, I'm ready,'' Maddy said, her smile a

clear indication that she was on to Matt's ploy. She pushed her chair back just as a middle-aged couple came to a stop next to Mac.

"Well, you certainly haven't lost your touch, Mac," the man said, grasping the pastor's extended hand. "Your spaghetti sauce was excellent…as always."

"Yes, it was wonderful, Mac," the woman chimed in. "I wish I could cook it as good as you."

More than a little surprised, Matt stared in bemusement as, with a flashing smile, David stood to thank the couple and exchange a few pleasantries.

"You cooked the spaghetti sauce?" Matt blurted out without thinking when the couple moved on.

"Yes." Not a hint of either false modesty or overt pride shaded his tone. He shrugged. "But I had a lot of help from our active parishioners."

"Nevertheless, you make a mean sauce, Mac," Maddy said, standing and offering her hand to him. "And it's been a pleasure meeting you."

"The pleasure was mine." David returned the compliment. "I'm glad you came." He sifted a gleaming glance at Matt. "You, too," he added softly.

"I enjoyed it," Matt lied, suddenly feeling pressured, her breathing constrained. Standing, she faced him—not quite eye to eye. Her eyes were more at the level of his chin. She didn't like the four or so inches in height he had over her. She didn't offer her hand, either.

"You know," he said just as Matt made to turn away. "I give a pretty mean sermon, too. I'd be pleased to have the both of you attend services some Sunday."

Not in this lifetime, Matt thought, and opened her mouth to tell him so. But her grandmother beat her to it.

"We just might take you up on that invitation," Maddy said, beaming at him.

David beamed back at her. Then gave a sidelong look at Matt. "I'll be looking forward to seeing you there someday."

Managing a weak smile and a mumbled response, Matt hustled her frowning grandmother away to collect their coats.

To her despair, David dogged their retreat, chatting with Maddy. His eyes laughing at Matt every foot of the way out.

Matt's constrained breathing didn't regulate until farewells had finally been exchanged and the door to the social room closed behind her—with David on the other side.

"What a charming man," Maddy said, her steps not as brisk on the return trip to the car.

"Yeah. Charming," Matt agreed through teeth gritted in baffling frustration.

"What's the matter with you?" Maddy demanded. "You've been acting strange all evening." She eyed Matt with obvious concern. "Are you coming down with a cold or something?"

On the verge of saying no, that she was feeling fine, Matt caught herself in time to grab at the excuse for her unusual behavior.

"I, uh, don't know. Maybe. I am feeling a little tired and washed out."

"Mmm," Maddy murmured, her sharp-eyed gaze skeptical. "Then I don't suppose you'll feel like accepting Mac's invitation to services tomorrow. Will you?"

Matt was once again on the verge of saying no when the realization struck her of her intended purpose for attending the church supper. She had planned to cast a professional eye over David's parishioners...and the only person there that she had really seen was David.

And there hadn't been one damn professional thing about her regard.

"Well?" Maddy's prodding voice held an edge of impatience at Matt's lengthy silence.

Matt sighed. She was a cop—with a job to do. She could not, would not, allow her personal feelings to interfere.

She didn't want to see David again. He unnerved her, made her experience confusing and conflicting emotions. In truth, he scared the hell out of her.

But...

"I don't know," she finally said, shrugging. "Let's wait until morning, see how I feel."

It was very late, and Mac was very much awake...awake and aching. He hadn't even attempted to court sleep. The bed was the absolute last place he wanted to be. It conjured thoughts both beguiling and bedeviling.

Standing at the bedroom window, Mac stared up into the clear, star-bright sky.

Is this a test, Sir? Mac asked his Maker in his less than traditional manner of praying. Military trained, he thought it the highest form of address for his ultimate Commander.

In Your infinite wisdom, have You visited this

*mental and physical affliction upon me to gauge
the depth of my devotion, faith and commitment?*

*But no... In Your infinite wisdom, You know the
depth of my commitment to Your service.*

*Still, there is this woman, this tall cop who turns
me on something fierce.*

What to do about it...and her.

*I know, I know... You endowed mankind with
intelligence and free will...the ability to reason
through our little problems, and hopefully arrive
at a rational and workable resolution.*

*On the other hand, You also endowed mankind
with sensuality, and the powerful urge to procreate, which necessitates the coming together of a
male and a female in the sexual act.*

*That inner drive within me, so long dormant,
has reasserted itself, and is now running hot and
strong in my system.*

*Is it wrong, Sir, to desire the company and com-
munion of another?*

What to do? How to proceed?

Sighing, Mac blinked, bringing the diamond-
bright sky back into focus. His expression contemplative, he turned away from the window, then
paused. He frowned for a moment before swinging back around. A faint smile feathered his lips

as he tilted his head to gaze once again up into the clear night sky.

The full meaning of the contents of his silent prayer echoed inside his mind.

Mankind was endowed with sensuality and the powerful urge to procreate.

Of course, he thought, wondering, as he had many times before, at the endless intelligence and love of the Supreme Being.

Thank you, Sir, for your depthless wisdom.

Pivoting away from the window, Mac began to undress for bed, his conscience no longer troubled. Savoring his renewed sexual vigor, he crawled between the cool sheets, his course set in his mind.

He had plans for Miss Matilda Wolfe, plans both sensual and honorable...as the Good Lord certainly knew.

Mac slept the peaceful sleep of the innocent.

Dressed in a white silk shirt and a chocolate brown suit that nearly matched the color of her eyes, Matt strode into the kitchen Sunday morning. Her grandmother was seated at the table, a half slice of toast in her hand, a cup of coffee in front of her.

''Morning, Gram,'' Matt said, glancing at the

clock and deciding she had time for a cup of the aromatic brew before they had to go. "I'll be ready to leave for church whenever you are."

"But…" Maddy frowned. "Have you forgotten?"

Her coffee poured, Matt crossed to the table and sat opposite her grandmother. "Forgotten?" Now she frowned. "Forgotten what?"

Maddy sighed—as mothers and grandmothers had sighed over the young since day one. "Matt, I told you last Monday that the Bakers would be picking me up for church this morning."

"Oh, yes." Her memory jogged, Matt did remember. "You said that after services you and the Bakers would be stopping somewhere for lunch before going to the nursing home to visit Mrs. Baker's sister."

"That's right," Maddy said, her smile one of patient acceptance of youth. "I also said we would probably stop for supper on the way home, if you'll recall. You assured me you could muddle through on your own."

"And I can." Matt could also understand how the information had slipped her mind. She had been rather distracted since the night of the incident at David's church. "You've trained me very well in that respect,'' she went on in a teasing tone.

Smiling, Maddy lifted her cup to take a sip of the coffee, a speculative gleam in her eyes. ''Are you still going to church?'' she asked.

''Might as well.'' Matt shrugged. ''I'm up and dressed for it.''

''You know…'' Maddy murmured, an almost too casual inflection in her voice. ''This might be a good time for you to take Mac up on his invitation and attend services at his church instead of ours.''

A thrill streaked down Matt's spine, part trepidation, part anticipation, and wholly excitement. The inner conflict kept her mute for a moment, sifting the pros and cons in her mind. The cons weighed heavily.

''Oh, Gram, I don't know…'' Her voice trailed away as she realized the merit of her grandmother's suggestion. Attending services at David's church would offer her the opportunity to perform the duty she had failed to complete last night—that of running a professional glance over the members of David's parishioners.

Of course, it would also give her opportunity of seeing and talking to—sparring with?—David again.

The pros gained the upper hand.

"Then again, perhaps you're right," she murmured, hiding behind the cup she'd raised to her lips.

"Of course, I'm right."

Matt shot a glance at her. Was she imagining things, or had there been a thread of satisfaction woven through her grandmother's placid tones?

Maddy avoided Matt's probing look by turning to peer at the clock.

"Oh, my, will you look at the time," she said, standing and carrying her cup and plate to the sink. "I've got to get a move on, or I won't be ready when the Bakers arrive to collect me."

Could her grandmother be playing matchmaker? Matt mused. Suspicion aroused, she watched the elderly woman flutter about, rinsing her dishes, stashing them in the sink, and averting Matt's contemplative gaze as she hurried from the kitchen.

Brooding, Matt absently drank her coffee. She had to be mistaken. Maddy had never before presumed to nudge Matt in the direction of a man, any man.

On the other hand, Matt mused, she couldn't recollect her grandmother ever fluttering before, either.

"The Bakers are here, and I'm off, Matt," the woman in question called from the living room. "Have a nice day, and be sure you have something substantial for dinner this evening."

"Okay, I—" Matt broke off at the sound of the closing door... Why bother to continue, she'd only be talking to herself.

The church parking lot was nearly as full of cars as it had been the previous night. It would appear, Matt mused as she wedged her car between a sports coup and a van, that David could draw a crowd.

After being swept along by a buffeting cold wind, she was glad to get inside the church where it was warm. It was also full. Skimming the interior, Matt noticed a space at the end of a row a little to the back of the room's center.

Perfect for her purposes, she thought, removing her coat as she strode down the center aisle, then slipped onto the hard wooden pew.

"Good morning," said the middle-aged gentleman seated in the pew a foot or so from her.

"Good morning," Matt returned, her greeting smile quickly turning to a frown. "I hope I haven't taken a place you were holding for someone."

"No." He gave a reassuring shake of his head. "The seat was up for grabs."

Smiling, she folded her coat into the space separating them.

The man offered her a hymnal, and the page number of the first hymn to be sung.

With a murmured, "Thank you," Matt searched out the correct page.

A moment later the service began.

The hymn was sung.

Then David was there at the pulpit—no, not David, but the Reverend Macdonough. He looked solemn, imposing and a bit intimidating. In his clerical robes, he appeared larger, taller than memory served.

He began the service.

Matt didn't hear a word of it for the sound of her thumping heart pounding against her eardrums. All she heard was the honeyed-gravel sound of his voice, stroking her senses, abrading her nerves.

She felt chilled, and then hot. She couldn't take her eyes off of him.

In minute detail Matt studied the stern set of his strong, rough-hewn features, the slight arch of his dark brows, the thrust of his squared jawline, the sensuous definition of his masculine mouth.

Longing, deep and primal, swept through her, firing her blood, and imagination.

She ached something awful.

Someone behind her coughed.

Reason reasserted itself.

Appalled by the intensity of her reaction, she reminded herself of where she was, and why she was supposedly there. Matt tore her rapt gaze from his alluring figure and applied herself to the congregation.

Trying to appear casual, she glanced around, and was immediately struck by the expressions on the faces she could see. Every one of them, young and old, appeared enthralled, either by the pastor's voice, or the content of his message.

Matt didn't see so much as a shading hint of guilt or furtiveness on any face. If the perpetrator of the desecration was there, he or she either felt no guilt or remorse, or had carefully hidden it.

Her questing gaze skimmed over, paused, then zapped back to hone in on a woman seated two rows farther back and to the other side of the aisle. The woman appeared to be in her mid-thirties...and not at all well. Her face, once attractive, Matt was certain, was pale and drawn, and she looked exhausted.

She had two children with her, a boy about

eighteen months or so, who she held on her lap, and a pretty girl about eleven years old.

Matt felt a pang of compassion when the woman quickly raised a hand to muffle a cough, causing the girl to glance at her in anxious concern.

The woman smiled and murmured something to the girl that eased the strain on the child's face.

Matt's gaze moved on.

When the service was over, and the final hymn sung, Matt moved with the crowd heading for the door…and the robed man exchanging greetings as they exited.

When she drew even with him, Matt accepted his extended hand. She had no other choice but to do so. But at least he was David again.

"Glad you could make it, Matt." David's hand was warm and strong around hers. He raised a brow. "But where is your grandmother?"

"She had a previous commitment," she explained, taking a step to move on. He kept her in place by tightening his grasp on her hand.

"I'd appreciate it if you'd hang around until I'm through here." Though soft, his voice held more command than request. "I'd like a word with you, hear the results of your observations."

She hesitated, wanting to stay yet somehow knowing that she shouldn't.

"I'll give you lunch."

Matt was beginning to feel embarrassed. Didn't the man care that he had an audience?

"Will you wait?" he persisted, giving evidence of his unconcern...or his knowledge of the regard in which he was held by his parishioners.

Matt caved.

"Yes, I'll wait."

Chapter 6

Not wanting to draw attention, and speculation, to herself, Matt didn't drive from the lot to his house. She waited in her car.

Five, ten, fifteen minutes she waited. It would appear his parishioners were a chatty bunch.

And all the time she waited, Matt chastised herself for agreeing to speak with him in private. Since she hadn't noticed anything out of the ordinary about any one member of his congregation, she had made no observations worth mentioning to him.

And she certainly hadn't agreed to wait because

he had promised her lunch; she could get lunch anywhere. Besides, she wasn't even hungry. She was too churned up inside, too edgy, too...

Not wanting to go where her thoughts were leading, Matt directed her attention to the cars exiting the parking lot in slow progression.

Finally, a woman hurried to the last remaining car. It was Corine, the woman David had introduced to Matt the night before, the one whose sad-eyed gaze had followed him when he had walked away.

Matt couldn't help but notice the quick look Corine shot at her car, or the expression of frustrated envy marring her pretty face.

Telling herself she needed another woman's antipathy like she needed a bout of the flu, Matt reached for the ignition key.

At that moment, David exited a side entrance of the church, his long-legged stride bringing him to her car in seconds. Opening the passenger door, he slid onto the seat beside Matt.

"Ready for lunch?"

Matt wanted to say no. And she would have, if his smile, his voice, hadn't been so...so friendly.

She caved again. "I suppose."

He indicated the turnoff driveway to his house. "Then, lead on MacWolf."

Failing to control the twitch of amusement on her lips, Matt rolled her eyes and set the car in motion.

"Is there something I can do to help?" Matt felt awkward and uncomfortable just standing in the center of David's kitchen.

Busy gathering ingredients to prepare their lunch, he slanted a quick smile at her over his shoulder.

"No, I've got everything under control." His hands and arms full of food, he backed away from the fridge and shut the door with his hip. "Have a seat. Coffee will be ready in a few minutes."

"But..." she started to protest.

He wasn't listening. "While I cook, you can fill me in on the observations you made in church."

Sighing, Matt slid into a chair. "What I observed was a group of normal, well-mannered, and very attentive, respectful people. I didn't spot one individual who appeared either disgruntled or guilty-looking."

The utter conviction in her voice brought him around to smile at her. His relief was obvious.

"That's a load off my mind." His smile faded. "But, that puts us right back at square one."

"'Fraid so." She nodded.

"I feel I must warn you that, if this was a random act of vandalism, we may never find the perpetrator."

He lifted his rather spectacular shoulders in a slight, hopeless-looking shrug.

"I know that—I knew it all along. I just thought it was worth your time to have a look at my congregation."

"It was," she agreed.

Nodding, he turned to the business of preparing lunch. His softened voice drifted to her. "I also thought it was an excellent excuse to see you again."

Matt didn't respond; she couldn't. She was too busy dealing with the tingling sensations his bald statement sent skittering through her.

This did not bode well, she warned herself. But her greedy gaze continued feasting on his tall, leanly muscled form.

Damn. No man should look that good in faded jeans and an old sweatshirt...most especially not a man of the cloth, she reflected.

"Are you sure there isn't something I can do to help?" she asked, feeling the need for a distraction from her own thoughts, and her hungry gaze.

"No." He turned from the sink to flash an unrepentant grin at her. "I'm afraid that I'm one of those infamous temperamental cooks who won't tolerate anyone else at the stove with me."

Matt returned his grin with a wry smile.

"But," he qualified, chuckling, "I have no objections to you setting the table."

"Okay...I can handle that." Matt got up from the chair. But before she took a step he halted her with his upraised hand.

"Not yet. I'll tell you when."

She lifted one eyebrow. "And what am I supposed to do in the meantime?"

His grin flashed again. "Make yourself at home. You can hang your coat there in the closet by the back door." He gave a flick of one hand. "And there's a powder room off the hallway there..." He flicked his hand in the opposite direction. "In case you want to freshen up...or something."

Matt stood there a moment, feeling useless. When he turned back to the sink, she heaved a sigh and carried her coat to the closet.

She wandered through the kitchen and into the hallway. After washing her hands in the powder room, she ambled into the living room.

As she had noticed when she had been there

before, the home's furnishings, while tasteful and of excellent quality, were spare. In the case of an area in front of the picture window, completely bare. Matt wondered if the lack of decorative touches was because of his being fairly new to the house or simply because of his bachelorhood.

She ambled into the dining room which was also sparsely furnished. But there was a large oak table set in the center of the room, the top nearly concealed by boxes of assorted sizes. Upon investigation, she was pleased to find the boxes contained a glittering array of Christmas decorations. This explained that bare spot in the living room. Obviously, David was planning to set his tree in front of the window.

"Coffee's ready, Matt," David called from the kitchen. "You can set the table now. Lunch is just about done."

And none too soon, she thought, her mouth watering at the aroma that greeted her when she entered the kitchen.

Since collecting the plates, utensils and such necessitated skirting around him, Matt knew at once she should have kept her mouth shut about wanting to help in some way. Other than to cease breathing, there was no way for her to avoid inhaling the distinctive scent of him—the combined smells of spicy soap, spicy aftershave, and even spicier pure male.

Heady stuff, for sure.

By the time David was ready to serve their lunch, Matt felt positive she could not manage to eat a thing.

"Where did you learn to cook like this?" Matt asked. She was savoring the last bite of the delicious, featherlight Western omelet which—despite her fears to the contrary—she'd devoured like a starving person.

"It's a long story," David said, rising to retrieve the coffeepot and refill their cups. "And not a particularly pretty one, at that."

"I have all day." Matt found her reply shocking. Yet she was intrigued despite her reservations about spending more time in his disturbing company.

"I was in the military—" he began.

"You were a cook in the army?" she interrupted in a burst of surprise. "Weren't you a chaplain?"

"No, Matt." His smile was wry. "I was in the Special Services."

"Oh." Matt frowned at the effort of making a

connection between the Special Services and the ministry.

"I know it's a reach," he said, grinning. "But there is a bridge between the two."

Did she really want to cross that bridge? Matt asked herself. She was curious—who wouldn't be? Even so, curiosity aside, did she really want to know his history, considering the effect he had on her? If she had an ounce of self-preservation, she mused, she'd stop him now, make her excuses and run like...

Too late, David led her onto that bridge.

His voice devoid of inflection, his words concise, he gave her a brief account of his service time, his special assignments. It was all very exciting, but not unexpected in light of his military status.

But then Matt felt her nerves quiver with apprehension when tension tightened his features, and his voice.

"My personal turning point came near the end of my second tour of duty." He paused to offer her a faint smile.

"I had planned to re-up, again." He shrugged, the movement looked anything but casual.

"We were assigned to Africa, to yet another emerging country torn by warring factions. Our mission was to distribute food—not interference, just bring food to the starving people who had fled their homes to escape the carnage.'' He closed his eyes a moment, as if marshaling his thoughts—and courage.

Without conscious direction, Matt reached across the table and grasped his hand. ''It erupted in your faces.'' It was an easy deduction; it had happened before, many times before.

''Yeah.'' He exhaled. ''The one faction hit us. I didn't even know which side, the current rulers or the supposed freedom fighters. They were all over us like a swarm of angry bees.'' He shook his head and gave a cynical laugh. ''It was sheer pandemonium. We were ordered to pull back.'' His voice rang hollow; his eyes looked haunted. ''That's when I saw him.''

'' 'Him'?'' Matt repeated, thinking he surely thought he had seen a vision of the Lord.

''The child,'' he said. ''A boy, around five or six. He was nothing but skin and bones, and he was injured and bleeding from a bullet wound in his side. And his eyes... Oh, God, his eyes.''

He fell silent. His own eyes, now the darkest blue, stared into the distance—or the past.

Matt was silent, too. What could she possibly

say? She tightened her hand around his. David blinked, and shuddered.

"He was lying by the side of the dirt road, staring at me. He didn't cry out in pain, or call to me for help. But then, he didn't need to say a word. His eyes were eloquent."

"You couldn't leave him behind." This guess was even easier than the first.

"No, despite orders of no physical involvement, I could not leave him behind," he said.

"What did you do?" she asked, aware of the penalties for disobeying orders.

"I scooped him up into my arms and ran like hell." His voice grew strained, and picked up speed.

"My unit had faded into the cover of the surrounding bush. I could hear my buddy yelling at me, urging me on. I had almost made it to the brush when I was hit." His body jerked, as if he'd actually felt the shot.

"You were captured?"

"No." David shook his head. "I barely felt it...then. I kept running, crashing into the brush, and straight into my buddy's arms." Pain, deep, emotional pain, flickered over his taut face. "It was all for nothing. I wasn't fast enough." His voice was raw. "The boy was dead."

The heavy weight of silence settled in the room, and into Matt's shocked mind. For long moments she couldn't think, react. Numb, she stared at him.

The crushing grip of his hand brought her back to reality. Matt half expected to hear her knuckles pop in response to his hard clasp on her fingers. Pain streaked up her arm; she clamped her lips against a cry of distress, wondering at the power of the protective surge she felt for him.

"David," she said calmly, softly.

His body jolted as if she had shouted at him. Then his eyes came into focus. "What?"

"You're..." Matt managed a strained smile. "You're hurting my hand."

"Good God." His fingers sprang apart, releasing her.

"Matt, I'm sorry...I—"

"No." She cut him off, shaking her head. "It's all right. I understand."

"It's not all right." Scowling, he gently cradled her abused hand in his palm. "Please, forgive me, Matt. I...er, wasn't really here." Then, slowly lifting her hand, he brought her palm to his lips.

A different sensation, the complete opposite of pain, streaked up Matt's arm. It shimmered like a sun-spangled waterfall through her body.

Matt caught back the gasp that rose to her throat, and from somewhere found the sense to distract him.

"And you...your wound?" Her eyes made a quick appraisal of his solid form. She'd never before noticed any apparent effects inflicted by the bullet. At least, there were no physical after-effects.

A self-deprecating smile shadowed his terse mouth.

"I was flown back to the States, to a military hospital. The physical wound healed." He went on, as if his thoughts had monitored hers. "But the mental damage was devastating—it damn near destroyed me."

That was the second time she had heard him swear in the retelling, which told her a lot about what he'd been through. Matt bit her lip until it hurt. She was almost afraid to ask, and yet, for reasons she had no desire to delve into, she had to know.

"How...how did you overcome the mental anguish?"

David laughed. It was not a pleasant sound. "For a long time, I didn't overcome it. I didn't even try."

"Your family?" Matt murmured.

''All gone.'' He winced. ''But that's another story. After losing my mother, then my father—'' he sighed ''—and then my younger sister, the military, the discipline, kept me from going off the rails.''

When he paused, Matt shivered, for his eyes had taken on that dark blue, distant expression once more.

''But after that debacle, the military became the cause, not the cure.'' His tones were as dark as his eyes. ''That boy's big, pleading eyes tormented me, wouldn't let me rest.''

''Oh, David,'' she murmured.

He moved his shoulders, figuratively shaking off her sympathetic concern. A self-derisive smile curled his tight lips.

''By the time my wound had healed, my tour of duty was out. I didn't reenlist. Instead, I plunged into self-pity. It was an easy move from there into alcohol, and from there into degradation.'' Disgust colored his voice. ''I wallowed in it…booze, women, panhandling, outright begging. You name it, I probably indulged in it.''

Disbelief widened Matt's eyes. This man? This pastor who had earned the obvious respect and devotion of his congregation? He was so gentle, so good. No. No. She could not, would not, accept it.

Matt wasn't even aware that she slowly moved her head in mute denial.

"Yes, Matt. It's true…all of it."

"Drugs, too?" Matt nearly choked on the words.

"Surprisingly…no." He gave a humorless chuckle. "Even in the deepest depths of despair, something inside me resisted that form of self-destruction."

"But looking at you now…" Confusion clouded her thoughts and speech. "How…"

"How did I make it from there to here?" A hopeful strand of genuine amusement enriched his velvet-coated, gravelly voice.

"Yes… I mean…" She shrugged.

"I know what you mean." He pushed away from the table and stood. "And I'll explain…after I get something to drink. All that talking has me parched."

"And me," she said, wetting her dry lips. It wasn't until the tension suddenly drained from her that Matt realized that throughout his recitation she had been wound up as tight as a spool of thread.

He smiled in understanding. "More coffee? Iced tea? Cola?"

"Something cold," she decided aloud. "Iced tea sounds wonderful."

"Coming up." Turning, David went to a cabinet and withdrew an automatic iced-tea machine, then set about brewing their drinks.

While he busied himself with the tea, Matt cleared the table of their forgotten plates, cups and utensils. She was wiping the table when he announced that the tea was ready.

Once again seated opposite each other at the table, tall ice-filled glasses in front of them, David launched back into his story.

"You wondered how I got from my self-created hell to here," he began.

A sip of tea in her mouth, Matt nodded.

He smiled in remembrance. "A very down-to-earth, very tough angel yanked me out of it."

Angel? Matt frowned.

David laughed. "Really." A flickering shadow banished his laughter. "She's gone now...hopefully to a justly earned reward. I received word of her demise a month or so before I was assigned here to Sprucewood." He slowly shook his head. "I hadn't even known she was ill, or I'd have gone to her...given my own life for her, if I could.'' He sighed. ''She knew that, of course, which was why she didn't let me know, I'm sure.''

''But...who was she?'' Matt asked, for some reason expecting to be given the name of a sister of mercy or a missionary.

''Her name was Rachel Rosenberg.''

''She was Jewish!'' Matt exclaimed without thinking.

''She was Jewish.'' His humor was back, tugging his lips into a soft smile. ''She was in her sixties, short, more than a little overweight—'' his eyes glowed with the light of pure love ''—and the most beautiful person it has ever been my privilege to know.''

An emotional lump lodged in Matt's throat. ''Tell me about her...please.''

He was quiet a moment, his expression contemplative. ''How to describe Rachel,'' he began, his voice touched with aching gentleness. He smiled. ''She loved the human race, no matter what color, creed, religious belief or station in life. To me, Rachel was the living, breathing embodiment of a handmaiden of the Lord. She was a very soft touch—and a very hard cookie.'' He chuckled. ''She lived, defined, the expression of tough love.''

"Sounds formidable," Matt murmured.

The sudden sparkle in David's eyes stole her breath—and melted her heart.

"You don't know the half of it. She was a veritable warrior in the service of saving supposed lost souls," he said, once again shaking his head, almost as if even he couldn't believe it. "I had been on the skids for about a year when she hauled me out of the gutter."

Matt gave a startled gasp.

He grinned. "Well, not precisely the gutter," he qualified. "Actually, I was curled up in a rat-infested, filthy alleyway—which didn't matter, because I was every bit as filthy. Filthy, malnourished, hungover, and sick as a dog from a batch of bad wine I'd greedily poured down my alcohol-raw throat."

Finding it harder and harder to equate David with the man he was describing, Matt could do no more than stare at him in astonishment.

Noting her expression, David smiled. "I know," he said. "It's hard to believe now, but I assure you every word is true."

"I wasn't doubting your veracity," Matt said. "No rational person would claim such a sordid past for mere shock value."

"And I am rational, have been for some time. Thanks to Rachel."

"You had to be a willing subject," Matt stated in his defense. "Or even she couldn't have turned you around so completely."

"Perhaps," he conceded.

"So, after hauling you out of that alley, how did she go about assisting this transformation?"

"The first thing she did was dry me out." He winced. "It was awful...I hope never to have to live through anything like that again. With that boy's reproachful eyes looking on, my mind, every cell in my body, screamed for the anesthesia of alcohol."

Grimacing in remembrance, he shook his head.

"Go on," Matt urged.

"I'd have taken off at a run, of course, if I could have," he continued. "But there was this big guy holding me down—man that guy was big, strong as a bull elephant, yet gentle as a spring lamb." His features were softened by affection. "His given name was Dwain, but everybody called him 'The Train.'" He grinned. "For obvious reasons."

Despite the seriousness of the topic, his grin was so infectious, Matt couldn't contain a smile. "Were you in a detox center?"

"No." He shook his head. "At least, not an official one. I was in the dry-out room of Rachel's home—the home she had turned into a shelter. She had inherited the house, and a small monthly annuity," he explained. "Don't ask me how she managed to keep the place viable, but somehow she always did.

"Of course, Rachel did receive some help, in the form of donations from the residents in the area—some money, but not much, for they weren't even close to middle class. But they were fairly generous with foodstuffs, used clothing, soaps, toothpaste, things like that."

"Obviously, you weren't the only person who loved her," Matt observed.

"No, I wasn't the only one." His smile was so tender it caused an odd, unfamiliar ache in her chest. "Everybody young, old, and in between, inside and outside the shelter loved Rachel. She was living proof of the scripture of reaping what you sow."

"I'm glad she found you in that alley."

"I will be eternally grateful." He heaved a sigh.

He was quiet for a moment. Not wanting to intrude on his somber mood, Matt was quiet, too.

Then he smiled at Matt in a way that instantly lightened the atmosphere, and her spirits.

"And so, we finally get to the original point of this long story. Rachel didn't only run a shelter, she ran a soup kitchen. And she taught me to cook." He laughed in remembrance. "She was a fantastic cook—nothing fancy, but good, solid, nourishing food. She taught every person, man, woman or child who stayed at her shelter, to cook. I was no exception. When she deemed me ready, I did kitchen duty...with Rachel by my side, directing every move."

"She was a superb teacher," Matt said, smiling. "My grandmother and I can vouch for that."

"I liked your grandmother, Matt." He smiled.

"She liked you." She smiled back at him. "You, and your spaghetti sauce."

"The sauce recipe is Rachel's, not mine. She gets the credit." He grinned. "Every recipe I use is hers. But that's okay, because she gave me permission to do so when I left the shelter."

"And when was that?"

"Not quite a year after she hauled me into it." He hesitated a moment, then continued. "She had always told me I'd know when I was ready to leave."

"And did you?"

"Oh, yes, I knew."

Curious, Matt took what she believed to be a sure guess. "Because you had decided to go into the ministry?"

David smiled, but shook his head. "No, I had decided on the ministry a few months before leaving."

Stymied, Matt frowned. "Then, how?"

"I knew when that boy's eyes no longer reproached, but smiled at me before leaving me in peace."

"Oh, David," she whispered, blinking against the sting of tears in her eyes.

Chapter 7

"Here now, none of that," David said, giving her hand a quick squeeze before pushing his chair back. "We've been sitting here too long," he said decisively. "I think we both could use some fresh air and exercise."

"But..." Matt began. His final mention of a child's eyes, while touching her heart, also jogged her memory of the little girl she'd noticed in church.

"No buts," he said, striding to the closet for her coat and his jacket, then returning to circle the table to grasp her hands and pull her upright.

"But," she protested, laughing as he thrust her coat at her. "I thought of something, someone in church I wanted to ask you about."

"Concerning the desecration?"

"No," Matt said, slipping into her coat. "Not that. Just something I thought might be of interest to you...especially now, after hearing your story."

"Mmm, intriguing," he murmured, shrugging into his ski jacket and ushering her to the back door. "You can explain while we walk."

After the artificial heat of the house, the cold air was a shock...as was David's backyard. Shivering, Matt slid her hands into the side pockets of her long coat and looked around in delight. Though the only color in the sectioned garden came from a few lingering chrysanthemums and several evergreens, she could easily imagine how it must look in summer, with the many various plantings in full and glorious bloom.

David slanted a knowing look at her. "Still no gloves, hmm?"

Matt laughed, feeling the cold breeze against her teeth. "No," she admitted, shivering again.

"You're cold." He made a half turn. "We'll go back inside."

"No." Matt slipped her hand from her pocket

to grasp his arm, halting him. "It was the shock. I'm fine. The cold air is refreshing. Let's walk." She motioned to the bricked pathways between the sections. "Did you design this garden?"

"Designed it and built it..." He laughed. "If 'build' is the correct term."

"Unimportant." Matt shrugged off the semantics. "I'm impressed. It's wonderful."

"Thanks." In a move so casual, it seemed the natural thing to do, he lifted her hand from his arm, threaded his fingers through hers, then started moving along the central pathway. "I like working with my hands, digging in the earth. It gives a man time to think."

"To ponder the mysteries of the universe?" Matt asked in a light, teasing tone. Her question was a bid to conceal her sudden attack of breathlessness caused by the warmth of his hand curled around hers.

He laughed. "Something like that."

What an incredible man, she mused, feeling her admiration for him go up another notch.

And what a complex man. In essence, three different and very distinct personalities, Matt reflected. The toughened soldier. The weakened derelict. The physically and morally strong, compassionate and determined pastor.

Add a garden builder, grower and philosopher into the bargain.

Incredible, indeed.

"The herb garden."

Until David spoke, drawing Matt from her reverie, she wasn't aware of staring at a straggly section of the garden.

"Oh...uh, I knew that." She hadn't; she hadn't even *seen* the squared area. "My grandmother grows her own herbs, too." She rushed on, feeling rattled, and wondering why. "But Gram grows hers on a shelf attached to the kitchen windowsill."

"So do I, in the winter." He flicked a hand at the plot. "This is my summer herb garden."

"I...see." Matt cast her gaze around. "And that next little area?"

"Vegetables...also in the summer." Silent laughter lurked in his dry voice.

Matt gave him an arched look. "No kidding?"

He laughed. "Moving right along, folks." He tugged on her hand to get her moving. "To your left, you'll notice the rose garden...in repose now, of course, but a riot of colorful, sweet smelling blossoms in the summertime." He smiled and tilted his head up as a lone white flake landed on his nose. "When it isn't snowing, that is."

Matt surrendered to the urge to laugh.

David rewarded her with a light squeeze on her hand.

With the lacy white stuff swirling lazily around them, they continued their short tour in the same vein. David pointed out the wildflower patch, the still-blooming mums, and the boxwood hedges separating each individual section. The tour ended at the far end of the garden, under the scant protection of a huge, now bare-limbed old chestnut tree.

Matt looked through the branches at the whitish-gray sky. A frown tugged her eyebrows together.

"Are you cold?"

"No...a little concerned." She lowered her gaze to his eyes, struck anew by the depth of their dark blue color. "Gram's out visiting with friends. I hope this snowfall doesn't amount to anything."

"Are the friends responsible people?"

"Oh, yes." She nodded. "It's not that, it's just..." She shrugged.

"You worry." He ended her unfinished remark.

Matt's smile was faint. "Yes."

"Understandable," he said, his smile as warm

as his hand, still clasping hers. "And commendable...but then, you're devoted to your family, aren't you?"

"Yes, certainly...but how do you know?"

He chuckled. "Oh, Officer Wolfe, your eyes glow with love whenever you speak of them."

"But..." Matt gave him a puzzled look. "The only family member I've mentioned is my grandmother."

"Not so." His lips curved into a chiding smile. "You mentioned them—briefly, I'll admit—on the night we met." Warm approval shaded his voice. "And your tone, your eyes, overflowed with sheer love for them."

"They're very special to me," Matt murmured, a bit self-conscious because of his praise.

"They should be." David's eyes darkened. "Until you've lost your loved ones, you can't know..." He stopped abruptly, took a deep breath, then went on. "Family should be the primary concern of everyone."

Sympathetic to the grief he obviously still suffered, Matt raked her mind for a topic to change the subject. Memory stirred, reminding her of the anxious concern in the eyes of the young girl in church that morning.

It wasn't exactly a change of subject, but she

felt sure the information would distract David from his somber recollections.

"Speaking of families, David," she said, her tone as casual as she could manage. "Do you remember I told you I had made one observation during service this morning that I thought you should hear about?"

"Yes, of course." Bright interest chased the darkness of pain from his eyes. "An observation unconnected to the vandalism. Right?"

"That's right." Matt agreed. "There was this small family—a mother and two children. The boy was eighteen months or so, and the girl was eleven or twelve."

Matt went on to describe the three individuals in a concise, professional way. "It was the anxious expression on the girl's face, the fear in her eyes when her mother coughed, that caught my attention. And also, David, the woman looked ill and somehow desperate."

Frowning in concentration, David slowly shook his head. "From your description I can't place them... They're not regulars, I can tell you. I know my regulars."

Matt didn't doubt that.

"But you can rest assured I'll look into it." His

voice was strong with purpose. "If the woman is ill and needs help, she'll receive it."

Matt didn't doubt that, either.

Recalling the fear in the girl's eyes, the woman's pale, drawn face, Matt shivered with relief, then started at the sudden tug on her arm.

"Come along, Officer Wolfe. You're shivering again." He strode out from under the tree, taking her with him. "Let's go back into the house and have some hot chocolate."

Matt wasn't cold; not seriously cold. But she didn't argue the point. Hot chocolate had appeal.

It wasn't until they were seated once more at the table, steaming mugs of the rich drink in front of them, that Matt became uneasy in her mind.

The attraction she had felt for David at first sight, startling as it had been, paled in comparison to the myriad feelings stirring inside her now.

There was respect, which was fine. In her opinion, he had earned the respect of everyone who knew him.

There was admiration. Also fine. He possessed many admirable qualities.

Matt could deal with the first two feelings; it was the deeper, hidden feelings that scared her silly. There were emotional responses to him quaking through her, causing her to shiver in the warmth of the house.

There was a strong physical attraction Matt didn't even want to think about, never mind deal with. After her one and only adventure into the realm of the physical senses, which in truth had not been an adventure, but more a disappointing fiasco, she had consigned her natural sexual urges to the deep freeze. Those urges, seemingly never very strong to begin with, had remained frozen solid ever since.

Until now.

At some time, out there in David's winter-chilled garden, a spring thaw had set in inside Matt, reactivating her libido. And that wasn't fine.

But that wasn't even the worst of it. Matt was very much afraid her emotional responses to him ran even deeper than the physical.

She could fall in love with the man. Matt gulped a swallow of chocolate, never even noticing that the hot liquid seared her tongue.

Her gaze flicked to him; her heart performed a funny little thump-thump.

Oh, hell…she was in big trouble.

It was time for her to get out of there, Matt told herself. Past time. Way past time.

She didn't have time for love. Falling in love

wasn't included in her agenda. It was strictly against her principles, her belief that being a cop, and being emotionally involved, was a dangerous combination. She had witnessed firsthand the proof of her beliefs in the fear revealed in the eyes of her mother, her aunts, no matter how hard they worked at concealment.

And Matt knew, as well, that, certainly clearer than she, her father and uncles had seen the fear, too. They'd seen it and lived with it every second they carried out their duties as law enforcement officers.

Yes, Matt reiterated to herself, it was time to get out of David's house, David's life.

He was dangerous to her.

Draining the still-hot drink that burned all the way down her throat, Matt set the mug on the table, pushed back her chair, and stood, ready to bolt.

Her abrupt action drew him from what appeared to be a reverie of his own—probably, she decided, concerning the mother and two children she had told him about.

"What's up?" he asked, smiling at her in a way that made her tremble inside.

"I've taken up enough of your day," she said briskly, damning the inner tremors. She started for the door on legs that were not as steady as she would have wished. "I'll be leaving now. But I'll be in touch if there's any new informa—"

"Wait a minute." He jolted up, shaking the table. "You can't leave now."

"Indeed?" Matt arched a brow.

"Yes, indeed." He mimicked her chilly tone. "And knock off the intimidating look." His eyes laughed at her. "I'm not impressed, because I've got your number."

"And what exactly does that mean?" She scowled.

He grinned, evidently still not impressed. "It means, my beautiful Officer Wolfe, that I know full well that you're an armor-plated marshmallow."

"What?" Matt frowned, at him, and the stupid thrill she got from hearing him call her beautiful. "What are you talking about?"

David laughed. "You. On the surface, you appear the tough, steel-encased cop. But I know that, inside, you're as soft and sweet as marshmallow."

"I am tough," she maintained, too firmly.

"Sure." His eyes fairly gleamed. "But my pot roast isn't."

"Huh?" Matt blinked. "Pot roast? What are you talking about? What pot roast?"

"The one I put together and shoved into the oven after church, for dinner," he explained.

After church? When after church? She had been there after church; had come into the house with him after church. She hadn't seen him put together a pot roast and shove it into the oven.

Matt gave him the look. Her special look that usually preceded the command "Assume the position."

David laughed in the face of her *look.*

"Don't tell me you didn't notice how long it was taking me to prepare our lunch," he chided. "Or did you assume I'm just an extra-slow mover?"

Well, of course she had noticed. How could she have helped but notice? Matt recalled. But she did have some manners...she wouldn't have dreamed of commenting on what had seemed to be his lack of speed.

"Aha," he crowed. "Condemned by your own silence. I'll have you know that as a rule, I'm a veritable dervish in the kitchen. There's little time for fussiness or finesse when you're cooking for a horde of hungry street people and vagrants."

What could she say? Clueless, Matt fell back on humor. "A dervish, huh?"

"Well, that might be stretching it a bit," he conceded. "But I do make a great Yankee pot roast, if I must say so myself. And I made it just for you."

Matt knew when she was outflanked. He had cooked dinner for her...just for her. She accepted defeat with a inner sigh for herself, and a smile for him.

"All right, David. I'll stay for dinner."

"Good." His smile was bright with pleased satisfaction. "We'll eat about six. Okay?"

"Fine." Matt glanced at the clock. It was 1:37. "What do we do till then?"

"Get comfortable. Read the paper. Whatever." He shrugged and held out his hand. "Come on, you can help me build a fire."

David led Matt into the living room and to the fireplace. To her surprise, he actually did allow her to help him...she handed the wood to him. When he had the fire going, he stepped back and indicated the grouped chairs and sofa.

"Make yourself at home," he invited, moving to a wide, russet-colored velour lounge chair. "Kick your shoes off and relax."

Matt hesitated an instant, then, slipping out of

her low-heeled pumps, curled up on the cream-and-green-striped sofa.

"Would you hand me the sports section of the paper, please?" He inclined his head. "It's there, at the other end of the sofa."

"Sure." Tilting to the side, she searched out the section and handed it to him.

"Thanks." He smiled; she fluttered. "You can have the rest...this will take me a while."

"Later, maybe," she murmured, absently staring into the flickering fire.

Quiet settled on the room, broken occasionally by the crackle of paper when he turned the page, and the softer crackle and pop of the burning wood. Mesmerized by the dancing flames, Matt cradled her head on the arm of the sofa. She was barely aware of the weight tugging on her eyelids.

She stirred at a light touch against her arm. Still half asleep, she opened her eyes to find David pulling an autumn-leaf-imprinted afghan over her.

"Sorry." His voice was soft, his eyes softer. "I didn't mean to wake you."

"'Sawright," she mumbled, raising a hand to cover a yawn.

"How long have I been asleep?" Without thought, she shifted onto her back and stretched out her legs.

"Not long. A half hour or so."

He was still bent over her; she could feel his breath feather her lips. Suddenly a hunger unrelated to pot roast sank its claws into her.

"I want to kiss you, Officer Wolfe." David's gravelly voice had lost its velvet coating. "I want to kiss you very badly."

"I—I hope you don't." Her voice was reedy, nearly nonexistent.

"Kiss you?" He sighed his disappointment.

"No," she whispered, a tremulous smile hovering on her lips. "I hope you don't kiss me very badly."

A flame brighter than any in the fireplace leaped in his eyes. His lips curved in a sensuous smile. He lowered his head; she caught the lingering scent of chocolate on his warm breath.

"You'll have to be the judge."

Matt heard his murmur an instant before she felt the light pressure of his mouth against hers.

Not yet fully awake, the taste of him, the excitement generated by his mouth molding to hers, sent her senses soaring into an altogether different realm of dreaming. It was Elysian. A paradise of pure blissful sensation.

With a low groan filling her mouth, David deepened the kiss. Matt raised her arms to coil them around his neck. His tongue glided along her bottom lip. Sighing, she opened, inviting the foray of his tongue.

Vaguely, Matt felt the afghan throw being whipped away, to be replaced by his weight. She felt the heat of him, the fullness of him, pressing into the material sheathing the juncture of her thighs.

Arching into him, she made a soft sound of frustration deep in her throat.

"I know the feeling," he murmured against her lips. "I want to touch you, kiss every inch of your soft skin." His voice roughened to a growl. "The clothes must go."

Sensation. Need. Raw desire burning away self-control, caution and inhibition. Matt surrendered to the moment, to her inner hunger...and to him.

"Yes."

Caught up in a haze of unleashed desire, the move was seamless from the living room to his bedroom. The first things to go were the pins anchoring her hair in a plait at the back of her head.

"Beautiful," he murmured, burying his hands in the gold-streaked mass. "I knew it would be."

Gently tugging on the long strands, he brought her mouth to his, not in demand, but in a mind-scattering seduction of her senses.

A searing flame of sheer sensation licking
through her, Matt moaned and reached for him.
At the same instant, he released her hair and
reached for her. With trembling fingers—his and
hers—the clothes were smoothed from quickening, quivering bodies.

David threw back the bedspread and covers.

Matt pulled him with her onto the bed.

With delightful, excruciating care, David ful-
filled his wish to touch her, kiss every inch of her
skin—which he declared both soft and silky.

In eager retaliation, Matt returned the pleasure
given, lingering over the hardest, silkiest part of
him.

"I...give up...Officer Wolfe..." He panted,
compulsively arching into her caressing strokes.
"I...can't...oh, have mercy, Matilda...I can't
take any more."

Grasping her shoulders, he pulled her up the
length of him. Matt shivered as the tips of her
breasts brushed over the curls matting his chest,
and the tip of his manhood brushed the curls matting her mound.

She let out a startled "Oh" when he heaved
himself up and then over, taking her with him.

"I'll be with you in a moment," he promised
in a passion whispery voice.

He reached over the side of the bed, and Matt heard him mutter to himself as he rummaged through a drawer in the nightstand, then exhale a deep sigh of relief. There came the sound of tearing foil. Matt watched as, leaning back, he sheathed himself in protection for them both.

The moments of separation could have been a cooling turnoff. Instead, watching him, empowered by the jutting proof of his desire for her, the flames of her desire for him turned into a roar.

Lowering himself to her once more, David cradled her face with his large, gentle hands, then crushed her mouth beneath his. His tongue teased her lips, avoiding her attempts to capture him, draw him inside.

Aroused to fever-pitch, Matt whimpered and arched into him in a silent demand.

Holding her lips with his, he slid his hands from her face, smoothing them slowly, maddeningly, down the sides of her body, pausing at every curve to stroke, to tease, to further inflame.

Her breathing shallow, Matt's hands mirrored his every caress. When his palms tested the smoothness of her inner thighs, her hands skimmed the bunched-muscled, hair-roughened texture of his.

When his fingers delicately dipped into the

moist readiness of her femininity, her fingers curled around the fully aroused hardness of his masculinity.

His own breathing growing harsh, uneven, he reached for her hips...then grasped...then lifted...then thrust into her, with his body and his tongue.

Matt gasped at the galvanizing double thrill of pleasure and, craving more, eagerly matched his driving rhythm of parry and thrust.

The pleasure spun out; beautiful pleasure; unbearable pleasure, until, with a muffled cry, Matt attained the pinnacle of all pleasure.

She heard David's echoing cry a moment later.

Chapter 8

Something had awakened him.

Disoriented, not fully awake, Mac sat up in the bed, frowning, trying to figure out what had startled him. A sound…yes, that was it. Some sound had penetrated the depths of his satiated slumber, penetrated and set off an alarm inside him.

Matt.

Reality came back in a rush. He turned his head, knowing what he'd see…or, more accurately, who he wouldn't see.

Matt was gone. The sound that had awakened him had been the door being shut.

A sigh whispered into the quiet, dusk-shadowed room as Mac tossed the covers aside.

Even though he felt certain she was gone, he crawled out of bed and pulled on his boxers and jeans.

Maybe she had left a note.

Holding the hopeful thought, Mac, bare-chested and barefoot, left the room. Mere minutes were required to make a circuit of the house. There was no sign of a note anywhere.

Shoulders slumped in dejection, Mac stood in the middle of the kitchen, not noticing the chill from the floor tiles permeating the soles of his feet, or the fragrant aroma of pot roast scenting the air.

Why had she left without waking him?

Mac made a snorting sound. The answer was obvious: Matt didn't want to speak to him.

And why didn't she want to speak to him?

Also obvious, he reasoned. She must be suffering pangs of regret for their lovemaking.

Dammit.

Mac directed his gaze to the darkening sky beyond the window.

Sorry, Sir, he respectfully addressed his Creator. *But, You see, I don't understand. How could*

Matt regret the very same act I found so incredibly beautiful?

I love her, he prayed, surprising himself with the truth he had not until now consciously acknowledged. *But, then, You knew that, didn't You?*

So, now what am I supposed to do? How do I proceed? If by walking away without a word, Matt has rejected not only the reality of our lovemaking, but me, as well...

Mac closed his eyes and shuddered. He had never been in love. Oh, he had experienced heavy infatuation—and during the dark years, even heavier sexual indulgence—but never had he felt anything near the depth of caring, concern, excitement and thrill of the love he was feeling for Matt.

To have known her once, to have felt he had touched her mind and soul as well as her body, only to awaken alone...

No. Mac shook his head and opened eyes glittering with purpose. Determination straightened his spine and squared his drooping shoulders.

No, Sir. I can't...I won't simply allow her to walk away. I swear to You, on my pledge of service to You, that I will not harm her, physically or emotionally. But I can't believe that after giv-

*ing herself to me in such joyous surrender, after
the near perfection of our union, Matt does not
care for me…love me.*

*In Your infinite wisdom, You know, I must know
what she is feeling.*

As always, having taken his problem, his concern, to the highest authority, Mac felt calmer.

She never would know if David's pot roast was
as good as he claimed.

Standing under a pounding shower spray, tears
running down her face, Matt sniffled, and told
herself she had more important things to consider
than a roasting piece of beef.

Things like deep-sixing every tenet and rule of
personal conduct she had set for herself when she
had decided on a career in law enforcement.

Things like her unexpected and unprecedented
flash-fire response to him.

Things like her willing—no, eager—plunge
into total abandonment to sensuality.

Things like the thrilling, unimaginable heights
she had attained with David.

And, most frightening, most bewildering,
things like the merging connectedness she had felt
with him when they had soared together into ecstasy.

''Frightening'' barely described it.

Matt's shivering intensified.

She had never believed the oft-told tales of the blending of mind and soul as well as body supposedly experienced by lovers.

She had dismissed such recountings as the stuff of fictional fantasy, spun from the fertile imaginations of poets and writers of romantic novels.

Experiencing for herself the truth of those age-old tales, while momentarily glorious and uplifting, was sobering, almost chilling, with the ramifications inherent in the aftermath.

Switching off the cascading spray, Matt stepped from the shower and wrapped herself in a towel. Her body quaked in reaction to the inner chill. She tossed back her wet-dark hair and glared at herself in the steam-clouded mirror.

She could do this, she told herself. She tried to stop her incipient sobs with hard repeated swallows. She could, and would, fight this unwanted, unasked-for development.

She loved David…was in love with David.

There, she'd admitted it.

It didn't change a thing.

Being in love weakened her.

She was a cop, dammit.

David was an ordained minister.

And the pairing of the cop and the pastor could not be a happening thing.

It wouldn't work.

Which meant, her work was cut out for her.

Which meant, she had to work at cutting him from her heart, her thoughts, her life.

Ignoring the shaft of pain the decision sent spearing into her chest, Matt dumped the sodden towel into the hamper. Stepping into her night-clothes, she strode from the bathroom to the kitchen.

She was amazed when a glance at the wall clock told her that less than an hour had elapsed since she had left David. Since she had crept, shattered and trembling, from David's bed, then his house, unable to face him in the afterglow of their soul-stirring lovemaking.

Figuring her grandmother wouldn't be home for another hour or two, she dashed off a terse note, saying she was home, and had gone to catch a nap before starting her shift at midnight. Then, assured she would not be disturbed by her loving grandparent, she went to her bedroom, crawled between the sheets, and curled into a ball of pure, unadulterated misery.

Her throat tight with trapped sobs, Matt silently

repeated her new mantra over and over again.

I can do this.

It was going to be a very long night, Matt predicted as she crawled from her bed. Long and boring. As a rule, the Sunday night shift was quiet and uneventful. For Matt, she somehow knew this night wouldn't prove the exception.

She hadn't slept, of course. She had heard her grandmother come home, putter about. She had feigned sleep when she'd heard Gram mount the stairs and open her door a sliver to peek in on her. She had heard the muted sounds issuing from the TV.

Matt had lain on her personal bed of nails until the last possible minute, allowing her only time enough to prepare for work.

She was uniformed, her hair smoothed back in her usual plait, applying an extra coat of concealing undereye makeup when her grandmother tapped on the door.

"Come on in, Gram," she called in a casual tone she was light-years from feeling. "I'm almost ready."

"Have a good nap, dear?" Maddy asked, standing in the open doorway.

"Not really." Matt pulled off a creditable

shrug and smile. "But then, I never do on the first night of this shift…as I'm sure you know."

"Too well." She nodded, her smile bittersweet. "I lived through it, first with your grandfather, then your uncle Jake…and now with you."

"You're a tolerant, patient and wonderful woman, Gram," Matt said, love for the woman plain in her voice. Giving a final swish of the blusher brush to her cheeks to camouflage the pallor, she turned, a genuine smile on her still unsteady lips. "I often wonder how—and why—you put up with all of us."

Maddy's washed-out blue eyes twinkled with inner amusement.

"I'm rather fond of my oversize bunch," she drawled. "Besides, looking after all of you keeps me off the street and out of trouble."

Matt laughed, even though it hurt her throat.

"I have fresh coffee ready for you." Maddy's voice was brisk. "How about some eggs?"

Matt's stomach heaved. "Ah…no, thanks."

"Cereal?" Maddy, a firm believer of a solid meal before going to work, persisted.

"I'm really not hungry, Gram." Matt swallowed the sour taste in her mouth. "I'll just have coffee."

Maddy leveled a stern look on her. "You

should have something in your stomach besides coffee.''

Too tired to argue, Matt sighed and relented. ''Okay, I'll have toast.''

''Toast,'' Maddy grumbled, turning away. ''Well, I suppose it's better than nothing.''

With her grandmother watching her like the legendary hawk, Matt managed to force down two pieces of toast.

''By the way,'' Maddy said, after settling into the chair opposite Matt. ''I didn't see you in church this morning. Did you cop out, no pun intended—'' she grinned, sweeping a glance over Matt's uniformed torso ''—or did you decide to attend services at David's church, after all?''

''I attended David's service,'' she said, nearly choking on a bite of toast.

''Well?'' Maddy prompted when Matt didn't elaborate. ''How was it?''

''He gives a very good sermon,'' she said, reflecting it was probably better if one actually heard it.

''I like that man,'' Maddy said decisively.

Matt cringed inside. ''So you said before.''

Though she had thought she'd kept her tone free of inflection, something in her voice must have alerted the older woman, for she frowned.

"You don't like David?"

No, I love him.

Naturally, Matt wasn't about to voice the first response that sprang into her beleaguered mind.

"Yes, of course I like him," she answered. "What's not to like about him?" Indeed, she added to herself, feeling the toast like lead in her stomach.

"I'll have to invite him over sometime," Maddy said in a musing tone. "Give him a taste of my cooking."

Oh, God. Matt quailed at the mere suggestion. Afraid she'd betray herself at any minute, she scraped back her chair and stood.

"Gotta go, Gram," she said, shoving her arms into her jacket sleeves, then scooping her holstered weapon from the corner of the table. "I'll see you in the morning," she rushed on, making for the back door. "Sleep well...and don't worry."

"Why should I change my habits at this late date?" Maddy retorted. "Take care."

Now, after the long night hours of tooling her squad car along empty streets and battling the yearning ache that slammed into her every time she drove past the turnoff to the church and Da-

vid's house beyond, Matt recalled her grandmother's parting remark with wry cynicism.

"Take care of what?" she asked herself. She
glanced at the dashboard clock, not for the first,
or even thirty-first time since she'd begun her patrol.

The clock read seven-twenty. Just forty minutes
remained of her shift.

"Four-one?"

Matt started at the crackling summons—the
first in a long while—and groaned. Sure. Why
not? she groused to herself. Far be it for the fates
to let her get through the entire night without a
major incident.

Resigned, she reached for the handset.

"Four-one," she repeated.

"Where are you located?"

"I'm just leaving the college circle, heading
north on Elm," she responded. "What's up?"

"We've received a report of a desecration of
church property on..."

No. Matt shook her head as the voice continued
to crackle particulars. Not even the most fickle of
fates could be this mean-spirited, she railed.

But, of course, the church property in question
was David's domain.

For an instant, just a millisecond, rebellion

flared inside Matt, then she just as quickly squashed it. She had realized she'd have to face him sometime.... But, hell, did it have to be at 7:25 in the morning? This morning, of all mornings?

"I'm on it," she responded, sighing as she replaced the handset.

Taking the fastest route, Matt cruised along the silent streets, inwardly girding herself for whatever she might have to endure when she saw David.

He was waiting on the road next to the crèche. From his surprised reaction when she stepped from the car, it was obvious he'd not been expecting her to respond.

"More paint, David?" she asked, miraculously managing to keep her voice crisp, cool and professional.

He moved closer to her. "Matt..." He reached for her hand. "We've got to talk about—"

"I'm on duty, Reverend," she interrupted, stepping aside to avoid his touch.

"I know that, but—"

"Let's see the damage." She again cut him off. Taking two steps to get a closer look at the wooden figures, she remained far enough back so as not to disturb any possible footprints in the ground which had been softened by the fitful snowfall the previous afternoon.

"You didn't…"

"No I didn't," David said over her voice. "As you'll notice, you don't have to be on top of it to see the strange handiwork of the vandal."

Matt could hardly believe what she saw. She stared in astonishment at the sight before her.

"Weird, wouldn't you say?" David said, coming to a halt beside her.

"Look on the bright side," Matt muttered, moving one step closer to the scene—and away from him. "At least there's no black paint to remove this time."

"True. All I have to do is pull that black trash bag from the figure of the Virgin Mary." He grimaced. "Of course, we don't know what's underneath the bag."

"Live in hope," Matt muttered one of her grandmother's sayings.

"Oh, I do." His voice held a wealth of meaning.

Matt chose to misunderstand his remark. "What is it with this perp?" she mused out loud. "First a spray of black paint to obliterate the figure's face, now a black bag over its head." She frowned. "I'm beginning to wonder if this could be the work of some cult member."

"I've been wondering the same thing ever since I noticed it around seven," he said, allowing her to get away with the diversionary tactic.

"On the other hand...you know..." Matt slanted a sidelong look at him. "If it wasn't for the proof of your big feet—" her glance came to rest on the large-size running shoes "—I might be tempted to consider you a suspect."

David's dark blue, amusement-filled eyes were waiting to pierce her when she slowly returned her gaze to his face. "No kidding?" he drawled. "And might I ask why you might be so tempted?"

She lifted her shoulders in half shrug. "Well, considering the strangeness of the hours you happen to notice the vandalism...the first one not long before midnight, and now so early in the morning—" She broke off, shrugging again.

"If you'll recall, I explained about the first incident. I was on my way home from visiting a parishioner." He smiled. "You've met Corine Baxter. She can tell you the exact time I left her house."

His mention of the blond woman's name caused an odd, unpleasant sensation in Matt's midsection—certainly not jealously, she assured herself. But what had he been doing at the other woman's home until after eleven o'clock that night, anyway?

"And this morning?" She arched her brows, dismissing Corine from her unsettling thoughts.

"This morning, Officer Wolfe," he said in a gritty voice, "I was attempting to walk off my frustration after a long, sleepless night."

"Oh." Beating a hasty retreat, Matt returned to the car to call base and request a lab crew.

As he had done days before, David was right behind her. He slid into the seat, right beside her.

"You're damned right, 'Oh,'" he said, slamming the passenger door. "Why did you run—no, sneak out on me without a word of explanation, or so much as a 'see ya, fella,' yesterday afternoon, Matt?"

"I'm on duty, Reverend," she repeated, using the excuse as a shield against him. "I can't talk now. I have to tape off the—"

"Bull," he retorted, slicing through her attempt to evade his question. "I helped you do that before, if you'll remember. It only took a few seconds. And it'll take a while for the lab crew to get here."

''David, I prefer not to discuss this now,'' she said, inwardly battling a resurgence of the shivers.

''I need to know, Matt,'' he persisted, grasping her arm as she moved to step out of the car.

Although his hold on her arm was gentle, it was firm. Nevertheless, Matt made a point of lowering her gaze to his hand, then raising narrowed eyes to his.

''Let me go, David.'' Her voice was soft in tone, but hard in authority.

''Sorry, Officer.'' He gave a quick shake of his head. ''I need to know why you left my bed, my house, and me, after the incredibly beautiful experience we shared.''

The inner shivers had matured into wrenching quakes, threatening to tear her apart and expose her true feelings, her love for him. Determined to conceal her emotions, she withdrew behind a brittle facade.

''We had sex,'' she said.

''We made love,'' he corrected her in sharp, impatient tones. ''I made love to you, and deny it now if you dare, you made love to me.''

''No...I...''

''Yes, Matt,'' he persisted, hammering at her already weakened defenses. ''I know, I was there, and fully involved. And...so...were...you,'' he said, spacing each damning word for emphasis. "And I want to stay involved with you. And not only to make love." He took a quick breath, then hammered relentlessly on. "Now I'll ask you again, why did you leave me without a word of explanation?"

Matt was nearly undone. This was worse than she had feared. It was bad enough that she was in love with him, but he was indicating, or at least hinting, that he was in love with her.

And she was convinced that any serious involvement—and he sure sounded serious—would definitely be unfair...to him.

She had been there, grown up in the midst of such involvements. Loving an officer of the law inflicted terror and mental torment along with its inherent joys and rewards.

No. David was too good, too fine a man to subject to that kind of uncertainty. He had suffered too much already. He deserved better, more than she could offer or guarantee.

She had set her course; she'd stay it.

"Let me go, David," she ordered, pulling against his grip. "I have to tape..."

"Answer me, Matt."

"I don't want to be involved, okay?" Matt shouted back at him, barely hanging on to what was left of her composure. "Yes, our lovemaking was wonderful...more than that," she admitted, the quakes inside working their way to the surface. "But it should not have happened. I lost my head for a while..." Her voiced hardened. "It won't happen again."

"But why?" David shook his head, as if clearing the effects of a blow. "Matt, didn't you hear, understand? I'm not looking for a brief period of fun and games. I'm telling you that I'm in lo—"

"Don't say it," she shouted, drowning him out. "I don't want to hear it." She gasped a harsh breath. "You have no idea what being involved with a law enforcement officer entails. I do. I have lived with it each and every day of my life."

"I don't care about that," David said when she paused for another gasp of air. "I care about you. I care about us. I don't care about—"

"I care enough for both of us." She again sliced through his words. "I must. I will not subject you, or any other man, to that kind of gut-wrenching, emotion-ripping uncertainty." Tearing free of him, she slid from the seat.

"Matt, wait," David demanded, flinging the door open and zipping around the car to her. "Listen..."

"The discussion is over, Reverend." Drawing

herself up to her full height, she stared into his eyes, and coldly, deliberately, cut him off at the knees. "The subject is closed."

Turning her back to him, feeling as though she was crumbling into tiny painful, sharp-edged shards inside her rigid frame, Matt strode to meet the police car coming up the driveway.

Chapter 9

Matt was tired, more tired than she could ever remember feeling. Her weariness was understandable, considering the amount of sleep she'd clocked, or more accurately, hadn't clocked; she had spent most of her time in bed tossing and turning. But at least her stint on the late-night shift was finally over.

As she had suspected would be the case, the lab crew had come up with little more evidence than before regarding the desecration. Instead of one, this time there had been two sneaker toe imprints, made by either a child or a short, slender adult. There had not been a print or any other mark on the figure under the bag.

In Matt's unvoiced opinion, the perp had been an adult, a young adult. Possibly a teenager who'd either held a grudge against David or the church, or had committed the crime for the sheer, upset-causing hell of it. She'd had occasions to deal with her share of such teenagers.

Not eager for another confrontation with David—and because she ached too much to see him—Matt asked the officer working the day shift patrol on that route to stop by to bring David up to speed on the case.

Her week was in. And now she was on official vacation leave until after the holidays.

Christmas was just four days away, and she was anticipating the arrival of her immediate and extended family.

Dragging her sleep-depleted body from her cover-rumpled bed, Matt padded barefoot down the stairs to the kitchen for a hopefully reviving cup of coffee. She found her grandmother there, in the process of baking Christmas good-ies…again.

"What is it this time, Gram?" Matt asked, smothering a yawn with her hand. "Not more cookies?"

"No." Maddy glanced up from the pastry rolled out on the tabletop to smile at her. "I'm baking those little pecan tarts your uncle Royce loves."

"Him and everybody else," Matt said, grinning as she made a beeline for the coffeemaker.

"Coffee's fresh," Maddy said, laying the rolling pin aside to begin cutting out small circles of pastry with a scalloped-edged cookie cutter. "I started it when I heard you moving around upstairs."

"You're a lifesaver," she vowed fervently, taking a mug from the cup tree on the countertop and filling it with the fragrant brew.

"And you look like you need saving," Maddy retorted, peering into Matt's face. "Are you coming down with something?"

"No, Gram, I'm just tired. You know I never sleep well when I'm on the late shift."

"Yes, I do know," she nodded, frowning. "But you look even more washed out than usual this time."

"Well...I suppose I'm a little excited about Mom, Dad and Lisa coming tomorrow," Matt quickly improvised, forgiving herself because she *was* eager for their arrival. "Maybe I'm not as grown-up as I like to believe."

Maddy chuckled. "Then that makes two of us kids, honey, because I'm just as excited as you are."

Matt laughed, then sat quietly, sipping her coffee and watching as the older woman swiftly put the little tarts together. Impressed by her grandmother's dexterity and talent—the woman was an excellent cook—Matt's mind drifted in the direction of another excellent cook. She wondered if David had bothered to prepare any special foods for the holiday, or if he had gotten around to putting up a tree for the decorations she'd seen littering his dining room table.

"Well, that's the first batch in," Maddy said, scattering Matt's errant thoughts. "Now, I'm going to take a coffee break before starting another batch."

"Good," Matt said, groping for a normal tone of voice, and an unaffected smile.

Pull it together, Wolfe, she chastised herself, annoyed with herself for her thinking of David every time she relaxed her guard.

"You have any plans for today?"

Jolted from her musings once more, Matt concealed her chagrin behind her mug. She drained the reviving liquid before responding to her grandmother's question.

"I need to finish my Christmas shopping," she said, rising to refill her mug. "Why, was there something you wanted me to do for you?"

"No." Maddy shook her head. "I was just wondering. Everything's under control here."

Her assertion elicited an easy laugh from Matt. "When don't you have everything under control, Gram?" she asked, a teasing smile curving her lips.

"I've had a lot of practice, honey," Maddy retorted. "Over sixty years of practice."

"And practice makes perfect?"

"Not always." Maddy smiled. "It helps if one's paying attention."

Something she hadn't been doing much of the past week or so, Matt acknowledged ruefully. She really did need to forget one too attractive, too tempting, too exciting man of the cloth, and get her act together.

Starting now.

Her resolve in place, Matt finished her drink, rinsed her mug, then headed for her bedroom with purposeful strides. "I'm gonna get dressed and get going, Gram," she said over her shoulder. "Make a list, if there's anything I can pick up for you."

"I'll think of something." Maddy's teasing response followed her along the hallway.

The mall was packed. Canned holiday music serenaded the harried-looking shoppers. Bright-eyed youngsters waited in line with eager anticipation to sit on the knee of the red-suited man to recite their list of wants.

Matt loved it all. She always had. She was one of a handful of people she knew who didn't groan whenever she heard some version or other of "White Christmas."

Since her own childhood, Christmas had been a magical time, a time of belief in the possibility of miracles. Attaining adulthood had not tarnished the special wonder of the holiday for her. Not even the harsh realities of her job had changed her feelings.

Matt didn't rush along with the horde. Absorbing the sights and sounds, she strolled the broad walkway, admiring the window displays and decorations. The green and red displays would disappear all too quickly in the New Year, replaced by cupids with bows and arrows, big red hearts, roses of every hue, and yards of trailing white lace. But that was okay. Matt liked Valentine's Day, too.

Toting an oversize shopping bag with an enlarged face of Santa Claus on the side, Matt had made every purchase on her grandmother's list, and all but one of her own. She still hadn't quite decided on a gift for her father—the man was difficult to buy for.

She was perusing the items displayed in the window of a men's store when her glance came to a halt on a loden green and white sweater.

David. The garment fairly shouted his name to her. David would look terrific in that sweater.

You're losing it, lady, Matt scathingly told herself. She dragged her gaze from the sweater—and her rebellious mind from the man.

Dad. Remember? Matt chided herself. She directed her gaze to the other articles displayed. What to get for the legendary Lone Wolfe?

In the end, Matt surrendered to whimsy. A hint of a devilish smile twitching the corners of her mouth, she selected an outrageously expensive silk dressing gown for the man who never even wore pajamas, never mind a robe.

Matt exited the mall with a jaunty stride, humming a refrain of "Jingle Bells."

David anchored the gold star to the topmost branch of the live blue spruce. Descending the ladder, he folded it and set it aside. After plugging in the tiny lights, he stepped back to admire his handiwork.

Beautiful, he decided…wishing Matt were there to admire it with him.

Over a week had passed since their contentious conversation. A week during which Mac had upbraided himself for giving in too easily to Matt's dictum, and condemning her for her lack of faith in him, his ability to deal with the dangerous aspects of her career.

He'd expected Matt to drop by to tell him the results of the lab report, as she had before. Mac had held out hope of coaxing her into the house, then taking the opportunity to convince her that his love for her was strong enough to withstand the uncertainties of being the mate of a law enforcement officer.

His hopes were dashed when earlier in the week the officer who had stepped from the squad car in front of his house had turned out to be a man.

Mac knew himself to be a patient man…he had acquired the quality the hard way. But he also recognized the warning symptoms when his patience rope was about played out. He had just about reached that point.

Staring at the star until it blurred around the edges, Mac sought comfort from his Supreme superior.

I'm pushing the patience envelope, Sir, running close to desperate. Loving her the way I do, I must see her, or at least call her, try to make her understand.

Mac heaved a sigh, then continued on in his silent communication.

I don't suppose You could find the time to whisper an encouraging word in her ear, perhaps? Or if not that, infuse her with a little spirit of the season of giving...maybe?

He blinked, and the star refocused in his sight.

Arrogant jerk, he derided himself, grimacing as he turned away. As if the Lord didn't have enough to contend with in the world. Where did he get off, bothering the Boss with his personal, emotional problems? Didn't the Bible say God helps those who help themselves?

With a rueful shake of his head, Mac picked up the ladder and started from the room. Then he stopped to pause, a serene smile softening the thin line of his lips.

Of course.

As often happened, Mac was struck by the

wonderful and mysterious ways of the Lord.... Who helped those who helped themselves.

His purpose firm, he went straight to the phone. Maddy answered.

After exchanging greetings with the young-at-heart older woman, Mac asked for Matt.

"She's not here, Mac, I sent her out for some last-minute grocery items." Maddy laughed. "I had thought I'd remembered everything I needed for the holidays," she went on chattily, bringing a tender smile to his lips. "But then I remembered that Matt's mother and sister prefer fresh lime in their seltzer water, and me with a crisper full of lemons."

Mac laughed along with her, but then his brows drew together in a frown. "That's right, Matt told me her family would be visiting for the holidays...from Colorado, right?"

"Yes." Barely suppressed excitement shimmered in her voice. "They arrive tomorrow. Matt's driving to Philadelphia International to pick them up."

"I'll bet she's anxious to see them."

"Anxious hardly describes it," Maddy said, chuckling. "She's been like a whirlwind these past few days—shopping, wrapping, cleaning an already-clean house, and getting underfoot, like a windup toy.''

Mac wanted to see her like that. Her cool reserve, her professional facade stripped away to reveal the warm and loving woman beneath.

''Well...'' He closed his eyes and smothered a sigh. ''You have a lovely Christmas, Maddy. You and Matt, and your family. I'll—''

''I'll have Matt return your call, Mac,'' she cut in to promise. ''As soon as she comes in.''

''No, she's busy,'' he said, certain she would definitely be too busy to listen to his plea. ''I'll get ba—''

''Mac?'' Maddy again cut him off.

''Yes, Maddy?''

''I know you must have a full schedule, and I'll understand if you can't, but...'' She hesitated, as if unsure about continuing.

''What can I do for you, Maddy?'' he asked gently.

''Well...I really would like you to meet my family,'' she explained. ''If you could find time— if only for a few minutes—would you stop by the house on Christmas night when they'll all be here?''

Mac didn't hesitate for an instant. ''Thank you for the invitation, Maddy. I'd like to meet your family. Would early in the evening be convenient?''

"That will be fine, Mac." Her voice was shades lighter. "I'll be looking forward to seeing you then."

It wasn't until after he had hung up the receiver that Maddy's phrasing registered. She had said they would all be there. Exactly how many Wolfe family members were there?

Then he shrugged. Made no difference. His primary interest was in one particular Wolfe, the she-Wolfe in cop's clothing.

Matt was having a wonderful time. She knew she was. She told herself so at least once an hour. She always had a wonderful time when the family was together. Yet this year, some of the shine was off the holiday glow.

The house was bedlam. But then, the house was always bedlam when the family gathered to celebrate anything—a holiday, a birthday, an anniversary, or just simply being together.

It was late in the afternoon. Christmas was almost over. The gifts had been opened, exclaimed over and, in the case of Matt's father, Cameron, hooted over by his three brothers.

The men, Maddy's four sons and six of her

eight grandsons, were in the kitchen, where they usually convened, because the beer was there.

The females of the family were relaxing in the living room, resting between the chores of serving then clearing away the remains of a huge traditional Christmas dinner, before some male decided it was time for a snack.

Sipping from a chilled glass of Chardonnay, Matt was enjoying a friendly argument with her sister over an obscure point of law when the doorbell rang.

"I'll get that," she volunteered, since she was seated nearest to the door.

People had been stopping by all day to say hello and offer holiday wishes. Expecting another neighbor or friend, Matt swung the door open, and froze, the words "Merry Christmas" withering on her tongue.

Before her, in the flesh—the pulse-leaping flesh—stood the very reason her day hadn't turned out as wonderful as she had anticipated it would.

"David." Less than a whisper, his name passed her lips on a breathy sigh.

"Merry Christmas, Matt." He didn't smile, just stood there, a large cardboard carton in his arms.

"Mac! Come in, come in," Maddy called, bustling to the door, her smile for him changing to a chiding frown for Matt. "It's cold out there."

"Thank you, and Merry Christmas," he repeated the greeting as he stepped inside. "And this is for you." He extended his arms, offering the carton to her. "Don't worry, it isn't heavy."

Maddy's smile held puzzlement and pleased surprise as she accepted the gift. "But whatever…"

"Why don't you open it and see, Grandmother?" The advice came in an amused drawl from Matt's sister Lisa, who had come to stand beside Maddy.

Brief as it was, Matt saw the fleeting expression of shock that flashed on David's face and in his eyes. Then, just as swiftly, the expression changed to comprehension and amusement.

"Twins," he murmured, his gaze probing Matt's. "You're identical twins."

"Yes." She nodded, looking cool, feeling hot. "Lisa, this is the Reverend David Macdonough. He's fairly new to the area." She mentioned the name and location of his church. "David, my sister Lisa."

"A pleasure, David," Lisa said, flashing her perfect white teeth as she extended her hand. "But…didn't my grandmother call you Mac?"

"The pleasure's mine, Lisa. And I'm Mac to some, David to...others." He smiled and shifted his glance from her to Matt. "Are you a cop, too?"

"Not I." Lisa grinned. "I'm a lawyer."

"Figures."

At that point, having opened the carton and removed the white freezer paper covering the contents, Maddy exclaimed, "Oh, my goodness! Mac, did you bake these?"

Naturally, her question sharpened the interest of the other four women in the room. Exchanging curious glances, after they left their chairs to have a look.

"It's bread," said Sarah, Jake's wife.

"It's a lot of bread," said Megan, Royce's wife.

"It's a lot of different kinds of bread," added Tina, Eric's wife, and the avid cook of the group.

"They smell divine," said Sandra, Cameron's wife, and Lisa and Matt's mother.

"You baked these?" It was a chorus, combined of every female voice there—but Matt's. She was otherwise occupied hanging David's coat in the closet.

"Yes," David answered, his eyes sparkling

with delight for the friendly women. "It's my contribution to Maddy…and her family."

"Mac, thank you, this is wonderful," Maddy said, lifting one of the individually plastic-wrapped loaves from the carton. "Italian bread. I love it."

"I know," David said, laughing at the confused look she gave him. "The church supper, remember?"

"And a batch of corn bread, my favorite," Megan said, taking another package from the box.

"Oh-hh, a long loaf of French," Sarah announced. "Jake's gonna devour this."

"Navajo fry bread!" Sandra laughed. "I haven't had that in forever."

"Look at this." Tina held an iced loaf aloft. "Stollen. I've never had success with stollen."

Of course, Lisa had to discover the last of the breads. "And Greek braided bread." She tossed a smile at David. "This is some multinational contribution."

"I lived in a multinational neighborhood for a while," David replied, sliding a conspiratorial look at Matt.

Suddenly remembering her manners, Maddy introduced David to her family. Then, carefully replacing the bread in the carton, she handed it to Matt.

"Matt take the bread, and Mac, into the kitchen, and introduce him to your father, uncles and cousins."

"How many uncles and cousins are there?" David murmured as they moved through the dining room.

"Three uncles, only six of the cousins," she answered. "Two of my cousins couldn't make it. This was their year to spend the holidays with their wives' families."

"And didn't you say that all of them are in law enforcement?"

Matt gave a brief nod. "Except my mother and Lisa, they're both lawyers," she said tersely, heading toward the sound of male voices and laughter. "Brace yourself," she warned. "They're a bit of a surprise."

Surprise was a woefully inaccurate description, Mac decided minutes later, upon coming face-to-face with a roomful of handsome blond giants.

It wasn't their height that struck him; not one of them topped him by more than an inch. Nor was it their male good looks that gave him pause. No, what most impressed Mac was the keen intelligence and bright humor that gleamed from the depths of the ten pairs of eyes that turned to assess him when he followed Matt into the kitchen.

And the sharpest of those eyes belonged to the oldest member of the group, Mac quickly discovered when he was introduced to Cameron Wolfe, Matt's father.

The man's grip might have been crushing…if Mac hadn't been able to match it.

The humor in Cameron's eyes spread to his lips and voice. "Nice to meet you, Reverend."

After apparently passing muster with Matt's father, meeting the others was a piece of cake. Although keeping the names straight was chancy.

There were the uncles, Royce, Eric and Jake. And the cousins, Justin, Edward, Andrew, Tim, Todd and Brian. Mark and Jeffrey were the two missing cousins.

"Baked all these yourself, did you?"

Mac thought the voice with the hint of ridicule came from Edward, Royce's son. He found a moment later that he'd guessed right.

"Don't knock it, son," Royce chastised his firstborn. "A man who can bake his own bread will never starve."

"I'll bet Tina freaked when she saw this." Eric displayed the stollen.

"And I'll bet Sandra's mouth watered when she spied the fry bread—she loves it," Cameron said, sharing a grin with his brother.

"What can we get you to drink, Reverend?" Jake asked, eyeing the long loaf of French bread.

"Name's Mac...or David," he said. "And I'll have a soda, thank you."

"Comin' up." Jake grinned, revealing yet another set of pearly whites. "Justin, get Mac a soda."

Within minutes, to Mac's heartfelt gratitude, the Wolfe males had drawn him into their very serious and highly contentious discussion on the pros and cons of the two teams most likely to go to the Super Bowl.

By ten that evening, it was pretty evident to Matt that every one of her family members, male and female alike, had taken to David's easygoing manner, his humor, and his obvious affection for people in general.

He had been invited to join the family for supper. A minor thing to some, perhaps, but a major consideration to Matt. It broke new ground, insofar as family suppers had always before been limited to actual family members.

But that wasn't even the worst of it. Matt suspected each and every one of her family members of indulging in a bit of matchmaking. The match being between her and David, of course. And her suspicions were not without reason or merit. She was wise to the little hints, the casual nuances, the offhand remarks—ostensibly made in jest— about how good they looked at one point while they were standing together.

Her suspicions were confirmed when, around ten-thirty, David made noises about leaving. Everyone suggested that Matt escort him to the door.

"Perfect," David murmured as soon as they were out of the room, and earshot. "I need to talk to you."

Harboring warring emotions of frustration at having to spend even a few minutes alone with him, and excitement at getting to spend even a few minutes alone with him, she led the way along the hall to the front door in a state of cool and withdrawn composure.

She was expecting him to renew his attack on her position of no involvement.

David surprised her.

"I located the woman and children you mentioned to me about noticing in church the other week." He smiled, as if aware of having thrown her a curve. "She lives about a quarter of a mile down the road from the church."

"Along my patrol route?"

"Yes."

"Is she ill...in trouble?" Matt asked, vividly recalling the woman's pallor, the anxious expression on the young girl's face.

"Yes, she is sick," he said. "And her financial situation is desperate."

"You put her in touch with the proper agencies?"

He shook his head. "She wouldn't hear of it. Said she'd starve before asking for charity."

"She'd let her children starve with her," Matt said, appalled by the very idea.

"No...she is feeding, taking care of the kids. She's just not taking care of herself."

"Her husband?"

He sighed. "Skipped out on her." A sad smile shadowed his lips. "She's not well disposed toward men at the moment...which is why I wanted to talk to you. I thought that perhaps if another woman spoke to her, explained that there was no shame in accepting help—" He broke off, frowning.

"You want me to stop by as a professional, explain to her—"

"No." David cut in with a quick shake of his head. "I feel the uniform might panic her."

"But then…how…" She gave him a helpless look.

He took a breath, then charged ahead. "I thought if we went to see her together, maybe, between the two of us, we could reassure her, convince her to allow us to help her through this rough period."

She hesitated, wanting and willing to do whatever she could, yet… There had to be any number of women who were active church parishioners who would be glad to accompany him in a visit to the woman; Corine, for instance.

The mere thought of the blond woman's name, the memory of the longing look in her eyes following David as he walked away on the night of the church supper, caused a twinge inside Matt.

Stirred to life, her memory expanded to the afternoon she had spent with David, in his house, in his arms, in his bed. A longing ache throbbed through her.

"I need your help, Matt."

Matt capitulated. He needed her.

"When?" The remote tone she contrived didn't even impress her.

"Tomorrow, if you're free, the circumstances are pretty dire."

"I'm free," she admitted. "What time?"

"Nine?" He raised a brow, and lowered his voice. "I could pick you up."

Matt hesitated once more, telling herself to play it safe by taking her own car.

"Matt?" His soft voice curled around her heart.

"I'll be ready."

Chapter 10

David explained to Matt about the woman's position in more detail during the drive to her house the following morning.

"Her name is April Henderson. Ever since her husband took off...apparently with another woman, she has been earning money by cleaning house for several women in the new development across the road. Do you know where I mean?"

Matt nodded. "Elm Tree Gardens."

"Yes." He sighed. "She has no transportation, and not only can she take her son with her, she can walk there. Of course, she's being paid under the table."

"The girl's in school?"

"Yes. Not this week, of course, with the schools closed until after the New Year. Mrs. Henderson told me—insisted—that she was doing fine, earning enough to get along, until she got sick. She calls it a cold, but I'm afraid it sounds like pneumonia."

"I gather she hasn't seen a doctor."

"No." He slanted a sad smile at her. "She said she can't afford it as, since she hasn't been able to work, the money's running out."

Sharp concern nagged at Matt. "We've got to convince her to let us help, David."

"I know." He turned off the road onto a short dirt drive.

Matt passed the property every working day, taking little note of it.

The house was small, one of many of the ranch houses thrown up at the end of World War II to accommodate the horde of servicemen returning from overseas.

The woman looked worse than she had that day in church; her eyes were hollow, her breathing harsh.

When she'd come to the door in response to David's knock, it was immediately apparent to Matt that she didn't want to let them in.

"Mrs. Henderson, I've brought a friend to meet

you," David said, his voice gentle, reassuring. "She'd like to explain the assistance available to you."

Caution and alarm sprang into the woman's eyes. But before she could refuse his offer, close the door in their faces, Matt took over.

"I do understand how you might feel about accepting charity, Mrs. Henderson," she said in strong yet calming tones. "I promise, I will not attempt to pressure you into anything."

The woman hesitated a moment more, during which she was convulsed by a racking cough. "I—I..." she began, between gasps for breath, and then she sighed and pulled the door open as she stepped back. "All right, you can come in, but..."

"I promise," Matt repeated.

She shyly ushered them into the small living room. It was spotlessly clean, the furniture old but well cared for. A small artificial tree stood in one corner, a few toys and a short stack of shirt boxes on the floor beneath it.

Thinking that at least the kids had had Christmas, Matt opened her mouth to offer greetings of the season. Before she could speak, a banging sound reverberated through the house from the kitchen. The tired-looking woman gave them a faint, apologetic smile.

"That's Andy," she explained with the limp wave of a hand. "If you don't mind coming into the kitchen...he wants his breakfast."

"Not at all," Matt assured her with a smile, motioning for the woman to lead the way. "Is there anything I can do to help?"

"No." She shook her head. "He's having cereal. We can talk while he eats."

The toddler was seated in an old wooden highchair, happily banging a plastic baby cup on the tray. Spying his mother, he began to chant a demand.

"Pup-eats, pup-eats."

"Yes, love, Mom's getting it for you." Her eyes, her smile, revealed pure love as she gazed at the boy. She turned to go to the countertop next to the sink, on which sat a box of cereal. Lifting the box, she shifted a wry look at Matt and David. "He loves puffed wheat," she said to interpret his demand. "Have a seat, this will only take a minute," she said, indicating the chairs neatly placed around the table.

After giving Andy his breakfast, the woman sat down across the table from Matt. "I better warn you," she said, her voice soft but decisive, "My parents were poor, but proud people. They never asked anyone for anything." Her voice grew firmer. "I won't go on welfare—my daddy would leave his grave and haunt me."

"All right." Matt accepted the woman's position without question. "But there are other organizations, church groups—" she indicated the silent man at the end of the table "—like Reverend Macdonough's, ready and willing to help in any way they can."

In a calm, steady voice, Matt spoke for some minutes, outlining the options available for those in temporary need of assistance.

"I'll be fine as soon as I can get back to work," the woman insisted, twisting the hands she'd folded on top of the table.

"You need to see a doctor," Matt said.

"I can't afford it." Her eyes burned with inner fever. "An office visit costs the earth these days."

"We'll take care of it." David spoke up for the first time. "Let us help you."

"I—I don't know. My daddy...I gotta think about it." Her movements jerky, she pushed her chair back and stood up. "I gotta call Jenny to eat." Casting a harried look at them, she rushed from the room.

With a sinking certainty that the woman was going to refuse their offer, Matt turned to stare at David in helpless despair of failure.

"David, I..."

"Pup-eats, pup-eats," Andy shouted, banging his empty bowl on the highchair tray.

Her mouth curving into an indulgent smile, Matt rose to accommodate him. "Hungry little tyrant, aren't you, big boy?" she said, laughing as he thrust the bowl at her. She had refilled the bowl with the cereal and milk and was placing it on the tray when his mother came running back into the room.

"She's gone...Jenny's gone," she cried, fear making her cold-roughened voice shrill.

David shot out of his chair. "What do you mean, she's gone?"

"She's not in the bedroom." Her head swiveled, as if hoping to see the girl materialize in front of her wild, wide-eyed gaze. "She's nowhere in the house." Her searching gaze came to rest on Andy; a sob erupted from her throat. "I've got to get him dressed. We've got to look for Jenny, find her!"

"Calm down," Matt said with gentle authority, automatically taking control. "You are not well, and it's very cold outside. David and I will look for Jenny. You stay here, indoors, with Andy."

"But...but..." the woman began in protest.

"Mrs. Henderson," David broke in, "I think now is the time to tell you that Matt here is a

policewoman with the Sprucewood Police Department.''

If anything, rather than reassuring her, the information seemed to instill sheer panic. ''Police!''
she exclaimed. Her eyes flew to Matt. ''Are you
going to report me for not paying income taxes?''

''No,'' Matt said sharply. Then, more softly,
''No, I am not going to report you, I'm going to
help you.''

The woman stared at Matt for a moment, then,
apparently satisfied with what she gleaned from
Matt's expression, she started to cry. ''Please,
please,'' she begged, sobbing. ''Find Jenny for
me. I—I couldn't bear it if anything happened to
her.''

''I'll do my best,'' Matt said, taking the
woman's hand and giving it a comforting squeeze.
''I promise.''

''I'm going to report this.'' Matt's voice was
tired. Her body was tired. Her mind was in rebellion.

''I know.'' David sounded every bit as tired as
Matt.

It was dark, past dinnertime. They had spent
the entire day searching for the missing girl. They
had combed the immediate area around her home,
the streets of Sprucewood and the surrounding

communities. Checking off the names of Jenny's friends and school mates on the list her mother had given them, they had talked to the girls' friends, their parents, Jenny's teacher, all without success. The child seemed to have vanished.

"Are you thinking that maybe her father—"

"Yes," Matt interrupted him, anger, frustration and a niggling fear making her voice harsh. "Her father...or another sick someone who... Dammit," she exploded, too aware of the possibilities.

"We have to contact Mrs. Henderson again, explain what has to be done," he said, his tone reflecting the anger and fear in Matt's.

They had been calling the woman periodically throughout the day, each time hoping the girl had returned home on her own. She hadn't.

"We'd better find a phone, it'll be faster than running back into the station."

"We'll go to my place," David said. "It's closer than any pay phone I know of."

Matt was quiet as he turned the car, heading back in the direction of his house. She raked her mind for something she might have overlooked, some place the child might have gone. She came up blank.

Sighing, she gazed through the windshield, staring at the familiar tree-dotted landscape lining the road leading to the driveway to the church.

Something, some movement, caught her eye as David approached the turnoff.

"Slow down," she said, her voice low, sharp, as she reached out to grasp his arm.

"Matt...what..." The car swerved, but David controlled it, slowed it to a crawl. "What is it?"

"I see something—or someone. A shape, little more than a shadow in the moonlight, moving through the trees—" She broke off to point. "There."

"I see," David said, his voice terse, tense. "A person...a small person, heading toward the church."

"Pull over," she ordered. "I'm going to follow on foot."

"*We're* going to follow," he corrected her, pulling the car onto the shoulder and bringing it to a stop.

She was out of the car like a shot.

He was right beside her.

Slowly, quietly, stealthily, they moved through the wooded area, alert for any sign, any sound. There was nothing but the rustle of the breeze through the stark, naked branches.

They were nearing the trees bordering the clearing around the church when they heard it...the unmistakable sound of a child weeping.

Matt and David came to a halt beside the large

evergreen. They exchanged looks of confusion
and consternation at the sight that met their startled eyes.

The girl was at the crèche, kneeling beside the
cradle, sobbing her heart out. In the moonlight-
bathed clearing, Matt could easily identify the
child as Jenny.

''What in the world?'' David breathed.

Matt shook her head, then raised a silencing
finger to her lips. She moved noiselessly toward
the scene. David stepped just as silently alongside
her. As they drew nearer, they could hear, and
understand, the girl's pleading confession.

''...And I'm sorry I hurt Your mother...
but...but, I prayed, so hard, to Her to help my
mommy. But she didn't. And my mommy got
sicker and...and sicker...and I got scared and angry...and I thought...I thought, if she can't see
my mommy...see how sick she was...then...then
no one should be able to see Your mother, either.
I took the can of paint my daddy used to cover
the dents he got in the car when he was drunk
and I...and I sprayed it to hide Your mother's
face. But they fixed it so I covered her up with a
trash bag....''

She sniffled. ''And...and then, just yesterday,
on Your birthday, that nice minister from the
church came to see mommy, came to help her.

And…oh, little Baby Jesus…now I think it was Your mother that sent the minister to my mommy. I feel so bad about what I did…I…was so ashamed, I ran away to hide. I hid in that old barn down the road forever. I had to come…I had to tell You…I love You so…and I'm so sorry.…'' Jenny's voice dissolved in her heart-wrenching sobs.

Deeply affected, Matt turned a tear-blurred gaze on David. Her soul melted, her resistance surrendered to the love and compassion glowing from the depths of his eyes.

She loved this wonderful man, Matt acknowledged. She loved him. All other concerns were secondary.

Wiping the back of her hand across her eyes, she stepped into the clearing to go to the girl. As before, David was right beside her. Matt prayed he would always be beside her.

Jenny screamed in fright when Matt laid a gentle hand on her shoulder.

''It's all right, Jenny,'' she said in soft, crooning tones. ''It's all right, now.''

The girl turned wide, tear-bright eyes up at Matt. ''Am I going to jail for what I did?'' she cried, her thin frame shaking with fear and sobs.

''No, Jenny,'' David answered, kneeling next to the girl. ''You're going home…to your mommy.''

Chapter 11

"Case closed." Matt smiled at David over the rim of her coffee cup.

"There'll be no problems with this at the station?" He asked, concern tingeing his smile.

Matt shook her head. "Not unless you press charges." She arched a brow. "Are you?"

He gave her a look that drew a laugh from her, the first in what seemed a very long time.

"Everything has resolved itself very well, all things considered," he said, rising to go for the coffeepot to refill their cups.

"Hmm." Matt nodded, musing on the events following their discovery of the girl at the crèche.

April Henderson had been tearfully overjoyed when Matt and David had arrived at the house, Jenny in tow. After hearing her daughter's story, and receiving Matt's word that she would handle the police matter, the woman broke down into sobs.

She also finally agreed to allow David and Matt to not only arrange a medical examination for her, but to set the wheels into motion for her to receive some assistance.

They had subsequently decided to get on it first thing in the morning. From the Henderson house, David had driven straight to his place.

Matt had been well aware of his purpose. At least, now, with her self-acknowledgment of her love for him, and her altered feelings about a relationship with him, she hoped she knew his purpose.

"I'd be a very happy man if my other problem, my primary problem, could be so satisfactorily resolved," David murmured, startling her out of her reverie.

He was standing next to her, the coffeepot forgotten in his hand. He stared down at her with blatant hunger in his eyes.

"What...problem is that?" she asked.

"You. Your lack of trust and faith in me. Your willingness to deny us both out of fear." He took a ragged breath and glanced at the coffeepot as if wondering how it had appeared in his hand. He slammed it onto the table with such force Matt was amazed it didn't shatter. Grasping her shoulders, he pulled her from the chair and into his arms, crushing her mouth with his.

His kiss seared her lips, stirred her soul, branded her his forever. Maybe the cop and the pastor could be a happening thing, after all.

"Dammit, Matt," David exploded when he raised his head. "I love you. Doesn't that mean anything to you?"

"It means everything to me," Matt said, her voice tight, thick with emotion, her heart full. "You mean everything to me."

He went rock still, staring into her eyes, hope flaring to life in his. "Are you saying what I'm almost afraid to believe you're saying?"

Matt smiled, flashing perfect white teeth.

"I'm saying," she said distinctly, "I love you. I'm saying my love for you is stronger than fear. I'm saying my faith in you is boundless. And I'm saying that I would trust you with my life."

David closed his eyes a moment. When he opened them again, the devilish gleam was back.

"I did warn you that I was stronger," he teased. "Didn't I?"

"Oh, my love, I wouldn't go that far." Suppressing a laugh, she gave him her assume-the-position look.

"How far would you go?" His eyes, those gorgeous blue eyes, danced with deviltry. "The bedroom?"

Matt lost control of her laughter. Pulling his head to hers, she kissed him, fast and hard. Then she placed her hand confidently in his.

"Lead on, Macdonough," she invited, excitement bubbling through her.

He didn't hesitate. Grasping her hand, he started for his bedroom.

"David, wait." Matt brought him up short with a sharp tug on his arm.

He groaned and closed his eyes. "Why?" His voice was ragged-edged with suppressed emotion.

"I...must call home."

His eyes flew open. "Call home? Matt..." he actually wailed before his voiced dwindled off, his expression revealing his confusion.

She gave him a helpless look and a hopeful smile. "They'll worry if it gets late and they don't hear from me. Not only Gram, but Lisa and my mother and..." She winced. "And my father."

"Uhh...huhh. Right. Your father. FBI. Big. Tough-looking. Not to mention your uncles... All big. All tough-looking. All law enforcement." He nodded. "Get on that phone, Matt."

Matt didn't even try to contain the laughter that bubbled into her throat. He sounded so intimidated...and looked so sexually frustrated. While she could believe the latter, the former was a joke.

As if David Macdonough could possibly be intimidated by her father or uncles. Her David, who had defeated his own personal Goliath.

Not in this lifetime.

The attack of giggles poured forth, rocketing through the kitchen.

And then, as quickly as Matt's laughter had begun, the giggles ceased, cut off by a sudden, startling, self-revelation.

Without conscious thought, she apparently had also defeated her own inner giant of trepidation—that of her determination against burdening a life partner with the fear and anxiety consistent with her profession.

David was frowning at her. "What?"

"I'm free." Matt heard the note of wonder in her voice, so wasn't surprised when his frown darkened.

"Excuse me?"

"I'll explain later," she said airily, turning to stroll to the wall phone. "Right now, I'm going to call Gram." She lifted the receiver, then paused, a smile curling her lips. "On second thought, I think I'll ask to speak to Mother..."

She tossed him a grin. "She's been there, she'll understand."

"I wish I did."

Matt heard his muttered comment over the sound of the phone ringing in her grandmother's house.

"Wolfe residence," Lisa answered.

"Hi, Lis, it's me. May I speak to Mom?"

"Sure…but where in the world have you been all day?" Lisa didn't wait for a response, but went on dryly, "Fooling around with the reverend, are you?"

"Actually, I was working," Matt returned, every bit as dryly. "We were both working…in fact, we solved a case of church desecration."

"Oh. I see." Lisa sounded so disappointed, Matt had to smile. "Well, then, congratulations."

"Thanks." Her amusement overflowed into her voice. "Now, may I speak to Mom?"

"Yes, of course. Hold on."

There were a few moments of murmurs in the background at the other end of the line, during which Matt slid a quick sparkling glance at David.

He sparkled back at her; only his sparkle contained more sensuousness than amusement.

Matt felt tiny pinpricks of excitement over every inch of her skin…and deeper. She took in a long, calming breath; it didn't help.

"Matt?"

She blinked at the smooth, serene sound of her mother's voice. "Oh...hi, Mom." Matt scowled at her own inanity.

"Hi, yourself," Sandra said in her natural unruffled manner. "You wanted to talk to me?" A gentle but determined maternal nudge.

"Yes, yes...er..." Matt wet her lips, took another deep breath, reminded herself that she was a mature, intelligent professional, then rushed into garbled speech. "I probably won't be home until late...so...ah, don't you, Gram, or any one of you wait up. I'm with David, and...I, er, well, we..."

"Matilda." Sandra's soft tone sliced through her daughter's incoherent explanation.

Matt sighed in self-despair. "Yes, Mother?"

"Are you trying to tell me—in your own inimitable way—that you and that most attractive man have a *thing* in the bud between you?"

Matt exhaled in relief. She really should have remembered that her mother was one very shrewd, very savvy lady.

"Yes, Mother, that is precisely what I'm trying to tell you," Matt answered with blunt candor.

"And could this *thing* evolve into something serious?" Sandra probed further.

Matt shot a quick look at David...and stopped breathing altogether for a moment. The sparkle was gone from his eyes. Those incredible blue eyes were staring at her with an open expression of adoration.

"Oh...I strongly suspect it could, Mother," Matt said, brilliantly illuminated to the depths of her being by the light of love for her glowing in David's eyes.

"I see. In that case, my blessing upon you both. And don't worry, no one will wait up."

"What about Dad?" she asked, well aware of her father's overprotective tendency toward his daughters.

"Don't worry about him, either." Sandra's laugh was soft. "I can handle your father."

Matt could attest to that. She was still smiling moments later when she hung up the receiver.

"What about your father?" David asked, concerned. "Is there a problem?"

She turned, her smile easy, her eyes reflecting the light of love back to him. "No, no problem," she said, extending her hand to him again.

Though he captured her hand with his, he hesitated. "But, I heard you say..."

She silenced him with a quick headshake. "Not to worry, Mother will take care of Dad."

"I like your mother." The deviltry was back in his eyes.

"And she approves of you." Needing no urg-

ing, she strolled beside him from the kitchen,
along the hallway, and into his bedroom.

"I like your father, too." David halted beside
his bed and pulled her into his arms. "And I like
your grandmother, your sister, your aunts, uncles
and cousins."

"I'm glad." She chuckled and curled her arms
around his neck. "And, from their response to
you last night, I know they like you, too. Now…"

Matt lowered her voice to a sexy murmur,
"Can we forget about the family…and concen-
trate on us?"

He smiled and lowered his head to brush her
lips with his. "I was afraid you'd never—"

His voice got lost inside her mouth.

His kiss was passionate, possessive, all-
consuming. Matt reveled in it, gloried in it, returned it with every cell and molecule in her body.

It was still the Christmas holiday season, but
for Matt, it might as well have been the Fourth of
July. She saw the rockets' red glares, felt the
bombs bursting, and surrendered to the sheer
delight of it…of David.

She tugged at his shirt buttons with eager, trembling fingers. He caught her hand in his.

"Slowly," he murmured against her kiss-
sensitized lips. "I want to savor the moment, savor you."

Aroused and anxious, Matt pulled her head back to gaze at him in frustration. "But...but..." she protested. "I want to touch you, David."

The expression that skittered across his face was one of unabashed joy. "Oh, my beautiful Matt, you can't begin to imagine how much I want you to touch me. And I want to touch you, touch you and kiss you, every inch of you." Raising a hand, he drew a finger down her cheek— which drew a longing sigh from her. "But slowly, my love. Let me show you how much you mean to me."

As before, he began with her hair, freeing the confined mass by removing the large butterfly clip anchoring the loose twist at the back of her head. The long, deeply waved strands tumbled onto her shoulders and into his hands.

"I love your hair. It's like autumn-burnished gold silk," he murmured, spearing his fingers into the tresses to pull her mouth to his.

This time his kiss was different. Applying the lightest pressure, he claimed her mouth with heart-wrenching care and gentleness.

Her senses seduced, Matt sighed and melted against the solid strength of his body.

With exquisite tenderness, David slowly removed her clothes, caressing her skin with featherlight strokes as each separate piece fell away.

His touch was so very tender, loving, Matt felt
both cherished and adored. She was quivering in
response by the time she at last stood naked and
unashamed before him in readiness.

Her hands moved once again to the buttons on
his shirt; this time David did not stop her. Past
subtlety, she divested him of his garments within
minutes.

When the last item was gone, Matt smoothed
her hands over his shoulders, his chest. Her palms
tingled from the friction of the wedge of dark hair
against her skin. Her senses whirled in response
to the strength of the trim, angular, muscled
length of him, her body quickening to the allure
of his musky aroused-male scent.

Groaning low in his throat, David pulled her
into his arms, letting her feel the power of his
need.

They sank as one onto the bed. Matt arched into
him in silent supplication.

"No, love. Not yet. Not yet," he whispered,
gliding his tongue over her lips.

Matt made a low throaty sound of protest when
he abandoned her mouth, then sighed as his lips
commenced a journey down the arch of her neck.
He paused to nip and lave at the curve of her
shoulder before stringing quick, stinging kisses
down her chest.

Matt bowed her spine.

David accepted her invitation to explore the rounded curves of her breasts. She cried out when at last, at last, he closed his lips around one taut, aching tip, and shuddered in response when he began to suckle.

He lavished his attention on her breasts for long, sense-whirling minutes, then abandoned them to continue his exploration. With his lips and tongue and warm breath setting her body on fire, he touched her everywhere, *everywhere,* making her frantic with need.

Her breath reduced to ragged gasps, Matt tangled her fingers in his hair, writhing beneath his erotic assault on her senses. Anticipation, excitement and tension spun wildly, on the very edges of control.

"David…please," she pleaded, tugging frantically on his hair. "I—I…can't bear any more."

"Yes…now," he said, his voice tight, strangled, as he surged up and over her. "Now."

Matt was beyond thinking, beyond noticing, beyond caring that there were no moments spent fumbling with foil-wrapped packages. Her desire to be joined with him, be one with him, had reached flash point.

With a whimper of relief when finally he was

inside her, she encircled his muscle-bunched flanks within the lover's embrace of her thighs.

David, the tendons rigid in his arched neck, did his best to control the pace, stretching it out to the nth of delicious pleasure.

But he had prepared Matt too well. Hungry, needful, she drove him on, to the very end of his tether, and with a groan of defeat, he gave in to the moment.

From there, their ride was wild, exhilarating; but it was short-lived.

Matt's outcry of ecstasy was followed within seconds by David's shuddering exclamation of completion.

It was late. Matt was lost to the world in slumber, her burnished gold hair a glorious drift of silk across the pillow.

Disentangling himself from her, Mac silently slipped from the bed.

She murmured a protest.

He froze.

The breath he was holding eased from his throat when she snuggled deeper into the covers, deeper into sleep. Then, naked as the day he came into the world, he walked to the window to stare out and up into the star-tossed, moon-bright sky.

Your servant, Sir, he addressed his ultimate Commander. *Just as I am…as the old hymn goes.*

I love her, as You surely know, love her so much, so very much, it's almost frightening. And, yes, Sir, I am afraid. I'm afraid to sleep, to close my eyes, for fear of waking up to find her gone again. I know…I know, it's unreasonable and precipitate, but I don't ever again want to wake up alone and without her.

I've been alone so long, as You also surely know. And I've waited so long…not even knowing what or who I was waiting for. But You knew, didn't You?

Did You choose her for me at the beginning?

Have I served well enough to deserve her love, her trust, her faith?

She, my beautiful Officer Wolfe, is a dedicated warrior in the battle between right and wrong. She is a woman with many strengths, purpose, principle. Whereas I, as only You know, have struggled against many weaknesses.

And yet, Sir, this most adored woman has declared her love for me.

I pray I prove worthy of the bounty and the blessing…Yours and hers…

A sensation woke Matt, a strange sensation of feeling bereft and alone. But that's silly, she thought, her mind still sleep-muzzy. She had slept alone all her life. Why would she now feel cold, alone and deserted?

David.

That quick, Matt was awake and alert. David was no longer with her, his body spooned to hers.

For an instant, panic flared...

Matt pushed herself up on one forearm and skimmed her gaze around the room. Her gaze came to rest on the naked solitary figure outlined against the window. Her sigh of relief whispered into the still night.

Leaving the warmth of the bed, the carpet silencing her movements, she went to him.

"David," she murmured, lifting a hand, yet hesitating to touch his motionless form. "What are you doing?"

He didn't hesitate for an instant. His stare remaining fixed on the sky, he reached out, curling an arm around her waist, pulling her to his side, to his chilled body.

"I was praying," he answered simply.

Praying? Matt cast a glance at the sky, embarrassment heating her cheeks. He—they—were standing at the window, naked and exposed before the twinkling eyes scattered across the night sky.

And the all-seeing eyes of their Creator.

She made a strangled sound of despair.

"What is it?" David shifted his stare to her, concern sharp in his voice. "What's wrong?"

"You're praying?" she whispered, finding it oddly difficult to drag her eyes from the sky. "Like this?" A sweep of her hand indicated their nudity.

He chuckled. "My sweet Officer Wolfe, do you honestly think it matters?"

Matt sent a fast, uneasy glance to the night sky. "Isn't it...well...disrespectful?"

His chuckle grew into a full-fledged laugh. "Oh, Matt," he murmured, the residue of laughter woven through his voice. "You must realize that layers and layers of the heaviest clothing could not conceal the most infinitesimal flaw, physical or mental, from His notice."

"I suppose," she conceded, although still not quite comfortable.

"The unadorned human form is His design," he reminded her, his arm tightening to pull her even closer, so close, she could feel the tiny goose bumps on his flesh.

"Yes, you're right," she agreed, though still uncertain.

He chuckled again.

Matt decided to change the subject.

"What were you praying for?" she asked,

snuggling closer, trying to warm him with her own body.

"Guidance." Again his answer was simple, to the point, his gaze returning to the star-bright sky.

"In what?" She looked up at him, loving the strength of his rough-hewn features, the devotion reflected in his eyes; loving him, the wonderful man that was David.

"All things...generally." Canting his head, he smiled at her. "But right now...you in particular."

"Me?" She frowned, feeling a twinge of unease. "I—I don't understand. Why would you seek—need—guidance for me in particular?"

"How to proceed." Again, a simple statement.

"David...really, you're going to have to do better than that," she protested. "Proceed with what?"

"With you."

"But...I don't know—" she began when, yet again, he didn't elaborate.

"No," he interrupted her. "Before I explain, I must ask you something. What did you mean earlier, when you said you were free? Free of what? To do what?"

"Free of the misguided resolve I'd made to never subject a man to the uncertainty and anxiety of being the mate of a law enforcement officer," she confessed, gazing up into his beloved face with her feelings for him as bared to his eyes as her nakedness. "Free to love you."

He seemed not to breathe for a moment, and when he did, it was shallow, uneven. "I can be trusted with your love, Matt. Please believe that."

She would have answered, but he went on.

"I will be anxious, uncertain, and flat-out scared when you are working. But I'll endure. I'll be waiting for you when you return to me. I will pray and keep the faith."

"I know that...now," she said. "And I will keep faith with you. Trusting you. Loving you."

David exhaled a heartfelt sigh. Then he swung his gaze back to the sky.

"Thank You, Sir."

Matt heard his barely audible murmur, felt the tremor of easing tension ripple through his body. So simple a thank you...and so very complex.

"David?" Her throat felt tight; her eyes felt the sting of tears.

"Yes, love?" His voice, so gentle, so tender, so very loving in tone, sent the tears over the barriers of her eyelids.

"You feel so cold...come back to bed." She moved to turn away; his other arm encircled her, held her still against his chilled form.

"I'm afraid."

She blinked. "Of what?"

"Of falling asleep." His lips curved in a self-deprecating smile. "And then waking later to find you have crept away from me again."

"I won't." Raising a hand, she touched fingertips to his cool cheek, his firm lips. "I'll sleep beside you through the night. I promise."

"Your family." He sighed. "Your father."

Yes, her family. Her father. Matt knew she had a tough decision to make; she made it in an instant.

"I love, respect and honor my family...most especially my father," she said, shivering as his cold pervaded her dwindling warmth. "But I have made my choice, David. From now on, my place is by your side," she vowed. "Wherever you may be."

"And if I should receive a call, be transferred?" he asked. "It happens in the ministry, you know."

"I love my work, David."

"I know."

"I love you more." Rising up, she kissed his mouth. "And I will never ask you to choose between me and your commitment to your faith."

"You'd go with me..." David's voice cracked with emotion. "Just like that?"

"Just try and get away from me." She gave

him a tear-sparkled, teasing look. "I'm a trained police officer, if you'll recall?"

"Yeah." Laughter shimmered in his voice. "So?"

"I'll follow you, find you, imprison you. Never let you go."

"It's a deal." The laughter escaping, David swept her up into his arms and carried her to the bed.

Laughing with him, Matt pulled him down with her when he lowered her to the cover-strewn mattress.

In scant seconds, desire chased the chill from her body.

Matt was content with the heat David generated within her. She was hoping for a long, cold winter.

*　*　*　*　*

The Winter Soldier
by
Diana Palmer

DIANA PALMER

got her start in writing as a newspaper reporter and published her first romance novel for Silhouette® in 1982. In 1993, she celebrated the publication of her fiftieth novel for Silhouette. *Affaire de Coeur* lists her as one of the top ten romance authors. Beloved by fans worldwide, Diana Palmer is the winner of numerous romance best-seller awards.

For J Nelson

One

It was Monday, the worst day in the world to try to get a prescription filled. Behind the counter, the poor harassed male druggist was trying to field the telephone calls, fill prescriptions, answer questions from patrons and delegate duties to two assistants. It was always like this after the weekend, Cy Parks thought with resignation. Nobody wanted to bother the doctor on his days off, so they all waited until Monday to present their various complaints. Hence the rush on the Jacobsville Pharmacy. Michael, the pharmacist on duty, was smiling pleasantly despite the crush of customers, accustomed to the Monday madness.

That group putting off a visit to the doctor until Monday included himself, Cy mused. His arm was throbbing from an encounter with one of his angry Santa Gertrudis bulls late on Friday afternoon. It was his left arm, too, the one that had been burned in the house fire back in Wyoming. The angry rip needed ten stitches, and Dr. "Copper" Coltrain had been irritated that Cy hadn't gone to the emer-

gency room instead of letting it wait two days and risking
gangrene. The sarcasm just washed right off; Coltrain could
have saved his breath. Over the years, there had been so
many wounds that Cy hardly felt pain anymore. With his
shirt off, those wounds had been apparent to Coltrain, who
wondered aloud where so many bullet wounds came from.
Cy had simply looked at him, with those deep green eyes
that could be as cold as Arctic air. Coltrain had given up.

Stitches in place, Coltrain had scribbled a prescription
for a strong antibiotic and a painkiller and sent him on his
way. Cy had given the prescription to the clerk ten minutes
ago. He glanced around him at the prescription counter and
thought he probably should have packed lunch and brought
it with him.

He shifted from one booted foot to the other with noticeable impatience, his glittery green eyes sweeping the
customers nearest the counter. They settled on a serene
blond-haired woman studying him with evident amusement. He knew her. Most people in Jacobsville, Texas, did.
She was Lisa Taylor Monroe. Her husband, Walt Monroe,
an undercover narcotics officer with a federal agency, had
recently been killed. He'd borrowed on his insurance policy, so there had been just enough money to bury him. At
least Lisa had her small ranch, a legacy from her late father.

Cy's keen eyes studied her openly. She was sweet, but
she'd never win any beauty contests. Her dark blond hair
was always in a bun and she never put on makeup. She
wore glasses over her brown eyes, plastic framed ones, and
her usual garb was jeans and a T-shirt when she was working around the ranch her father had left her. Walt Monroe
had loved the ranch, and during his infrequent visits home,
he'd set out improving it. His ambitions had all but bank-
rupted it, so that Lisa was left after his death with a small
savings account that probably wouldn't even pay the interest on the loans Walt had obtained.

Cy knew something about Lisa Monroe because she was

his closest neighbor, along with Luke Craig, a rancher who was recently married to a public defender named Belinda Jessup. Mrs. Monroe there liked Charolais, he recalled. He wasn't any too fond of foreign cattle, having a purebred herd of Santa Gertrudis cattle, breeding bulls from which made him a profitable living. Almost as prosperous as his former sideline, he mused. A good champion bull could pull upward of a million dollars on the market.

Lisa had no such livestock. Her Charolais cattle were steers, beef stock. She sold off her steer crop every fall, but it wouldn't do her much good now. She was too deeply in debt. Like most other people, he felt sorry for her. It was common gossip that she was pregnant, because in a small town like Jacobsville, everybody knew everything. She didn't look pregnant, but he'd overheard someone say that they could tell in days now, rather than the weeks such tests had once required. She must be just barely pregnant, he mused, because those tight jeans outlined a flat stomach and a figure that most women would covet.

But her situation was precarious. Pregnant, widowed and deeply in debt, she was likely to find herself homeless before much longer, when the bank was forced to foreclose on the property. Damned shame, he thought, when it had such potential for development

She was clutching a boxed heating pad to her chest, waiting her turn in line at the second cash register at the pharmacy counter.

When Lisa was finally at the head of the line, she put down her heating pad on the counter and opened her purse.

"Another one, Lisa?" the young female clerk asked her with an odd smile.

She gave the other woman an irritated glance as she dug in her purse for her checkbook. "Don't you start, Bonnie," she muttered.

"How can I help it?" the clerk chuckled. "That's the

third one this month. In fact, that's the last one we have in stock.''

"I know that. You'd better order some more.''

"You really need to do something about that dog,'' Bonnie suggested firmly.

"Hear, hear!'' the other clerk, Joanne, seconded, peering at Lisa over her glasses.

"The puppy takes after his father,'' Lisa said defensively. He did, she mused. His father belonged to Tom Walker, and the mostly German shepherd dog, Moose, was a local legend. This pup was from the first litter he'd sired—without Tom's knowledge or permission. "But he's going to be a lot of protection, so I guess it's a trade-off. How much is this?''

Bonnie told her, waited while she wrote the check, accepted it and processed it. "Here you go,'' she told the customer. She glanced down at the other woman's flat stomach. "When are you due?''

"Eight months and two weeks,'' Lisa said quietly, wincing as she recalled that her husband, away from home and working undercover, had been killed the very night after she'd conceived, if Dr. Lou Coltrain had her numbers right. And when had Lou ever missed a due date? She was uncanny at predicting births.

"You've got that Mason man helping you with the ranch.'' Bonnie interrupted her thoughts. "You shouldn't need a dog with him there. Can't he protect you?''

"He only comes on the weekends,'' Lisa replied.

Bonnie frowned. "Luke Craig sent him out there, didn't he? But he said the man was supposed to spend every night in the bunkhouse!''

"He visits his girlfriend most nights,'' Lisa said irritably. "And better her than me! He doesn't bathe!''

Bonnie burst out laughing. "Well, there's one bright side to it. If he isn't staying nights, you only have to pay him for the weekends...Lisa,'' she added when she saw the guilty expression on the other woman's face, "you aren't still paying him for the whole week?"

Lisa flushed. "Don't," she said huskily.

"Sorry." Bonnie handed her a receipt. "It's just I hate the way you let people take advantage of you, that's all. There are so many rotten people in the world, and you're a walking, talking benevolence society."

"Rotten people aren't born, they're made," Lisa told her. "He isn't a bad man, he just didn't have a proper upbringing."

"Oh, good God!" Cy said harshly, glaring at her, having kept his mouth shut as long as possible without imploding. The woman's compassion hit him on a raw spot and made him furious.

Lisa's eyes were brown, big and wide and soft through the plastic frames of her glasses. "Excuse me?"

"Are you for real?" he asked curtly. "Listen, people dig their own graves and they climb into them. Nothing excuses cruelty."

"You tell her!" Bonnie said, agreeing.

Lisa recognized her taciturn neighbor from a previous encounter, long ago. He'd come right up to her when she'd been pitching hay over the fence to her cattle one day and told her outright that she should leave heavy work to her husband. Walt hadn't liked that comment, not at all. It had only been a few days after he'd let her do the same thing while he flirted with a pretty blond parcel delivery employee. Worse, Walt thought that Lisa had encouraged Cy's interference somehow and they'd had a fight—not the first in their very brief marriage. She didn't like the tall man and her expression told him so. "I wasn't talking to you," she pointed out. "You don't know anything about my business."

His eyebrows rose half an inch. "I know that you overpay the hired help." He looked pointedly at her flat belly.

"And that you're the last person who should be looked upon as a walking benevolence society."

"Hear, hear!" Joanne said again from behind Bonnie.

Lisa glared at her. "You can be quiet," she said.

"Let your erstwhile employee go," he told her. "I'll send one of my men over to spend nights in the bunkhouse. Bonnie's right about one thing, you don't need to be by yourself after dark in such a remote place."

"I don't need your help," she said, glowering at him.

"Yes, you do. Your husband wouldn't have liked having you try to run that ranch alone," he added quietly, even though he didn't mean it, and he hoped that his distaste for the late Walt Monroe didn't show. He still recalled watching Lisa heft a huge bale of hay while her husband stood not ten paces away flirting with a pretty blond woman. It was a miracle she hadn't miscarried, the way she hefted heavy things around. He wondered if she even knew the chance she was taking…

She was looking at him with different eyes now. The concern touched her despite her hostility. She sighed. "I guess you're right," she said softly. "He wouldn't have."

He hated the way that softness made him feel. He'd lost so much. Everything. He wouldn't admit, even to himself, how it felt to have those dark eyes look at him with tenderness. He swallowed down the ache in his throat.

She let her gaze fall to his arm, the one that had just been stitched, and her soft gasp was audible. "You've been hurt!"

"Two prescriptions, Mr. Parks," Bonnie said with a grin, holding up a prescription sack. She bent to pick up the package, a strand of her short blond hair falling around her pretty bespectacled face. "And Dr. Coltrain said that if you don't take this pain medication, he'll have me flogged," she added impishly.

"We can't have that, I guess," Cy murmured dryly.

"Glad you agree." She accepted his credit card as Lisa turned to go.

"You drive into town?" Cy asked the widow.

"Uh, well, no, the car's got a broken water pump," she confessed. "I rode in with old Mr. Murdock."

"He'll be at the lodge meeting until midnight," he pointed out.

"Just until nine. I thought I'd go to the library and wait."

"You need your rest," Cy said curtly. "No sense in waiting until bedtime for a ride. I'll drive you home. It's on my way."

"Go with him," Bonnie said firmly as she waited for Cy to put his credit card back into his wallet and sign the ticket. "Don't argue," she added when Lisa opened her mouth. "I'll phone the lodge and tell Mr. Murdock you got a ride."

"Were you ever in the army?" Cy asked the young woman with a rare twinkle in his green eyes.

She grinned. "Nope. But it's their loss."

"Amen," he said.

"Mr. Parks..." Lisa began, trying to escape.

Cy took her arm, nodded to Bonnie and herded Lisa out of the pharmacy onto the street where his big red Ford Expedition was parked. On the way they ran into the second pharmacist, a dark-eyed woman with equally dark hair.

"Hi, Nancy!" Lisa said with a grin.

Nancy gave a gamine smile. "Don't tell me, the line's two miles long already."

"Three. Want to go home with me?" Lisa asked.

Nancy sighed. "Don't I wish. See you!"

Nancy went on toward the pharmacy and Lisa turned back to let Cy open the door of the Expedition for her. "Imagine you with a red vehicle," she said dryly. "I would have expected black."

"It was the only one they had in stock and I was in a hurry. Here." He helped her up into the huge vehicle.

"Gosh," she murmured as he got in beside her, "you could kill an elephant with this thing."

"It's out of season for elephants." He scowled as she fumbled with the seat belt. "That's hard to buckle on the passenger side. Here, like this..." He leaned close to her and fastened it with finesse despite his damaged left hand and arm. It required a closeness he hadn't had with a woman since his wife and son died in the fire. He noticed that Lisa's eyes were a very soft dark brown and that her complexion was delicious. She had a firm, rounded little chin and a pretty mouth. Her ears were tiny. He wondered what that mass of dark gold hair looked like at night when she took the hairpins out, and his own curiosity made him angry. With compressed lips, he fastened the seat belt and moved away to buckle his own in place.

Lisa was relieved when he leaned back. He made her nervous when he was that close. Odd, that reaction, she thought, when she'd been married for two months. She should be used to men. Of course, her late husband hadn't been that interested in her body. He didn't seem to enjoy sleeping with her, and he was always in such a rush that she really didn't feel any of the things women were supposed to feel. She recalled that he'd married her on the rebound from the woman he really wanted, and the only thing about Lisa that really appealed to him had been her father's ranch. He'd had great ideas about starting an empire, but it was only a pipe dream. A dead dream, now. She stared out at the small town as they drove through it on the way out to their respective ranches.

"Do you have anyone managing the ranch for you?" he asked when they were on the lonely highway heading out of town.

"Can't afford anyone," she said wistfully. "Walt had big plans for the place, but there was never enough money to fulfill them. He borrowed on his salary and his life insurance policy to buy the steers, but he didn't look far enough ahead to see the drought coming. I guess he didn't realize that buying winter feed for those steers would put us in the hole.'' She shook her head. ''I did so want his plans to work out,'' she said wistfully. ''If they had, he was going to give up undercover work and come home to be a rancher.'' Her eyes were sad. ''He was only thirty years old.''

''Manuel Lopez is a vindictive drug lord,'' he murmured. ''He doesn't stop at his victims, either. He likes to target whole families. Well, except for small children. If he has a virtue, that's the only one.'' He glanced at her. ''All the more reason for you to be looked after at night. The dog is a good idea. Even a puppy will bark when someone comes up to the door.''

''How do you know about Lopez?'' she asked.

He laughed. It was the coldest sound Lisa had ever heard. ''How do I know? He had his thugs set fire to my house in Wyoming. My wife and my five-year-old son died because of him.'' His eyes stared straight ahead. ''And if it's the last thing I ever do, I'll see him pay for it.''

''I had…no idea,'' she faltered. She winced at the look on his face. ''I'm very sorry, Mr. Parks. I knew about the fire, but…'' She averted her eyes to the dark landscape outside. ''They told me that Walt only said two words before he died. He said, 'Get Lopez.' They will, you know,'' she added harshly. ''They'll get him, no matter what it takes.''

He glanced at her and smiled in spite of himself. ''You're not quite the retiring miss that you seem to be, are you, Mrs. Monroe?''

''I'm pregnant,'' she told him flatly. ''It makes me ill-tempered.''

He slowed to make a turn. ''Did you want a child so soon after your marriage?'' he asked, knowing as everyone locally did that she'd only married two months ago.

''I love children,'' she said, smiling self-consciously. ''I guess it's not the 'in' thing right now, but I've never had dreams of corporate leadership. I like the pace of life here in Jacobsville. Everybody knows everybody. There's precious little crime usually. I can trace my family back three generations here. My parents and my grandparents are buried in the town cemetery. I loved being a housewife, taking care of Walt and cooking and all the domestic things women aren't supposed to enjoy anymore.'' She glanced at him with a wicked little smile. "I was even a virgin when I married. When I rebel, I go the whole way!"

He chuckled. It was the first time in years that he'd felt like laughing. "You renegade."

"It runs in my family," she laughed. "Where are you from?"

He shifted uncomfortably. "Texas."

"But you lived in Wyoming," she pointed out.

"Because I thought it was the one place Lopez wouldn't bother me. What a fool I was," he added quietly. "If I'd come here in the first place, it might never have happened."

"Our police are good, but…"

He glanced at her. "Don't you know what I am? What I was?" he amended. "Eb Scott's whole career was in the Houston papers just after he sent two of Lopez's best men to prison for attempted murder. They mentioned that several of his old comrades live in Jacobsville now."

"I read the papers," she confessed. "But they didn't mention names, you know."

"Didn't they?" He maneuvered a turn at a stop sign. "Eb must have called in a marker, then."

She turned slightly toward him. "What were you?"

He didn't even glance at her. "If the papers didn't mention it, I won't."

"Were you one of those old comrades?" she persisted.

He hesitated, but only for a moment. She wasn't a gossip. There was no good reason for not telling her. "Yes," he said bluntly. "I was a mercenary. A professional soldier for hire to the highest bidder," he added bitterly.

"But with principles, right?" she persisted. "I mean, you didn't hire out to Lopez and help him run drugs."

"Certainly not!"

"I didn't think so." She leaned back against her seat, weary. "It must take a lot of courage to do that sort of work. I suppose it takes a certain kind of man, as well. But why did you do it when you had a wife and child?"

He hated that damned question. He hated the answer, too. "Well?"

She wasn't going to quit until he told her. His hands tightened on the steering wheel. "Because I refused to give it up, and she got pregnant deliberately to get even with me." He didn't stop to think about the odd way he'd worded that, but Lisa noticed and wondered at it. "I curtailed my work, but I helped get the goods on Lopez before I hung it up entirely and started ranching full-time. I'd just come back from overseas when the fire was set. It was obvious afterward that I'd been careless and let one of Lopez's men track me back to Wyoming. I've had to live with it ever since."

She studied his lean, stark profile with quiet, curious eyes. "Was it the adrenaline rush you couldn't live without, or was it the confinement of marriage that you couldn't live with?"

His green eyes glittered dangerously. "You ask too damned many questions!"

She shrugged. "You started it. I had no idea that you were anything more than a rancher. Your foreman, Harley Fowler, likes to tell people that he's one of those dashing professional soldiers, you know. But he isn't."

The statement surprised him. "How do you know he isn't?" he asked.

"Because I asked him if he'd ever done the Fan Dance and he didn't know what I was talking about."

He stopped the truck in the middle of the road and just stared at her. "Who told you about that? Your husband?"

"He knew about the British Special Air Services, but mostly just what I told him—including that bit about the Fan Dance, one of their rigorous training tests." She smiled self-consciously. "I guess it sounds strange, but I love reading books about them. They're really something, like the French Foreign Legion, you know. A group of men so highly trained, so specialized, that they're the scourge of terrorists the world over. They go everywhere, covertly, to rescue hostages and gather intelligence about terrorist groups." She sighed and closed her eyes, oblivious to the expression of the man watching her. "I'd be scared to death to do anything like that, but I admire people who can. It's a way of testing yourself, isn't it, so that you know how you react under the most deadly pressure. Most of us never face physical violence. Those men have." Her eyes opened. "Men like you."

He felt his cheeks go hot. She was intriguing. He began to understand why Walt had married her. "How old are you?" he asked bluntly.

"Old enough to get pregnant," she told him pertly. "And that's all you're getting out of me."

His green eyes narrowed. She was very young, there was no doubt about that. He didn't like the idea of her being in danger. He didn't like the idea of the man Luke Craig had sent over to look out for her, either. He was going to see about that.

"How old are you, if we're getting personal?" she asked.

"Older than you are," he returned mockingly.

She grimaced. "Well, you've got scars and lines in your face, and a little gray at your temples, but I doubt you're over thirty-five."

His eyebrows arched almost to his hairline.

"I'd like you to be my baby's godfather when he's

born," she continued bluntly. "I think Walt would have liked that, too. He spoke very highly of you, although he didn't say much about your background. I was curious about that. Now I understand why he was so secretive."

"I've never been a godfather," he said curtly.

"That's okay. I've never been a mother." She frowned. "Come to think of it, the baby hasn't been a baby before, either." She looked down at her flat belly and smiled tenderly, tracing it. "We can all start even."

"Did you love your husband?"

She looked up at him. "Did you love your wife?" she countered instantly.

He didn't like looking at her belly, remembering. He started down the road again, at a greater speed. "She said she loved me, when we married," he said evasively.

Poor woman, Lisa thought. And poor little boy, to die so young, and in such a horrible way. She wondered if the taciturn Mr. Parks had nightmares, and guessed that he did. His poor arm was proof that he'd tried to save his family. It must be terrible, to go on living, to be the only survivor of such a tragedy.

They pulled up in front of her dilapidated ranch house. The steps were flimsy and one of the boards was rotten. The house needed painting. The screens on the windows were torn, and the one on the screen door was half torn away. In the corral, he could hear a horse whinny. He hoped her fences were in better shape than the house.

He helped her down out of the truck and set her gently on her feet. She was rail-thin.

"Are you eating properly?" he asked abruptly as he studied her in the faint light from the porch, scowling.

"I said you could be the baby's godfather, not mine," she pointed out with an impish smile. "Thank you very much for the ride. Now go home, Mr. Parks."

"Don't I get to see this famous puppy?"

She grimaced as she walked gingerly up the steps, past

the rotten one, and put her key in the lock. "He stays on the screen porch out back, and even with papers down, I expect he's made a frightful mess... That's odd," she said when the door swung open without the key being turned in the lock. "I'm sure I locked this door before I... Where are you going?"

"Stay right there," he said shortly. He opened the truck, took out the .45 automatic he always carried and cocked it on his way back onto the porch.

Her face went pale. Reading about commandos was very different from the real thing when she saw the cold metal of the pistol in his hands and realized that he was probably quite proficient in its use. The thought chilled her. Like the sight of the gun.

He put her gently to one side. "I'm not going to shoot anybody unless I get shot at," he said reassuringly. "Stay there."

He left her on the porch and went carefully, quietly, through the house with the pistol raised at his ear, one finger on the trigger and his other hand, in spite of its injury, supporting the butt efficiently. He swept the house, room by room, closet by closet, until he got to the bedroom and heard a sound inside. It was only a sound, a faint whisper. There was a hint of light coming from under the door, which was just slightly ajar.

He kicked the door open, the pistol leveled the second he had a clear view of the bed.

The man's face was a study in shock when he saw the expression on Cy Parks's dark face and the glitter in his eyes. Bill Mason, Luke Craig's erstwhile cowboy-on-loan, was lying on the bed in his shorts with a beer bottle in one hand. When Cy burst in the door, he sat up starkly, his bloodshot eyes blinking as he swayed. He was just drunk enough not to realize how much trouble he was in.

"You're not Mrs. Monroe," he drawled loudly.

"And you're not Mr. Monroe. If you want to see daylight again, get the hell out of that bed and put your clothes on!''

''Okay. I mean yes, sir, Mr. Parks!''

The man tripped and fell, the beer bottle shattering on the floor as he sprawled nearby. ''I broked it,'' he moaned as he dragged himself up holding onto the bedpost, ''and it was my...my last one!''

''God help us! Hurry up!''

''Okay. Just let me find...my pants...'' He hiccuped, tripped again and fell, moaning. ''They must be here somewhere!''

Muttering darkly, Cy uncocked the pistol, put the safety on, and stuck it into the belt at his back. He went to find Lisa, who was standing impatiently on the porch.

''I saved you a shock,'' he told her.

''How big a shock?''

''The great unwashed would-be lover who was waiting for you, in your bed,'' he said, trying not to grin. It wasn't really funny.

''Oh, for heaven's sake, not again,'' she groaned.

''Again?''

She was made very uncomfortable by the look on his face. ''Don't even think it!'' she threatened angrily. ''I'm not that desperate for a man, thank you very much. He gets drunk one night a week and sleeps it off in Walt's bed,'' she muttered, oblivious to both her phrasing and his surprised look. ''I lock him in, so he can't cause me any trouble, and I let him out the next morning. He's got a drinking problem, but he won't get help.''

''Does Luke Craig know that?''

''If he did, he'd fire him, and the poor man has no place to go,'' she began.

''He'll have a place to go tomorrow,'' he promised her with barely contained fury. ''Why didn't you say something?''

"I didn't know you," she pointed out. "And Luke meant it as a kind gesture."

"Luke would eat him with barbecue sauce if he knew what he was doing over here!"

There was a muffled thud and then the tipsy man weaved toward the front door. "So sorry, Mrs. Monroe," Mason drawled, sweeping off his hat and almost going down with it as he bowed. "Very sorry. I'll be off, now." He hesitated at the top step with one foot in the air. "Where's my horse?" he asked blankly. "I left him out here somewhere."

"I'll send him to you. Go back to Craig's ranch."

"It's two miles!" the cowboy wailed. "I'll never make it!"

"Yes, you will. Get in the truck. And if you throw up in it, I'll shoot you!" Cy promised.

The cowboy didn't even question the threat. He tried to salute and almost fell down again. "Yes, sir, I'll get…get right in the truck, yes, sir, right now!"

He weaved to the passenger side, opened the door and pulled himself in, slamming the door behind him.

"I'd sleep on the sofa," Cy advised Lisa. "Until you can wash the sheets, at least."

"His girlfriend must be nuts. No woman in her right mind would sleep with him," she murmured darkly.

"I can see why. I'll send a man over to the bunkhouse. And he won't get drunk and wait for you in bed," he added.

She chuckled. "That would be appreciated." She hesitated. "Thanks for the ride home, Mr. Parks."

He hesitated, his narrow green eyes appraising her. She'd taken her husband's death pretty hard, and she had dark circles under those eyes. He hated leaving her alone. He had protective feelings for her that really disturbed him.

"I'll want to meet that pup when I come back again."

She managed a smile. "Okay."

"Go in and lock the door," he instructed.

She clutched her heating pad and her purse to her chest and glared at him, but he stared her down. *Oh, well,* she thought as she went inside, *some men just didn't know the meaning of diplomacy.* She'd have to make allowances for that little character flaw.

He waited until she got inside and locked the door before he climbed into his truck. He wondered why she'd said Walt's bed and not *their* bed. The question diverted him as he drove the intoxicated but quiet cowboy over to Luke Craig's house and showed him to Luke. The blond rancher cursed roundly, having closed the door so that his new wife, Belinda, wouldn't overhear.

"I'm very drunk," the cowboy said with a lopsided grin, swaying on the porch.

"He was stripped to his shorts, waiting for Lisa in her bed," Cy said, and he didn't grin. "I don't want this man sent over there again."

"He won't be. Good God, he's hidden it well, hasn't he?"

"I'm very drunk," the cowboy repeated, and the grin widened.

"Shut up," Cy told him. He turned back to Luke. "I'm sending one of my own men over to sleep in the bunkhouse. Can you handle him?"

"I'm *veerrryy* drunk," the cowboy interjected.

"Shut up!" chorused the two men.

Belinda Jessup Craig opened the front door and peered out at the tableau. "He's very drunk," she pointed out, and wondered why they looked so belligerent. "You'd better bring him inside, Luke. We can sober him up in the kitchen. You can't leave him stumbling around like that. I'll phone the Master's Inn and see if they've got room for him." She glanced at Cy's puzzled expression. "It's a halfway house for alcoholics. They offer treatment and continued support."

"She wants to save the world," Luke muttered, but he grinned at her.

"And he wants to control it," she shot back with a wink. "Care to come in for coffee, Mr. Parks?"

"No, thanks," he replied. "I have to get home."

"I'm sorry about the trouble," Luke said.

"Your heart was in the right place. She's special," he added in spite of himself.

Luke smiled slowly. "Yes. She is."

Cy cleared his throat. "Good night."

"Good night," Luke answered.

"Good night!" the cowboy echoed before Luke propelled him firmly into the house.

Two

Cy took his medicine and had the first good night's sleep he'd enjoyed in days. He'd sent a capable, older cowboy over to Lisa's ranch the night before to sleep in the bunkhouse and keep an eye on things. He'd also arranged covertly for sensitive listening equipment to be placed around her house, and for a man to monitor it full-time. He might be overly cautious, but he wasn't taking chances with a pregnant woman. He knew Manuel Lopez's thirst for revenge far too well. The drug lord had a nasty habit of targeting the families of people who opposed him. And Lopez might not know Lisa was pregnant. Cy wasn't willing to risk leaving Lisa out there alone.

The next day he drove over to Lisa's house and found her struggling with a cow in the barn, trying to pull a calf by hand. He couldn't believe she was actually doing that!

He'd barely turned off the engine before he was out of the big sports utility vehicle and towering over her in the barn. She looked up with a grimace on her face when she realized what a temper he was in.

"Don't you say a word, Cy Parks," she told him at once, wiping the sweat from her forehead. "There's nobody but me to do this, and the cow can't wait until one of my part-timers comes in from the lower pasture. They're dipping cattle…"

"So you're trying to do a job that you aren't half big enough to manage. Are you out of your mind?" he burst out. "You're pregnant, for God's sake!"

She was panting, sprawled between the cow's legs. She glared up at him and blew a stray strand of hair out of her eyes. "Listen, I can't afford to lose the cow or the calf…"

"Get up!" he said harshly.

She glared at him.

For all his raging temper, he reached down and lifted her tenderly to her feet, putting her firmly to one side. He got down on one knee beside the cow and looked at the situation grimly. "Have you got a calf-pull?"

She ground her teeth together. "No. It broke and I didn't know how to fix it."

He said a few words under his breath and went out to his truck, using the radio to call for help. Fortunately one of his men was barely two minutes away. Harley, his foreman, came roaring up beside Cy's truck, braked and jumped out with a length of rope.

"Good man, Harley," Cy said as he looped the rope around the calf's feet. "If we can't get him out ourselves, we can use the wench on my truck. Ready? Pull!"

They were bathed in sweat and cursing when they managed to get the calf halfway out.

"He's still alive," Cy said, grinning. "Okay, let's go again. Pull!"

Three more firm tugs and the calf slipped out. Cy cleared his nose and mouth and the little black-baldy bawled. The cow turned, gently licking away the slick birth membranes covering her calf.

"That was a near miss," Harley observed, grinning.

"Very near." Cy glowered at Lisa. "In more ways than one."

"Excuse me?" Harley asked.

"It was my cow," Lisa pointed out. "I thought I could do it by myself."

"Pregnant, and you think you're Samson," he said with biting sarcasm.

She put her hands on her hips and glared up at him. "Go away!"

"Gladly. When I've washed my hands."

"There's a pump over here," Harley reminded him, indicating it.

"You go ahead, son," Cy muttered, glancing at his stitched arm. "I've got a raw wound. I'll have to have antibacterial soap."

Harley didn't say anything, but his face was expressive. He thought his poor old crippled boss was a real basket case, barely fit to do most ranch work.

"Antibacterial soap, indeed. The germs would probably die of natural causes if they got in you!" Lisa muttered.

"At least my germs are intelligent! I wouldn't try pulling calves if I was pregnant!"

Lisa almost doubled over at the thought of a pregnant Cy Parks, which only served to make him angrier.

"I'll get back to your place and start the men culling cattle for the next sale, boss man. I can wash up there!" Harley called, and didn't wait for an answer. The amused expression on his face was eloquent—he wanted to get out of the line of fire!

"Craven coward," she muttered, staring after the cloud of dust he and the truck vanished in. "Are all your men like that?"

He followed her into the kitchen. "He's not afraid of

me," he said irritably. "He thinks I'm pitiable. In fact, he has delusions that he's soldier of fortune material since he spent two weeks having intense combat training with a weekend merk training school," he added with pure sarcasm. "Have you got a hand towel?"

She pulled one from a drawer while he lathered his arms, wincing a little as the water and soap stung the stitches.

"You don't want to get that infected," she said, studying the wound as she stood beside him with the towel.

"Thanks for the first-aid tip," he said with failing patience. "That's why I asked for antibacterial soap!" He took the towel she offered, but his eyes were on her flat belly even as he dried away the wetness. "You take chances," he said shortly. "Dangerous chances. A lot of women miscarry in the first trimester, even without doing stupid things like heavy lifting and trying to pull calves. You need to think before you act."

She studied his quiet, haunted face. Discussing pregnancy didn't seem to make him feel inhibited at all. "You must have been good to your wife while she was pregnant," she said gently.

"I wanted the baby," he replied. His face hardened. "She didn't. She didn't want a child until she was in her thirties, if then. But I wouldn't hear of her terminating the pregnancy," he added, and there was an odd, pained look in his eyes for an instant. "So she had the child, only to lose him in a much more horrible way. But despite everything, I wanted him from the time I knew he was on the way."

She felt his pain as if it were tangible. "I won't have anyone to share this with," she said, her voice husky with remembered loss and pain. "I was over the moon when they did the blood test and said I was pregnant. Walt wouldn't even talk about having children. He died the night after I conceived, but even if he'd lived long enough to

know about the baby, he would have said it was too soon."
She shrugged. "I guess it was."

She'd never told that to another soul. It embarrassed her
that it had slipped out, but Cy seemed unshockable.

"Some men don't adjust well to children," he said simply. It went without saying that he wasn't one of them. He
didn't know what else to say. He felt sorry for her. She
obviously took pleasure in her pregnancy, and it was
equally obvious that she loved children. He sat down at the
table with her. Maybe she needed to get it out of her system. Evidently she could tell him things that she couldn't
tell anyone else.

"Go on," he coaxed. "Get everything off your chest.
I'm a clam. I don't tell anything I know, and I'm not judg-
mental."

"I think I sensed that." She sighed. "Want some coffee?
I have to drink decaf, but I could make some."

"I hate decaf, but I'll drink it."

She smiled. She got up and filled the pot and the filter
and started the coffeemaker while she got down white
mugs. She glanced at him with pursed lips. "Black," she
guessed.

He gave her an annoyed look. "Don't get conceited because you know how I take my coffee."

"I won't."

She poured the coffee into the cups and sat back down,
watching as he cupped his left hand around it. "Does it
still hurt?" she asked, referring to the burns on his hand.

"Not as much as it used to," he said flatly.

"You don't have anyone to talk to, either, do you?"

He shook his head. "I'm not much for bars, and the only
friend I have is Eb. Now that he's married, we don't spend
a lot of time together."

"It's worse when you hold things inside," she murmured
absently, staring into her coffee. "Everybody thinks I had
a fairy-tale marriage with a sexy man who loved danger

and could have had any woman he wanted.'' She smiled wryly. ''At first I thought so, too. He seemed like a dream come true. Boy, did my illusions leave skid marks taking off!''

''So did mine,'' he said flatly.

She leaned forward, feeling daring. ''Yes, but I'll bet *you* weren't a virgin who thought people did it in the dark fully clothed!''

He burst out laughing. He hadn't felt like laughing since…he couldn't remember. Her eyes bubbled with joy; her laugh was infectious. She made him hungry, thirsty, desperate for the delight she engendered.

She grinned. ''There. You look much less intimidating when you smile. And before you regret telling me secrets, I'd better mention that I've never told anybody what my best friend did on our senior trip to Florida. And I won't tell you now.''

''Was it scandalous?''

''It was for Jacobsville.'' She chuckled.

''Didn't you do anything scandalous?''

''Not me,'' she popped back. ''I'm the soul of propriety. My dad used to say that I was the suffering conscience of the world.'' Her eyes darkened. ''He died of a stroke while he was using the tiller out in the garden. When he didn't come in for lunch, I knew something was wrong. I went out to find him.'' She moved her coffee cup on the table. ''He was sitting against a tree with his thermos jug of coffee still in his hands, his eyes wide-open, stone dead.'' She shivered. ''Mom had died when I was in sixth grade, of cancer. Dad loved her so much. He loved me, too.'' She lifted her sad eyes. ''I suppose I'd rather have had him for a short time than not to have had him at all. Walter felt sorry for me and asked me to marry him, because I was so alone. He'd just lost the woman he loved and I think he wanted to marry me just to spite her. The ranch was a bonus. I was really infatuated with him at first, and he liked me and loved this ranch. I figured we had as good a chance of making a marriage work as people who were passionately in love.'' She sighed again. ''Isn't hindsight wonderful?''

He leaned back in his chair and looked at her for a long time. ''You're a tonic,'' he said abruptly. ''You're astringent and sometimes you sting, but I like being around you.''

''Thanks. I think,'' she added.

''Oh, it's a compliment,'' he murmured. ''I wouldn't offer you anything except the truth.''

''That really is a compliment.''

''Glad you noticed.''

''What happened to the drunk cowboy?'' she asked.

''Luke's wife is getting him into a halfway house,'' he mused. ''A real crusader, that lady. She is a bleeding heart.''

''She likes lost causes,'' she countered. ''I've heard a lot about her, and I like what I've heard. If I can get this ranch back on its feet, I'd like to help her.''

''Another latent crusader,'' he teased.

''A lot of people need saving, and there aren't a lot of reformers around,'' she pointed out.

''True enough.''

''Thanks for sending that other man over to keep a lookout. He's very nice. Did you know that he likes to do needlepoint?'' she asked matter-of-factly.

He nodded. ''Nels does some exhibition-quality handwork. Nobody teases him about it, either. At least, not since he knocked Sid Turpen into the water trough.''

She chuckled. ''He looked like that sort of man. I knit,'' she said. ''Not very well, but it gives me something to do when I'm by myself.''

''You're always by yourself,'' he said quietly. ''Why don't you come home with me one or two evenings a week

and we can watch television after I've finished with the
books. I could come and fetch you.''

Her heart jumped. She didn't need telling that he'd never
made that invitation to anyone else. He was like a wounded
wolf in his lair most of the time. ''Wouldn't I be in the
way?'' she asked.

He shook his head. ''I'm alone, too. You and the baby
would be good company; before and after he's born. You
don't have a husband anymore. I don't have a family,'' he
said bluntly. ''I'd like to help you through the next few
months. No strings,'' he added firmly. ''And absolutely no
ulterior motives. Just friendship.''

She was touched. He made her feel welcome, warm and
safe. She knew that a lot of people were intimidated by
him, and that he was very standoffish. It was a huge compliment he was paying her. ''Thanks,'' she said genuinely.
''I'll take you up on that.''

He sipped his coffee and put the cup down. ''It might
be good for both of us to spend less time alone with the
past.''

''Is that what you do, too, thinking about how it might
have been, if...'' She let the word trail away.

''If,'' he agreed, nodding. ''If I'd smelled the smoke
sooner, if I'd gone to bed earlier, if I'd realized that Lopez
might send someone after me even from prison...and so
forth.''

''I kept thinking, what if I hadn't got pregnant so soon
after I married,'' she confessed. ''But I'm not sorry I did,
really,'' she added with a tiny smile. ''I like it.''

He searched her dark eyes for longer than he wanted to
and dragged his attention away. All at once, he glanced at
his watch and grimaced. ''Good Lord, I almost forgot! I've
got a meeting at the bank this morning that I can't miss—
refinancing a loan so that I can replace my combine.'' He
got to his feet. ''No other problems except for drunk cowboys in your bed?'' he asked whimsically.

She glared at him. "Don't look at me, I didn't put him there!"

His eyes roamed over her. and he smiled slowly. "His loss."

"You get out of here, you fresh varmint," she said, rising. "And there's no use trying to seduce me, either. I'm immune."

"Really?" he asked with raised eyebrows and a twinkle in his green eyes. "Shall we test that theory?" He took a step in her direction.

She flushed and backed up a step. "You stop that," she muttered.

He chuckled as he reached for his hat. "Don't retreat. I'll keep to my side of the line in the sand. Keep that door locked," he added then, and not with a smile. "I'm having you watched, just in case Lopez does try something. But if you need me, I'll be as close as the telephone."

"I know that. Thank you."

"Your car has a busted water pump," he added, surprising her that he remembered. "I'll have one of my men come get it and overhaul it for you."

She was all but gasping. "But, you don't have to...!"

"I know I don't have to," he said, eyes flashing. "You can't be stuck out here without transportation, especially now."

She didn't want to accept what she knew was charity, but the temptation to have her little red car fixed and running again was too much. She couldn't afford an extra spark plug. "Thank you," she said a little stiffly. It hurt her pride to know that he was aware of her financial situation.

He searched her face quietly. "No need for thanks. I'll take care of you. And the baby."

She stared at him while confusing sensations washed over her like a gentle electric current. She'd never felt such a surge of emotion, with anyone.

"I don't have any ulterior motives, Lisa," he said, speaking her name for the first time. It sounded soft, mysterious, even beautiful in his deep, measured tones.

"Then thanks, for seeing about my car," she said gently. "And if you get sick, I'll take care of you. All right?"

His heart ran wild. He'd never had anybody offer to look after him. His wife hadn't been compassionate. It hit him right in the gut that Lisa thought of him with such kindness. He searched for an answer and couldn't find one.

"I'm sure you never get sick," she said quickly, a little intimidated by his scowl. "But just in case."

He nodded slowly.

She smiled, reassured.

He turned and went out the door, speechless for the first time in recent memory. He couldn't have managed a single word to save his life.

Lisa went onto the porch and watched him drive away with confused emotions. She shouldn't let things intensify. She was a recent widow and he hadn't been widowed all that long ago. People would gossip, if for no other reason than that Cy Parks was the town's hermit. On the other hand, she was lonely and a little afraid. She remembered what Walt had told her about Manuel Lopez and the men who worked for him in the narcotics underworld. She knew what they did to people who sold them out. A shiver ran down her spine. They'd killed Walt and they might not stop until they wiped out his whole family—that was the reputation that Lopez had. She wasn't going to put her baby at risk, regardless of what people thought. She touched her flat belly protectively.

She smiled. "I'm going to take such wonderful care of you."

The smile remained when she thought how Cy would care about the baby, too. He wasn't at all the sort of man he seemed on first acquaintance. But, then, who was? She went back inside to work in the kitchen, careful to make sure the doors were locked.

Cy used his cell phone to have a local wrecker service take Lisa's small car over to his ranch, where he had one of his two mechanics waiting to fix it. Harley was good with machinery, but he had the mechanic do the work instead. For reasons he didn't understand, he didn't like having his good-looking foreman Harley around Lisa.

He went to the meeting with his banker and then on to Ebenezer Scott's place, careful to phone ahead. There were men on the gate who didn't like unexpected company and might react instinctively.

Eb met him at the front door, more relaxed than Cy had seen him in years.

"How's it going?" he asked the newly married man.

Eb grinned. "Funny how nice a ball and chain can feel," was all he said, but his eyes were twinkling with delight. "How's it going on your end?"

"Let's go inside," Cy said. "I've found out a few things."

Eb took him into the kitchen and poured coffee into mugs. "Sally's teaching. I don't usually do more than grab a sandwich for lunch…"

Cy held up a hand. "I haven't got time, thanks. Listen, they've got the beehives on site around that new warehouse on the land adjoining mine. There's a lot more activity there, panel trucks coming and going and deliveries after dark. I've spotted a number of unfamiliar faces. They don't look like beekeepers to me. Besides," he added curtly, "I saw a couple of Uzis."

"Automatic weapons at a honey plant," Eb murmured thoughtfully. "They must have armed, militant bees." He grinned at his own whimsy. "I'd hoped that Lopez might hesitate after his failed attempt on Sally's family." Sally, along with her aunt Jessica and Jessica's young son, Stevie, were targeted for vengeance by the drug lord. Luckily Lopez hadn't succeeded in his mission.

"We knew that Lopez had mentioned to one of his slimy followers that he needed a new distribution center. What better place than a little Texas town not far from the Gulf of Mexico, with no federal officers around?"

"He knows we're around," Cy pointed out.

"He only knows about me," came the reply. "Nobody locally knows about you. And he thinks I won't do anything because he's backed away from harming Sally's family. He figures the two guys who are taking the fall for him will keep the wolves from his door."

"I don't like it."

"Neither do I, but unless we can prove he's channeling drugs instead of honey through here, we can't do anything. Not anything legal," he added slowly.

"I'm not going up against Uncle Sam," Cy said firmly. "This isn't the old days. I don't fancy being an expatriated American."

Eb sighed. "We're older."

"Older and less reckless. Let Micah Steele go after him. He lives in Nassau and has connections everywhere. He wouldn't be afraid of getting kicked out of the States. He doesn't spend much time here anyway."

"His stepsister and his father live here," Eb pointed out. "He isn't going to want to put them in harm's way."

"From what I hear, his father hates him and his stepsister would walk blocks out of her way to avoid even passing him on the street," Cy said curtly. "Do you think he still cares about them?"

"Yes, I do. He came back with the express purpose of seeing his father and mending fences, but the old man refused to see him. It hurts him that his father won't even speak to him. And I've seen the way he looks at Callie, even if you haven't."

"Then why does he live in Nassau?"

Eb glanced around warily. "He's over here doing a job for me, so watch what you say," he cautioned. "I don't want him on the wrong side of me."

Cy leaned back in his chair and sipped coffee. "I suppose we all have our crosses to bear." He narrowed one eye at his oldest friend. "Do you think Lopez will make a try for Lisa?"

"It's possible," he said flatly. "Down in Mexico, a 'mule' crossed him. He killed the man's whole family except for one small child."

"That's what I thought. I sent Nels Coleman over to her ranch to stay nights in the bunkhouse. He used to work for the Treasury Department back in the late seventies."

"I know him. He's a good man."

"Yes, but not in Lopez's class. Your guys are."

Ebenezer nodded. "I have to have good people. The government and I are more than nodding acquaintances, and I run a high-tech operation here. I can't afford to let my guard down, especially now that I've got Sally to think of."

"It's been a long time since I've had to consider a woman," Cy replied, his green eyes quiet and thoughtful.

"Lisa Monroe is sweet," Ebenezer said. "She'll love that child to death."

"She's like that," Cy agreed, smiling. "I wish she wasn't so bullheaded. I went by to see her this morning and found her out in the barn, trying to pull a calf all by herself with her bare hands."

Ebenezer chuckled. "I won't turn your hair white by mentioning some of her other exploits, before she got pregnant."

"This isn't the first time she's done something outlandish?"

"Let's see." Ebenezer pursed his lips, recalling gossip. "There was the time she stood in the path of a bulldozer that was about to take down the huge live oak in the square that a peace treaty with the Comanche was signed under.

Then she chained herself to a cage in the humane society when they were going to put down half a dozen dogs without licenses.'' He glanced at Cy. ''The Tremayne brothers suddenly developed dog fever and between them, they adopted all six. Then there was the time she picketed the new chain restaurant because they refused to hire immigrants…''

''I get the idea,'' Cy murmured dryly.

''We were all surprised when she married Walt. He was a real man's man, but his job was like a religion to him. He didn't want anything to tie him down so that he couldn't advance in the agency. If he'd lived, that baby would have broken up the marriage for sure. Walt said often enough that he wasn't sure he ever wanted children.'' He shook his head. ''He wasn't much of a husband to her, at that. Most of us felt that he married her on the rebound from that model who dropped him. He felt sorry for Lisa when her dad died and she was left all alone. Even after the wedding, he flirted with every pretty woman he saw. Lisa went all quiet and stopped staying home when he was around. He wasn't around much of that two months they were together, either. He volunteered for the undercover assignment the day they married. That shocked all of us, especially Lisa, and he got killed the same day he was introduced to Lopez.''

''They knew who he was,'' Cy guessed.

''Exactly. And it was Walt's first undercover assignment, to boot. The only reason Rodrigo hasn't been discovered infiltrating Lopez's distribution network is that he's still a Mexican national and he has at least one cousin who's been with Lopez for years. The cousin would never sell him out.''

''Lucky man,'' Cy remarked. ''I hope we don't get him killed.''

''So do I,'' Eb said with genuine concern. ''Rodrigo's been in the business for a lot of years and he's the best undercover man I know. If anybody can help us put Lopez away for good, it's him. But meanwhile, we have to keep Lisa safe.''

Cy went thoughtful. ''She's a kind soul.''

''Kind and naïve,'' Eb replied. ''People take advantage of her. That baby will wrap her right around its finger when it's born.''

''I love kids,'' Cy said. ''I miss mine.''

''Lisa will love hers,'' came the quiet reply. ''She'll need a friend, and not only because of Lopez. She can't run that ranch by herself. Walt was good with horses, and the men respected him. Lisa can't keep managing those two cowboys who work part-time for her, and she can't get a foreman because she hasn't enough capital to pay the going rate. Besides all that, she doesn't know beans about buying and selling cattle.''

''Didn't her father teach her?''

''Not him,'' Ebenezer chuckled. ''He didn't think women were smart enough to handle such things. He ran the ranch until the day he died. She was kept right out of it until then. Walt proposed to her at her father's funeral and married her shortly after.''

''She loved her father, I gather.''

''Of course she did, and he loved her. But he was a nineteenth-century man. He would have fit right in after the Civil War.'' He shook his head. ''That ranch isn't solvent. Lisa's going to lose it eventually. She needs to go ahead and put it on the market and get the best price she can.''

''I might see if she'll sell to me. I could rent her the house and have my own men work the ranch.''

Ebenezer grinned. ''Now, that's constructive thinking.'' He leaned forward, emptying his coffee cup. ''As for those so-called beehives, I think we'd better send somebody over to have a quiet look after dark and see if there are really any bees in them.''

''Good idea. Then we can start making plans if it looks

like Lopez is sending drugs through here." Cy got to his feet. "Thanks for the coffee."

"Anytime. Watch your back."

Cy smiled. "I always do. See you."

When Cy got home, Harley was out in the front yard having an animated conversation with a foreigner in an expensive pickup truck. He turned as Cy drove up in front of the house. He cut off the engine and eyed the newcomer's vehicle with knowing eyes. Here was an opportunity not only to meet one of Lopez's executives, but to throw them off the track about him as well.

"Hey, boss, this is Rico Montoya," he said with a grin. "He's our new neighbor with the honey export business. He just dropped by to say hello."

Sure he did, Cy thought, but he didn't reply. He got out of the utility vehicle slowly and deliberately favored his left arm as he moved to the pickup truck.

"Glad to meet you, Mr. Montoya," Cy said with a carefully neutral expression. "My men noticed the warehouse going up." He tried to look worried. "I don't really like bees close to my purebred Santa Gerts," he said without preamble. "I hope you're going to make sure there aren't any problems."

The man's eyebrows rose, surprised at Cy's lack of antagonism. Surely the rancher knew who he was and whose orders he was following. Or did he? His dark eyes narrowed thoughtfully. Parks was holding his crippled left arm in his right and he had the look of someone who'd seen one tragedy too many. Lopez had been worried about interference from this rancher, but Montoya was certain there wouldn't be any. This wasn't an adversary to worry about. This was a defeated man, despite his past. He relaxed and smiled at Cy. "You're very straightforward," he said with only a trace of an accent. He was wearing a silk suit and his thick hair was not only cut, but styled. There was a slight bulge under his jacket. "You have nothing to fear from our enterprise," he assured Cy. "We will be meticulous about our operation. Your cattle will be in no danger. I give you my word."

Cy stared quietly at the other man and nodded, as if convinced. Near him, Harley was gaping at the lack of antagonism that Mr. Parks showed to most visitors. It wasn't like him to favor that burned arm, either.

"I am very pleased to make your acquaintance, Mr. Parks," Montoya said with a grin. "I hope that we will be good neighbors."

"Thank you for taking the time to stop by and introduce yourself," Cy said with a noticeable lack of animation. He got a firmer grip on his injured arm. "We don't get many visitors."

"It was my pleasure. Good day, Señor." Montoya smiled again, this time with faint contempt, and pulled his truck out of the driveway. Cy watched him go, arrow-straight, his mouth making a firm line in his lean, taut face.

"Mr. Parks, you are the oddest man I know," Harley said, shaking his head. "You weren't yourself at all."

Cy turned to him. "Who do you think that was?"

"Why, our new neighbor," Harley said carelessly. "Nice of him to come over and say howdy," he added with a scowl. "Your arm bothering you?"

"Not in the least," Cy said, both hands on his lean hips as he studied the younger man. "What did you notice about our new hardworking neighbor?"

The question surprised Harley. "Well, he was Latin. He had a bit of an accent. And he was real pleasant..."

"He was wearing a silk suit and a Rolex watch," he said flatly. "The truck he was driving is next year's model, custom. He was wearing boots that cost more than my new yearling bull. And you think he makes that kind of money selling honey, do you?"

Harley's eyes widened. Once in a while, his boss threw

him a curve. This was a damned big curve. He frowned. How had Cy noticed so much about a man he only saw for a minute or two when Harley, a trained commando he reminded himself, hadn't?

"That was one of Lopez's executives," Cy told the younger man flatly, nodding at his wide-eyed realization. "I want you to go work cattle over near that warehouse and take a pair of binoculars with you," Cy told his foreman. "Don't be obvious, but see who comes and goes for a few days."

"Sir?"

"You told Eb you wanted to help keep an eye on Lopez's operation. Here's your chance."

"Oh, I see, Mr. Scott told you to send me out there." Harley grinned from ear to ear. "Sure. I'll be glad to do it!"

"Just make sure you aren't caught spying," Cy told him flatly. "These people are killers. They won't hesitate if they think they're being watched deliberately."

"I can handle myself," Harley said with faint mockery.

"Yes, I know, you're professionally trained," Cy drawled.

The tone made Harley feel uncertain. But he put it down to jealousy and grinned. "I know how to watch people without getting noticed," he assured his boss. "Does Mr. Scott want tag numbers as well as descriptions of the people?"

"Yes, and pay attention to the trucks that come in."

"Okay."

Cy wanted to add more to those instructions, but he didn't want Harley to know everything. "Be sure you keep your mouth shut about this," he told Harley. "Eb won't like it if he thinks you're gossiping."

"I wouldn't want him mad at me!" Harley chuckled. "I'll keep quiet."

"See that you do."

Cy walked back to the house with a quick, sharp stride that reflected his anger. He'd just met a new link in Lopez's chain, probably one of his divisional managers. It would work to his advantage that he had just convinced the drug lord's associate that he was a crippled rancher with no interest in the bees except where his cattle were concerned.

Lopez thought he had it made with his "honey business" as a blind, here in little Jacobsville. But Cy was going to put a stick in his spokes, and the sooner, the better.

Three

Harley drove the little red car with its new water pump back to Lisa Monroe early the next morning, with Cy following in his big utility vehicle.

Lisa was overjoyed at the way the engine sounded as Harley pulled up at the front porch and reved it before he turned it off.

"It hasn't ever sounded that good before!" she enthused. "Thank you, Harley!"

"You're very welcome, ma'am," he said, making her a mock bow with his hat held against his chest. "But I didn't fix it. I'm just delivering it."

She laughed and Cy glowered. She and Harley were close in age, or he missed his bet. The man, despite his bravado, was honest and hardworking and basically kind. Cy wondered how old Lisa was. Well, at least she was young enough to find Harley's company stimulating—probably much more stimulating than the company of an aging mercenary who was half-crippled and cynical....

"Won't you both come in for a cup of coffee?" she invited.

"I will," Cy told her. "Harley, go take a look around and see what needs doing. Then find Lisa's part-time help and get them on it."

"My pleasure, Mr. Parks," he said with a wicked grin and turned to follow the tersely given instructions.

Lisa gave Cy a speaking look.

"Go ahead," he invited. "Tell me that chores are getting done by people other than you. Tell me that the south pasture is being hayed before the predicted rains day after tomorrow. Tell me," he added mockingly, "that you've got your new calf crop vaccinated and tagged."

She got redder by the minute. She didn't want to tell him that she couldn't get the men to take her suggestions seriously. They were throwbacks to another age, most of them were twice her age, and the madder she got, the more indulgent they became. Once they threatened to quit, they had her over a barrel and she gave up. Hands were thin on the ground this time of year. She could barely afford to pay her employees as it was.

"Harley will get them moving," he told her.

Her lips compressed and her eyes sparked. She looked outraged.

"I know," he said helpfully. "It's a new age. Men and women are equals. You pay their wages and that means they need to do what you say."

She made a gesture of agreement, still without speaking.

"But if you want people to obey, you have to speak in firm tones and tell them who's the boss. And it helps," he added darkly, "if you hire people who aren't still living in the last ice age!"

"They were all I could find to work part-time," she muttered.

"Did you go over to the labor office and see who was available?" he asked.

The suggestion hadn't occurred to her. Probably she'd have found young, able-bodied help there. She could have kicked herself for being so blind.

"No," she confessed.

He smiled, and that wasn't a superior smile, either. "You aren't aggressive enough."

"I beg your pardon?"

"If you're going to hire that type of man, you have to have the whip hand. I'll teach you."

"If that means I'll end up being a local legend like you, I'm not sure I want to learn it," she replied with a twinkle in her dark eyes.

"Old lady Monroe," he recited, chuckling, "carries a shotgun and emasculates men in the barn."

She flushed. "Stop that."

"Isn't that a nicer image than sweet little Lisa who hasn't got the heart to fire a man just because he lies in wait in her bed dead drunk and stinking?"

"Cy!"

He grinned as she curled one hand into a fist. "Much better," he said. "Now hold that thought when you speak to your lazy hands next time. In fact, don't smile at them ever again. Be decisive when you speak, and don't ask, tell. You'll get better results."

She had to admit, she wasn't getting any results at all the way she was. On the other hand, she was still young, and feeling her way through leadership. She wasn't really a drill sergeant type, she had to admit, and the ranch was suffering because of it.

"I don't suppose you'd like a ranch?" she asked whimsically, and was startled when he replied immediately that he would.

"Oh." She stared at him, poleaxed.

"I'll give you the going market price. We'll get two appraisals and I'll match the highest one. You can rent the house from me and I'll manage the cattle. And the cowboys,'' he added wryly.

"It's not in very good shape,'' she said honestly, and pushed her glasses back up onto her nose.

"It will be. If you're willing, I'll have my attorney draw up the papers tomorrow.''

"I'm very willing. I'll be happy to sign them. What about the appraisals?''

"I'll arrange for those. Nothing for you to worry about now.''

"If only my father hadn't been such a throwback,'' she murmured, leading the way into the ramshackle house. "He thought a woman's place was in the kitchen, period. I'd much rather be working in the garden or doctoring cattle than cooking stuff.''

"Can you cook?''

"Breads and meats and vegetables,'' she said. "Not with genius, but it's mostly edible.''

She poured black coffee into a mug and handed it to him. When she sat down across the table from him, he noticed the dark, deep circles under her eyes.

"You aren't sleeping much, are you?'' he asked.

She shrugged. "I'm still halfway in shock, I guess. Married and widowed and pregnant, and all in less than two months. That would be enough to unsettle most women.''

"I imagine so.'' He sipped his coffee. She made the decaf strong and it tasted pretty good. He studied her narrowly. "You haven't had any more problems at night, have you?''

"None at all, thanks.'' She smiled. "And thank you for having my car fixed. I guess if people are going to own old cars, they need to be rich or know a lot about mechanics.''

"They do,'' he agreed. "But I'll keep your little tin can on the road.''

"It's not a tin can,'' she said. "It's a very nice little

foreign car with an—'' she searched for the right words ''—eccentric personality.''

''Runs when it feels like it,'' he translated.

She glared at him. ''At least I don't have to have a ladder to get into it.''

He smiled. ''Remind me to have a step put on just for you.''

She didn't reply, but that statement made her feel warm and safe. God knew why. She was certain he wasn't really going to modify his vehicle just for her. She'd only been in it once.

''Do you like opera?'' he asked out of the blue.

She blinked. ''Well, yes...''

''*Turandot?*''

''I like anything Puccini composed. Why?''

''It's playing in Houston. I thought we might go.''

She pinched her jean-clad leg under the table to see if she was dreaming. It felt like it, but the pain was real. She smiled stupidly. ''I'd really like that.'' Then her face fell. She moved restlessly and averted her eyes. ''Better not, I guess.''

''You don't have to wear an evening gown to the opera these days,'' he said, as if he'd actually read her mind. He smiled when her eyes came up abruptly to meet his. ''I've seen students go in jeans. I imagine you have a Sunday dress somewhere.''

''I do.'' She laughed nervously. ''How did you know I was worried about clothes?''

''I read minds,'' he mused.

She sighed. ''In that case, I'd love to go. Thank you.''

He finished his coffee. ''Friday night, then. I'll go round up Harley and see what he knows about your place.'' He got up, hesitating. ''Listen, there are some things going on around here. I don't want to frighten you, but Lopez has men in and around town. I want you to keep your doors locked and be careful about strangers.''

"I always am," she assured him.

"Do you keep a gun?"

She grinned. "No. I have Puppy Dog."

"Puppy Dog will get under a bed if there's trouble," he assured her flatly. "I've still got Nels staying in the bunkhouse at night, and he's armed. All you have to do is yell. He'll hear you. He's a very light sleeper."

"You can't be sure that Mr. Lopez means me harm."

"I'm not. But I'm a cautious man."

"All right," she said. "I'll keep both eyes out for trouble."

"I'll pick you up Friday night about five. Okay?"

She nodded. "I'll be ready." She went with him to the front door and stood behind the screened door to study him, frowning. "Cy, is it too soon for this?"

"Because you've been a widow such a short time?" He shook his head. "I know you miss Walt. I'm not offering anything heavy, just a trip to the opera. It's very unlikely that we'll see anybody who knows us in Houston."

"I guess you're right." She folded both arms around herself. "The walls are beginning to close in on me."

"I don't doubt it. A night at the opera isn't exactly a cause for gossip."

"Of course not." She smiled. "I'll see you Friday, then. And...thanks."

"I get lonely, too," he said with surprising candor. He gave her one last grin and walked out to find Harley.

His foreman was tight-lipped as he came striding out of the barn. When Harley forgot to be irritating, he was a cowboy and a half. Most of the men walked wide of him in a temper already. "The whole damned place is about to fall to pieces," he said without preamble. "The hay hasn't been cut, the corn hasn't been put in the silo, there are breaks in half the fences, the calves don't even have a brand.... What the hell kind of men did Mrs. Monroe hire?"

"Lazy ones, apparently," Cy said tightly. "Find them and put them all on notice. Lisa's selling me the place. We'll put on four new men to work this ranch and share chores with my own."

"That's a wise decision on her part," Harley said. "She doesn't seem to know much about the business end of cattle ranching."

"Her father thought women weren't smart enough to learn it," Cy mused.

"What an idiot," Harley replied. "My mother can brand cattle right along with the cowboys, and she keeps the books for Dad."

"A lot of women are big-time ranchers, too," Cy agreed. "But Lisa doesn't really have the knack, or the love, for it. Cattle ranching is hard work even if you do."

Harley nodded. "I'll put her part-timers on notice and get the boys over here with a tractor and a combine to hay those fields and harvest the corn."

"When you get that organized," Cy said, "I want to know what you saw over at the honey warehouse last night."

"Not much," Harley had to admit. "And I got challenged on your land by a man with a rifle. Good thing there was a cow down in the pasture for me to show him," he added with a grin. "I told him we had a problem with locoweed and offered to show him where it grew. He went back on his side of the fence and didn't say another word."

"That was a stroke of luck," Cy remarked. "Because we don't have any locoweed."

"We do now," Harley murmured. "I set out a couple of plants and netted them, just in case I get challenged again. Now that I have a legitimate reason to be out there, they won't pay much attention to me. And if they go looking for locoweed," he added with a mocking smile, "why, they'll find it, won't they?"

Cy smiled at the younger man. ''You're a treasure, Harley.''

''Glad you noticed, boss, and how about that raise?''

''Don't push your luck,'' came the dry reply. ''I'll talk to you later.''

''Sure thing.''

Cy drove to the lawyer's office the next morning to discuss the land buy. Blake Kemp was tall, thirtyish, with a gray streak in his black, wavy hair, and pale blue eyes. He was the terror of the Jacobsville court circuit, although he looked mild-mannered and intelligent. Deceptive, Cy mused, studying him, because Kemp had a bite like a rattlesnake in court.

''I'm going to buy the Monroe place,'' Cy said without preamble. ''Lisa can't run it alone, and she hasn't the capital to make improvements or even necessary maintenance.''

''Good decision on her part,'' Blake told him. ''And on yours. It's good land, and it adjoins your property.'' He pursed his chiseled lips. ''Is that the only merger you're contemplating?''

Cy's eyes narrowed. ''She's only been widowed two weeks,'' he pointed out.

Blake nodded. ''I know that. But she's going to have a hard time paying rent. She doesn't even have a job anymore.''

Cy studied him evenly.

''Well, I guess I could use a receptionist,'' he said. ''Callie Kirby is my paralegal, and she can't really handle the research and the phones at the same time. Besides, Lisa worked for a colleague of mine last year. She knows her way around a law office.''

''What happened to the brunette who works with Callie?'' Cy asked.

''Gretchen's gone off to Morocco with a girlfriend from

Houston," Blake said with a chuckle. "She spent the past few years nursing her mother through a fatal bout of cancer," he added solemnly. "And then the first man who took a shine to her insurance money broke her young heart. She needed a change of scene, and she said she doesn't want to work in a law office when she comes back. So there's a job available, if Lisa wants it."

"I'll tell her. Thanks."

He shrugged. "We all like Lisa. She's had a rough deal, one way or another."

"She has indeed. Now, about those appraisals…"

When Cy came to pick Lisa up for their trip to the opera, he was wearing a navy sports coat with dark slacks and a white shirt. His tie combined red and navy in a paisley print. He looked dignified and very handsome. Lisa was glad he hadn't worn a dinner jacket, because she had nothing that dressy in her small wardrobe. The best she could find was a simple gray jersey dress with long sleeves and a skirt that fell to her calves. She covered it with her one luxury, a lightweight black microfiber coat that was warm against the unseasonably cool autumn winds. Her hair was in a neat, complicated braid and she wore more makeup than usual to disguise her dark-circled eyes. She slept badly or not at all lately, and not completely because she missed Walt. She was having some discomfort that concerned her. She knew that pregnancies could fail in the early weeks, and it bothered her. She really needed to talk to her doctor when she went for the next visit. It might be nothing, but she didn't want to take any chances with her baby.

"Not bad at all," Cy mused, watching her pull on the coat over her clinging dress. She had a pretty figure.

"Thank you," she said, coloring a little. "You look nice, too."

"I talked to my attorney about the property," he said after he helped her into the utility vehicle and started the engine. "He's contacted two appraisal firms. They'll be out next week to see the ranch and give you an estimate."

That worried her. She hated seeing the family ranch go out of the family, but what choice did she have? She smiled wanly. "Walt was planning a dynasty," she recalled. "He talked about all sorts of improvements we could make, but when I mentioned having kids to inherit it, he went cold as ice."

Cy glanced at her. "Not much point in working yourself to death just to have the empire go on the market the minute you're in the ground."

"That's what I thought." She turned her small purse over in her lap. "It's just as well that you'll have the ranch," she added. "You'll know how to make it prosper."

"You'll still be living there," he pointed out. "I'll be a damned good landlord, too."

"Oh, I know that." She stretched. "I'll still have to get a job, though. I'll want to put what I get for the ranch into a savings account, so the baby can go to college."

She surprised him constantly. He'd thought she might want to brighten up the house, even buy herself a decent car. But she was thinking ahead, to the day when her child would need to continue his education.

"Nothing for you?" he asked.

"I've got everything I really need," she said. "I don't have expensive tastes—even if Walt did. Besides, I've got a little nest egg left over from some cattle Walt sold off before he…before he died."

"I know of a job, if you want it."

He distracted her, which was what she supposed he'd intended. "Really?"

"Kemp needs a receptionist," he said. "Gretchen's gone off to Morocco and she isn't coming back to work for him. So now Callie Kirby's up to her ears in work. Kemp said you'd be welcome."

"What a nice man!" she exclaimed.

"Now there's a word that doesn't connect itself with Kemp." He gave a soft laugh. "Or didn't you know that people talk in whispers around him?"

"He doesn't seem that bad."

"He isn't, to people he likes." His eyes softened as they searched her averted face. "He'll like you, Lisa Monroe. You're good people."

"Thanks. So are you."

"Occasionally."

She glanced in his direction and smiled. "It's funny, isn't it, the way we get along? I was scared to death of you when you first moved here. You were so remote and difficult to talk to. People said you made rattlesnakes look companionable by comparison."

"I moved here not long after I buried my wife and son," he replied, and memories clawed at his mind. "I hated the whole world."

"Why did you move here?" she asked curiously.

He wasn't surprised that she felt comfortable asking him questions. He wouldn't have tolerated it from anyone else. But Lisa, already, was under his thick skin. "I needed someone to talk to, I guess," he confessed. "Eb lived here, and he and I go back a long way. He'd never married, but he knew what it was to lose people. I could talk to him."

"You can talk to me, too," she pointed out. "I never tell what I know."

He smiled at her. "Who would you tell it to?" he drawled. "You don't have close friends, do you?"

She shrugged. "All my friends got married right out of high school. They've got kids of their own and, until fairly recently, I didn't even date much. I've been the odd one out most of my life. Other girls wanted to talk about boys, and I wanted to talk about organic gardening. I love growing things."

"We'll have to lay out a big garden spot for you next spring. You can grow all sorts of stuff."

"That would be nice. I've got a compost pile," she added brightly. "It's full of disgusting things that will produce terrific tomatoes next summer."

"I like cattle, but I'm not much of a gardener."

"It's a lot of work, but you get lovely things to eat, and they aren't poisoned by pesticides, either." She glanced out at the long, flat dark horizon. "I guess you aren't big on people who don't like to use chemicals."

"Haven't you heard?" he chuckled. "I go to cattlemen's association meetings with J. D. Langley and the Tremayne brothers."

"Oh, my," she said, because she'd heard about the uproar at some of those gatherings, where the Tremaynes had been in fistfights over pesticides and growth hormones. Their position against such things was legendary.

"I enjoy a good fight," he added. "I use bugs for pest control and organic fertilizer on my hay and corn and soybean crops." He glanced her way. "Guess where I get the fertilizer?"

"Recycled grass, huh?" she asked, and waited for him to get the point.

He threw back his head and roared. "That's one way of describing it."

"I have some of that, too, and I use it in my garden. I think it works even better than the chemical ones."

The subject of natural gardening and cattle raising supplied them with topics all the way to Houston, and Lisa thoroughly enjoyed herself. Here was a man who thought like she did. Walt had considered her organic approach akin to insanity.

The parking lot at the arts center was full. Cy managed to find one empty space about half a city block away.

"Now that's a full house," he remarked as he helped her down from the vehicle and repositioned her coat around her shoulders. "This thing sure is soft. Is it wool?" he asked, smoothing over it with his fingers.

"It's a microfiber," she told him. "It's very soft and warm. The nights are pretty chilly lately, especially for south Texas."

"The weather's crazy everywhere." He nudged a long, loose curl from her braided hair behind her ear, making her heart race with the almost sensual movement of his lean fingers. "I thought you might wear your hair loose."

"It's…difficult to keep in place when it's windy," she said, sounding and feeling breathless.

His fingers teased the curl and slowly dropped to her soft neck, tracing imaginary lines down it to her throat. He could feel her pulse go wild under his touch, hear the soft, broken whip of her breath at his chin. It had been far too long since he'd had anything warm and feminine this close to him. Restraints that had been kept in place with sheer will were crumbling just at the proximity. He moved a full step closer, so that her body was right up against him in the opening of her coat. His hands were both at the back of her neck now, caressing the silky skin below her nape.

"I haven't touched a woman since my wife died," he said in a faintly thick tone, his voice unusually deep in the silence. The distant sound of cars and horns and passing radios faded into the background.

She looked up, straight into his green eyes in the glow from a streetlight, and her heart raced. That look on his face was unfamiliar to her, despite her brief intimacy with her late husband. She had a feeling that Cy knew a lot more than her husband ever had about women.

Cy's thumbs edged around to tease up and down her long, strained neck. Her vulnerability made him feel taller, more masculine than ever. He wanted to protect her, care for her, watch over her. These were new feelings. Before, his relationships to women had been very physical. Lisa made him hungry in a different way.

She parted her lips to speak and he put a thumb gently over them.

"It's too soon," he said, anticipating her protest. "Of course it is. But I'm starving to death for a woman's soft mouth under my lips. Feel." He drew one of her hands to his shirt under the jacket and pressed it hard against the thunderous beat of his heart.

She was more confused than ever. This was totally unfamiliar territory. Walt had never said anything so blatantly vulnerable to her, not even when they were most intimate.

His free hand went around her waist and drew her slowly closer, pressing her to him as his body reacted powerfully to the touch of her soft warmth. He lifted an eyebrow and smiled wickedly at her frozen expression.

"Why, Mrs. Monroe, you're blushing," he chided softly.

"You wicked man...!"

His nose brushed lazily against hers in a tender nuzzling. "I've probably forgotten more about women than Walt ever knew in the first place," he said. "You don't act like a woman who's ever known satisfaction."

That was so close to the truth that it hurt. She stiffened.

He lifted his head and searched her eyes. His own narrowed. He moved her lazily against him and felt her breath catch, felt her hands cling to his lapels as if she were drowning.

"Oh...no," she choked as a surge of pure delight worked its way up her spine. She hated herself. Her husband was only buried two weeks ago...!

While she was thinking of ways to escape, and fighting her own hunger, Cy backed her very gently against the big utility vehicle and edged one of her long legs out of his way to bring them into more intimate contact.

"This is the most glorious thing a man and a woman can do together," he murmured as his mouth lowered to hers. "He cheated you. I won't. Open your mouth."

Her lips parted on a shocked little gasp, and his mouth ground into them, parting them. He wasn't hesitant or tentative. He demanded, devoured. His mouth was a weapon, feinting, thrusting, biting, and all the while her body rippled with a thousand stings of new pleasure as she clung hard to his strength. Sensations she'd never known piled one upon the other until a hoarse moan tore out of her strained throat and went up into his mouth.

Another minute and he knew he wouldn't be able to pull back at all. He had her hips pinned with his, and his body ached for satisfaction.

With a rough curse he dragged his head up and moved away from her. She looked at him with dazed eyes in a flushed face, her mouth swollen from his kisses, her body shivering with new knowledge.

He drew himself up to his full height. His eyes glittered like green diamonds in a face like stone. He had to fight to get a normal breath of air into his lungs.

She tried to speak, but she couldn't manage even a whimper. Her body was still flying, soaring, trembling with little shivers of pleasure that made her knees weak.

He reached out and caught her small hand in one of his big ones, linking their fingers. "We'd better go inside," he said quietly.

"Yes." She let him pull her away from the truck and lead her toward the arts center. She was amazed that she could walk at all.

Four

Turandot was beautiful. Lisa cried when the tenor sang "Nessun Dorma," one of her favorite arias. The sets were elegant, colorful, the Chinese costumes glittery and resembling fantasy more than reality. The dragon was a masterpiece of sound and fury and color. All in all, it was a magnificent production, and Puccini's glorious music brought it alive. Lisa had never seen an opera except on the public broadcasting television channel. She knew that she'd never forget this for as long as she lived, and every time she remembered it, she'd remember Cy sitting beside her in the dark.

Meanwhile, Cy was cursing himself silently for what had happened in the parking lot. It was months too soon for that. She was a pregnant, newly widowed woman and he'd let his emotions get out of control. His jaw tautened as he remembered the silky feel of her in his arms. He wanted to take care of her, and it looked as though she was going to need protection after all—from him.

Somehow he was going to have to get them back on a simple friendly footing. It wouldn't be easy. He had no idea how she felt about what had happened. She sat quietly beside him, obviously enjoying the opera. She even smiled at him from time to time. But if she was angry, it didn't show. He remembered her soft moan, her clinging arms. No, he thought, she'd gone in headfirst, too, just as he had. But he had regrets and he suspected that she did as well. He had to draw back before he put the delicate new feeling between them at risk. Lisa was off limits in any physical way, and he was going to have to remember that.

Lisa saw his scowl and wondered if he had regrets about what had happened. Men got lonely, she knew, and he was a very masculine sort of man to whom women were no mystery. He was probably wondering how to tell her that it wasn't about her a few minutes ago, that any woman would have produced that reaction in a hungry man.

She would save him the trouble, she decided, the minute they started home. He'd already done so much for her. She couldn't expect him to take over where Walt had left off; not that Walt had ever really felt passion for her. Walt had enjoyed her, she supposed, but there hadn't been any sizzling attraction between them. It shamed her to admit that what she'd felt in the parking lot with Cy had been infinitely more pleasurable than anything she'd ever done with her late husband. She didn't dare think about how it would be if they were truly intimate...

Her hand jerked in Cy's as the final curtain fell and the applause roared. She clapped automatically, but made sure that both her hands were tight on her purse when they started to leave.

"It's a beautiful opera," she remarked as he escorted her to the exit.

"Yes, it is," he agreed pleasantly. "I've seen it in a dozen different cities, but I still enjoy it."

"I guess you've been to the Metropolitan Opera in New York City?" she mused wistfully.

"Several times," he agreed.

She imagined him there, with some beautiful woman in an expensive evening gown and wrapped in furs. It wasn't far to imagine them going into a dark room together, where the coat and the evening gown were discarded. She swallowed hard and tried not to think about that.

He could feel tension radiating from her. She was clinging so hard to that tiny purse that she was leaving the indentations of her nails in the soft leather.

When they reached the Expedition, he opened the door for her, but held her back when she started to climb inside.

"I'm sorry about what happened earlier," he said gently. "I've made you uncomfortable."

Her wide eyes met his. "I thought I'd made you uncomfortable," she blurted out.

They stood just looking at each other until his lean face went harder than ever with the effort not to give in to the hunger she kindled in him.

"You poor man," she said huskily, wincing as she saw the pain in his eyes. "I know you're lonely, Cy, that you just needed someone to hold for a few minutes. It's all right. I didn't read anything into it."

His eyes closed on a wave of pain that hit him like a bat. She reached up and pulled his face down to her lips. She kissed him tenderly, kissed his eyes, his nose, his cheek, his chin, with brief undemanding little brushes of her mouth that comforted in the most exquisite way.

He took a ragged breath and his lean hands captured her shoulders, tightening there when he lifted his face away from her warm mouth. "Don't do that," he said tersely.

"Why not?" she asked.

"I don't need comforting!" he said curtly.

She moved back a step. He looked as if she'd done something outrageous, when she'd only meant to be kind. It irritated her that he had to be antagonistic about it. "Oh, I see," she said, staring up at him. "Is this how it goes? 'Men are tough, little woman,'" she drawled, deepening her voice and her drawl, "'we can eat live snakes and chew through barbed wire. We don't want women fussin' over us!'" She grinned up at him deliberately.

He glared at her, his eyes glittering.

She raised her eyebrows. "Want me to apologize? Okay. I'm very sorry," she added.

His broad chest rose and fell heavily. "I want you to quit while you're ahead," he said in a tight voice.

She stared at him without guile. "I don't understand."

"Don't you?" His smile was full of mockery and he was seeing a succession of women from his wild days who liked to tease and run away, but not too far away. His lean hands tightened on her shoulders as his eyes slid down her body. "Your husband didn't tell you what teasing does to a man?"

"Teasing…?" Her eyes widened. "Was I?" she asked, and seemed not to know.

That fascinated expression was real. He did scowl then. "What you were doing…it arouses me," he said bluntly.

"You're kidding!"

He wanted to be angry. He couldn't manage it. She did look so surprised.… He dropped his hands, laughing in wholesale defeat. "Get in the damned truck."

He half lifted her in and closed the door on her barely formed question.

She was strapped in when he pulled himself up under the steering wheel, closed the door and reached for his seat belt.

"You were kidding," she persisted.

He looked right into her eyes. "I wasn't." He frowned quizzically. "Don't you know anything about men?"

"I was married for two months," she pointed out.

"To a eunuch, apparently," he said bluntly as he cranked the vehicle and pulled out of the parking lot and into traffic.

"I *am* pregnant," she stated haughtily.

He spared her an amused glance. "Pregnant and practically untouched," he replied.

She sighed, turning her attention to the city lights as he wound south through Houston to the long highway that would take them home to Jacobsville. "I guess it shows, huh?" she asked.

He didn't say anything for half a block or so. "Did you want him?"

"At first," she said. Her eyes sought his. "But not like I wanted you in the parking lot," she said honestly. "Not ever like that."

A flash of ruddy color touched his cheekbones. He was shocked at her honesty.

"Sorry, again," she murmured, looking away. "I guess I haven't learned restraint, either," she added.

He let out a long breath. "You take some getting used to," he remarked.

"Why?"

His eyes met hers briefly before they went back to the highway. Rain was beginning to mist the windshield. He turned on the wipers. "I don't expect honesty from a woman," he said curtly.

She frowned. "But surely your wife was honest."

"Why do you think so?"

"It's obvious that you loved your little boy," she began.

His laugh had the coldest ring to it that she'd ever heard. "She wanted an abortion. I threatened to take away her credit cards and she gave in and had him."

"That must have been a difficult time for you," she said softly.

"It was." His jaw clenched. "She was surprised that I wanted her baby."

"Hers, and not yours?" she ventured.

"Hers by one of her lovers," he said bitterly. "She didn't really know which one."

There was an abrupt silence on the other side of the truck. He glanced at her frozen features with curiosity. "What sort of marriage do you think I had? I was a mercenary. The women you meet in that profession aren't the sort who sing in church choirs."

"How did you know I sang in the choir?" she asked, diverted.

He laughed, shaking his head. "I didn't, but it figures. You're her exact opposite."

She was still trying to understand what he was saying. "You didn't love her?"

"No, I didn't love her," he replied. "We were good together in bed and I was tired of living alone. So, I married her. I never expected it to last, but I wanted a child. God knows why, I assumed it was mine."

"Why did she marry you if it wasn't?"

"She liked having ten credit cards and driving a Jaguar," he said.

That produced another frown.

"I was rich, Lisa," he told her. "I still am."

She pulled her coat tighter around her and stared out the window, not speaking. She was shocked and more uncertain about him than ever. He was such a complex person, so multifaceted that just when she thought she was getting to know him, he became a stranger all over again.

"Now what is it?" he asked impatiently.

"I hope you don't think I agreed to come out with you...that I was eager to let you buy the ranch because..." She flushed and closed her mouth. She was so embarrassed that she wanted to go through the floor.

"If I'm rich, it's because I know pure gold when I see it," he said, casting her an amused glance. "Do you think I'll assume that you're a gold digger because you came out with me?"

"I kissed you back, too," she said worriedly.

He sighed with pure pleasure and relaxed into the seat, smiling to himself. "Yes, you did."

"But it was an accident," she persisted. "I didn't plan it…"

"That makes two of us." He pulled up at the last streetlight before they left the city behind and turned to her. His eyes were narrow and very intent. "There are things in my past that are better left there. You'd never begin to understand the relationship I had with my wife, because you don't think in terms of material gain. When I was your age, you were the sort of woman I'd run from."

"Really? Why?" she asked.

He cocked an eyebrow and let his eyes run over her. "Because you told me once that you hadn't slept with Walt before you married him, Lisa," he drawled.

She glared at him. "I would have if I'd wanted to," she said mutinously.

"But you didn't."

She threw up her hands, almost making a basketball of her small purse. She retrieved it from the dash and plopped it back into her lap.

"You're the kind of woman that men marry," he continued, unabashed. "You like children and small animals and it would never occur to you to be cruel to anyone. If you'd gotten involved with me while I was still in my former line of work, you wouldn't have lasted a day with me."

"I don't suppose I would have," she had to agree. She looked through the windshield, wondering why it hurt so much to have him tell her that. Surely she hadn't been thinking in terms of the future just because of one passionate kiss? Of course, her whole body tensed remembering the pleasure of it, the exciting things he'd said…

"And you weren't Walt's usual date, either," he said surprisingly. "He liked experience."

She grimaced. "I found that out pretty quick. He said I

was the most boring woman he'd ever gone to bed with. Except for our wedding night, and the night before he was killed, he slept in a separate bedroom.''

No wonder she was the way she was, he mused as the light changed and he sent the big vehicle speeding forward. She probably felt like a total failure as a woman. The child must have been some sort of consolation, because she certainly wanted it.

''I'll bet you hate admitting that,'' he said.

''Yes, I do. I felt inadequate, dull, *boring*,'' she muttered. ''He liked blondes, but not me.''

''He liked that parcel service driver plenty,'' he recalled, his eyes narrowing. ''You were pitching hay over the fence to the cows and he was flirting with her, right under your nose. I never wanted to hit a man more.''

Her lips parted on a quick breath. ''You saw…that?''

''I saw it,'' he said curtly. ''That's why I stopped by later and said something about the way you were pitching hay by yourself.''

She shifted in the seat. ''He said they were old friends,'' she replied. ''I guess he really meant they were former lovers. He never treated me to that sort of charm and flirting. He really wanted Dad's ranch. It was a pity I went with the deal.''

''It was his loss that he took you for granted,'' he corrected. ''You're not inadequate. You proved that earlier tonight, in the parking lot.''

She cleared her throat. ''An incident best forgotten.''

''Why?''

''Why?'' She stared at him. ''Walt's only been dead two weeks, that's why!''

He stopped at a four-way stop and turned in his seat on the deserted road to look at her. ''Lisa,'' he said quietly, ''it wouldn't have mattered even if he'd still been alive, and you know it. What happened was mutual and explosive.''

"It was a fluke..."

His hand reached out and his fingers traced her lower lip. She couldn't even speak. "Would you like me to prove that it isn't?" he asked quietly. "There are plenty of dirt roads between here and home, and the seats recline all the way."

"Cy Parks!"

"Best of all," he mused, "we wouldn't even have to worry about pregnancy, would we?"

Her face was scarlet; she knew it was. He was making her breathless with that torturous brush of his fingers, and she was vulnerable. She'd never really known desire until tonight, and she wished she could turn the clock back a day. Life was difficult enough without this new complication.

He drew in a long breath and lifted his hand back to the steering wheel. "God knows I want to," he said shortly, "but you'd die of shock and never speak to me again afterward."

"I...certainly...would," she faltered, pushing her hair back unnecessarily just for something to do.

He shook his head. He'd known her such a short time, really, but she seemed to hold his attention even when he wasn't with her. Every future event he thought of these days, he considered her part in. It was disturbing to know that he considered her part of his life already.

She fiddled with the top button on her coat. Her eyes were restless, moving from the dark horizon to the occasional lighted window flashing past as the utility vehicle picked up speed. What he'd said disturbed her, mostly because she knew it was true. She'd have gone anywhere with him, done anything with him. It made her guilty because she should be mourning Walt.

"Don't brood," Cy told her. "You're safe. No more torrid interludes tonight, I promise."

She fought a smile and lost. "You're a terrible man."

"You have no idea how terrible." He paused to look both ways before he crossed a lonely intersection. "Harley's fired your part-time hired hands, by the way."

"He's what?"

"Calm down. They were being paid for work they didn't do. That's economically disastrous."

"But who'll get in the hay and brand the calves...?" she worried.

"You didn't hear the noise? Harley got the tractors out in your hay field early this morning. The haying's done. The corn crop is next. I'm hiring on four new men. Harley will supervise them, and your place will live up to its promise." He glanced at her. "You haven't decided not to sell it have you?"

"I can't afford to keep it," she confessed. "I'm glad you don't plan to build a subdivision on it or something. It's been in my family for a hundred years. Dad loved it with all his heart. I love it, too, but I have no idea how to make it pay. I'd like to see it prosper."

"I think I can promise you that it will."

She smiled, content with just being next to him. He turned on the radio and soft country music filled the cab. After a few minutes, her eyes slid shut as all the sleepless nights caught up with her.

She was vaguely aware of being gently shaken. She didn't want to be disturbed. She was warm and cozy and half-asleep.

"No," she murmured drowsily. "Go away."

"I have to," came a deep, amused voice at her ear. "Or we'll have a scandal we'll never live down. Come on, imp. Bedtime."

She felt herself tugged out of the seat and into a pair of warm, hard arms. She was floating, floating...

Cy didn't wake her again. He took off her shoes, tossed the cover over her, put her glasses on the bedside table and left her on the bed in her nice dress and coat. He didn't dare start removing things, considering his earlier passionate reaction to her. But he stood beside the bed, just watching her, enjoying the sight of her young face relaxed in sleep. He wondered how old she was. She never had told him.

He turned and went back out into the hall, pausing to check the lock on the back door in the kitchen before he went out the front one, locking it carefully behind him. He still wasn't convinced that Lopez wouldn't make a beeline for Lisa if he thought his men could get away with harming her. Cy was going to make sure that he didn't.

He stopped by the bunkhouse to have a word with Nels before he went home and climbed into his own bed. He stared at himself in the bedroom mirror, his eyes narrow and cynical as he studied his lean, scarred face and equally scarred body. He was only thirty-five, as Lisa had already guessed, but he looked older. His eyes held the expression of a man who'd lived with death and survived it. He was wounded inside and out by the long, lonely, terrible years of the past. Lisa soothed the part of him that still ached, but she aroused a physical need that he'd almost forgotten he had. She was a special woman, and she needed him. It was new to be needed on a personal level. He thought about the child she was carrying and wondered if it would be a boy or girl. She'd need someone to help her raise it. He wanted to do that. He had nobody, and neither did she. They could become a family—for the child's sake.

He turned off the lights and went to bed. But his dreams were restless and hot, and when he woke up the next morning, he felt as if he hadn't slept at all.

Harley got the calves branded and the corn in the silo in quick order.

"You've got a knack for inspiring cowboys to work, Harley," Cy told him one afternoon a few days later.

"I get out there and work with them, and make them

ashamed of being lazy,'' Harley told him with a grin. ''Most of them can't keep up with me.''

''I noticed.'' Cy leaned back against the corral fence and stared at the younger man evenly, without blinking. ''You were out near the warehouse last night. What did you see?''

''Three big trucks,'' Harley said solemnly. ''One had some odd stuff on the back. Looked like oil drums lashed together.''

That was disturbing. Cy knew that drug dealers threw portable bridges across rivers to let trucks full of their product drive to the other side. What Harvey was describing sounded like a makeshift pontoon bridge. Cy and the mercenaries he'd worked with had used them, too.

''Did you get a look at what was in the trucks?'' he asked.

Harley shook his head. ''The doors were closed and locked. I was afraid to risk trying to pick a lock, with all that hardware around. Those guys had Uzis.''

''I know,'' Cy said without thinking.

Harley's eyebrows went up, and he grinned in a fairly condescending way. ''Do you now? Are you using Uzis to load cattle these days, boss?''

Cy realized what he'd said and chuckled. ''I wasn't listening. Sorry.''

''No problem. I noticed a couple of new faces over there,'' he added. ''Tough-looking men, and they weren't wearing suits.''

''Get back out there tonight,'' Cy told him. ''And be very careful, Harley. I've got a bad feeling about this whole thing.'' He didn't add that he was worried about Lisa. He saw her every other day, and the paperwork had just been completed and signed, ready for the transfer of money and deeds. He wouldn't be surprised to learn that Lopez had an informant in town who'd tell him that. It might prompt the drug lord to hasty action, if he thought Lisa was selling the ranch in order to move away. He couldn't know that Cy planned to rent her the ranch house. He wouldn't like having to search for her.

Knowing that bothered him, and he mentioned it to Lisa when he stopped by to see her the next day. Harley had seen yet another unfamiliar face on the warehouse property, and he'd also seen flat after flat of jars being moved inside the structure. The drug dealers were getting ready to begin operations. Things would heat up very soon, or Cy missed his guess. He didn't want Lisa in the middle of it.

"Have you got family you could visit out of state?" he asked without preamble as he joined her in the living room, where she had gas logs burning in the fireplace.

She curled up on the sofa in her jeans and knit turtleneck white sweater and stared at him curiously. "I don't have family anywhere," she confessed. "Maybe a cousin or two up around Fort Worth, but I wouldn't know where to look for them."

He sighed heavily and leaned forward in the chair with his arms crossed over his knees. "All right," he said, seeming to come to a decision. "If you leave the house from now on, I want to know first. If you can't get me, you call Eb Scott."

"Why?"

He knew she was going to ask that. He didn't have a very logical reply. "I don't know what Lopez is up to," he said honestly. "He may have given up on ideas of targeting you. On the other hand, he may be lulling us into a false sense of security. I'd rather err on the side of caution."

"That suits me," she said agreeably.

"Do you have a phone by your bed?"

"Yes," she said. "It makes me feel more secure."

He stood up. "Don't forget to keep your doors locked, even in the daytime, when you're home alone."

"I'm not, much," she said without thinking. "Harley

comes by every day to check on me, sometimes twice a day.''

His eyes narrowed. He didn't like that, although he said, ''Good for Harley.''

She caught a nuance of something in his tone. ''Do you mind?'' she asked deliberately. He'd been remote and she'd hardly seen him since the night of the opera. She wondered if he'd been avoiding her, and she concluded that he was. His manner now was standoffish and he seemed in a hurry to leave. She wanted to know if he was the least bit put out by Harley's attentiveness.

''It's your life,'' he said nonchalantly, tilting his wide-brimmed hat over one eye. ''He's a steady young man with a good future.''

He couldn't be thinking…or could he? She started to tell him that Harley was friendly, and that she had no romantic interest in him. But before she could, Cy was already on his way out the door.

She went after him, trying not to be undignified and run. She didn't catch up to him until he was going down the steps.

''When do we close on the sale?'' she asked, having no other excuse for following him.

He turned at the door of the utility vehicle. ''The first of next week, Kemp said. It will take that long to get the paperwork filed.''

''Okay. You'll phone me?''

''I will. Or Kemp will.''

That sounded less than friendly. She wrapped her arms around her chest and leaned against one of the posts that held up the long porch. ''That's fine, then,'' she said with forced cheer. ''Thanks.''

He opened the door and hesitated. ''Are you in a rush to close?''

She shrugged. ''Not really. I just wanted to know when

I'd need to start paying rent. I was going to go see Mr. Kemp next week about that job.''

She thought he didn't want her around, and that was so far from the truth that it might as well have been in orbit. But he didn't want to rush her, frighten her. Hell, he didn't know what he wanted anymore.

''I'll see you Monday,'' he said, and got into the vehicle without another word. He didn't even look back as he drove away.

Lisa stared after him with her heart around her ankles. So much for her theory that he was attracted to her. She supposed that he'd had second thoughts. It might be just as well. He was mourning his son, whom he'd obviously loved even if it wasn't his own child, and she was a recent widow expecting a child of her own. She'd been spinning daydreams and it was time to stop and face reality. Cy wasn't her future even if she'd hoped he was hers. She turned and went back into the lonely house, pausing to close and lock the door behind her.

Five

The first time she heard the noise at the window, Lisa thought it was a squirrel. The old house seemed to attract them. They often scurried over the roof and came leaping down into the limbs of the big pecan trees that surrounded the porches. But she usually didn't hear them in the wee hours of the morning, and so loud that they woke her up. She tried to go back to sleep, but then the noise came again. This time it didn't sound like a squirrel. It sounded more like a window being forced open.

Lisa slipped out of bed in her sweatpants and white cotton top, hesitating at the door that led into the hall. The noise had come from the room next door, the one Walt had occupied for most of their married life.

She heard a faint rubbing noise, like one a man might make climbing in a window. Her heart began racing and she dashed down the hall in her bare feet, down the wooden steps and into the kitchen. Her glasses were still in the nightstand drawer by her bed, and she could barely make out familiar objects in the dim light. She was headed for the back door when she was caught and lifted and a big, gentle hand was clapped over her mouth while she struggled pitifully in an embrace of steel.

"It's all right," Cy Parks whispered at her ear. "It's all right, we know there's someone trying to break in upstairs. Micah's rappeling from the roof down to the window of the room across the hall. He'll have him in a minute. Don't scream or you'll give him all the warning he needs to get away. Okay?"

She nodded.

He eased her back onto her feet, taking her soft weight against the black sweater he was wearing with black jeans, one lean arm holding her just under her breasts. She saw the glimmer of metal in his other black-gloved hand. Her frightened eyes drifted up to his face, and all she could see of it was his eyes. He was wearing some sort of black mask.

While she was studying him, she heard a loud thud, followed by a louder groan.

"All clear!" came a loud, deep voice from upstairs.

"Stay here." Cy let her go and went past her and up the staircase with an economy of motion that made her very glad she wasn't the enemy.

She leaned back against the counter and almost jumped out of her skin when the back door opened and Eb Scott came in pulling his mask off, grinning.

"Sorry," he said quickly. "But the man Cy had staying in the bunkhouse spotted two suspicious figures outside your window. Unless you're expecting Romeo, it's a bit late for social calls."

"I was asleep," she said, shaken. "I heard the noise and thought it was a squirrel. I was trying to get out the back door when Cy grabbed me." She whistled. "I thought my number was up."

"Good thing you slept light," Eb said solemnly. "We barely got here in time."

"Who is it, do you think?" she asked.

"One of Lopez's goons," Eb told her flatly. "And this definitely confirms our worst fears. Lopez is after you."

"But I didn't do anything!" she said, still shaken from the experience. "Why is he after me?" She brushed back the long, tangled curtain of hair from her flushed cheeks. She felt sick.

"He's going to set an example for anybody else who might consider trying to infiltrate his organization," Eb told her. "It doesn't matter what you did or didn't do. He doesn't care. Your husband betrayed him and he wants you to pay for it, too. He wants all the government agencies to know the price for selling him out—their lives and their families' lives."

The fear made a tight knot in the pit of her stomach. She sank down into one of the kitchen chairs with a protective hand over her belly. She felt twice her age.

She heard heavy footsteps on the staircase and out the front door before Cy came back into the room, tearing off his mask. He looked even more formidable than usual, and that said something about his present demeanor, Lisa thought.

"Micah's taking the guy over to the sheriff," he said. "He suddenly doesn't speak English, of course, and his friend lit a shuck while he was breaking into the house. We won't be able to prove a thing beyond the obvious."

"He'll be out on bond by tomorrow afternoon and out of the country an hour later," Ebenezer added.

Cy's expression was homicidal before he turned his glittery green eyes on Lisa. "You can't stay here a day longer," he said flatly. "Lopez doesn't make the same mistake twice. You've been put on notice. The next time, there won't be a near miss."

She ground her teeth together. "This is my ranch. I haven't sold it to you yet, and I'm staying here," she said furiously. "I'm not going to let some sleazy drug kingpin force me into hiding out like a scared kid!"

"Commendable courage," Cy remarked with a stoic expression. He reached into his belt and pulled out something dark. "Here."

He tossed her his automatic. She caught it and then dropped it with a gasp of pure horror.

"You'd better pick it up and learn to shoot straight and under fire," he said coldly. "You'd better learn to shoot to kill while you're at it. Because that," he indicated the gun, "is the only way you'll survive if you insist on staying here alone. We were almost too late tonight. Next time, we might not be so lucky."

She glared at him, but she didn't argue. "I hate guns."

"Good God, so do I," Cy told her. "But when you get in a war, you don't throw potatoes at the enemy."

"Then what do I do?" she asked Cy.

Cy told her. "Go pack a bag. You're leaving."

"Leaving for where?" she demanded, standing up with both hands on her hips. "I told you already, I've got no family, no close friends, and no place to go to!"

"Yes, you have. The Expedition's outside. I'll send Harley over in the morning to pick up your VW and bring it over, too."

Her dark eyes widened. It didn't help much, her glasses were upstairs on the bedside table and all she could see of Cy was a blur. "I can't go home with you. I've only been widowed a short time!"

"I've only been widowed three years," he reminded her. "So what?"

"I can stay with Callie Kirby!"

"Callie's apartment isn't big enough for Callie, much less Callie and you," he said. "I've got three bedrooms. You can even have a bathroom of your own."

She didn't want to give in. But the memory of someone

trying to break in the house scared her. She knew that she couldn't shoot an intruder. That left her few options.

"When you make up your mind, I'll be in the truck," Cy told her.

He actually walked out the door. Eb followed him with an amused grin that he didn't let Lisa see.

Lisa glared after him, hesitant and bristling with hurt pride. But in the end, she went upstairs, changed into jeans and a shirt and packed a small bag. Ten minutes later, he opened the door of the utility vehicle so that she could climb in with her tote bag.

"If Harley so much as grins, I'll kick him in the shins," she said after she'd fumbled her seat belt together.

"So will I," Cy promised her.

She glanced at him from the warm folds of her flannel-lined denim jacket. "Would you have shot that man?"

"If there hadn't been another way to stop him, yes."

"I couldn't shoot anybody," she said.

"I know. That's why you have to stay with me until we get Lopez." He glanced at her. "It won't be so bad. I can cook."

"So can I."

"Good. Fair division of labor." He glanced at her with a faint smile. "When the baby comes, we'll take turns getting up for his meals."

She felt a warm glow wash over her. She smiled, too. "Oh, I wouldn't want to sleep if he was hungry," she mused dreamily. "I'd get up, too."

He remembered his wife complaining bitterly about lost sleep, making formula, giving bottles. She hated everything to do with the baby, and couldn't begin to understand his affection for the tiny little boy, who wasn't even…

He closed his mind to the anguish that memory fostered, and concentrated on his driving instead.

Apparently Cy's men were asleep in the bunkhouse, because the ranch house was quiet when they arrived. He helped Lisa out of the vehicle and carried her suitcase into the house.

"You'll probably like this room. It faces the rose garden," he added with a smile.

She looked around at the simple, old-fashioned room with its canopied double bed and gauzy white curtains and white furniture. "It's very pretty," she murmured.

"The house belonged to an elderly woman, who was the last living member of her family," he said. "She had to go into a nursing home. I learned the history of the house from her. It belonged to her father, who was one of the better known Texas Rangers. She raised two kids and three grandkids here. One of her grandsons was a congressman, and another worked for the U.S. Secret Service. She was very proud of them."

"Is she living in Jacobsville?"

He nodded. "I go to visit her every other week. You might like to go along occasionally. She's a walking history of Texas."

"I'd like that." She was studying him with open curiosity. He looked so different in that stark black outfit that she wondered if she would even have recognized him if she'd seen him on the street. Her husband had been in law enforcement, but even he hadn't looked as dangerous as Cy Parks in commando gear.

He lifted an eyebrow.

"Sorry," she murmured with a shy smile. "You look different, that's all."

"Think of it as a covert ops business suit," he mused. "The object is to blend in with the night."

"Oh, you did that very neatly," she agreed.

He chuckled. "Get some sleep. There won't be anybody to bother you here, and you can sleep as late as you like."

She grimaced. "What about Puppy Dog?"

"What?"

"Puppy Dog," she said. "He's all shut up on the back porch…"

"I'll fetch him at daybreak," he said. "But if he eats one of my chickens, he's dog bone stew. Got that?"

"You've got chickens?"

"Five," he said. "Rhode Island Reds. I like fresh eggs."

She smiled. "I like them, too."

"A woman after my own heart." He moved toward the door. "The windows are electronically wired, by the way," he added with the doorknob in his hand. "If anyone tries to open them from the outside, they'll think we're being bombed."

"That's reassuring."

"So it is. Sleep tight."

"You, too."

He spared her a glance. "Don't get up until you want to. I'll haul Puppy Dog over here at daybreak."

"He likes to chew up things," she said worriedly.

"You shouldn't let him eat heating pads, while we're on the subject."

"He can reach the shelf I keep them on," she said. "I didn't realize it until I saw him jump up to pull it down. By then I'd lost two and I thought I'd left them on the sofa." She shook her head. "He's already very tall. His father, Moose, is almost five feet tall when he stands on his hind legs."

"He'll be good protection for you when he's trained."

"He seems to be training me," she said on a wistful breath.

"I'll take care of that. 'Night."

She smiled. "Thanks for rescuing me."

"I had good help," he told her.

She stood staring after him even when the door closed. Her life had just gone up two notches on the complications scale. She forced herself not to think of how hungry he'd made her the night they'd gone to Houston to the opera, of how much she liked being close to him. He'd been very standoffish since, so it was obvious that he didn't like the small taste of her he'd had. She was safe with him. Safe, pregnant and a widow. She shouldn't be thinking about kissing Cy. The thought made her uncomfortable, but she slept soundly all night long.

Harley walked in the kitchen door with a wicker basket full of eggs and a disgusted look on his face. He stopped short when he saw Lisa, in jeans and a sweatshirt with her dark blond hair in an unruly bun, making coffee.

She gave him a challenging look back. "Where's Cy?" she asked.

"Gone to town to have his truck cleaned."

That sounded intriguing. "Does he do that a lot?"

"Only when dogs throw up in it."

"Oh, dear," she said.

"Seems your puppy doesn't like to go for rides," he murmured with a grin. He put the basket of eggs on the table. "He's out in the barn with the boss's collie."

"I didn't know Cy had a dog."

"He didn't know he had one, either, until it got run over week before last," he remarked. "He picked it up and took it to the vet. It was a stray that somebody had put out, half-starved, full of fleas, almost dead from lack of care. Amazing what some dog shampoo, flea medicine, regular meals and attention can do for a mangy old cur." He shook his head. "For a hard-nosed man, he sure has some soft spots. He'd never make a soldier, let me tell you." He held up a hand when she started to speak. "Don't tell him I said that," he added. "He pays me a good salary and he's a fine man to work for. He can't help it if he isn't exactly G.I. Joe. Considering what he's been through, I guess he's got some grit in him somewhere."

She almost bit her tongue through trying not to tell Harley what she knew about his soft-centered employer. But that was Cy's business, and she didn't want to get on his bad side when she'd only arrived.

"I rode over to your place with the boss and drove your little VW back with me. It's in the garage. None of my business, but are you staying awhile?" he asked curiously.

"I guess so," she sighed. She poured coffee into a cup. "A man broke into my house last night. Cy let me come over here."

"Broke into your house? Why?"

She grew pensive. "My husband was an undercover DEA agent," she told him. "He was infiltrating a drug lord's organization when he was exposed and executed. Apparently the drug lord likes to set examples, like wiping out whole families of people who oppose him. I'm on his list."

"Then you sure came to the right place," Harley said with a beaming grin. "As it happens, you'll be safer here than anywhere else in the county, except maybe with Ebenezer Scott." He seemed to stand two feet taller. "I was in the Army Rangers for two years and I've had commando training. Nobody can slip by me."

"I can't tell you how much better I feel, knowing that," she said, smiling pleasantly.

He almost blushed. "Good. Well, I'll get back to my chores. Glad you're okay, Miss...Mrs. Monroe," he corrected, tipping his hat on his way out.

"Thanks for bringing my car," she said.

"No problem." He shot a grin back at her as he left.

She sat down at the kitchen table beside the eggs and shook her head. He didn't have a clue what was going on. His life was apparently so dull that he couldn't live without the illusion of bravery. She wondered how he would respond to a real threat, and hoped she never had to find out. He seemed a nice sort of man, but she had a feeling that he wasn't quite as formidable as he made out.

* * *

Cy came in for lunch, helping himself to bread, mayonnaise and luncheon meat while Lisa poured iced tea into tall glasses.

"I can make sandwiches," she offered.

He gave her a grin. "I'm used to doing it myself. Want a couple?"

"Just one, thanks," she agreed and sat down at her place beside his at the small table. "I'm sorry about Puppy Dog messing up your truck."

His eyebrows lifted under disheveled black hair. "Who told you?"

"Harley." She gave him a gamine look. "He said that he'd be glad to protect me from potential attackers, seeing as how he's a trained commando."

Cy chuckled softly. "I was his age once. Seems like fifty years ago, now."

She put her elbows on the table and propped her chin on her hands, watching him make sandwiches. "Did you swagger, too?"

"Probably. At least, I did until I saw combat for the first time. Nobody tells you that people scream when they get shot. On television they just grunt or groan and hold the part that's been shot." He shook his head. "It's a lot more…vivid…in real life."

"Were you afraid, the first time?"

"I was afraid every time," he corrected with a level stare. "Only a fool pretends he isn't. You learn to face the fear and deal with it, just like everyone else does."

"It's difficult, isn't it?"

"Difficult to watch people die, yes," he told her. "Difficult to live with what you do, too. I remember a young boy in Africa who was fighting the rebels. He carried a carbine in his hands and ammunition belts that probably weighed more than he did, strapped around his chest. His name was Juba." He smiled as he worked. "He had a passion for chocolate bars. We always had a few in our packs, just a taste of something sweet to remind us of civilization. One day, Juba ran ahead of us into a building the rebels had just evacuated. We hadn't swept it for traps and he wouldn't stop when we tried to warn him. He broke a trip wire right in the doorway and blew himself up.'' His hand hesitated on the knife as he spread mayonnaise on the bread. His eyes were solemn and quiet. "He didn't die right away," he added grimly. "We gave him morphine from one of our medical kits. Then I sat under a silk cotton tree with him in my arms and talked to him until he died." His eyes fell back to his task. "He was eleven years old."

She winced. "That's very young to be fighting a war."

"He'd already lost his parents and two sisters in the crossfire," he recalled. "He was alone in the world, except for us. We'd thrown in with the government forces. They were overwhelmed by the rebels and advertised for mercenaries. My unit went in. I started with thirty men and came back with three." He passed her a plate with a sandwich on it and started making two more for himself. "The rebels took over the capital and formed a government of their own. It stood for two months before outside troops joined forces with the overthrown government, moved in and took back possession of their country. Before they did, ten thousand people were shot or blown up in the streets."

"I'm sure I wouldn't make a good soldier, even if Harley thinks he would," she remarked somberly.

"I wanted to make enough money to retire while I was still a young man," he mused. "I planned to come back home, buy a ranch, get married and settle down." He finished his own sandwiches and poured cream into his coffee. "It almost worked. But along the way, I helped a government agency get hard evidence on that drug lord Lopez," he said, searching her eyes. "As I mentioned a while back, he had my house in Wyoming set on fire. The hitch was, my son was supposed to be rescued before the incendiary device was placed. Lopez's henchman didn't think one kid more or less would matter.'' He traced an invisible pattern on his coffee mug. ''The only consolation I had was that Lopez had the assassin eliminated for that slip-up. He doesn't kill children.''

''I'm so sorry,'' she murmured, watching him.

''So am I. But all the regrets in the world won't bring back that little boy.''

His face was harder than rock. She sketched it with her eyes. ''You can help me take care of my little boy.''

He glanced at her. ''What makes you think it's a little boy?''

''Wishful thinking, I guess. I love baseball and soccer and working around the ranch. I know girls can do those things, too, but I'd love a son.''

''You'd love whatever you get,'' he chided.

''Yes. I would.'' She grimaced.

''What's the matter.''

''I don't know.'' She laughed nervously. ''I have these mild cramps sometimes. I read a book about being pregnant, and it said some women have fleeting cramps during early pregnancy.''

He scowled. ''That doesn't sound good.''

She picked up her sandwich. ''Maybe it's just nerves. It's been a rough few weeks.''

''Sure it has. But if those cramps get any worse, you go see a doctor.''

''I will.''

After lunch, he took her out to the huge, airy barn to see Puppy Dog, who was comfortably contained in a huge stall with a drain in the concrete floor, and fresh wheat straw making a comfortable place for him to sleep.

''Hello, Puppy Dog,'' she said, going into the stall to pet the frisky, enormous puppy. ''Did you miss me?'' She glanced past him at the clean containers of dog food and water, and the dog toys liberally scattered along the wall. "Maybe not, considering all the toys."

"Dogs need something to play with. Keeps them active and healthy. I got half a dozen for Bob, too."

"Bob?"

He motioned to her. She gave Puppy Dog a last hug and went out of the stall. He whined for a minute and then went back to pick up a ball he liked.

In the stall next door was a huge white-and-tan collie with an intelligent face and soft brown eyes. There were still traces of malnutrition in the coat, but Bob was beginning to shape up into a beautiful animal.

"He's a doll," she said, smiling at him.

"*She's* a doll."

She hesitated. Turned. Raised her eyebrows.

"*She's* a doll," he repeated.

"Bob is not a female name…"

"If a boy can be named Sue, a girl dog can be named Bob."

"You listen to too many Johnny Cash songs," she accused with a chuckle.

"He's great, isn't he?" he asked. "The boy named Sue was great, but I loved everything he ever recorded."

"I have two of his albums myself," she confessed.

He grinned. "I knew you had good taste."

She liked the way his eyes twinkled when he smiled. He was something of a curiosity around town, because he had a reputation for being a hard case and unsociable. But here, on his home ground, he was relaxed, pleasant, even amusing. She wondered how many people ever got to see this side of him. Probably not many.

"What happened to that man who broke into my house?" she asked abruptly.

"Sheriff's got him locked up," he told her. "We left the crowbar right where it dropped. The man wasn't even wearing gloves. There are enough fingerprints on it to convict him. He'll make bond, of course, and then he'll go home.''

"Home?"

He turned toward her. "A man wearing an Armani suit drove up here a few days ago and introduced himself as my new neighbor. There's a honey packing warehouse on my border. But it's not honey they're distributing, if you understand what I mean."

She stilled. "Drugs?"

"Raw cocaine," he replied. "Or, rather, cocaine paste. At least, that's what we suspect they're stockpiling in that warehouse."

"Here, in Jacobsville?" she gasped.

"Right here," he said.

"Then tell the sheriff and let him send some men out to arrest the owners!"

"They won't find cocaine if they do," he said carelessly. "In fact, I'd bet my boots that they'll phone in a tip about themselves just to draw the law out there to check around. And while they're checking, all the honey in the jars will be real honey, and even a drug-sniffing dog won't find a trace of cocaine. Having searched the place once and found nothing, local law enforcement will logically hesitate before they go back out there a second time. At least, not without some concrete evidence of malfeasance. It's easy to get sued for harassment, and believe me, Lopez would howl at the idea of taking our sheriff to court over it."

"You sound very cynical," she told him.

"I know how these people operate. In my checkered past, I've dealt with drug dealers, gun runners, diamond smugglers, hit men…"

Her eyes were growing wider by the second. "You outlaw, you."

"Count on it," he told her. "I did what the job called for. Wars make strange bedfellows. Got to have guns and ammunition, you know, not to mention explosives, communications equipment, medicines. You can't walk into the nearest superstore and buy those.''

''You can buy guns,'' she began.

''Registered guns,'' he emphasized. ''They're required by law to do a background check before they sell a gun, and there's a waiting period. If you know where to go, you can get everything from Uzis to C-4, and no waiting.''

''I had no idea,'' she murmured, shaking her head.

''It's almost impossible to shut these drug cartels down. They are run on a corporate structure. In a sense, they're multinational corporations. They have a hierarchy, complete with divisional managers and regional distribution networks. When you understand the way they work, you also understand why it's such an uphill battle. You can't arrest every gang member in the country. That's what it would take to stop it. And even then,'' he added, ''there would still be dealers. You know why? Because where there's demand, there's supply. As long as there are people willing to pay for illegal drugs, there will be people who sell them.''

''That's very demoralizing,'' she pointed out.

''Of course it is. But you can't fight a war unless you know the enemy. Every time we shut down one of the cartels, we come one step closer to cutting off the supply. It's discouraging to see the statistics, but there are a lot of dedicated people trying to stop the drug trade. I like to think that one day, they'll succeed.''

''I'd be very happy if they could put Mr. Lopez someplace where he can't shoot me,'' she told him.

He smiled. ''At least,'' he said, ''we've got *you* someplace where he can't. Now eat that sandwich. Waste not, want not.''

She laughed softly and bit into the sandwich.

Six

Lisa settled in at the ranch, much to the interest of Cy's cowboys, who walked around with stunned expressions every time they saw her. Most people around Jacobsville had the same attitude, because of Cy's remoteness. Of course, he had dropped the charges against Belinda Craig's rebellious young charge at her summer youth camp when the lad had been caught trespassing on his property. And he'd taken Candy Marshall, that nice young woman from the local cattlemen's association out to the bar to look for Guy Fenton when he'd been drunk for the last time before he fell in love with Candy and married her. But other than those two incidents, he kept to himself and had little if anything to do with women. Now here was Lisa Monroe, a young widow alone and pregnant, living with him. It was delicious gossip.

As Cy had predicted, the man who was arrested for breaking into Lisa's house had skipped bond and left the country. That didn't let her out of the woods, though, he assured her. Lopez wouldn't stop until he accomplished whatever goal he'd set. Since it was common knowledge that Lisa was staying with Cy, the drug lord wouldn't have far to look to find her.

Also, as Cy had predicted, an anonymous tip led sheriff's deputies to the "honey warehouse" behind Cy's ranch. The flats of jars and the beehives Harley had watched them unload were searched and searched again, by deputies, DEA agents and drug-sniffing dogs. Predictably, they found nothing illegal and went away. It didn't take a genius to realize that it would be hard to get the law enforcement people out there again without vivid concrete evidence of illegal operation. Gossip was that the owners of the new "business" had already threatened a multimillion lawsuit against the various agencies for just setting foot on the property. Jacobsville was a small town in a small county and its sheriff's department already had such a tiny budget that they hadn't had a raise in two years. The county commissioners went pale at the thought of even a small lawsuit. Like it or not, the sheriff was constrained by politics and capital.

There was one encouraging new development. Rodrigo, the Mexican national who'd successfully infiltrated Lopez's distribution network, managed to get a brief message to Eb Scott, saying that a huge shipment of cocaine paste was scheduled to be shipped into the country soon through Mexico. He had few details as yet, but would keep his eyes and ears open and report anything pertaining to the shipment as soon as he heard it.

Lisa overheard Cy talking with Eb Scott on a shortwave radio—an odd way to communicate, she thought, when the telephone was right beside him.

When he gave his call sign and cut the unit off, she asked him about it.

"This—" he indicated the set "—has a scrambler. It's high-tech, not a conventional shortwave device."

She shook her head as she studied the array of electrical gadgets in the study where Cy did his bookwork. "I've never seen so many strange-looking things."

"Didn't Walt have equipment like this?" he asked curiously.

"If he did, he kept it someplace else." She sighed, thinking of Walt's horrible end and their very brief marriage. Absently her hand went to her belly.

"You were up walking the floor last night," he commented. "Why?"

She shifted. "I had some more cramps," she murmured. But she wasn't too concerned. When she called the doctor she was told it wasn't so unusual to have twinges now and again.

He scowled, watching her. "This isn't the first time you've had cramping. You need to call a doctor."

"I did, day before yesterday," she reminded him. "He said it's a fairly common complaint in early pregnancy, and as long as there's no bleeding there's no reason to worry. Actually I feel better than I have for weeks."

Cy managed not to say that she looked delectable, but she did. Her long, soft hair was loose around her shoulders and even with glasses on, she was pretty. He liked the little tip-tilted nose and the full, soft bow of a mouth. He liked the way she watched him, like a curious little bird, when he worked around the ranch. He especially liked the way she looked in cutoff jeans that showed the curves of her legs up to the thighs, and the way her knit blouse outlined her firm, small breasts. He remembered the feel of her in his arms, the softness of her young mouth, and his whole body clenched. She didn't know, couldn't know, what an ordeal it was for him to be in the same house with her and never touch her. But he didn't want her to feel threatened. She was at risk, and she had no place else to go.

She lifted both eyebrows when she saw that the dark

scowl over his green eyes was getting more ominous by the minute. "What's wrong?" she asked.

"Don't go out in the yard like that," he said abruptly.

She looked down at herself and then back at him, puzzled. "I beg your pardon?"

"You heard me." He stood up, towering over her. That was a mistake because now he could see the upper curves of her breasts that her knit blouse left visible. "I don't want my men leering at you." Especially Harley, he thought angrily.

Her eyes kindled with humor. "You're leering at me right now," she pointed out, grinning because he obviously found her attractive. Her knees suddenly felt wobbly.

"I'm not leering. I'm noticing. But I've got some young men with bucking hormones and to them a woman in a steel drum would probably look sexy. Wear jeans and a blouse that buttons to your throat."

"Bucking hormones," she mused. "That's a new one."

"You aren't that naïve," he grumbled. "You were married. You can tell when a man wants you."

Not really, she wanted to tell him. Walt had only slept with her twice, and apparently had to force himself both times. He wasn't really attracted to her physically, and the feeling had been mutual. It wasn't that way with Cy. She looked at him and her knees went weak.

"I'm not wearing a steel drum around the place to do housework," she informed him. "Hormones or no hormones. Heavens, I'm pregnant! Who's going to make a pass at a pregnant woman?"

"Any man under eighty who sees you dressed like that," Cy said flatly. "Up to and including me."

Her heart jumped into her throat as her eyes lifted to his and were captured. She felt the breath rush past her parted lips as the look intensified, making her feel odd in the strangest places, even more strongly than the night at the opera. She remembered the taste of his mouth on hers, and no matter how disloyal it might have been to her late husband, she wanted it again.

"Would you really?" she asked.

He looked uncomfortable. "We were talking about how you dressed. When you go outside around the men, don't wear shorts and low-cut blouses."

"Are you telling me that grown men can't control themselves and I have to go around in a coat all summer to keep from disturbing them?" she wanted to know. "That's not fair."

"Oh, hell, of course it's not fair! But men are going to look when there's something to see. All the legislation in the world won't kill a basic human instinct, and that one is hundreds of thousands of years old!"

Her eyes dropped to his hard mouth and she remembered, not for the first time, how delicious it felt when he kissed her. Then she felt guilty for even the thought. She was forgetting Walt, something that Cy hadn't. He hadn't touched her again since she moved in. He was respecting her husband's death. She was sorry about Walt, but when she got close to Cy, her emotions were all over the place.

"Harley seems to spend a lot of time in the house lately," he remarked unexpectedly.

"He gathers the eggs for me," she replied, fighting down the excitement she felt as his green gaze slid over her once again. "Ever since you found that chicken snake in the henhouse, I've been nervous about putting my hand in the nests."

"We moved the chicken snake into the barn," he reminded her.

"Well, it isn't in handcuffs or anything, now is it?" she demanded. "It can go wherever it wants to, and I've noticed that snakes seem to feel violent attractions to anyone who's scared of them."

"In that case, I don't suppose even the house is safe."

She immediately started looking around her feet and he burst out laughing.

"Never mind," he said on a sigh. "I guess Harley's better than a snake, at that."

"I know he isn't what he pretends to be," she replied with a smile. "But he's nice. Besides," she added with a calculating look that he missed, "isn't he helping to keep an eye on those people who set up the honey warehouse next door to you?"

He didn't like that, not one bit. Eb had agreed to let Harley spy on the drug dealers if he kept his mouth shut. Quite obviously he'd been bragging about his exploits to Lisa.

"Did he tell you that?" he asked quietly.

She didn't quite trust the look in his eyes. She didn't want to get Harley in trouble. On the other hand, she didn't like telling lies.

"He mentioned that he was watching them to make sure the bees didn't threaten your purebred cattle," she said, which was the truth. Or, at least, what Harley had told her.

"I see." He relaxed visibly and she knew she'd said the right thing. She wondered why he was so concerned about bees, when plenty of people around Jacobsville kept them. Maybe he had a hidden fear of flying insects.

Cy's green eyes narrowed. Harley was young, in his late twenties, and despite his bravado, in peak physical condition. Cy was thirty-five and scarred, inside and out. Perhaps Lisa couldn't help liking the younger man. And he had been kind to her.

"If you'd rather I asked someone else to fetch the eggs, I can," she began, trying to find a way to erase that dark scowl on his lean face.

"Of course not," he said at once. "Why should I mind?"

He left her wondering about that, and she went back to what she'd been doing.

* * *

Two days later, Cy came into the kitchen and found Harley holding Lisa's hand in the living room.

Both of them turned and jerked at his sudden appearance. Harley's high cheekbones colored as Cy's green eyes glittered at him like a poisonous snake uncoiling.

"Hi, boss!" he said with forced enthusiasm. "I was, uh, just showing Lisa…Miss…Mrs. Monroe how to break a hold."

"Yes, he was," Lisa said quickly. She had on those same tight jeans and a yellow sweater with a vee neck that was much too low when she bent over. Cy's unsmiling scrutiny made her feel as if she'd just committed adultery. She'd put on the outfit deliberately, not for Harley, but for Cy. He hadn't been near her until now. Harley had.

"I'd better get back to the garage now, I guess," Harley said, still flushed. He was wearing a white T-shirt and jeans with a red rag sticking out of his back pocket. "I'm overhauling the cattle truck, boss."

"Good. Hadn't you better go do it?" Cy asked with a bite in his voice that he seldom used these days. He looked dangerous, something Harley noted with surprise.

"Sure thing!" Harley went through the kitchen and out the back door without another word.

"He really was showing me how to get out of a hold," she told Cy with her hands on her hips.

Cy moved toward her, too jealous to think properly. "Was he now? And you've learned the lesson? Show me. Let's see you get out of this hold!"

He had her around the waist and flush against every line of his lean, powerful body before she could speak. She opened her mouth to protest and his lips claimed hers, hungry and rough and demanding.

She wanted to fight. She really did. But the closeness of him, the warmth, the strength of him drained her of every semblance of protest. With a tiny little cry, she slid her arms under his and pushed as close as she could get, answering that hard kiss with all the pent-up longing of the weeks since he'd touched her. She felt a shudder go through him even as her own body rippled with passion.

He said something against her mouth that she didn't hear, didn't understand. Her mouth pushed up against his, answering the devouring fierceness of his hard lips. It wasn't a practiced sensuous kiss at all. It was flash-fire need, hunger, desire, out of control. It gave her an odd feeling of pride that she could throw him off balance. And as much as it shamed her to admit it even in the privacy of her mind, his jealousy of Harley made her even hungrier for him.

His body began to swell and old instincts jerked him out of her embrace. He stepped back, fighting the desire that tautened every muscle he had. The unexpected explosion left him shocked and uncertain.

They were both breathing unsteadily, staring at each other more like combatants than lovers.

"I don't like Harley touching you," he said bluntly, bristling with possessive instincts he hadn't known he had.

"I noticed." She sounded breathless.

His green eyes slid down her body and back up again with desire and possession equally mixed. "You're pregnant."

She nodded. Somewhere deep in her mind she wished it was Cy's baby. That was disloyal to Walt and she should be ashamed. Her hand went protectively to her waistline.

He muttered something under his breath and stepped back. "I shouldn't have touched you," he bit off. "God knows, I'm trying not to! I might manage it if you'd stop tempting me with tight jeans and shirts cut to the navel in front!"

So that was why he'd kept his distance. She was pregnant and he felt that he should be trying to take care of her, not make love to her. But he wanted her. She knew it in every cell of her body. It made her glow with new delight; with hope.

He got his breath back and glared at her. "Harley's fixing the truck. Make sure he stays out of here. If you don't tell him, I will, and I won't be diplomatic."

She wasn't offended by the possessive note in his deep voice. She liked it. "All right, Cy."

His eyes narrowed. Her compliance, unexpected, knocked the fire off his temper. "Stay inside and keep the doors locked."

"Okay."

"Don't assume that you're safe just because Harley's in the garage," he added tautly. "He isn't half as savvy as he thinks he is, and he's never dealt with men like Lopez."

"Okay," she repeated with a smile.

He drew in a heavy breath. "There's a loaded pistol in my middle desk drawer. Just in case."

"I'll remember."

Her mouth was swollen from the pressure of his, and it gave him a feeling of pride to see her disheveled and flustered because of him. He didn't smile, but his eyes did.

"Are you leaving?" she asked breathlessly.

"Yes." He dragged his eyes away from her to check his watch. "I've got to drive up to Kingsville to see a man about some new bulls."

She knew where he was going the minute he mentioned the town, and her soft sigh was all too audible. "I went on a tour of that ranch once, with Dad," she said. "It made our little operation look like a milkmaid enterprise. They had some beautiful breeding stock."

"I like Santa Gertrudis cattle," he said. "No better place to buy them than where the foundation herd originated." His eyes narrowed again as he studied her. "While I'm gone, don't go out of the house for any reason. Harley will have the house in sight all the time, and I've got surveillance equipment linked to Eb Scott's place. If anything happens that Harley can't handle, Eb can be here in five minutes. You aren't afraid by yourself?''

''By myself?'' she exclaimed. ''Cy, have you noticed those fifteen cowboys who work for you…?''

''Only six of them work here full-time. And none of them are around the ranch house for most of the day, except early in the morning and late in the afternoon,'' he told her. ''Harley's working on one of the cattle trucks, which is the only reason that he'll be nearby. If you need him, push the intercom button and he'll come right up.'' He indicated the button next to the wall phone in the dining room. He hated having to tell her that. He hated the idea of Harley anywhere near her. ''And keep all the doors locked.''

''You're worried,'' she gathered.

''I've heard a few things. Yes, I'm worried. Humor me.''

She shrugged and smiled up at him. ''Okay, boss.''

His eyebrow lifted and he smiled back. ''Oh, that sounds sweet,'' he drawled. ''Pity I know it's just lip service. You smile and nod your head when I tell you, for your own good, not to do something. And then you go right out and do it the minute my back's turned.''

''It always worked with Dad,'' she mused. ''It's a waste of time to argue with some men,'' she added.

He reached for his hat on the wall rack. ''And some women,'' he countered. ''Watch yourself.''

''You do that, too,'' she returned smartly. ''You're not on Lopez's good list, either.''

He propped his hat on his head as the back door opened to admit Harley. He glanced at Lisa from under the wide brim. ''Yes, but Lopez doesn't like to take unnecessary chances, and he's already had one bad brush with the law,'' he began as Harley's footsteps became audible behind him. ''He won't come here unless he gets pretty desperate…''

''Because he knows I'm here, Mrs. Monroe,'' Harley interrupted with an irrepressible grin at his boss and their houseguest. "Nobody's going to lay a finger on you while I'm on the job."

"Of course," Lisa said and didn't dare look at Cy.

"I just came in to get a soft drink. It's thirsty work. You, uh, don't mind, boss?" he asked Cy warily.

"I don't mind," Cy lied. "But don't get careless," he told his young foreman, and with more than usual caution. "Lopez won't."

Harley dismissed Lopez and his entire organization with a flick of his hand. "All the same, he won't come around here."

Cy wanted to argue the point, but the younger man was in a concrete mind-set and he wouldn't listen to reason. He'd just have to hope that Harley wouldn't do something stupid.

"I'll be back late. Remember to keep the doors locked," he cautioned Lisa.

"You bet."

He left rather reluctantly.

Harley got himself a cold drink out of the refrigerator and paused at the back door. Lisa went to the kitchen counter and got out a bowl and a knife and some potatoes and began peeling them for potato salad. "I wanted to make sure I hadn't got you in trouble," Harley said sheepishly. "Mr. Parks was pretty hot when he came in."

"It's all right," she assured him with a smile. "He's protective of me because of the baby," she added.

Harley grimaced. "I should have realized that. He isn't a man who has much to do with women, you see." He shrugged. It had seemed like violent jealousy to Harley, but now Mr. Parks's ill temper seemed justified. He wouldn't want anybody making passes at her when she was pregnant. Of course, he added silently as he looked at her, she did seem somewhat flustered and her mouth was swollen. He wondered...

"Don't you want that soft drink in a glass with some ice?" she asked. His scrutiny was making her nervous.

"No, thanks, this is fine. Well, if you need me, just call, Mrs. Monroe. I'll be trying to find the oil leak in that engine."

He looked as if he'd found several, she mused, judging from all the black stains on his once-white sweatshirt. It never ceased to amaze her that Harley always found something white to put on when he was going to do a dirty job.

"I know where the intercom button is," she assured him. "But I don't think I'll need to use it."

"You never know. I'll lock the door as I go out. See you later."

"Sure."

He locked the door and moved slowly toward the garage. Lisa watched him walk back to the garage with a slight frown between her eyes. Cy was unusually worried about Lopez, and it made her uneasy. Surely the man wasn't going to risk having any more men picked up by the sheriff. After all, he'd lost two in the midnight raid on Lisa's house that had prompted Cy to bring her here to stay with him.

On the other hand, she had to admit, if the man based his reputation on keeping his word, he couldn't afford not to make good on a threat. But she was fairly certain that Lopez was long gone. Otherwise why would Cy have gone off in the first place?

Reassured, she went to the kitchen, put Lopez forcefully out of her thoughts and peeled the rest of the potatoes.

Harley finished most of his repairs on the truck and came back into the house for another drink, liberally stained with grease and a noticeable cut on the back of one lean hand. It was bleeding. There was even a little grease in his crew-cut sandy hair.

"Here," Lisa said at once, leading him to the kitchen sink. "Wash that with antibacterial soap while I find a bandage."

"It's nothing much, Mrs. Monroe," he protested, but very weakly.

She smiled to herself as she fetched adhesive bandages from the kitchen cabinet and began peeling one apart to cover the deep scratch after it was clean.

"I wish you'd been with us in Africa," he observed wryly, his blue eyes twinkling. "Several of us got banged up out in the bush."

"In the bush? With the lions?" she exclaimed.

He held out his dried hand for her to put on the bandage. "Didn't see any lions," he remarked. "But there were plenty of guerrillas. Not the furry kind, either." He sighed and smiled dreamily. "That's the life, Mrs. Monroe, fighting for principles and a king's ransom in loot. When I get another two or three training courses under my belt, that's what I'm going to do; I'm going back to Africa to make my fortune."

"Or get yourself shot," she observed.

"Not a chance. I'm too handy with close quarter weapons." He looked as if he could strut sitting down as he said it. "My instructor said he'd never seen anybody who was such a natural in martial arts. And I can throw a knife, too."

"It wouldn't do you much good if the other guy had a gun, would it?" she asked innocently.

"It isn't so hard to disarm a man, if you know how," he said confidently. "They taught us a lot of tricks. I guarantee there isn't a man alive who could threaten me with a gun. I know my business."

Lisa almost winced at the certainty in his tone. He was young, probably not much older than she was, and she couldn't help thinking that a little knowledge could be a dangerous thing.

"Thanks for patching me up," he told her with a grin. "I found the leak. Now all I have to do is put all the parts back on the truck without having any left over."

She laughed as she put away the bandages. "I'd have

bagsful left over," she mused. "I can cook and work horses and cattle, but I don't know a thing about engines."

"My dad's a mechanic," he told her. "He has his own garage. I grew up learning how to fix things. It comes in handy on a ranch this size, even though we have a full-time mechanic on the payroll." He shook his head. "It must cost a fortune to run a place like this. I guess Mr. Parks inherited his."

She went back to her potatoes, her head down as she asked, "You don't think he might have worked for it?"

"Not many professions that pay the kind of money he has, from what I've heard," he said. "Besides, he's not exactly a risk-taker. He doesn't do much of the heavy work around here and he really favors that left arm from time to time. I guess it still hurts him sometimes."

"I guess." She didn't add that he might change his mind about Cy if he ever saw him dressed in black and carrying an automatic weapon.

"Thanks for the first aid," he told her as he retrieved another soft drink from the refrigerator and closed it. "Better get back to work."

He went out and the door locked behind him. Lisa forced herself not to think about that hungry kiss she and Cy shared in the living room or if Cy was going to draw back into his shell again. He was a complex and attractive man, but she seemed to be off limits. Pity. They had so much in common...

Seven

It was late afternoon when Lisa heard a truck pull up out by the barn. She was sure it was Cy. Without thinking, she got up from the kitchen table where she'd been rearranging a messy kitchen drawer and went right out the back door.

It wasn't Cy. It was three men, all foreign-looking. Harley saw them and came out of the garage, wiping his hands on a red work cloth.

"Can I help you boys?" he asked with faint menace.

"We are looking for Mr. Parks," the flashily dressed one said with an ear-to-ear grin.

"He's gone to Kingsville to look at bulls," Harley said obligingly. "I don't know when he'll be back."

"How convenient," the man drawled, and pulled an automatic weapon from under his jacket.

Harley froze in place and his jaw dropped.

Lisa realized the danger immediately. She closed and locked the back door and ran to Cy's study, locking herself inside. She grabbed the mike of the shortwave set, already positioned to the Scott ranch, and gave out a Mayday call.

"Stay in the house," Eb's calm but very hushed voice came over the air instantly. "Cy's on his way."

He left before she could ask what he meant. She didn't know whether to lock herself in and wait, or go to a window and try to see what had happened to poor Harley. She felt guilty that she hadn't been able to do anything for him, but she was one person against three men, one of whom was dangerously armed.

In the end, she grabbed the loaded pistol Cy had told her he kept in his center desk drawer and went cautiously down the hall. She peered out the curtain that covered the upper, glassed portion of the kitchen door. Harley was in the grip of a man at least his physical equal, a pistol at his throat. One of the other men was looming with that automatic weapon and she just glimpsed the third wandering into the garage, out of sight.

She ground her teeth together and held the huge .45 automatic pistol tighter, wondering what she should do. She'd never fired a pistol in her life, but if she had to use it, she thought she could. Shivering with nerves, her heart pounding, her mouth dry, she heard the sound of a truck approaching very fast. Cy's big red Expedition roared up in the yard. He was out of it seconds after the engine died.

But it wasn't the Cy she was used to seeing. He walked slowly toward the two visitors in plain sight, his tall figure bent slightly forward, and he was cradling his burned left arm in his right hand.

"You are Cy Parks," the man with the automatic weapon called in a cold tone.

"Yes," Cy replied quietly. He glanced at Harley, who was red-faced and nervous, held securely in the grip of the second man.

"We want the woman," the flashily dressed visitor continued. "You will bring her out to us. Now."

"She's a widow. She's pregnant," Cy began.

"This is nothing to us," the man replied. "We were told to bring the woman back. It will cost us our lives not to comply with the instructions we were given."

Cy sighed audibly. "I'll go get her," he said with resignation.

"Mr. Parks!" Harley burst out, horrified. "Man, you can't...you can't let them have Mrs. Monroe!"

"They'll shoot us if we don't, son," Cy told the other man in a subdued tone that matched his bent stance. As he spoke, he let go of his burned arm and let it dangle at his side. The right hand moved, just a fraction, but his limping posture had the full attention of the armed men. They didn't notice the movement under his long sleeve. "You might let poor old Harley go," he added. "He just works for me."

"Let a trained mercenary loose on the three of us?" The man laughed. "We heard him talking to the woman in the kitchen about his exploits in Africa."

Which meant, Cy deduced, that they had the house bugged. He'd have to do something about that, and quickly. He glanced at Harley and prayed that the younger man wouldn't panic and do something stupid.

"It was a lie. Honest!" Harley swallowed hard. "I'm not a merk. I'm just a simple, working cowboy...!"

"Why, of course he is. And do I look like any sort of threat to armed men?" Cy asked softly. "I mean, look at me. I'm just a poor cripple."

Harley grimaced. It hurt him to see poor old Mr. Parks grovel like that. If only he could get that pistol away from his throat. He might be able to do something to save Mrs. Monroe and his boss! His fears were still present but subsiding a little as he realized the danger his boss and Lisa were in. He had to conquer the fear. He knew what to do. Even if he'd had little training, he remembered the moves. And he'd been an army ranger when he was in the service, only a short time before he came to work for Cy Parks. He wasn't a coward. He could do what he needed to do, to protect Cy and Lisa. He could do it. His head lifted and new purpose narrowed his eyes as he watched the armed men.

The man with the automatic weapon shrugged. "I see that you are injured. But this man told the woman that he had commando training and would not hesitate to use it," he told Cy. "Am I to believe now that he is harmless?"

"No," Cy drawled. "It's more than enough if you believe I am," he said enigmatically and glanced at Harley. "You just stay put, Harley," he added in a tone that made Harley frown. "I'll just go get Mrs. Monroe…" His head turned abruptly to the left of the gunman and he pointed. "Good God, look at that!!"

The man with the automatic weapon reacted predictably and was diverted for a few precious seconds. It was enough. Cy's hand moved so fast that his knife was in the man's shoulder before he could turn his head back, causing him to drop the automatic weapon as he groaned in shock and pain. Even as that knife hit the target, Cy whirled and sent a second knife slicing through the air. It hit the man holding the pistol at Harley's neck, pinning his forearm, pistol, sleeve and all, to the wood of the barn wall behind him. The man cried out and Harley ducked and got out of the way immediately.

Green eyes blazing, Cy rushed forward, aimed an explosive high kick at the first man's stomach, bringing him down instantly. He fell, trying to extricate the knife from his shoulder at the same time, with little success.

"There's…another man…in there!" Harley called urgently through his shock.

"There was." A deep chuckle accompanied the words. Eb Scott came out of the barn with a miserable-looking man in denims held at gunpoint. "He made a fatal error. Never turn your back to a dark corner. Nice timing, Cy."

Cy didn't answer. He jerked up the automatic weapon

and spared a glance for the groaning man on the ground and the other one, pinned to the wall of the barn.

"I didn't want to do it like this," Cy said calmly, walking to the man his second knife had pinned to the barn wall. "But if you're going to set a trap, it's best done on your home ground and in your own time. Oh, shut up for God's sake," he growled at his victim as he jerked the knife out and wiped it on the man's shirtsleeve. "You're barely nicked! When you get a Bowie knife sticking out of your arm, you can complain."

Harley was still staring at his boss with wide eyes. He hadn't said a single word. He felt his head to make sure it was where he'd left it.

"You all right, Harley?" Cy asked curtly.

"Shh…sure," he stammered.

"I'll just check on Lisa." Cy strode off toward the house.

Harley stared after his boss as if he'd never seen him before. "Did you see that?" Harley asked Eb Scott. "Did you see it? He had the second knife in the air even before the first one hit its target!"

"You said he was no threat!" the assailant with the formerly pinned forearm growled at the man in the suit. Both were holding their wounds.

"I thought he was crippled!" the flashily dressed man growled. The knife was still in his shoulder, and he didn't dare pull it out for fear it might hemorrhage at withdrawal.

"So did I," Harley murmured, but only Eb heard him.

"Cy's not quite what he seems," was all Eb had to say about it.

On the porch, Lisa had watched with surprise and disbelief as Cy easily took care of the two armed men, while Harley stood shellshocked nearby. If she'd ever worried about him, her mind rested easier after she saw the ease with which he subdued the armed assailants. She watched him with covetous, protective eyes, almost limp with relief. She'd been so worried that he might die right in front of her eyes. She opened the door as Cy mounted the steps and rushed out to throw herself against his chest, oblivious to his shocked delight. She was still holding the gun in one hand.

He took it from her, keeping the other arm around her, and put the safety back on. "Were you going to come out shooting and rescue me?" he asked with a grin.

"If I got the chance, I was," she said huskily, clinging harder. "I certainly wasn't going to cower in the house and let them kill you."

His eyes were warm with affection as he lifted his dark head to search her flushed face. "Nice to know I can count on backup when I need it," he told her, tracing a soft pattern down her flushed cheek.

She smiled at him and only looked away when she heard sirens and saw two sheriff's cars pull up in the driveway with their lights flashing. "Speaking of backup," she gestured. "Did you plan this?"

He shrugged. "Eb planned it and convinced me to go along," he said quietly. "All those surveillance gadgets paid for themselves this afternoon. Eb was already in the barn when I left here. He waited to act after the guns were drawn because he didn't want to get Harley killed." He shook his head as he saw Harley standing morose and miserable against the barn with his arms folded while the deputies handcuffed the three men. Barely two minutes later, an ambulance joined the patrol cars. "What I didn't know was that Lopez had the house bugged," he added curtly. "When we get these guys in custody, I'm going to sweep the house and get rid of them."

"They can hear what we do in the house?" she asked worriedly.

He glanced down at her and knew she meant what they were doing in the living room before he left. He smiled slowly. "Not all of it," he murmured wickedly. "Probably they only had listening devices in the kitchen, since we spend so much time in there."

"Oh." She sighed with relief.

"I'd better go and have a word with the deputies," Cy told her. "You okay?"

She grinned. "Never better. Are you?"

"Can't hurt a weed," he replied, winked and walked back down the steps.

Eb and Cy explained what had happened to the deputies. Cy agreed to swear out a warrant so that the three men could be held. He was furious that Lopez had dared to send men onto his own place after Lisa. He wasn't ever going to get the chance to do that again. He swore it.

As the two wounded prisoners were being loaded up in the ambulance and the other one confined in the patrol car for the trip to jail, Cy joined Harley at the barn door.

"I'm all hot air," Harley said with cold self-contempt. He couldn't meet the older man's eyes. "All that damned bragging about what I could do, and how I could take care of everybody. And look at me! I was taken by surprise and overpowered by a man half my size. I'm a fraud, Mr. Parks. You ought to fire me on the spot."

Cy only smiled. Harley was showing the first signs of wisdom. And even if he'd been overpowered, he'd conquered whatever fears he had. Cy knew that the younger man's pride was in shreds at being surprised and captured. He'd been in similar situations himself. No need to rub it in, just because he'd overreacted at Harley holding Lisa's hand.

"If I fire you, who's going to gather Lisa's eggs every morning?" Cy asked.

Harley couldn't believe he'd actually heard that droll question. He forced his shamed eyes up, and found his boss's eyes twinkling.

"You don't want to fire me?" he asked.

"Not today," Cy replied. "Get back in there and finish getting that cattle truck fixed. We'll need it tomorrow to haul calves."

"It's finished," Harley said with a faint smile. "I was just putting it back together when those guys drove up and caught me off guard."

Harley still felt a little disoriented. Mr. Parks, on the other hand, didn't have a hair out of place and seemed supremely calm. Despite the cool weather, Harley felt perspiration on his forehead. He wiped his sweaty brow on his arm and let out a heavy breath. He even managed a grin. "I guess you learned how to throw a knife when you were in the military. You, uh, were in the military?"

"Somewhat."

"Well, it was amazing, what you did with those knives," Harley continued. "That's some aim you've got, Mr. Parks."

"I get in a little practice now and then."

Harley moved away from the barn. "You sure had those guys foxed about how helpless you were," he said, chuckling. "They bought every word."

"To their cost," Cy said easily, without breaking stride. "You never underestimate an adversary, if you want to live."

"You've, uh, been in a few fights then?"

Cy's green eyes were enigmatic as he glanced back at the younger man. "Stop fishing, Harley. Get that truck running."

He turned again and started toward the house. Harley watched him go with raging curiosity. On an impulse he didn't even understand, Harley picked up the pistol his captor had dropped where it lay forgotten in the straw. He tossed it toward Cy Parks's back.

As if he sensed danger, Cy whirled immediately and caught the weapon in midair. He had it cocked and leveled at Harley's nose in the space between one heartbeat and the next. Harley stopped breathing as he looked down the barrel for seconds that seemed like hours.

Cy cursed harshly and lowered the gun. "If you ever do that again, so help me, I'll shoot you in the foot, Harley!" he growled, furious. He snapped on the safety and walked toward the sheriff's deputies to leave the weapon with them.

Harley let out the breath he'd been holding. He'd served two years in the army himself, in the rangers. He didn't know a single man who could have done what Cy Parks just had. That was a sort of training that men only got in some elite fighting force, and it wasn't regular military. He forced himself to walk back to the garage without casting another glance at his enigmatic boss. He felt as if his legs had turned to rubber.

Lisa was uneasy all night. She kept hearing noises. She dreamed that Cy was in front of the man with the machine gun, but that he hadn't managed to throw those knives in time. She woke up crying, in a cold sweat.

The door opened, the light came on and Cy stood over her, dressed in pajama bottoms with his broad, hairy, scarred bare chest. His dark hair was touseled, his eyes narrow with concern.

"You screamed," he said.

She sat up in her sweatpants and pullover white cotton T-shirt and hugged her knees. She couldn't quite see him because her glasses were in the drawer of the bedside table. She could imagine how she looked with her eyes red and wet with tears and her long hair tangled all around her.

"Sorry if I woke you," she said miserably. "It's been a rough day."

"For me, too," he replied. "I'm sorry you ever got mixed up in this business."

"So am I, but there's not much we can do about that

now." She pushed back her long, sweaty hair. "Now Lopez seems to be after you, too."

"No. He's after you. This was a test run, to see if he could get to you on my ranch."

"He didn't."

"No, he didn't."

"You think he'll try again."

"They say Lopez will follow a man to hell to get even with him," he said quietly. "I believe it."

"What am I going to do? I can't keep on staying here…"

"Why not?"

"Well…"

He came around the side of the bed. "Move over," he said, sitting down beside her on the bedspread. "Now listen. I've got a big house and plenty of room. As long as you're here, right here, I can protect you, and I will. You've got a baby coming and you need someone. There's no reason you can't stay."

She looked worried. She picked at the cover. "Cy, people are already talking about us…"

"They'll stop when we get married."

She didn't seem to breathe for a space of seconds. She looked up at him with a curious mixture of shyness, excitement and pleasure. "Married."

"Married."

She picked at a fingernail while she turned the proposal over in her mind. She was barely widowed. Whatever would people think of her?

"We don't advertise what's going on in this town, but the people who count know that you're staying here because you're in danger," he said quietly. "As for all the rest, if we marry, no one will have any reason for talk. I'm not proposing for any hidden agenda," he added. "We'll have a marriage of convenience. Period."

That was vaguely disappointing, and she hoped she could keep him from seeing how it affected her.

"Okay," she said after a minute. "But you can kick me out when this Lopez thing is over," she added and managed a smile.

"Fair enough," he agreed, his face carefully schooled not to let any hint of emotion show through. "But only if you want to leave by then. I wouldn't make that offer to any other woman. I've had a bad time with marriage. If Lopez hadn't decided to target you, I wouldn't have proposed in the first place."

"I know that," she said.

"Not that you aren't attractive," he said unexpectedly. "I think you know that under different circumstances, you'd be first on the endangered list. I haven't made a secret of the way you affect me. But you're pregnant and a very recent widow. Under the circumstances, it would hardly be appropriate to take advantage of the situation."

He was talking in riddles and she was very puzzled by the look in his eyes when he spoke to her. Odd, how reluctant he sounded to have her leave. But surely he was marrying her for the reasons he'd mentioned. He'd been through his own time of pain. She knew that there must be times when he ached for the child who had died in such a terrible manner. But for whatever reason, he was offering Lisa a marriage of companionship, protection for her baby. She couldn't have turned it down to save her life. Living with him would be heaven, even if he kept her at arm's length.

"Are you sure it's the right thing to do?" she asked worriedly.

"Yes, I am," he said firmly. "And the sooner, the better."

She toyed with a fold of her sweatpants. "I might be in the way."

His chest rose and fell heavily. His eyes narrowed. He

looked at her with such hunger that it was blatant when she met his eyes.

Involuntarily she let her knees down. The T-shirt was thin and his eyes went instantly to the thrust of her breasts against it. Her mauve nipples were very noticeable, making soft peaks under the fabric.

His breathing changed. Her own eyes went to that broad chest and she wondered how it would feel against her.

"Don't push your luck," he said in a husky tone. "It's been three years. More than that. I didn't want her after my son was born, and the feeling was mutual."

Her eyes lifted to his. "You want me."

He nodded, very slowly. His eyes went back to the T-shirt and her own roamed over his bare chest like seeking, exploring fingers. In the silence of the bedroom, the sound of their breathing was harsh and loud. She could hear her own heartbeat in her ears, see his at the base of his strong throat.

She shivered and his teeth clenched.

"That baby is just starting to develop," he said, almost choking on his own voice in a throat as dry as desert sand. "And you've had cramping. I won't risk it."

"I wasn't offering, really," she managed unsteadily. She bit her lower lip and frowned as she searched his lean, hard face. "I don't understand. I never...felt like this. I'm scared."

"Felt like what?" he asked, not at all embarrassed. "Tell me, Lisa."

She flushed. "I can't!" she bit off.

He took her by both arms and pulled her gently across him, so that her head lay in the crook of his powerful arm. His free hand went to her throat and caressed its way under her long, loosened dark blond hair. She relaxed against him helplessly, her breath coming in tiny little jerks as she looked up into his quiet, gentle eyes.

"Then I'll tell you," he said softly. "You want to pull

the fabric out of the way and show yourself to me," he whispered. His thumb moved slowly over her parted lips. "You feel hot and swollen all over, and you aren't quite in control. That's what frightens you."

She shivered again. "It wasn't like this with Walt."

His big warm hand slid from her neck down to her collarbone and as he held her wide eyes, it moved blatantly over the hard peak of one small breast and pressed there.

She whimpered, closing her eyes with a faint shudder. Her hand pressed hard into his hair-roughened chest and she leaned her hot face against the cool, hard muscle of his upper arm.

His cheek lay gently against hers. He caressed her almost absently, with a slow, restrained tenderness that made her whole body tremble with passion.

Her nails bit into his chest as the hunger grew with every soft brush of his fingers.

She felt his mouth on her closed eyelids as his hand found the hem of the T-shirt and moved under it. She arched helplessly to the sensuous delight of that expert touch.

He smiled against her mouth as he kissed her very tenderly. All the while his hand explored the softness of her silky skin, arousing a need that made her moan helplessly.

She moved closer, her eyes opening, wide, dazed, soft as a doe's.

He slid the fabric under her chin and looked at the firmness of her young breasts while he traced them. Odd, he thought, that her breasts showed no evidence of a pregnancy that should be approaching its fifth week. He'd seen his wife's body, and he remembered the changes pregnancy made in it. He wondered if women differed in the physical signs.

"I'm very small," she whispered unsteadily.

"Do you think size matters?" he murmured with a wicked, soft smile.

"If it didn't, men wouldn't buy those picture magazines..."

He bent and brushed his mouth against hers. "The men who buy those magazines don't have real women to practice on."

"Is that why?" she asked, laughing breathlessly through her shyness.

"You're just right," he breathed, letting his fingers sketch her body. "And if you weren't five weeks pregnant, I'd do more than talk about it."

"Would you?"

He lifted his head and looked down at the soft thrust of her creamy pink breasts. His eyes narrowed as he imagined the feel of them under his mouth. He felt his body tense with desire. It made him ache.

"You want to put your mouth on me, don't you?" she asked daringly. "I...would let you."

"I know," he said in a choked tone. His eyes met hers. "And what do you think would happen then?"

Her face colored helplessly as images flashed through her whirling mind.

His eyes narrowed. "I haven't wanted a woman for a long time. I want you very badly. Don't make it hard for me to walk away."

She forced herself to breathe slowly, to deny the ache inside her. She was suddenly ashamed of the way she'd behaved, and she grimaced as she tugged her T-shirt down and lifted herself out of his loosening arms.

"I'm sorry," she said without looking at him.

"No need to apologize." He got to his feet. His arousal was noticeable but he didn't turn away. He looked down at her with lingering traces of desire, and she looked at him the same way.

"First, we get married," he said in a subdued tone that didn't match his stormy eyes. "Then we talk to your obstetrician. If it's safe, I'll make love to you. Assuming that you want me to.''

''I want you to,'' she said honestly, avoiding his probing gaze.

''That makes two of us.''

She slipped back under the covers and only then lifted her eyes back up to meet his. ''I'm glad those men didn't hurt you,'' she said.

''Harley took it hard,'' he replied.

''Of course he did. He's not so bad,'' she added with a smile.

He didn't like hearing her say that. She was young and she had all the normal urges. He wanted to marry her right away, before Harley got to her. Maybe she'd have felt the same desire for anyone who offered her tenderness. She'd barely been married and she hadn't wanted her husband. She was ripe for an affair. If it happened, it was going to be with him. He wasn't letting Harley near her.

''You look angry,'' she commented.

He forced a smile. ''Frustrated,'' he said, deliberately letting his gaze slide over her.

''Oh.''

''Your breasts aren't swollen,'' he remarked bluntly, ''and your nipples aren't enlarged or dark. Has the doctor explained the normal changes pregnancy will make in them?''

''Well, yes,'' she said, fighting embarrassment. ''I imagine I'm not far enough along for it to show much.''

''That makes sense.'' He moved back to the door. ''If you need me, sing out.''

''Would you like musical comedy or grand opera?'' she mused. ''Because I can start right now and save you the trip back to your own bed.''

He chuckled softly. ''Not yet,'' he told her deliberately. ''First the ring, then the doctor. First things first.''

She sighed. "Okay. You're the boss."

"Yes, I am," he mused. "But that won't last much longer, I imagine," he murmured, and left her sitting there with puzzlement all over her face.

Eight

A week later, with Eb and Sally Scott for witnesses, Cyrus Jonathan Parks married Lisa Jane Taylor Monroe in a quiet civil service in front of a justice of the peace. She wore a simple beige dress and carried a small bouquet of orange autumn maple leaves and yellow chrysanthemums that seemed just right for an autumn wedding.

They'd discussed rings and chose simple gold wedding bands with no ornamentation, just right for a marriage of convenience.

Except that it was more than that. Lisa began to tremble every time she got within five feet of her handsome, taciturn new husband. He knew that she wanted him. He wanted her, too. But despite the flare of desire between them, all he'd really offered her was a refuge, not love eternal. He'd said quite bluntly that he wouldn't have married her at all unless she'd been in danger, and he didn't plan to stay married to her after Lopez was arrested or subdued. She had to remember that.

There was time for a small reception at the Jacobsville Methodist Church fellowship hall, where friends still suffering from belated shock at the sudden wedding of Jacobsville's most reclusive rancher had laden a table with delicious tidbits while cakes for both bride and groom graced a side table. Cy and Lisa were required to cut the bride's cake together and share the first piece. As she looked up into his eyes, the photographer Cy had hired took a photograph so revealing that when Lisa would see it a week later, she would be too embarrassed to show it to anyone. She'd looked like a woman absolutely besotted with the man beside her.

They went back to his ranch together after the reception, and she went inside quickly, to spare him the humiliation of not being able to carry her over the threshhold with his damaged arm. Incredibly, the well-meant action ignited an argument that had explosive consequences.

The front door slammed audibly as Lisa went down the hall. He caught up with her in the bedroom she'd been occupying.

Green eyes blazing, he closed the door behind him. And locked it.

"Why didn't you paint a sign and have it hung on the front door?" he asked in a menacing tone. "We both know I have limited use of this," he extended his left arm. "But I could have carried you over the threshold. You aren't exactly a challenging weight!"

She just stared at him, stunned by the furious anger in his lean face. "I was only trying to spare your pride," she said tightly. "I never meant to insult you."

He threw off his jacket and tossed it onto a chair. His strong fingers went to his tie. That followed the jacket. He unbuttoned his shirt, all the while walking deliberately toward Lisa.

She'd never had cause to be afraid of him. She wasn't now, although her knees felt weak as water under her. He was devastatingly attractive to her, and if her heartbeat was shaking her, it wasn't out of fear. She wondered if he knew.

His hands caught her by the waist and brought her against him firmly. His glittery eyes searched her wide, surprised ones. His fingers contracted. He wasn't behaving rationally, and it wasn't much of a surprise. He'd gone without a woman for over three years and here was Lisa, his wife, who made him hungry as he'd never been hungry before. He thought briefly of the child she was carrying, and hesitated.

"Did you speak to the doctor about the baby…?"

"Since I haven't had any more cramps, he said it's all right," she said huskily, drowning in the strong arms enfolding her.

She was hardly aware of meeting him halfway when his head bent. He kissed her slowly, softly, and then with a hunger that made fires in her blood. She reached up on tiptoe to press hard against his strong body, clung as the kiss deepened and became slow and hungry, devouring her soft mouth.

Her submissive moan made him wild. He lifted her quite easily with his right arm, catching her neatly under her knees with the left one, and carried her to the bed with his mouth still demanding and rough on her eager lips.

It was broad daylight. The sun filtered in through the blinds, but she didn't feel inhibited by the light. Walt had always wanted the darkness, but Cy didn't seem to care at all. He caressed her out of her neat beige dress and the things under it, his mouth ardent and expert in a way she'd never experienced with her husband. Walt had always been in a hurry. Cy wasn't. Long before his shirt came off, she was twisting under him in a veritable orgy of pleasure, her nails biting into his shoulders, her gasps audible as each pleasure was eclipsed by a new one. It was like the night he'd proposed, but without his stoic restraint. He didn't seem to mind her knowing that he was desperate to have her, although he was patient and tender and restrained.

She wouldn't have believed that a man who'd gone without a woman for so long could be so patient. He acted as if he had all the time in the world. He laughed softly at her obvious desire, but he didn't satisfy it. His mouth worked its way lazily down her soft body to her breasts while she trembled in the wake of new and mysterious pleasures. She seemed to hang in midair as his mouth hovered over the hard peak of her breast. Then, tenderly, his mouth worked its way completely over it and began to suckle her, and she cried out in surprised ecstasy.

Her headlong response delighted him. She'd mentioned once that her husband hadn't been patient, and now he was willing to believe it. Despite her marriage and her pregnancy, she acted like a woman who'd never been intimate with anyone. Her ardent clinging, her soft cries of pleasure, her trembling made him feel more like a man than ever before. His own wife had hated this part of marriage, hated her child, hated him. In the old days, before his marriage, there had never been a shortage of women. But since he'd been widowed, there had been no one. Not until now. And this soft, eager woman beneath him was his wife. He groaned harshly against her breast as a wave of hot pleasure swept over him. His control was suddenly gone.

He wrestled the rest of his clothes off and jerked back the bedspread, moving Lisa onto the cool, crisp sheets. His body covered hers, feeling the heat and eagerness of it. He heard her faint gasp and felt the ripple of her soft body as she moved to accommodate him.

"Cy...!" she whispered, her nails gripping his upper arms.

His mouth closed her lips as he eased down. "Don't be afraid. I'll be careful with you," he whispered, reading the helpless fear in that soft exclamation. "Very, very careful. I won't hurt the baby."

That wasn't at all what she was thinking, to her shame, but she was too shy to tell him that she wasn't sure her slender body could adjust to his. He wasn't made like Walt, she could tell…

She gasped again as he moved lazily and a violent spasm of pleasure shook her entire body. Her nails bit into him and when he lifted his head to look at her, she knew her eyes must be like saucers. She was aware of her legs relaxing, her slender hips arching, her body trying to incite him to repeat that lazy movement of his body, to give her that shock of ecstasy again.

His soft, possessive eyes met hers. "Is this what you want me to do?" he whispered lazily, and he smiled as he moved and she tensed again, trembling.

She couldn't get the words out, but he didn't seem to need them. He shifted their positions and the next time he moved, she closed her eyes on a shuddering moan of exquisite pleasure. Never like this. She hadn't dreamed that a woman could feel such…!

He heard her voice, barely audible, pleading with him, sobbing at his throat. He was near the end of his endurance, but from the sound of her, he needn't be patient any longer. He caught her mouth firmly under his and moved deliberately, roughly, quickly, feeling her body take up the rhythm and echo it. The silken brush of her skin took the last of his control. He could feel her going up the spiral with him, he could hear the pleasure in her choked sobs, feel it in her clinging hands and arching body, in the grip of her long, elegant legs as they curled around his and tightened in spasms.

It was more than he'd hoped for. She fell with him into the white-hot heat of ecstasy, throbbed with him as reality became nothing more than a glimpse of light somewhere in the distance. He felt his body stiffen even as hers convulsed under the pressure of him. It was like being buried in warm, soft velvet…

"No!" she cried out as the pleasure fell away from her just as she'd grasped it. "No, no…!"

"What is it?" he asked huskily at her ear, his body shivering a little in the aftermath as he lay heavily above her. "Did I hurt you?"

"It didn't last," she sobbed, clinging. "I couldn't… make it last…!"

He understood at once. His mouth moved softly over her damp eyes, across her wet cheek and down to her parted lips where her breath came in husky little jerks. "Pleasure like that would be lethal in long doses," he whispered into her lips. He bit at her lower lip gently and then rubbed his mouth over it in soft little caresses.

She moved experimentally and felt the intimate pressure of him. Her eyes lifted to his, a little shy, and very soft.

His thumb brushed her lower lip while he searched her eyes in a silence so profound that she could hear their accelerated heartbeats.

"It was like making love to a virgin," he said in a deep, slow tone.

"It was like being one," she whispered honestly. Her fingers smoothed over the hard muscles in his upper arms. The one that had been damaged was only noticeable from the elbow to the hand, she observed. The rest of him, despite a few scars and depressions, was absolutely perfect.

He brushed back the loose strands of blond hair and, impulsively, took all the hairpins out to let it fall around her shoulders.

"That's better," he murmured, smiling.

They were still intimately joined, and her eyes searched over his lean, dark face with wonder.

His hips moved very sensuously and her whole body clenched visibly.

He reached to put the hairpins on the side table. He looked down into her eyes and moved again, with deliberate sensuality, watching her lift toward him helplessly.

He bent and put his mouth tenderly over hers, shifting onto his side with both lean hands on her hips as one long, powerful leg slid between both of hers. He felt her shiver as the pleasure began all over again. His last sane thought as she pressed into his body was that he hoped he had the stamina to survive what they were going to do to each other this time…

Much later, after a shower and a change of clothes, they had a small wedding supper of bacon and eggs and toast and coffee at the small kitchen table. Cy couldn't force himself to take his eyes off Lisa, and the attraction seemed to be mutual just at first. She couldn't stop touching him, even just to pass him the sugar or refill his cup. It was more than physical desire. It was a sort of intimacy he'd only seen in old movies. He'd had brief affairs, liaisons, even a wife. But with none of the other women had he felt this deep emotional bond.

His green gaze dropped to her belly and a surge of jealousy caught him unaware. She was carrying another man's child. When he'd first taken her in, protected her, it had been more out of pity and affection than anything else. But slowly desire and the need to possess had replaced his initial attraction, and jealousy had become a constant companion since he'd seen Harley holding her hand. But after what they'd shared in bed, he was unexpectedly jealous of her late husband and the baby as well. He didn't understand his own riotous feelings. He was upset at the level of intimacy they'd attained and disturbed by the sense of possessiveness he felt for her. This hadn't been the plan at all. He'd married her to protect her and the baby from Lopez, not with any long-term relationship in mind. He'd proposed a marriage of convenience, which was interesting when he considered how quickly he'd maneuvered her into bed with the flimsiest of excuses. Abstinence alone wouldn't have caused hunger that sweeping.

He didn't understand his sudden lack of restraint, and because he didn't, he was broody. At least he'd had the presence of mind to ask about the risk to the baby first. But that wasn't much comfort at the moment. He'd crossed the line, his own line, and he couldn't put her at risk again. He'd have to keep his uncontrollable urges to himself. As that thought persisted, he forced himself not to stare at Lisa. If he was going to practice restraint, he'd better get a head start, and right now.

She noticed the faint scowl on his heavy brow and looked at him quizzically as she sipped her second cup of coffee. "Is something wrong?" she asked.

He made a dismissing gesture with a movement of his shoulder. He smoothed his thumb absently over the fork he was holding. He seemed deep in thought and he was even more silent than normal.

She was getting more insecure by the minute. In bed, she'd felt as if she belonged to him completely, as if no two people on earth could have been any closer, any more intimate. Now, she was as far away from him as if they were still just neighbors. She wondered if she'd done something wrong. Maybe she'd been too…eager. She flushed, remembering her passionate, wanton behavior. He might be one of those men who didn't like aggressive women in bed. She swallowed the lump in her throat and averted her eyes from his taciturn expression. He hadn't complained, but he was very remote since they'd left the bedroom. She'd have to remember that he didn't like her undisciplined ardor, and not be so uninhibited again. Maybe if she could curtail her headlong response, it would ease the sudden tension between them.

She forced a smile to her face. "Would you like some more coffee?" she asked pleasantly.

He pushed his cup toward her to let her refill it, and finished the last of his eggs. He was furious at himself for the jealousy that had attacked him so unexpectedly. He'd married her to protect her from Lopez and help her take care of the child, and that was just what he was going to do. He'd be better off if he could keep in mind that passionate interludes in the bedroom weren't part of their deal, and stop trying to create new problems for himself and Lisa in the first days of their marriage. He'd broken faith with her by seducing her. Besides, he reminded himself, they still weren't out of the woods where Lopez was concerned. The man wouldn't stop just because Cy had married Lisa. In fact, he was willing to bet that the marriage would tempt Lopez to even further improvisation.

Meanwhile, he still had the problem of Lopez's warehouse behind his property. Since the blatant attack on Harley and Lisa, Cy had pulled Harley off the night surveillance, certain that Lopez's people would have night scopes now that would catch anyone spying on them. That excuse about locoweed worked once, but it wouldn't work again. Still, there was surveillance equipment that was undetectable by infrared glasses, and Cy initiated it. He hadn't shared it with Harley. The younger man hadn't quite recovered from the shock of seeing his supposedly crippled boss take down two professional assassins. He'd stopped asking questions, but he watched Cy from a safe distance and did nothing to upset him. He wouldn't even talk to Lisa unless Cy was around lately. It was almost comical.

She got up to put the dishes in the sink and he stacked his cup and saucer on his plate to simplify the chore for her. She smiled as she finished clearing the table and began to fill the sink with soapy warm water.

"I need to buy you a dishwasher," he said abruptly. "There wasn't much need for it when I lived alone, but we'll have dinner guests from time to time…"

"I don't mind washing dishes in the sink, Cy," she faltered, her wide dark eyes in their big lenses searching his.

He leaned against the counter, watching her deliberately, his face scowling and remote. "I wasn't as gentle as I should have been. Do you feel okay? Any queasiness or discomfort?" he asked bluntly.

"I feel great!" She smiled. "No cramping and I haven't had a hint of morning sickness since I've been pregnant."

Cy frowned. It had been a long time since his late wife had been pregnant, but he remembered everything he'd read on the subject. It was hard to overlook the lack of visible changes in Lisa's soft body, especially her breasts. He felt suddenly uneasy. Pregnancy tests weren't foolproof. Maybe she wasn't pregnant after all. But if she wasn't pregnant with her late husband's child, she could quite easily be pregnant with his right now. Especially, he thought ruefully, after his exhaustive lovemaking. He hadn't held anything back and he hadn't tried to protect her—useless when she was already pregnant, which he'd thought at the time. He'd proposed a temporary marriage to protect her. Making her pregnant with his own child wasn't part of the plan. He didn't want a binding relationship…did he?

She noticed his curious stare. "Why are you looking at me like that?" she asked uneasily.

"I like your hair loose around your shoulders," he said evasively.

"Do you?" She pushed the heavy fall of it back over her shoulders with a tiny smile. "It's a nuisance to wash and dry."

"I had Harley bathe Puppy Dog, by the way," he mentioned, searching for a neutral subject.

"Did you? That was nice."

"Bob needed a bath, too," he said. He didn't add that putting Harley to work bathing dogs had made him feel pretty good. He was still brooding about the way Harley had tested his reflexes with the pistol. He hadn't wanted any of his men to know about his old life. That was wishful thinking, he supposed.

She hesitated, washing the same plate until it threatened to rub the pattern off.

"Speaking of Puppy Dog," he said, "didn't he stay in the house with you before you moved over here?"

"Yes," she agreed, "but he's big and clumsy, like his father, and you've got lots of breakable stuff. Anyway, he seems to like being out in the barn with Bob. It's almost as warm in there, with the doors closed, as it is in the house. And it's amazingly sanitary. For a barn."

"I like healthy stock. Sanitation is important." He glanced around the kitchen. "I thought I was a fairly decent housekeeper, but you've brightened the place up considerably."

"I like housework," she said absently. "I do know a few things about the cattle business, but I enjoy cooking and cleaning and even ironing shirts." She fingered his. "I always thought I'd take to family life like a duck to water. I just never had the chance to prove it."

He scowled, thinking of the difference she'd made here. He'd gotten used to finding her in the kitchen or the living room when he came home every evening. He liked the little touches, the frilly curtains in the kitchen, the silk flowers on the table, the visible signs of her presence in his life. He thought about having her move back into her old house, and it was distasteful. He refused to pursue that line of thought.

His eyes went to her waistline and quickly away. She noticed and bit her lower lip while she finished washing utensils and put them in the other side of the sink to rinse.

"Does it bother you that I'm pregnant?" she blurted out.

He hesitated. He didn't know how to answer her. "The baby must be a comfort to you," he said slowly, "with your husband gone."

She didn't even feel as if she'd been married, she thought to herself. She'd slept with her husband exactly twice and the rest of the time he'd either been away from home or pretending that she wasn't there. He'd married her on the rebound.

He'd proposed to Lisa, having already confessed about the woman he'd loved leaving him. Lisa had no hope of marrying anyone else and she'd been very lonely since her father's death. A marriage of convenience wouldn't be so bad, she'd told herself. But Walt couldn't love her, and she couldn't love him. Now here she was in a second marriage of convenience with a man who didn't want her permanently any more than Walt had.

"I've always wanted children," she said noncommittally.

He was remembering the little boy who hadn't been his, and how painful it had been to lose him in such a violent manner. That led him to thoughts of Lopez and revenge.

Lisa saw the expression on his face and frowned. He hadn't wanted to harm her child, but it was obvious that he regretted their intimacy. She wished she could, but it had been the only time in her life she'd felt as if she belonged to someone.

"I'm sorry, by the way," she said quietly. "About not letting you carry me over the threshold," she added, avoiding his sudden intent gaze. "I really was trying to spare your pride."

He stared at her for a few seconds before he spoke. "There was some nerve damage and loss of muscle tissue to my arm after the fire," he said. "But I can do almost anything I could before. I don't advertise it," he added slowly. "It gives me a psychological advantage if people think I'm less capable than I am—especially since Eb's line of work became public knowledge."

"You don't want people to know what you did," she said with understanding. "Well, you may fool everyone else, but Harley goes out of his way not to upset you these days," she murmured.

"He's lucky I didn't shoot him," he muttered. His eyes narrowed. "Did you see it?"

She nodded.

"And you still didn't think I could carry you into the house."

She cleared her throat. "I was terribly shy of you, if you want the truth," she told him. "Walt was an ordinary man who never made me nervous. But my knees started shaking the minute I saw you. I didn't know what you'd expect of me. I was a little afraid of you."

"Why?"

Her shoulders rose and fell. "I haven't been completely honest with you about a few things. Not important things," she was quick to emphasize. "But I'd only been intimate with Walt twice and it was uncomfortable and quick and embarrassing. I…knew you were experienced, and that you'd expect more from a woman than Walt had. I thought I wouldn't be enough for you. If you meant us to have a real marriage, I mean, and not just one on paper."

So that was why. She hadn't been challenging him at all. She'd been afraid of the very thing her behavior precipitated.

"I'm sorry. I didn't understand," he added irritably.

"Not your fault. I sort of got carried away, too." She blushed.

A lot of things were becoming clear to him, predominantly her total lack of experience with intimacy. If she'd only slept with her husband twice and hadn't liked it, the past few hours must have shocked her speechless. Funny, most women weren't naïve these days. His gaze darkened as he stared at her. She seemed mature sometimes. And then she'd throw him a curve, from out of nowhere. He couldn't fathom her.

"Are we going to sleep together at night?" she asked before her courage failed.

"No," he said flatly. "This afternoon should never have happened. I'm not going to put your baby at risk a second time."

She worked not to let her disappointment show. Now she

was certain that she hadn't pleased him. She seemed to be an ongoing disappointment to men in bed, and she didn't know how to change it. "Okay," she said with forced carelessness.

He was glad she was taking it so calmly. She might not have loved her husband, but she genuinely wanted the baby and there was still a chance that she was pregnant, despite the lack of symptoms. He recalled now that some women did have cramping in the early stages, and it usually went away, just as hers had. And a lot of women never had morning sickness.

If she really was pregnant with Walt's child, he wasn't going to be the cause of her losing her baby. Nor was he going to touch her for the duration of their marriage of convenience. Once the threat of Lopez was removed, he was going to let her go back home and go to work for Kemp. They could have the marriage quietly annulled and it would be the best thing for both of them. He wasn't going to let himself love anyone ever again. He couldn't go through the hell of losing anyone else.

Lisa felt embarrassed, but she didn't let it show. It shouldn't have surprised her that she'd disappointed him in bed, considering the sophisticated women he'd probably attracted before his marriage. She was just a country woman with no experience, and thank God he didn't know her real age or he'd be doing more than clamming up when they talked. "I'll have supper when you come in," she said.

"I'll be late."

She nodded. "Okay."

He went to the door, hesitated, looked back and a flash of possessiveness showed in his green eyes as he stared at her. Her face colored and he forced himself to look away. She wasn't the first woman he'd taken to bed, and she wouldn't be the last. He had to stop seeing her as some sort of permanent fixture in his life. There was simply no future in it. He grabbed his hat off the rack, slanted it over one eye and walked out without another word.

Lisa went back to her dishes on shaky legs. She wondered if he had any idea what that smoldering look of his did to a woman.

Nine

Two more weeks passed with the occupants of the Parkses' house being polite to each other and not much more. Cy had swept the house for "bugs" the same day Lopez's men made their assault, making sure that he didn't miss any of Lopez's little listening devices. He had no idea how long the drug lord's men had been eavesdropping, but there hadn't been that many opportunities for them to get into the house. He didn't imagine it had been long.

He checked his surveillance tapes periodically as well, noting that the warehouse on the land behind his property had been joined by what looked like a small processing plant, supposedly for honey from the row upon row of bee-hives on the property. He saw nothing to indicate a drug presence, but Lopez had added several more men to the site, and there were several big eighteen-wheel trucks on the premises now. It looked very much as if Lopez planned to start shipping his product fairly soon.

Meanwhile, Cy had gone to see Eb Scott to check on

Rodrigo's progress, and the status of the cocaine shipment he'd already reported.

"Narcs got it down in the Gulf," Eb murmured coolly. "The Coast Guard homed in on the boats that were carrying it and strafed them with gunfire. Needless to say, they gave themselves and their shipment up. The DEA made several arrests and confiscated enough cocaine paste to addict a small country."

"Damn," Cy murmured angrily. "So here we sit."

"Don't knock the confiscation," Eb mused. "I'd love to see them make that kind of haul on a daily basis."

"So would I, but I want to catch Lopez with his fingers in the cookie jar," the other man said. And soon, he could have added, because his hunger for his wife was growing less controllable by the day. He looked at her and ached. Anger made new lines in his lean face. "Meanwhile, he sits on the edge of my property like a volcano about to erupt and I can't do a damned thing about it. I suppose you know that the sheriff's department and the DEA were all over it because of an 'anonymous' tip."

"I know," Eb replied. "One of Lopez's men phoned in the tip, apparently, and then the man in charge of the honey operation threatened to sue everybody for harassment if they came out again and did any more searches." He shook his head. "You have to admire the plan, at least. It was a stroke of genius. Nobody's going to rush out there again to look around unless there's concrete evidence of drugs."

"And that," Cy agreed, "will be hard to come by now."

"Exactly." He leaned forward in his chair and studied Cy intently. "You look older."

Cy scowled. "That's what marriage does to a bachelor."

"It had the opposite effect on me," his friend replied. "I've had a streak of good luck since I married Sally."

"I noticed. Is Micah Steele still in town?" he asked abruptly.

"He's in and out. He had an assignment and he's due

back next week. Had an apparently disastrous argument with his stepsister Callie Kirby over his father before he left."

"Callie isn't much for arguments," Cy pointed out. "If there was an argument, he started it."

"Could be."

"I wish we could nab Lopez and get Rodrigo out of there before he gets himself shot," Cy said, changing the subject. "He's good people. I don't want him killed on our account."

"Same here. He's been in the business at least as long as Dutch and J.D. and Laremos," he replied. "And they taught him everything he knows."

"They were the best."

"We weren't bad, either," Eb said on an amused laugh. "But I suppose we either settle down or die. Personally I consider marriage an adventure."

"Some do," he said without enthusiasm and changed the subject.

"Did you hear that Sally's aunt Jessica married Dallas and moved back to Houston with their son Stevie?" Eb asked unexpectedly. "Nobody was exactly surprised about it."

"At least she'll be looked after," Cy remarked.

"That's true." Eb frowned as he stared at his friend. "It's none of my business, but is it true that Lisa's pregnant?"

He was going to say yes, but Eb was watching him with the insight of years of friendship and he let his guard drop. "That's a good question," Cy replied, leaning forward. "I thought that she was, just after Walt was killed," he added. "But she had some symptoms I don't like and she doesn't show the normal signs of pregnancy." He grimaced. "We don't talk about it."

"She's young," Eb agreed. "I don't imagine she knows very much about pregnancy, since she was an only child more or less raised by her dad. He wasn't the sort to discuss intimate issues with her.''

"She's young, you said," Cy returned quickly. "How young?"

"You mean to tell me that you're married to her and you don't know how old she is?"

"She hid the marriage license," he muttered. "Put her thumb over the birthdate while I was signing it and confiscated it as soon as the JP signed it. Every time I've asked, she's changed the subject."

"I see."

"Well?" Cy prompted.

Eb grimaced. "She ought to tell you."

"Eb!"

The other man shifted restlessly. "She's twenty-one. Barely."

Cy's face went white. He leaned back in his chair as if he'd been shot. He took off his hat and wiped his sweaty brow on his sleeve. "Dear God!"

"That's legal age," Eb pointed out. "And you don't need me to tell you that she's amazingly mature for that age. Some women grow up quicker than others. She never really had a childhood. From what I've heard, from the age of six, she was riding horses in competitions and working around the ranch. For all that her Dad wouldn't teach her management, there isn't much she doesn't know about the daily routine of ranch hands."

"Fourteen years my junior," Cy groaned. "I could never get her to tell me."

"Now you see why," his friend remarked. "You'd never have married her if you'd known."

"Of course I wouldn't have married her if I'd known, Lopez or no Lopez! I don't rob cradles!"

Eb chuckled. "She's no kid. Around Jacobsville we pay more attention to family than we do to age differences. Lisa comes from good people. So do you."

Cy had his face in his hands. "Walt wasn't even thirty," he remarked. "And damned Harley is barely twenty-eight. He's still in and out of the house all the time flirting with her when he doesn't think I see him. I caught him a couple of weeks ago showing her how to break handholds, right in my own living room."

"You know how to handle that," Eb said easily.

Green, glittery eyes came up to meet his. "I can't handle it. She's too damned young for me and I don't want to stay married to her!"

Eb's eyebrows went up at the vehemence of the statement. "What do you plan to do, then, kick her out and let Lopez…"

"Oh, for God's sake, you know I wouldn't do that! I just don't want her getting comfortable in my house," he added irritably. "I think she's still in shock at Walt's death and latching onto the first pair of comforting arms she can find."

"So that's it. And you don't want to take any chances until you know for sure."

Cy glared at him. "Don't psychoanalyze me!"

"Wasn't trying to," Eb said with a grin. "But she and Walt didn't marry for love eternal. He'd just lost Becky Wayne and his heart was broken. Everybody knew he married Lisa on the rebound. And she'd never been in love with anybody. She assumed it came naturally when you put on an engagement ring. That isn't the case."

"You ought to know," Cy said. "You got engaged to Maggie Barton, and I know for a fact you didn't love her."

"I was lonely," he said simply. "But until Sally stormed back into my life, I didn't know what love was. I do now."

Obviously. It was written all over him. Cy turned his eyes away.

Eb's expression became covertly amused. "If you don't want Lisa for keeps, you might let Harley get on the inside track. He's got potential…"

"Damn Harley!" Cy burst out, his eyes were blazing. "If he goes near her again, I'll feed him to my chickens!"

So much for Cy's true feelings, even if he wouldn't admit them. Eb chuckled. "I haven't forgotten what happened at your place when Lopez's men made a try for Lisa," Eb murmured. "Talk is that Harley's given up throwing pistols at you and he walks a mile around you lately."

"Some men have to learn the hard way that they aren't invulnerable. Harley got overconfident. It almost cost him his life. You know that the two assailants made bond and left the country?"

"I know. What was it, a million in bond, each?"

"Yep. Pocket change to Lopez, but the judge set bond as high as she could. I don't blame her."

"She's a good judge at that," Eb agreed.

Cy stood up, feeling shaky. "I've got to get back home. If you hear from Rodrigo, let me know. I'm still trying to keep an eye on the honey plant. Nothing's shown up so far."

"Wouldn't it be a hoot if Lopez had decided to turn respectable and it's a real honey processing plant?" Eb mused.

"Sure, and pigs will fly."

"Not on my place, they won't," Eb said. He got up, too, and walked the other man to the front door. "But bullets may, before this mess is over," he added in a somber tone. "I don't like all this sudden quiet from Lopez's warehouse. They're up to something."

"That's exactly what I'm afraid of," Cy agreed, and he didn't smile.

As another week crawled by, Lisa could see that Cy was brooding about something. He continued to be standoffish and remote after their tempestuous afternoon in bed together, and he'd been somber and unapproachable altogether since he'd gone to see Eb Scott. But his eyes always seemed to be on her. She caught him watching her when she worked in the kitchen, when she washed clothes. He'd bought her a dishwasher, as he'd promised, and every sort of kitchen utensil and cookware any gourmet would have cherished. He surprised her with the romance novels she liked to read, and even scarce out-of-print editions of authors she enjoyed. He was forever buying toys for Puppy Dog and Bob, and coaxing Lisa into stores where he had accounts. She was spoiled constantly. But he never touched her.

One evening when they'd just finished watching the news, she cut off the television and followed him daringly into the office where he kept his computer and printer and fax-modem. He looked up from behind the massive oak desk with an expression of surprise.

"Can I come in?" she asked from the doorway.

He shrugged. "Help yourself."

That didn't sound welcoming, especially from a man to his new wife, but she smiled and walked up to the desk.

"Something bothering you?" he asked quietly.

"Yes."

"What?"

She stuck her hands into the pocket of her pretty embroidered purple apron. "I feel like an unwanted house guest lately," she said flatly. "I want to know what I'm doing wrong."

He scowled and put down the pencil he was holding over a spreadsheet of figures. "You haven't done anything wrong, Lisa," he said.

"I must have. You can't seem to force yourself to come within five feet of me." Her voice sounded raw and she didn't quite meet his eyes.

He leaned back in the chair. A harsh sound came out of his throat and his lips made a thin line as he studied her. "You didn't tell me you were just twenty-one."

She looked suddenly uncomfortable. "Does it matter?"

"Good God in heaven!" he exclaimed, explosively pushing himself up and out of his desk chair. "Of course it matters! You're still a kid and I'm thirty-five years old!"

She let out an expressive breath.

"You don't look your age," he muttered, walking away from her to stand in front of the dark window. The horizon was a faint silhouette in the distance, flat and cold-looking.

"That's what Walt used to say," she recalled. She leaned her hip against his desk and stared at his long back. "But I'm not as immature as you're making me out to be."

His shoulder moved jerkily. "If you were ten years older…"

"But I'm not. So what do you want to do about it?" she demanded, blowing a wisp of loose hair out of her mouth. "Do you want me to move back over to Dad's ranch and go to work for Mr. Kemp and pay rent? I'm willing."

He felt his heart stop. His expression was vulnerable for those few seconds, and he actually winced.

"Don't look so tormented. It won't cause any gossip if I go back home, wedding ring or no wedding ring. We can get an annulment."

"The gossips would have a field day over that!"

"I can't believe you care what people might say," she bit off. "I certainly don't."

"It isn't that." He rammed his hands into the pockets of his jeans and stared at her worriedly. "You've never been out of Jacobsville. You don't know beans about men." He drew in a slow breath. "You should have gone to college or at least seen a little more of the country and the world before you married."

"There was never enough money for travel," she said shortly. "My dad was a small rancher, not an aristocrat. If I went to college it would be to study veterinary medicine or animal husbandry, and I don't really see how I could do that with a baby on the way!"

He hesitated. Should he tell her what he suspected about

the baby? It might be the best time to do it. But he couldn't think clearly. All he could think about was her age. He should have realized how young she was. He felt as if he'd taken unfair advantage of her, even if it had been the only way to protect her from Lopez. She had been married already, he reminded himself. It wasn't as if he'd snatched her from a cradle.

Her hand went to her waistline. "I'd much rather have the baby than a degree, if you want the truth," she said.

His face hardened. He couldn't tell her. Not yet. For all he knew, she might truly have loved her late husband. What would it do to her if she wasn't pregnant? He turned back toward the desk. "I don't want you to move out. Lopez may be laying low, but I guarantee he hasn't gone away. I won't risk your life."

She stood glaring at him. "Fair enough. When he's finally caught, I'm out of here," she said flatly. "I am not living with a man who can't bring himself to touch me because I'm pregnant with another man's child!" she added, making a stab in the dark. It seemed to have paid off when he went rigid all over.

She turned and started out the door, sick at finally knowing the truth he hadn't wanted to tell her. It wasn't her age that bothered him, not really—it was Walt's baby!

"Damn it, that's not why!"

She whirled. "Then what is?"

He glared at her. She had a temper that easily matched his, despite her youth, and with her dark eyes flashing and her face flushed, she gave him a very inconvenient ache.

"It's strange that you don't have any pregnancy symptoms," he said flatly. She didn't answer him for several tense seconds. "All right," she said finally. "I'll make an appointment first thing tomorrow."

"See that you do," he returned curtly.

She searched his drawn face, seeking answers to questions she didn't want to ask. "We were so close, the day we married,'' she said hesitantly. ''You were…different. I thought you cared about me.''

He managed a smile that mixed equal parts of self-contempt and mockery. ''Didn't anyone ever tell you that men get sentimental after sex?''

She seemed to close up like a flower. She turned away from him without another word and left the room, quietly pulling the door closed behind her.

He ran an angry hand through his dark hair and cursed himself silently for that cruel remark. He'd never been so confused. He didn't know if she was carrying Walt's child or not. He didn't know how he really felt about her. He was sick at heart to realize how very young she was. On top of that, he was frustrated because Lopez wouldn't come out in the open and make a move. One thing he was sure about, though, was that Lisa had to be protected. He was going to take care of her the best he could. Then, when it was over, and she was safe, she could have a chance to decide whether or not she wanted to spend her life with a maimed ex-mercenary.

He wasn't going to continue to take advantage of her, even if it was killing him to stay out of her bed. If she wasn't pregnant, he wasn't going to take the slightest chance of making her that way. She was going to be completely free to decide her future. Even if it was with damned Harley.

Lisa went to the doctor and had the pregnancy test, and came back to the ranch looking more disturbed and worried than ever.

Cy was waiting for her in the living room. He stood up, his face strangely watchful. ''Well?'' he asked abruptly.

She moved restlessly, dropping her purse into a chair. She was wearing the same beige dress she'd worn the day they married, with a lightweight brown coat, and her hair was in a bun. She looked pale and quiet and not very happy.

''The test was positive,'' she said, avoiding his eyes.
''He said pregnancy symptoms sometimes don't show up
right away. He said there was nothing at all to worry
about.''

Cy didn't say anything. Apparently he'd been wrong
right down the line. She was pregnant, and her child was
Walt's. It was uncharitable of him to be disappointed about
that, but he was.

She'd noted the expression that crossed his face and it
wounded her. She knew that men were said to grow possessive once they'd been intimate with a woman, and it
wasn't totally unexpected that he resented Walt's place in
her life. It wouldn't be easy for a man to accept and raise
a child that wasn't his.

''Are you sure you don't want me to leave?'' she asked
in a subdued tone.

''Of course not,'' he said automatically.

She lifted her eyes to his. ''I won't get in your way.''

''You aren't in my way.''

She moved jerkily away. ''Okay. Thanks.''

She seemed to hesitate at the door, but only for a second.
She went out, leaving Cy to watch her exit with a tangle
of emotions.

He stopped by his office to check his messages before
he retrieved his shepherd's jacket and slanted his hat across
his green eyes. He went out by way of the kitchen so that
he could tell Lisa where he was going.

Harley had just come in with the eggs, and he was leaning against the counter smiling at Lisa, who was smiling
back. They were both so young...

''Sorry I didn't get them in first thing this morning,''
Harley was telling her, ''but I had some work to do on the
fence line.''

''That's okay. I had an appointment in town,'' Lisa replied.

''I'll be late tonight,'' Cy said from the doorway. They

both jumped, surprised by his sudden appearance. Harley cleared his throat, nodded at Lisa and went rushing down the steps toward the barn.

Cy didn't understand why until Lisa actually backed up against the sink.

"Now, what, for God's sake?" he demanded shortly.

"You ought to see your face in a mirror," she retorted.

His green eyes narrowed. "Harley spends too much time in here," he said flatly. "I don't like it."

Her eyebrows arched. "How would you know? You're never here!"

His lips made a thin line. He was bristling with unfamiliar emotions, the foremost of which was pure jealousy.

She glared up at him from her safe vantage point at the sink. "I didn't cheat on Walt and I won't cheat on you," she said coldly. "Just in case you wondered."

He glared back at her. His eyes, under the wide brim of the hat, glistened like green fire.

"I never should have agreed to come here," she said after a minute, her breath sighing out as she leaned back against the counter. "I've never been so miserable in my whole life."

That was worse than a slap in the face. His whole body tightened. "That makes two of us," he lied. "Don't worry. It won't be much longer before we'll have everything resolved. Once the sale of the ranch goes through, you'll have enough money to do what you please."

He turned and walked out. He didn't look back.

Lisa felt like breaking things. She was crazy about the stupid man, and he wouldn't give an inch. He didn't want her talking to Harley, he was resentful of her baby because it was Walt's, he alternately ignored and spoiled her. Now he'd offered to let her leave. She didn't want to. She'd grown used to living with him, even if it was like being alone most of the time. But he had said that she could go when things were resolved. Did that mean they were close to dealing with Lopez? She hoped so. The memory of the assault on her bedroom and then the attempted assault here still worried her. She felt safe with Cy, even with Harley. If she went home, she'd be watched, but she wouldn't feel safe.

Cy, driving toward town in his truck, was fuming. So she wanted to go home. Well, he'd see what he could do to hurry things up for her. First he went to Kemp's office and told him to push the paperwork through as fast as possible. Then he started toward Eb's place. There had to be some way to force Lopez to stick his neck in a noose.

But on the way, he decided to swing by the old Johnson house. It would be deserted now, of course, and there was only one other house on the stretch of outlying road. He didn't really know why it occurred to him to go that way. Maybe, he considered, his old instincts still worked at some level.

He pulled off the paved road and turned down the small county road that led to the Johnson place. He remembered Eb talking about the members of Lopez's cartel who had rented a house nearby and had accosted Sally Johnson before she'd married Eb. It was a crazy notion, and he needed his head read. All the same, he told himself, it never hurt to play a hunch.

He noticed the lack of traffic on the road, which was nothing unusual. This far out, there weren't a lot of people who opted for the badly kept county road instead of the newer highway that led to Victoria. The late autumn landscape was bleak and uninviting. All the leaves were off the trees now, and the last bunches of hay were cut and stacked in barns for winter forage. The weather had a nip in it. Nights were cold. He remembered winter nights when he and Eb were overseas, trudging through ice and snow. Life was much simpler here, if not overly comfortable.

He was watching the scenery, not paying a lot of attention to anything, when he noticed two huge tractor-trailer rigs parked near an old Victorian house. He didn't slow down or show any obvious interest in the once-deserted dwelling. But it was painfully clear why Lopez's "honey operation" was sitting still. He had a distribution center up and running already, only it wasn't behind Cy's property. The beehives were only a blind. Here was the real drug operation, complete with huge renovated barn and dangerous-looking employees sitting around the big rigs, which were backed up to the barn. Cy knew without looking that there would be locks on those barn doors and men with automatic weapons patrolling around it. He knew, too, that it wasn't hay that was being loaded into the trucks.

They'd been foxed. And now it was almost too late to close down the operation. He'd have bet money that this was Lopez's follow-up shipment to the one that had been confiscated down in the Gulf of Mexico. The odd-looking oil drums were scattered around, and had obviously been used to bridge rivers between Texas and the Gulf so that the men hauling the cocaine had been able to cross at places where the border patrol wouldn't be waiting for them.

He drove straight past the place without looking again. As he passed the deserted Johnson homeplace, with its For Sale sign standing awry and uninviting, he knew that what they'd all dreaded was already taking place. Lopez was back in business, right here in Jacobsville. And if Cy and his friends were going to stop them, there wasn't much time to plan an assault.

At the end of the road, he turned back into the highway and burned rubber getting to Eb's place.

Ten

Eb was surprised by the news.

"Right under our damned noses," he exploded. "No wonder we couldn't find any evidence of drug smuggling at the honey warehouse. That was a blind, and we fell for it, just like raw recruits!"

"The question is, what do we do now?" Cy asked coldly. "And since Rodrigo didn't warn us about this, have they found him out and disposed of him?"

"I hope not," Eb said sincerely. "But I can't help thinking that he would have warned us if he'd been able to." He ran his hand through his hair. "Hell of a time to make this sort of discovery, when Lopez is ready to ship his new supply out to his distribution network."

"It gets worse. From what I saw, I'd say he's ready to go tonight."

"We'll have to go in now," Eb said at once. "Or we'll miss the chance. And we'll have to have help," he added. "I counted at least twelve men. Even with our experience, we won't be able to take that many men armed with machine guns.''

"I know. But we can't do it without authorization, either,'' Cy returned. "We live here. I don't know about you, but I don't want to end up as an ex-patriated American.''

"Neither do I.'' Eb's eyes narrowed. "There's another consideration, too. If Rodrigo's with them, still undercover, the feds won't know and they'll shoot him. We have to go in with them. I have a few contacts. I can call in favors.''

"So can I,'' Cy agreed. "Let's compare notes. With a little luck, we may be able to bring down Lopez's local network and save Rodrigo all at once.''

It was rushed and hectic to get the necessary people notified and in place, but they managed it, just. The sheriff pulled two deputies off patrol and called in two more special deputies. The DEA only had three men who could get to Jacobsville in time to assist with the surprise attack, but they were dispatched immediately. Two of the best officers from the local police department, Palmer and Barrett, volunteered to go along with the sheriff's force to help. They might still be outnumbered, but hopefully it would be possible to take the drug dealers by surprise and close down their operation. Nobody wanted a drug cartel operating out of Jacobsville.

Cy was putting on his night gear when Lisa came into his room and gasped.

"Where are you going?'' she exclaimed.

He turned, black face mask in hand, to study her. She was wearing sweats, yellow ones that made her blond hair look more blond. It was loose, around her shoulders, and she had that peculiar radiance that pregnancy bestowed on a woman's face.

"Lopez's goons are ready to haul their shipment out tonight. We're going to stop them,'' he said honestly.

Her worried eyes never left her taciturn husband, from

his tall, powerful figure in black to his lean, scarred face and glittery green eyes. He was devastating to her, physically as well as mentally. He took her breath away. She hated knowing what he meant to do.

She went right up to him, her dark eyes looking even darker through the lenses of her glasses. "No," she said shortly. "No, you don't! There are plenty of people in law enforcement who do this for a living. I'm not letting you go after those drug dealers!"

He took her by both shoulders, pulled her against him, and bent and kissed the breath and the protest right out of her. His arms enfolded her, cradled her, while his hard mouth devoured her soft, parted lips. It was a long time before he lifted his dark head.

"If Lopez is allowed to set up an operation here, none of us will ever be safe again, especially you," he said quietly. "If we don't stop it now, we never will."

"You could be killed," she said miserably.

The worry on her face made him feel funny. He couldn't remember anyone caring if he lived or died, especially not his erstwhile wife who'd only wanted creature comforts. His welfare was of supreme unimportance to her. But Lisa was cut from another sort of cloth. She was brave and honest and loyal. He searched her face and realized with a start that he could give up anything, even his own life, easier than he could give up Lisa. She was too young for him, of course...

He kissed her again, long and hard, ignoring all the reasons why he should do his best to send her out the door and out of his life. For her own good, of course, he rationalized. Sadly, none of those reasons made any difference when he was within five feet of her. Her arms curled around him and she gave him back the kiss with every bit of strength in her body. It was like walking on hot coals. She couldn't get close enough.

She was breathless when he lifted his head, but the resolve was still there, in those narrow green eyes. "It amazes me," she whispered huskily, "what lengths you're willing to go to...in order to stay out of my bed."

He laughed despite the gravity of the situation. "Is that what you think?"

"Walt was my husband," she said quietly. "I was fond of him. I'm not sorry that I'll have his child, so that a part of him will live on. But you and I could have children of our own as well. It isn't biology that makes a man a father; it's love. And you aren't ever going to convince me that you wouldn't love a baby, even if it wasn't yours genetically."

He sighed gently and smoothed back her disheveled hair. "I keep mixing you up with the past, when you're nothing like my late wife. I don't resent Walt's baby." He shrugged. "It's not the age difference, either, really. But you're young and I'm older than my years make me. Maybe you need someone closer to your own age."

"Someone like Harley?" she asked deliberately.

His face hardened and his eyes flashed dangerously. *"No!"*

Hope, almost deserted, began to twinkle in her eyes. "That's what I thought you said." She pulled his head down and kissed him tenderly. "I know you can take care of yourself. I've seen you do it. But don't take chances. I want to be married a very long time."

"You do?" he murmured.

"Yes. I'm not going back to Dad's ranch. If you won't let me live in the house, I'll live in the barn with Puppy Dog and Bob and tell everybody in Jacobsville that you won't let me live with you...."

He was kissing her again. It was sweet and heady, and he didn't have time for it at all. He just couldn't seem to stop. He was starting to ache and that would never do.

"And I'm moving into your bedroom while you're

gone," she added, her voice thready with passion. "So there."

"Maybe I can think up an objection before I come back," he murmured against her lips.

"You try to do that." She grinned.

He loosened her arms and put her gently away from him, his strong hands tight on her shoulders. "While I'm gone, stay in the house with the doors locked. I've got Nels on the front porch and Henry watching the back door. They're both armed. Stay away from the windows and don't answer the phone. You know where the spare pistol is," he added, and she nodded. "It's loaded."

She bit her lower lip, realizing from his demeanor how dangerous it would be for both of them. "Okay. I'll use it if I have to. But don't you let yourself get shot," she told him firmly.

"I know, come back with my shield or on it."

She smiled and nodded. "That's right. Because you're not a 'summer soldier' like Thomas Paine wrote about. You're a winter soldier, fighting through blizzards. But you have to come back to me in one piece."

"I'll do my best to oblige," he mused, smiling back. Her eyes were soft and dark. He almost got lost in them. His gloved hand came up to touch her flushed cheek. "What did I ever do in my life to deserve someone like you?" he asked in a breathlessly tender voice. He moved away from her before that softness captured him. "I'll be home when I can."

She put up a brave front. "Okay," she said, and without further protests.

He paused at the doorway for one long, last look at her. She was a hell of a woman. And he wasn't giving her up, whether or not it would have been for her own good. He read the same resolve in her own face. She didn't cry or complain or try to stop him. She stood there very bravely and kept smiling, even though her eyes were too bright to be normal. She was still standing there when he went out into the hall and disappeared.

Harley was sitting on the front porch with Nels, waiting for him with a lit cigarette and a scowl. He got to his feet when Cy came out the door dressed in black and wearing a face mask. Harley had on jeans and boots and a camo jacket left over from his army ranger days.

"You aren't leaving here without me," Harley said belligerently.

"Who says I'm leaving?"

"Don't insult me." Harley opened his jacket to disclose a .45 automatic. "I may not be a full-fledged merk, but I was a crack shot in the Rangers," he added. "And no matter how many men are going, I might still be useful."

That was much better than bragging that he had combat training, Cy supposed. He hesitated, but only for a minute.

"All right. Let's go. Nels, guard her with your life," he added to his man on the porch, who nodded solemnly.

Harley headed for the Expedition, but Cy shook his head. He indicated a black Bronco of questionable vintage, parked under a tree. There were two men already in it. Harley was shocked that he hadn't seen it at all until now.

He wasn't surprised to find Eb Scott in the front seat with an unfamiliar man much bigger than Eb or Cy, and both of the newcomers dressed similarly to Cy.

"Here," Eb said, handing a small container of black face paint to Harley. "You'll shine like a new moon without a mask."

Harley at least knew how to use camouflage paint. He wanted to ask half a dozen questions, the foremost of which was why his boss was going along on what was obviously a search and destroy mission. Then he remembered the way Cy had used that knife on the two intruders and the way he'd caught the pistol Harley had thrown at his retreating back. It had long since dawned on him that his boss hadn't always been a rancher.

"Stubbs and Kennedy are going to rendezvous with us at the old Johnson place," Eb said tautly. "We've got the sheriff's department out in force, too. You and Micah and I will set up a perimeter with the deputies and let the feds go in first."

"Who are Stubbs and Kennedy?" Harley asked.

"DEA," came the cold reply. "Walt Monroe was one of theirs. They get first crack at these mules."

Mules, Harley recalled, were the drug lords' transportation people. He handed the face paint back to Eb. "You said the old Johnson place," Harley began. "But the warehouse is right behind Mr. Parks's place."

"That was a damned blind," Cy said shortly. "To draw attention away from the real distribution point. I could kick myself for not realizing it sooner."

"No wonder we never saw any drugs changing hands," Harley realized.

"Listen," Eb said as he eased the Bronco off the main highway and down the back road that led first to the Johnson place and then to the rental house near it, "I want a promise from you, just on the off chance that Lopez is around. No storm trooper stuff."

"Mr. Scott, I wouldn't dream…!" Harley began.

"Not you," Eb said impatiently. "Him!"

He was staring in the rearview mirror straight at Cy, whose eyes were glittering.

"He set fire to my house," Cy said in a menacing tone, "killed my wife and my five-year-old son. If he's there, he's mine, and no power on earth will save him. Not even you."

"If you kill him, the DEA will string you up on the nearest courthouse lawn!"

"They're welcome," Cy returned grimly.

"And what about Lisa, when you're gone?" Micah

Steele interjected. "This isn't Africa. You're not on your own. You have to think about Lisa and her baby."

"Africa was a long time ago," Cy said irritably, noting Harley's intent stare.

"None of us have forgotten it," Micah persisted. "You walked right into a nest of snipers with machine guns firing. Your clothes were shot to pieces and you took ten hits in the body, and you kept right on going. You saved us from certain death. We won't forget how much we owe you. That's why we're not letting you near Lopez. If I have to knock you down and sit on you, I'll do it."

"They were lousy shots," Cy muttered.

"They were crack shots," Eb countered. "But you psyched them out by walking right into the gunfire. It won't work with Lopez's men. We have to let the DEA take point. We aren't even supposed to be in on this. I had to call in markers from all over Texas to get even this far. And to boot, I had to confess to Kennedy why we're here—to protect Rodrigo from everybody in case he's among these guys. Don't forget that we haven't heard a word from Rodrigo. He may also be with them and unable to get a message to us."

"They may have killed him already, too," Cy added.

"We won't know until we get there. Harley—" Eb glanced over the seat "—you stick close to Cy."

Harley was weighing the dangers of that position when Micah Steele began to chuckle. "That's all he'll be able to do, or don't you remember that it took Laremos and Brettman and Dutch all together to bring him down just after Juba was killed, and he went right after a company of crack government troops?"

Harley's gasp was audible. "Laremos and...!"

"Who do you think taught us all we know?" Eb mused. "Now put a sock in it, Harley. This is where things get dicey."

He pulled up at the old Johnson place and cut off the

engine. He handed out high-tech night scopes and listening devices to Micah and Cy. Cy gave Harley a level stare.

"This isn't a weekend at a merk training school," he told the younger man in a firm tone. "If there's a firefight, you stay out of it. Eb and Micah and I are a team. We know to the last ditch how far we can trust each other and we work as a unit. You're the odd man out. That being the case, you could get somebody killed. You're backup, period. You don't shoot until and unless one of us tells you to."

Harley swallowed. He was getting the idea, and an odd sickness welled up in his stomach. He could hardly talk, because his mouth was so dry. "How will we know the bad guys from the good guys?"

"The DEA boys will have that imprinted on the back of their jackets in big letters. Palmer and Barrett from the police department and the deputies from the sheriff's department will all be in uniform. The bad guys will be trying to protect their product. This is important," he added intently. "If you should be captured, make damned sure that you're on the ground when we come in. Because if that happens, if we have to storm the house, the first thing we'll do is to take out everybody standing. Have you got that?"

"I've got it," Harley said. "But I'm not going to get myself captured."

The others synchronized watches, and piled out of the Bronco. With Eb in the lead, they made their way so stealthily that Harley felt like an elephant bringing up the rear. He realized at once that his so-called training session was nothing but a waste of money. And that his inexperience could prove deadly to his comrades.

Eb deployed Micah and Cy at the edge of the woods behind the barn. One of the feds motioned to them, and to the five sheriff's deputies. As he waved, four other men in DEA jackets split and went around both sides. Everybody hesitated.

Harley crouched with his heart beating him half to death. He'd been in the United States for his entire tour of duty with the Rangers, except for a brief stint in Bosnia, where he hadn't managed to get out of headquarters. He'd seen people who'd been in combat and he'd heard about it. But he had no practical experience, and now he felt like a high school freshman getting ready to give a book report in front of the whole class—on a book he hadn't read. His knees felt like rubber under him.

Time seemed to lengthen as the seconds ticked by. Then, quite suddenly, one of the government agents raised his arm high and brought it down.

''Move out!'' Eb called to his team.

It was pandemonium. Lopez's men were in civilian clothing, not the black gear that Cy and the others were wearing. The sheriff's deputies and the police officers were in uniform, and the DEA boys had visible identification on their jackets. Everybody seemed to be firing at once.

Harley hesitated at the sharp firecracker pop of guns going off, the sound so ominous and deadly in real life, so unlike the enhanced gunfire used in movies and television. He got a grip on his nerve, clutched his pistol in both hands and moved out a few seconds in the general direction where Cy and Eb had just vanished. He started to run, but he wasn't quick enough to get to cover. He ran right into the path of a submachine gun, and it wasn't held by one of his team. He stopped, his breath catching in his throat as he looked certain death in the face for the first time in his young life.

The small, dark man in jeans and checked shirt facing him ordered him in perfect English to drop his pistol. The leveled automatic weapon he was holding looked very professional. Harley's pride took a hard blow. He'd walked right into that by being careless and he steeled himself for what was coming. He knew that the man wouldn't hesitate to fire on him. With a muffled curse, he dropped his automatic to the ground.

"One less to worry about," the foreign man said with a vicious smile. *"Adios, señor…!"*

Harley heard the loud report as a shot was fired and he tensed, eyes closed, waiting for the pain to start. But the weapon spilled out of the other man's hands an instant before he crumpled and fell forward.

"Get the hell out of there, Harley!" Cy raged.

Harley's eyes opened to find his opponent lying very still on the ground, and Cy standing behind him. Cy picked up Harley's .45 and threw it to him.

"Get around in front of the barn. Hurry!" Cy told him.

Harley felt shaky, but he caught the pistol and walked rapidly past the downed man. He glanced at him and had to fight the rise of bile in his throat. He'd never seen anyone like that…!

His heart was racing crazily, his mouth felt as if it had been filled with cotton. As he cleared the side of the building, he saw firefights. Some of the drug dealer's men were undercover, firing from behind the big transfer trucks. Others were in the barn. They were cornered, desperate, fighting for their lives if not their freedom.

The DEA guys moved in, motioning to their backup, their own weapons singing as they brought down man after man. Most of the wounds were nonlethal, but the noise from the men as they fell made Harley sick. Groans, screams…it wasn't like that in the movies. He watched the police officers, Palmer and Barrett, walk right into the gunfire and drop their opposition neatly and without killing them. He envied them their cool demeanor and courage. He reminded himself never to tick them off once this was all over!

His whole body seemed to vibrate as he followed his boss. What had he been thinking when he enrolled in that mercenary training school? It was all just a lot of baloney, which had made him overconfident and could have gotten him killed tonight. The comparison between himself and these professionals was embarrassing.

Cy went into the barn alone, but now Harley didn't hesitate. He took a sharp breath, ground his teeth together and went right in behind him, ready to back him up if he was needed. He fought the fear he felt and conquered it, shaky legs, shaky hands and all. He'd made a fool of himself once. He wasn't about to do it twice. He wasn't going to let Cy and the others down just because he had butterflies in his stomach. His lean jaw tautened with new resolve.

There was a man in an expensive suit with an automatic weapon firing from behind several bales of odd-looking hay in the barn. Harley noted that he was the man who'd come to Cy's ranch in the pickup truck to "introduce himself."

Cy's instincts were still honed to perfection. He pushed Harley to one side and stepped right into the foreign man's line of fire and raised his own weapon, taking careful aim. Not even the head of the other man was visible now as he crouched behind the bales.

"Drop the gun or I'll drop you, right through your damned product," Cy warned.

The foreign man hesitated, but Cy didn't. He fired. The bullet went right through the hay and into the man, who cried out, clutching his shoulder as his weapon fell.

"Same arm I got with the knife, wasn't it?" Cy asked coldly as he approached the man and dragged him to his feet. He pushed him back against one of the wooden posts that supported the hayloft and held his pistol right to the base of the man's neck. "Where's Lopez?"

The drug dealer swallowed. He saw his own death in Cy's masked face, in those terrible glittering green eyes.

Harley felt that familiar cold sickness in the pit of his stomach as the muzzle of Cy's .45 automatic pressed harder into the adversary's neck just for a few seconds. It wasn't a training exercise. The gun was real. So was the threat.

He looked at his boss, at the man he thought he knew, and realized at once that Cy wasn't bluffing.

"Where's Lopez?" Cy repeated, and he pulled back the trigger deliberately.

"Please," the foreigner gasped, shivering. "Please! He is in Cancún!"

Cy stared at him for just an instant longer before he jerked the man around and sent him spinning away from the protection of the bales.

"Hey, Kennedy!" he called.

One of the DEA men came forward.

"Here's the site boss," Cy told him, pushing the injured man ahead. "I think you'll find him more than willing to talk. And if he isn't, just call me back," he added, watching the drug lord's man go even paler.

"I'll do that. Thanks," Kennedy said. "The sheriff's deputies and those police officers have most of them cuffed and ready to transport. We're going into the house. At least three of them managed to hole up in there. And there's a fourth man still missing. Watch your back."

"You do the same," Cy said. He glanced at Harley. "Let's check out the perimeter of the barn."

"Sure thing, boss," Harley drawled, but he was pale and somber and all traces of his former cockiness were gone. He held his pistol professionally and followed his boss out the door without a trace of hesitation. For the first time, Cy was really proud of him.

They trailed around back, watching as shadows merged with other shadows. There was a sudden crack of twigs and Harley spun around with his .45 leveled as another man carrying an automatic weapon stepped suddenly from behind one of the big trucks. His lean face was unmasked, and he was definitely foreign.

Harley fired, but Cy's hand shot out and knocked the barrel straight up.

"Good reflexes, Harley," Cy said, smiling, "but this

guy's on our side. Hi, Rodrigo,'' he called to the unmasked newcomer. "Long time no see."

"*Muchas grácias* for the timely intervention," Rodrigo replied on a husky chuckle. He moved forward, his white teeth showing even in the darkness. "It would be a pity to have come this far and be shot by a comrade."

"No danger of that," Cy said with a smile as he clapped the other man on the shoulder. "We were afraid they'd killed you. How are you?"

"Disappointed," came the reply. "I had hoped to apprehend Lopez, but he remained in Cancún and refused to participate. Someone is feeding him information about the movement of the government agents. He knew you were coming tonight."

"Damn!" Cy burst out.

Eb Scott and Micah Steele, the taller man who'd accompanied them, came forward. "Rodrigo!" he greeted, shaking the other man's hand. "We thought you'd been killed when we didn't hear from you."

"Lopez was suspicious of me," he said simply. "I couldn't afford to do anything that might tip my hand." He waved his hand toward the barn. "As it is, he was warned in time to divert the cocaine shipment and substitute this for it," he added, indicating the neat bales. "This has a significant street value, of course, but it is hardly the haul we hoped for."

Harley was inspecting the "hay." He frowned as he sniffed a twig of it. "Hey! This is marijuana!"

"Bales of it," Cy agreed. "I noticed when we came in that the barn had a padlock on it."

"Now that's what I call keeping a low profile," Harley murmured dryly. "Locking a barn full of hay."

"It would have been coca paste, if Lopez hadn't been warned," Rodrigo told Cy. "What he'd set up behind your ranch was a small processing plant that would have turned coca paste into crack cocaine. If I'd had just another week…!''

Cy smiled. "We'd rather have you alive, Rodrigo. We aren't through yet."

"No, we aren't," Micah Steele said coldly. "I have a contact in Cancún who knows Lopez. He can get someone in the house."

"An inspired idea," Rodrigo said. "Just don't share it with your friends over there," he added bitterly. "They don't have much of a track record with infiltration. Someone else infiltrated Lopez's home once before and died for it."

"Excuse me?" Micah asked.

"They lost an agent who worked for Lopez as a housekeeper," Rodrigo said. "He pushed her off his yacht." His face tightened. "Then he took a fancy to my sister, who was singing in a night club. He assaulted her, and she committed suicide at his house by throwing herself…onto the rocks below."

Eb's eyes narrowed. He was remembering some of the crazy things Rodrigo had done before he took this assignment, behavior that had marked him as a madman. Now they made sense. "I'm sorry," Eb said simply.

"So was I." Rodrigo glanced at the government agents rounding up the stragglers. "I'd better get out of here before that guy with Kennedy recognizes me."

"Who, Cobb?" Eb asked, frowning.

Rodrigo nodded. "It was his office I ransacked," he murmured. "They say he'll follow you to hell if you cross him. I'm inclined to believe it."

Rodrigo murmured, "Well, whether or not Cobb recognizes me, I don't want to risk being apprehended while Lopez is still loose. I can't do any good in prison."

"You were never here," Eb replied, tongue-in-cheek.

"Absolutely," Cy agreed. "I haven't seen you in years."

Micah Steele lifted one huge hand to his eyes. "Forgot my glasses," he murmured. "I couldn't recognize my own brother without them."

"You don't wear glasses, and you don't have a brother," Cy reminded him.

Micah shrugged. "No wonder I couldn't recognize him." He grinned.

Harley listened to the byplay, wondering how these men could seem so calm and unconcerned after what they'd all been through. He was sick to his stomach and shaking inside. He was putting on a good enough front to fool everyone else apparently, though. That was some small compensation.

"Get going," Eb motioned to Rodrigo. "Kennedy's heading this way."

Rodrigo nodded. "I'll be around if you need me again."

"We'll remember," Cy said. "But it won't be infiltrating Lopez's gang next time."

"No, it damned sure won't," Micah Steele said with ice in his deep voice. "Next time, we'll go at him head-on, and he won't walk away."

"I will count the days." Rodrigo melted back into the darkness before Kennedy came around the barn and paused beside the small group.

"The four of you had better do a quick vanishing act," Kennedy told them. "Cobb's over there asking a lot of questions about you guys, and he won't overlook a breach of departmental procedure. Since he outranks me, that wouldn't be good. As far as I'm concerned, officially, you were special agents undercover and I don't know who you are for your own protection. You infiltrated Lopez's gang and took a powder the minute the firefight was over. Since I never knew your names, I couldn't confirm your involvement." He gave them a big grin. "Unofficially, thanks for your help. At least we've managed to shut down one of Lopez's little enterprises." His eyes narrowed. "The man you dropped in the barn,'' Kennedy added, talking to Cy, ''was the one who popped a cap on Walt Monroe. We've been hoping to happen onto him. Cobb says he'll go down for murder one, and I guarantee he'll make it stick. Monroe was one of his new recruits. He doesn't like many people. He liked Walt.''

''I'll pass that along to his widow,'' Cy said. ''She'll be glad.''

He nodded. ''Walt was a good man.'' He looked around. ''I only wish we'd had something really nasty to pin on these guys. Distribution of cocaine would have suited me better than distribution of marijuana.''

''Yes,'' Cy agreed, ''but even if this was small pickings, it will hurt Lopez to have a hefty portion of his transportation force out of action, not to mention the lab he set up next to his beehives on my back property line. He's lost a big investment here tonight, in manpower, material and unrecoverable goods. He'll really be out for blood now. None of us will be safe until we get Lopez himself.''

''Dream on,'' Kennedy said quietly. ''He's more slippery than a greased python.''

''Even pythons can be captured.'' Micah Steele's eyes glittered through his mask. ''I've got a few friends in Nassau. We'll see what we can do about Lopez.''

''I didn't hear you say that,'' Kennedy replied.

''Just as well,'' Micah chuckled. ''Since I was never here.''

''There's a lot of that going around,'' Kennedy murmured. ''Get going before Cobb gets a good look at you. I'll take it from here.''

Eb nodded and the others joined him for a quick jaunt back to the Johnson place where they'd left the truck.

Harley hadn't said a single word. Eb and Cy and Micah talked about Lopez and discussed options for getting to him. Harley sat and looked out the window.

It wasn't until Eb dropped the two men off at Cy Parks's

ranch, several hundred yards from the house, that Cy was able to get a good look at his foreman.

Harley had the expression now, the one any combat veteran would recognize immediately. The experience tonight had taken the edge off his youth, his impulsive nature, his bravado. He'd matured in one night, and he'd never be the same again.

"Now," Cy told him quietly, "look in a mirror. You'll see what was missing when you were talking about your 'exploits' on the mercenary training expedition. This is the real thing, Harley. Men don't fall and then get back up again. The blood is real. The screams are real. What you saw tonight is the face of war, and no amount of money or fame is worth what you have to pay for it in emotional capital."

Harley's head turned. He looked at his boss with new eyes. "You were one of them," he said. "That's what you did before you came here and started ranching."

"That's right," Cy said evenly. "I've killed men. I've watched men die. I've watched children die, fighting in wars not of their making. I did it for fame and glory and money. But nothing I have now is worth the price I paid for it." He hesitated. "Nothing," he added, "except that woman in my house right now. She's worth dying for."

Harley managed a wan smile. "I could have gotten you all killed tonight, because I didn't know what I was doing."

"But you didn't get us killed," Cy returned. "And when the chips were down, you conquered your fear and kept going. That's the real definition of courage." He put a big, heavy hand on the other man's shoulder. "You have a way with ranch management, Harley. Believe me, it's a better path than hiring yourself out to whatever army needs foreign help. At the very least, you accumulate fewer bullet wounds."

Harley nodded. "So I saw. Good night, boss."

"Harley."

The younger man turned.

"I've never been prouder of you than I was tonight," Cy said quietly.

Harley tried to speak, couldn't, and settled for a jerky smile and a nod before he walked away.

Cy walked on toward the house, smiling faintly as he contemplated the movement of the curtains in the living-room window.

Before he even reached the porch, Lisa was out the front door and flying toward him. He caught her easily as she propelled herself from the second step. He folded her close, whirled her around and kissed her with his whole heart.

She held on to him for dear life, tears raining down her face as she thanked God that he'd come back to her in one piece.

"Can I keep you?" she whispered at his lips as he picked her up and carried her inside.

His heart jumped wildly. "Keep me?" he murmured, kicking the door shut with his foot. "Try to get rid of me...!"

She smiled under the fierce hunger of his mouth, savoring its coolness, its beloved contours, as he carried her into the bedroom and kicked that door shut as well. She could feel the adrenaline surging through his powerful body even before she felt the aftereffects of passion in his hungry, devouring kisses. She had a feeling that it was going to be the most explosively sensual night of their married lives. And she was right.

Eleven

Two feverishly exciting hours later, Lisa lay trembling against the powerful body beside hers in the tangled covers of Cy's big bed. She stretched and moaned helplessly as the movement triggered delicious little aftershocks of pleasure.

"If you weren't already pregnant," he murmured huskily, "you would be, after that."

She lifted herself up and propped her forearms on his damp, hair-roughened, deeply scarred chest. She brushed her mouth against one of the scars lovingly. "I went back to the doctor again yesterday," she confessed.

"Why?" He was concerned now, his green eyes narrowing on her face.

She traced his hard mouth with her fingertips. "To have a sonogram to date the pregnancy and to have some blood work done." She looked straight into his eyes. "The baby is yours, Cy."

He shivered. She could feel the ripple of muscle go right down him. "What?" he asked.

"I'm only a few weeks along. That means the baby is yours—not Walt's." She slid down beside him and pillowed her cheek on his chest, letting one slender, pretty leg slide over his muscular, hairy one. "He told me he did some checking and the results from my first pregnancy test after Walt died were switched with someone else's. It was a mix-up at the lab. That explains why I haven't had any pregnancy symptoms until now."

He stroked her long hair absently. "I can't believe it."

"Me, either. But it makes sense. I didn't know, but before we married, Walt…had a vasectomy. I checked with his doctor to get information on Walt's RH factor."

Every tendon in his body pulled tight. He rolled over and looked down into her flushed face incredulously.

"He said he didn't want children," she confessed. "The doctor said that he wanted to make sure he didn't have any. The doctor wanted him to tell me. He never did."

He was speechless with wonder. His baby. She was carrying his baby. He thought of his late wife and the child she'd borne that belonged to another man. He'd married Lisa believing that she was pregnant with her dead husband's child. But here he was with a miracle. He was going to be a biological father, for the first time in his life. He felt moisture sting his eyes as his big, lean hand smoothed over her flat stomach gently.

The expression on his face made her feel warm inside, safe, cocooned. "No need to ask if you're pleased," she said in a tender, amused tone.

He laughed self-consciously. "Pleased? I'm ecstatic. I don't suppose my feet will touch the ground for weeks."

She smiled and pressed close. "Mine won't, either, and not only because of the baby."

"Why else, then?" he teased.

She sighed, drawing her fingers across his mouth. "Because you love me."

He didn't hesitate or deny it. He only smiled. "Sure of that, are you?"

"Yes."

"How?"

She linked her arms around his neck and pressed her mouth gently to his damp throat. "It shows, in so many ways. All the time."

His fingers tangled contentedly in her long hair. "Like what you feel about me shows," he murmured, holding her closer.

"Does it?"

"We nurture each other," he said softly. "I never realized married people could be close like this, tender like this, loving like this. I've been standing outside warm houses all my life, looking in, and now I'm right inside by the fireplace." His arms contracted. His face nuzzled gently against hers. "I love you with all that I am, all I ever will be. More than my life."

She moaned and pressed closer, shivering. "I love you more than my life, too," she breathed at his lips. "I'm going to give you a son, Cy."

"And a daughter," he whispered back, delighted. "And a few others, assorted."

She smiled against his mouth. "You'll be a wonderful daddy."

He kissed her with aching tenderness, almost overwhelmed with emotion. Out of such tragedy and anguish had come this woman, this angel, in his arms. He was still amazed that she could love him, want him, need him as she did, with his past, with his scarred body and scarred emotions. He'd never dared hope for so much in his life. He closed his eyes and thanked God for the biggest miracle he'd ever had.

"I'll take care of you as long as I live, Lisa."

"And I'll take care of you as long as I do," she murmured happily. "I hope we live a hundred years together."

He laughed softly and agreed, drowning in the warm delight of her body curled so close into his. It was unbearably sweet to love, to really love, and be loved in return.

Her leg moved sensuously against the inside of his and she felt his breath go jerky. She was more sure of herself now, eager for new lessons, new techniques, new adventures with this man, this winter soldier, she loved.

"Cy?" she whispered as her hand smoothed over his chest and then steadily down.

It was hard to talk. "What?" he managed in a husky tone.

"I want you to teach me."

"Teach you…what?" he bit off as her hand moved again.

"How to please you."

He would have answered her, if he'd been able. But his soft groan and the shivering of his powerful body as he eased over hers were more than enough to convince her that she was pleasing him already. She stretched like a contented cat under the warm, sinuous press of his lean hips and then moaned as the fever burned so high that she thought she might become ashes in his arms. Life had never been so sweet. And this was only the tip of the iceberg, the very beginning of their marriage. She pressed her mouth into his and held on tight, following him into the fire.

With Lopez's Jacobsville connection closed down, and all his local assets seized by the feds, it seemed a good guess that the drug lord would set up operations elsewhere. But he still had people, unknown people, acting as his eyes and ears. He also had someone inside the federal agency, Rodrigo had said, to tip him off about drug busts. Cy worried about who it was. Cy worried more about another possible attempt on Lisa, after the successful sneak attack on Lopez's shipment of marijuana.

Cy had gone to Eb's ranch at his friend's request to discuss future plans, and they were talking over cups of black coffee in the living room when Micah Steele came into the room. He was taller, bigger than both the other men. He had thick, straight, medium blond hair cut conventionally short. He was wearing a beige Armani suit that seemed perfect for his tall frame. It made his dark eyes look even darker. He wore a watch like Eb's on his left wrist and no other jewelry. Thirty-six years old, the former CIA agent spoke several languages fluently and had a temper that was explosive and quiet. Dutch van Meer used to say that Micah could get more results with a steady look than he could with a weapon.

"Why are you still in town?" Cy asked curiously.

"That's what I asked you over to tell you." Eb grimaced. "We've still got problems."

"When have we had anything else lately?" Cy said with resignation.

"The word is that Lopez's bosses in Colombia think he's slipping. First, he got arrested. Then he lost a shipment to the Coast Guard. We cost him a tidy sum in men and equipment here, not to mention marijuana. Yesterday, another group of his men were driving plastic bags of cocaine paste in several transfer trailer trucks bearing the logo of a grocery store chain. The DEA was tipped off, probably by Rodrigo, and the feds got all the trucks plus their cargo. The haul would have been worth millions, if not billions, in crack cocaine sales if it had been processed and put out on the streets. It's the largest confiscation by the DEA in years. Lopez's bosses are furious. They're ready to dump Lopez, and he's cut some sort of deal to keep his connection. The word is, he's making plans to eliminate the obstacles to his local smuggling traffic."

"That's no real surprise," Eb pointed out.

Micah's dark eyes narrowed. "No. But I didn't expect this quite so soon. He can't get to either of you without some difficulty, now that his operation here has been shut down. Any group of strangers in town would stick out like sore thumbs, and the local authorities are on alert. But one of my contacts said that Callie and my father might become targets, and that the last he heard, Lopez was going to call in a mechanic. One man, alone, might succeed where a larger group failed."

It went without saying that a "mechanic" meant a professional killer. "Why your family and not ours?" Cy asked.

Micah leaned against the mantel above the fireplace in Eb's study. He smiled mockingly, looking more elegant than a male model with his striking good looks. "You only helped shut down a small operation of Lopez's. But I tipped the DEA guys about the multimillion dollar cocaine shipment that was confiscated."

Cy whistled. "Did Rodrigo pass that tidbit along?"

"Not Rodrigo," came the reply. "It was a last act of defiance by his cousin, who," he added grimly, "is now dead. They pulled him out of a vat of industrial chemicals. They were only able to identify him by dental records."

"Any idea where Rodrigo is?" Eb wanted to know.

"Hiding out in Aruba, I gather from my sources. But he may not be safe, even so. Lopez has a long reach. He's got people everywhere."

"Plus an informant with the feds who's spilling the beans to Lopez about our government's attempts to bring him down," Cy added.

"That's how Lopez knew I blew the whistle on him. You'd better believe that Kennedy and Cobb are doing their best to find out who it is," Micah replied. "But I expect it's someone in a high position who's beyond suspicion. It won't be easy to ferret him out."

"He's risking a lot on Lopez's account, whoever he is," Eb mused.

"Lopez is paying him a million a tip," Micah interjected.

"Well, that would make it worth the risk for most people, I'm afraid," Eb said.

Micah dropped down into an easy chair and lit a cigar. Eb turned on the smokeless ashtray and handed it to him. Micah chuckled, taking it in one big hand.

"That will kill you," Eb said with a grin.

"In my line of work, bullets will probably get me long before smoking does. Besides, I don't expect to be here long." He checked the big watch on his wrist. "Callie gets off work in five minutes. I'm going to waylay her before she goes to pick up Dad at the senior citizen center."

His face changed when he mentioned his former stepsister. His dark eyes narrowed and his jaw went taut. He smoked absently, his mind obviously far away.

"If worse comes to worst, you could take her and your father down to Nassau with you and keep her out of Lopez's reach," Eb suggested.

Micah gave him a hellish glare. "Neither of them will talk to me right now, much less agree to go to Nassau. Haven't you heard?" he drawled. "I'm anybody's friend but theirs."

"You always start the fights," Eb pointed out. "You can't blame Callie for defending herself."

Micah took another draw from the cigar and thumped ashes in the ashtray. "I blame her for everything," he said icily. "If it hadn't been for her and her damned mother, my father would want to see me occasionally."

"Surely he doesn't still blame you for his divorce?" Cy remarked.

"He blames me for everything." He put out the cigar impatiently and turned the smokeless ashtray off. "I blame her mother."

"Whatever happened to her?" Eb asked.

"I have no idea," Micah said abruptly. "She dumped Callie and left town even before the divorce was final. She hired a lawyer to bring the papers to her in England so that she wouldn't have to see any of us again. Some mother."

"Callie never talks about her," Eb said thoughtfully. "It's not surprising. Her mother treated her like the hired help. Callie wasn't pretty enough or sophisticated enough to please her mama."

"There's nothing wrong with Callie," Micah replied absently. "She's naïve, of course, but looks aren't that important. She's a good woman, in the true sense of the word. I should know," he added with a harsh laugh. "I've left a trail of the other kind behind me over the years."

"I won't argue with that," Eb had to agree. "They used to follow you around like flies after honey. Really beautiful women."

"Window dressing," Micah said carelessly. "Underneath they all had one thing in common—greed. Being rich and single has its drawbacks as well as its perks."

There was a brief silence while all of them recalled other times, other places.

"How's Lisa, by the way?" Micah asked. "Is the baby all right?"

"The test results got mixed when she had the first test, just after Walt was killed," Cy replied. He began to smile. "But she's pregnant now."

Eb scowled. "With Walt's baby. I know."

Cy shook his head. "Not Walt's baby. Mine." His eyes were brimming with pride, joy, delight. "Walt had a vasectomy before they married. He didn't want kids at all."

The other two men chuckled softly. "I thought you said she was too young for you," Eb said mischievously.

"I changed my mind. She's old for her age and I'm young for mine." He couldn't seem to stop smiling. "It's like a second chance. I never thought I'd get one."

"I'm glad for you," Eb said. "Glad for myself, too. We've made good marriages."

"I wish you could stop talking about it," Micah said disgustedly, glancing from one of them to the other. "I'll break out in hives any minute."

"Mr. Confirmed Bachelor," Eb said, jerking a thumb at the blond man.

"Napoleon before Waterloo," Cy agreed.

Micah got up out of his chair. "I'm going to see Callie. I brought Bojo over here with me, but he flew to Atlanta to see his brother. I guess it's just as well. If I had him tail her, he'd probably attract a little attention."

"Dressed in a long white silk robe and babushes on his feet? Who'd notice that in Jacobsville, Texas?" Eb asked dryly.

"He's Berber. The beard and mustache are traditional, like the accoutrements. He wouldn't blend, that's for sure," Micah said. He sighed. "I've had a hard time replacing Dallas since he got shot up and then left to marry Sally's aunt Jessica. Good men are really hard to find these days."

"They were just as hard to find back when we started out, too," Eb said. "Well, there's always Harley. He's hooked on adventure."

"No, he isn't," Cy said firmly. "He's the best foreman in two counties and I'm not recommending him for a target."

"He did pretty good that night," Eb said. "When the chips are down, he can keep his head."

"I want him to keep his head," Cy said. "That's the whole point of keeping him at home."

"How about Rodrigo?" Eb suggested.

Micah nodded slowly. "He could come to Nassau. He'd be safer there, with Bojo and me. I'll see if I can find him on my way home."

"Take care of yourself," Cy said.

Micah shook hands with him. "You do the same."

He left the two of them still talking about Rodrigo and climbed into the racy black Porsche he drove. It was like him, power and grace conventionally packaged and deceptively straitlaced. Micah was a law unto himself.

Micah drove to the side street near Kemp's law office, where Callie's little yellow VW beetle was sitting. He liked the updated style of the body, and the color suited her. She was bright and sunny. Or she had been, until her mother ruined all their lives.

It was five o'clock on the dot, and he waited and watched the rearview. Sure enough, less than a minute later, Callie Kirby came out of the law office and went down the sidewalk toward her car, lost in thought as she dug in her purse for her car keys. It amazed him that everything didn't fall out on the pavement at her feet. He remembered Callie being all thumbs, a gangly teenager suffering from embarrassment, lack of social graces and a bubbly personality despite her drawbacks.

But this Callie had changed. She had pale blue eyes and an ordinary sort of face, but it had a gamine charm all its own. She wore her dark hair short. She was only medium height, a little thing compared to him. But for her size, she packed a wallop when she lost her temper. He was sorry they couldn't be friends. He didn't have many, and she would have had the distinction of being the only woman among them. His affairs had tarnished him in Callie's quiet eyes. She had no use for playboys. Especially Micah Steele. Like his father, she blamed him for the divorce and the anguish that came after it. She thought that he'd been having an affair with her mother. That was ironic, when her mother was the one woman on earth he'd ever considered totally repulsive.

Well, you couldn't go home again, they said. They were right. That door was closed forever. His father was old and weak and illness had taken much of the spirit out of him. He hated the separation between them. He loved his father.

He was glad that Callie did, too, and that she took such good care of the old man. He thought about Lopez and the possibility of a hit man with those two gentle people as the targets, and his blood ran cold. He didn't want them to die for his actions. Lopez would know that, and it would please him. His teeth clenched as unwanted pictures of some nebulous tragedy began to take shape in his mind.

Callie came toward her car, noticed the low slung Porsche and stopped dead in her tracks, staring at it.

Micah climbed out of the car with his usual elegance of movement and went to join her beside her car.

"We need to talk."

She clutched her purse against her small breasts and looked up at him with faint hauteur. Her heart was racing. He could see her blouse move jerkily above her breasts. He remembered vividly the feel of her in his arms that once…

"*We* never talk," she informed him. "You say what you want to, and then you walk away."

She had a point. He pulled the half-smoked cigar from its holder and lit it.

"That's illegal in the mall," she said with unholy glee. "Light up there, and they'll arrest you."

"You'd love that, wouldn't you?"

She wasn't going to be drawn into another verbal firefight with him. She straightened. "I'm tired and I still have to pick up Dad at the senior center. He stays with me now."

"I know." He hated the thought of Callie being his father's nurse and protector. It was one of many things he resented. "Have you heard from your mother?" he added mockingly.

She didn't flinch. But her eyelids did, just barely perceptibly. "I haven't heard from my mother since the divorce," she said calmly. "Have you?" she added with pure venom.

His dark eyes glittered at her.

She decided to cut her losses. "What do you want?" she asked bluntly.

Now that he had her attention, he didn't know how to put it. She had no idea what he did for a living. Even his father didn't know. He'd kept his profession secret from both of them. He'd inherited a large trust from his mother, which would never have been enough to furnish him with Porsches and Armani suits. They didn't seem to realize that, so he left them to draw their own conclusions. Now, with Lopez looming over him, his profession might get them both killed. He had to find a way to protect them. But how?

"I don't suppose you and Dad would like to come down to Nassau for a vacation?" he asked speculatively.

Her chin lifted proudly. "I'd rather holiday in hell," she said with a cold smile.

He let out a husky, hollow laugh. "That's what I thought."

"Your father is all right," she said, anticipating what she thought was wrong. "It was just a mild stroke."

"When did that happen?" he asked abruptly, with concern.

"No one called you?" She shifted her purse. "Sorry. We've all watched him carefully since that heart attack. It was two weeks ago, he lost the feeling on the left side of his face and couldn't move it. As I said, it was mild. It was a light stroke. But they were actually able to clean out the artery that was clogged and put a shunt in it. He's on blood thinners, and he has a good prognosis. You don't have to worry about him. I'm taking good care of him."

"On your salary," he said flatly, angered.

She stiffened. "I make a decent living and he's an economical guest. We struggle along together just fine. We don't need financial help," she added firmly. "In case you wondered," she added, reminding him that he'd accused her of being money-hungry just like her mother. It was one of many things he'd said to her that still hurt.

The words went right through him, but he hid his reaction. He wished he could forget the accusations he'd made, the hurtful things he'd said to her. But there was no going back. "Did you know your own father?" he asked, curious.

Her face grew taut. "I don't know who my father was. My mother's first husband was positive that it wasn't him. That's why he didn't press for custody when she divorced him."

She said it with savaged pride, and he was sorry he'd forced the admission from her. "So my father's standing in for him?" he probed gently.

"Jack Steele was kinder to me than anyone else ever was," she said tightly. "It's no great burden to look after him. And you still haven't said why you're here."

He fingered the burning cigar and tried to find the words. "I've made an enemy," he said finally. "A very bad man to cross. I think he might target you and my father to get back at me."

Callie frowned. "Excuse me?"

His dark eyes met hers. "He's a drug lord. He heads one of the Colombian cartels. I just cost him several million dollars by tipping the DEA about a massive shipment of cocaine he sent over here."

Her blood ran cold. She worked in legal circles. She knew about drugs, not only their dangers, but also the penalties for using or selling them. She also knew about the Colombian cartels, because they were on the news most every night. They were graphic about how drug dealers got even with people who cost them money. She couldn't even shoot a gun, and Jack Steele, Micah's father, was practically an invalid despite his remarkable recovery. The two of them together would never be able to protect themselves from such an adversary, and she couldn't afford to hire a bodyguard.

She stared at Micah blankly. "Would he be that ruthless?" she had to ask.

"Yes."

Her chest rose and fell heavily. "Okay. What do we do?"

Straightforward. No accusations, no rage, no exaggerated fear. She simply asked, trusting that he'd know. And he did.

"I'm going to send someone over here to watch you and Dad," he replied. "Someone trustworthy."

"And what are you going to do?" she wanted to know.

"That's my business."

He looked, and sounded, harder than nails. She felt exposed, vulnerable. She was eighteen again, hearing him accuse her of setting him up with his father. He'd already been angry at her for what had happened when they'd been alone that last Christmas they'd all lived together. He'd given in to temptation and it had taken all his willpower to get away from her at all. He'd lectured her about being so free with her kisses, so wanton and forward. He'd left her in tears. It had only dawned on him much later that she'd had something alcoholic to drink. He'd walked out into the hall, where her mother had seen him in a state of unmistakable arousal and had made a blatant play for him, thinking *she'd* aroused him in her low-cut dress.

In the seconds it took his dimmed brain to react, his father had come out of the study and found him in the hall with Callie's mother, in a compromising position. Micah and his father had almost come to blows. Callie and her mother were summarily booted out the door and Micah had accused Callie of sending her father out there to catch him with his stepmother, out of revenge because he wouldn't kiss her. It had broken Callie's heart. Now, she withdrew from Micah Steele as if he were molten lava. She had no wish to repeat the lesson he'd taught her.

"Very well," she said demurely. "I'll look after Dad while you do...whatever you're going to do. I've got my grandfather's shotgun and some shells. I'll protect him at night.''

He looked at her in a different way. ''Can you shoot it?''

''If I have to,'' she replied. Her face was very pale, but she wasn't flinching. ''Was there anything else?''

His dark eyes slid down her slender, graceful body and he remembered Callie in bathing suits, in flimsy gowns, in her one fancy dress at her birthday party—her eighteenth birthday party. She'd been wearing deep green velvet, cut low and sensuous, and he'd refused her invitation to attend the celebration. Like so many other things he'd said and done, he'd hurt her that day. She still looked impossibly young. She was barely twenty-two, and he was thirty-six, over a decade her senior.

He wanted to prolong the meeting. That was unlike him. He shrugged one shoulder indifferently instead. ''Nothing important. Just watch your step. I'll make sure nobody gets close enough to hurt either of you.''

She gave him one slow, eloquent look before she turned to her small car and unlocked it. She got in and drove off, without another word. And she didn't look back.

Twelve

Cy and Lisa were having a late supper at the kitchen table. They watched each other hungrily with every bite as they discussed the changes the baby would mean in their lives. They were delightful changes, and they spoke in low murmurs, smiling at each other between bites. The loud squeal of tires out front caught them unaware and made them tense. Surely it wasn't another attack by Lopez or his men...!

Cy was out of the chair and heading for the front door seconds later, his hand going automatically to the phone table drawer where the loaded .45 automatic was kept. He made a mental note to himself to keep his gun locked up once the baby arrived. He motioned Lisa back and moved cautiously out onto the porch. Seconds later, he lowered the weapon. It was Micah Steele, but he was hardly recognizable.

His thick blond hair was disheveled, and he needed a shave. He looked as if he hadn't slept.

Cy didn't waste time asking questions. He caught the taller man by the arm and pulled him inside. "Coffee first. Then you can tell whatever you need to."

"I'll bring it to the study," Lisa offered.

Cy smiled at her and bent to kiss her cheek. "I'll bring it to the study," he corrected tenderly. "Growing mamas need their rest. Go watch TV."

"Okay." She kissed him back, sparing a curious and sympathetic glance for Micah, who nodded politely before he preceded Cy into the kitchen.

When Lisa was out of earshot, Cy poured coffee into two mugs and put them on the table.

"Would you rather talk in the study?" Cy asked him.

"This is fine." Micah cupped the mug in both hands and leaned over it in a slumped posture that said all too much about his mental condition.

Cy straddled a chair across from him. "Okay. What's wrong."

"Lopez has Callie," he said in a husky, tortured voice.

Cy sat stock-still. "When? And how?" he exploded.

"Yesterday, not five minutes after I spoke to her outside her office building," he said dully. "We had a brief conversation. I warned her that someone I knew might possibly target her or my father. She listened, but she didn't pay much attention. I told her I was going to have someone watch them for their own safety. But I'd barely gotten back to my motel when Eb phoned and said he'd had an urgent message from Rodrigo that Callie was going to be snatched. I phoned the adult day care where she leaves Dad every day and they said she hadn't picked him up." He looked absolutely devastated. "You can set your watch by Callie. She's always early, if she isn't right on time. I went looking for her, and I found her car about a block from the senior center on a side street. The driver's door was standing wide-open and her purse was still in it.''

Cy cursed roundly. ''Did you call the police?''

Micah shook his head. He ran a big hand through his hair restlessly. ''I didn't know what to do.'' He looked at Cy in anguish. ''Do you know what that snake will do to her? She's untouched, Cy. Absolutely untouched!''

He had a pretty good idea what Lopez would do, and it made him sick to consider it. Judging by Micah's behavior, his stepsister meant a lot more to him than he'd ever admitted; possibly, more than he'd realized himself.

''The first thing we do is call Chet Blake.''

''A lot of good a local police chief is going to do us,'' Micah said miserably. ''By now, Lopez has her out of the state, if not out of the country.''

''Chet is a distant relation of our state attorney general, Simon Hart,'' Cy interrupted, ''and he has a cousin who's a Texas Ranger. Lopez's men left some sort of trail, even if it's just a paper one. Chet has connections. He'll find out where Lopez has taken her. If she's in Mexico, we can contact the Mexican authorities and Interpol…''

Micah's steely glare interrupted him. ''All I need to know is where she is,'' he said tautly. ''Then I'll pack up Bojo and Rodrigo, and we'll play cowboys and drug dealers.''

Cy wanted to try to reason with him, but the man was too far gone. He'd seen Micah in this mood before, and he knew there was nothing he could say or do to stop him. He spared a thought for Callie, who was probably terrified, not to mention Micah's father. The old man had already had a major heart attack and a stroke, and the news might easily be too much for him. Micah would have to make up a story and tell it to whoever was nursing him. He said as much.

"I've already taken care of that," Micah said heavily. "One of the freelance homebound nurses who sometimes visits him at the center went home with him. I've arranged for her to stay there until I come back—or until Callie does. I told her to say that Callie had an emergency out of town, a cousin in a car wreck. He doesn't know that she has no cousins. He'll believe it, and he won't have to be upset."

"Good thinking," Cy said. "What can I do?"

Micah finished his coffee. "You can keep an eye on Dad for me while I'm out of the country. You and Eb," he added. "If you don't mind."

"Certainly I don't mind," Cy told him. "We'll have somebody watch him constantly. I promise."

"Thanks," Micah said simply. He stood up. "I'll let you know when I've got her safe."

"If there's anything else you need, all you have to do is ask," Cy told him.

Micah smiled wanly. "Remember that old saying, that we don't appreciate what we've got until we lose it?"

"She'll be all right."

"I hope so. See you."

"Good luck."

Micah nodded and went out as quietly as he'd come in. Cy poured himself another cup of coffee, took out a glass and filled it with milk for Lisa before he closed up the kitchen and went to join her in the living room.

Her eyes lit up when he sat down on the sofa beside her, put the drinks down and slid his arm behind her to watch her knit.

"What was wrong with him?"

"Lopez got Callie," he said.

She grimaced and groaned. "Oh, poor Callie! Can he rescue her, do you think?"

"As soon as we find out where she is. I've got to make some phone calls in the study. Go on to bed when your program goes off. I'll be there in a little while."

She put her hand on his cheek and caressed it softly. "I love going to bed with you," she said softly.

He smiled at her, bending to kiss her lips tenderly. "I love doing everything with you," he said.

"Will it be enough for you, me and the baby?" she asked solemnly. "Will it make up for what you've lost?"

He drew her close and hugged her. "I'll always miss Alex," he replied, naming his five-year-old son who died in the Wyoming fire. "And I'll always blame myself for not being able to save him. But I love you, and I want our baby very much." He lifted his head and looked down into her dark eyes hungrily. "You'll be enough, Lisa."

She smiled again, and kissed him hungrily before he got up from the sofa. "I love you."

"I love you, too." He ruffled her long hair and grinned at her. "You've changed my whole life. I look forward to waking up every morning. I have such a pretty view in my bed."

She chuckled. "I have a very nice one of my own." She sobered. "Will Lopez hurt Callie?"

"I wish I knew. We'll do what we can to help Micah find her."

"Even when Lopez is not here, he's still here," she said. "One of these days, he's going to be called to account for all the evil things he's done."

"And he'll pay the price," Cy assured her.

He went to make his phone calls. He paused in the doorway to take one long look at his wife. Despite his sympathy for Micah Steele, he was grateful that he hadn't lost Lisa to Lopez's violence. His life was new again, fresh, full of promise and joy. After the storm, the rainbow. He smiled. The winter soldier had found a warm, loving home at last.

* * * * *

Don't miss the next exciting book in Diana Palmer's
SOLDIERS OF FORTUNE series!

THE LAST MERCENARY—

Micah and Callie's romance—will be available in
May 2002 from Silhouette Special Edition®.

17th August 2001
Lone Stallion's Lady   By Lisa Jackson

21st September 2001
His Forever Bride   By Laurie Paige

You Belong To Me   By Jennifer Greene

19th October 2001
The Marriage Bargain   By Victoria Pade

Honourable Intentions   By Marilyn Pappano

16th November 2001
The Baby Quest   By Pat Warren

One Wedding Night   By Karen Hughes

21st December 2001
The Birth Mother   By Pamela Toth

Rich, Rugged...Ruthless   By Jennifer Mikels

18th January 2002
The Magnificent Seven   By Cheryl St. John

Outlaw Marriage   By Laurie Paige

15th February 2002
Nighthawk's Child   By Linda Turner

MONTANA BRIDES

0901/MB/RTLb

The
Christmas
that changed
everything

Mary Lynn Baxter Marilyn Pappano
Christine Flynn

Available from 16th November

*Available at most branches of WH Smith,
Tesco, Martins, Borders, Eason, Sainsbury's,
and most good paperback bookshops.*